Yahweh

To: MME Storm Chantal
Fr: R. F[signature]

Rhoan Flowers

authorHOUSE

AuthorHouse™
1663 Liberty Drive
Bloomington, IN 47403
www.authorhouse.com
Phone: 1-800-839-8640

© 2011, 2012 Rhoan Flowers. All rights reserved.

No part of this book may be reproduced, stored in a retrieval system, or transmitted by any means without the written permission of the author.

Published by AuthorHouse 11/15/2012

ISBN: 978-1-4685-2508-3 (e)
ISBN: 978-1-4685-2509-0 (hc)
ISBN: 978-1-4685-2510-6 (sc)

Library of Congress Control Number: 2011962518

Any people depicted in stock imagery provided by Thinkstock are models, and such images are being used for illustrative purposes only. Certain stock imagery © Thinkstock.

This book is printed on acid-free paper.

Because of the dynamic nature of the Internet, any web addresses or links contained in this book may have changed since publication and may no longer be valid. The views expressed in this work are solely those of the author and do not necessarily reflect the views of the publisher, and the publisher hereby disclaims any responsibility for them.

Introduction

The time had arrived for the creator of the earth to reclaim his planet, after centuries of allowing Satan the Devil to govern over it. This epic adventure details the catastrophes, which the entire globe experience during the coming of the Almighty Lord. Following the manifestation of symbols in the skies, that beckons the arrival of the lord throughout the entire globe, humans who haven't repented their sins, began flocking to churches, mosques, synagogues and other places of worship to seek forgiveness, while others ignored the warnings with the belief that the proclamation was a hoax.

The governments of the world, which feared that the symbol in the skies suggested the destruction of the entire globe by a planet on a collision course with the earth, orchestrate means of destroying the approaching planet. Every country armed with nuclear missiles united to launch missiles at the approaching planet, in order to either destroy it or blast it off course. The present ruler of the earth who is the only one knowledgeable that his reign has neared it end, authorize his human subjects to deploy their means of defense, in hopes of abolishing the threat destined to remove him from grace. The planet named Heaven that is feared to be the reason for the warning in the skies eventually slows its approach although human governments proceed with their decision to vanquish the planet.

Lucifer aka Satan the Devil who refuses to release his strangle hold over the earth, plots to destroy the armies of the Heaven, which are God's anointed forces sent to eradicate all wickedness from the earth. The Devil instead of surrendering, utilizes the inventions of humans to increase his battalions in order to combat the angels of Heaven. The Devil, after the shortcomings of a few of his Archangels, releases the monstrosities from his dungeon upon the earth, in order for them to remind his human subjects of who truly is their sovereign king. Through the insolence of the earthly governments, the Almighty God eventually punishes everyone on the face of the earth with plagues, which increase their suffering. The lord also curses them with turbulent weather, which magnified the destruction across the globe.

The universal soldiers from Heaven are sent to earth, where they have to battle different armies from Hell, across the different continents. These fierce battles erupts between the angels of God and their nemesis, who obeys and worships their leader Satan the Devil. While the combatants clash, the monstrosities from Hell are tackled by the defending animals from Heaven, which are all carnivorous creatures that are obedient only to their masters. The Devil hides and remains in seclusion, as his different armies face off against the single army of universal warriors, which police and protect the entire galaxy. The final clash between Satan and God's anointed son releases the earth from its sinful state, where the lord himself brings forth the final judgment upon mankind.

Chapter 1

Orleans Ontario, Canada;
Present day:

I entered the Toronto Dominion bank on the corner of Trim Road and Watters Avenue after casing the facility for nearly a week. After joining the short line-up, I glanced up at the huge clock behind the center bank teller and noticed that it was 11:35am. There were five customers ahead of me, two elderly females, a United Parcel Service male employee, a young Caucasian male bobbing his head to the tunes transmitting from his I-Pod, and a father gently holding his daughter in his arms. As I gazed around the facility, I began wondering which of the three tellers would be my service representative as the first of three customers were served. As the line shortened, two female friends who worked at the Tim Horton across the street joined the line behind me, while gossiping about some annoying customer they attended to earlier that morning.

At 11:50, the bank manager approached one of her female tellers and told her to take her lunch break. As I approached the front of the line the teller placed her, 'next wicket please', sign atop the counter, and then finalized her affairs before proceeding to lunch. A well-attired businessman entered the bank and walked towards the business wicket, as I watched the father, with his daughter, exit through the transaction machines section.

"Next in line please!" declared the teller to my right, as a male customer entered the bank, but opted for the transaction machines services.

I walked up to the teller and noticed her name tag that read Stacie before placing my backpack on the counter and slid her a note which read, "this is an armed robbery, calmly place funds in the bag!" A jolt of terror overtook the blond-hair teller as I showed her a glimpse of the revolver packaged in the front pouch of the backpack. The young Caucasian beauty nervously emptied her cash drawer, while I ensured everything was normal inside the bank by gazing over my shoulder at the other patrons inside.

"Here you go sir." the female teller frightfully mumbled.

I kindly thanked the female for her hospitality and grabbed my backpack from atop the counter, before briskly walking out of the facility. Everything appeared normal around the area as I checked out the surroundings before mounting my Yamaha R-1 getaway machine. The faint sounds of police sirens could be heard in the distance, while I fired up the racing bike and fled the scene. My R-1 twin engine roared as I sped down the hill on Trim Road on my way towards Interstate 174.

There was a police cruiser en route to the robbery scene as I blew through the intersection at Trim Road and St. Joseph Boulevard. The cruiser had halted along the eastbound lane and paused at the intersection for a few seconds before it began pursuing me as I sped towards the highway. As I came up to the commencement of the interstate, the traffic light prevented me from entering, while motorists sped by from both directions. With the police cruiser quickly approaching, I decided to disobey the traffic signal and run the red light.

The problem with my decision was the fact that I was traveling northbound, with the intention of going west along a busy roadway where the eastbound traffic was scanty throughout. The momentary break in the eastbound traffic flow soon gave me the opportunity to cross over to the center median. However, joining the westbound traffic was a separate challenge in itself. I tightly gripped onto the R-1 front brakes, while revving up the bike's RPMs before releasing the brake grip, which fired off the motorbike against oncoming traffic. My Yamaha R-1 quickly cleared the eastern portion of the highway, as I clamped onto the brakes to prevent the bike from sailing into the busier section of the highway.

There was a tractor trailer passing a Volks Wagon Beetle, which was slouching along the interstate. The driver of the tractor-trailer saw me from a distance and believed I was going to continue without yielding, due to my aggressive demeanor when crossing the eastbound section of the highway. The conductor of the semitractor jammed his brakes after he'd increased his speed to 118mph in order to pass the Volks Wagon. The air-brakes on the semitrailer locked the tires, as the vehicle screechingly slid towards me.

With the trailer bearing down on me, I decided to take off to avoid a collision, which would have undoubtedly been fatal. The front tire of my R-1 motorbike railed up into the air as the rear tire burned rubber against the asphalt. The Yamaha speedster took off like a jet, and I was forced to muscle the bike in order for the front end to level out. The high speed that the trailer was travelling caused the cargo filled semi to begin jack-knifing, as the driver attempted to avoid splattering me across the roadway by turning into the median. The front bumper of the semi came inches from my rear tire, before its rear trailer completely dislodged from the engine compartment.

With daylight ahead, I clutched up and muzzled the gas as the front tire reconnected with the asphalt. I glanced over my shoulder at officer who was forced to wait for the traffic to clear before entering the intersection. The vehicles ahead of the police cruiser eventually created enough space for the copper to squeeze through, but the accident involving the tractor trailer and three other vehicles, took precedent for the officer who ceased pursuit and radioed emergency assistance. The officer raced to assist the conductor of the semitractor whose vehicle had flipped over, causing the roof to cave in and trap the driver inside.

I was almost to the next ramp before I realized that the cruiser would no longer pose a threat, though I continued hammering the Yamaha. There were six vehicles entering the highway at Tenth Line Road, but it wasn't until I was about to pass the exit that I realized that the two center cars were actually undercover officers. Not wanting to surrender their element of surprise, the cops waited until they'd almost entered the highway before applying their sirens. I blasted by the on-ramp at 180mph, seconds before noticing the vehicles ahead of me all pulling off to the medians, like Moses separating the Red Sea.

Everyone who exited to the side medians began looking to the skies, as if

Rhoan Flowers

there was an air show in progress, which helped me by opening the speeding lanes ahead. The skies, which were as clear as water, began exhibiting a series of symbols, which were legible from as far as the eyes could see. The symbols across the skies weren't in English. However, momentarily, a certain voice would translate the meaning to every amazed viewer. The actions of motorist along the roadway intrigued me, as I took a second to gaze up at the skies, where the bold black symbols glistened under the scorching sun. As I gazed at the symbols, a female's voice spoke into my ears as if she was my companion aboard the Yamaha, "Your God and creator is returning!"

"What the Hell?" I muzzled to myself, while looking over my shoulder to verify that there was no-one on the bike with me. A terrifying sensation shocked through my body as I was forced to weave around a Hummer in the fast lane.

There was a special transit lane along interstate 174 for public transportation use only. At that point even the city buses were pulling off to the soft shoulders, with their passengers and conductors vying to witness the spectacle. Interstate 174 itself was a fifteen mile stretch of roadway, which merged into interstate 117 from the eastern provincial route, that travels back to Montreal. Prior to the highway merger, there was an off-ramp strictly for city busses, by which I exited as I attempted to flee the pursuing officers. Aboard one of the undercover police cruisers was a devoted Christian who after witnessing the symbols, felt compelled to attend to his family rather than continue his pursuit. The officer detached himself from the chase and exited the highway at Jeanne D'Ark Boulevard without notifying anyone of his decision.

While gearing down to safely exit the public transit's off-ramp, I glanced back through my side mirror at the lone ranger in pursuit who was a slight distance behind me. The transit roadways stretched across the entire metropolitan area of Ottawa and made it easier for public transit busses and disabled vehicles to travel throughout the city. With the belief that utilizing the transit roadways would serve as an attribute, I saw no greater opportunity to rid myself of my pursuers, as I sped along the narrow private roads towards centre town. Along the public transportation roadways was a series of busses with everyone dismounted and fascinated at the developments across the skies. There were people video-taping the spectacle with their cell-phones and other devices, while others nervously contacted their friends and family to disclose what they've witnessed.

I exited the transit way at Nicholas Street and Laurier Avenue to the sight of skeptical citizens staring in amazement at the symbols, while debating amongst themselves about the meaning of and the persons responsible for producing the symbols. As I slowed drastically to weave my way through the crowd of spectators, I overheard a female positively identifying the author of the writings as an angel. The trailing police cruiser soon came up to the crowd of spectators, which was mainly comprised of students from the University of Ottawa, who were as menacing to the public servant as they were towards me. As I turned right on Laurier Avenue, I came across a blockade of vehicles, which were mainly vacated by their operators, who sought to personally witness the spectacle. My Yamaha motorbike provided me the opportunity to weave through the abandoned vehicles, while the protruding undercover cruiser was forced to abandon his chase.

There was a Baptist church on the corner of Laurier Avenue and Cumberland Street with a host of people banging down the doors seeking entry. My movements were limited to a crawl due to the hundreds of spectators gazing about like zombies, as they stared up at the clouds. Without the sounds of the police cruiser following, I swerved through the many obstacles along Cumberland Street en-route to the Alexandra Bridge, which links the province of Ontario with Quebec. The second church I rode by at Cumberland and Daly had scores of people forcing themselves into the structure, regardless of the fact that the building was already packed to capacity. Every church I rode by prior to the bridge had a magnitude of visitors forcibly seeking entry, as if the structure itself was to be their saving grace.

I safely got to the Alexandra Bridge and crossed over into Quebec where my second glance at the symbols was as clear and legible as it was on the Ontario landscape. I rode by two police cruisers whose occupants had begun ignoring the tasks to which they were assigned, as everyone appeared to be interested in salvation all at once. I drove along Fournier Boulevard for approximately seven miles before arriving at my destination at the Lotus Motel in Gatineau. I parked my get-away vehicle at the rear of the motel where it was impossible to be seen from the main road. I gazed around to ensure I wasn't being watched before removing the fake license plate that I'd attached prior to my escapade.

I had rented a motel suite that was located on the secluded third floor. While mounting the rear staircase, I passed the motel's owner who indicated that the front office would be closed until further notice. However, I was offered the opportunity to remain at no additional cost, provided that I watched over the structure in his absence. I agreed to the owner's terms before continuing my ascent, as I was rather eager to seclude myself. While walking towards my suite, I gingerly hid my face from a few visitors who stood by the stair rails as they stared up at the symbols. Before entering the suite I gazed up at the symbols again and was again dumbstruck by the female's voice again translating he symbols.

Once inside the motel suite I quickly bolted the door behind me, before drawing the curtains closed for maximum privacy. I grabbed the television remote from atop the double bed and tuned into the local news channel, as I proceeded to the bathroom where I began removing the disguise I wore to hinder my identity. I first removed the false wig from my head and tossed it into the sink before gingerly removing the beard and mustache and I proceeded to wash the makeup from my face. Once I'd finished I hopped into the shower for a quick bath, after which I packed the clothing and disguise articles into a garbage bag and cleaned up the area.

I walked over to the window and slid a tiny peep hole through the curtains, which offered me substantial viewing of the main boulevard. Once I became content about my safety, I took the backpack and emptied the contents onto the bed before proceeding to calculate the spoils of my treachery. While counting the money, I momentarily changed the channel in search of possible reports regarding the heist, which I thought would be broadcasted throughout the surrounding areas. Every channel I managed to surf through was all televising the same phenomenon, which was said to be a global event, reported by news organizations from the smallest islands to the largest continents. The reports indicated that the symbols appeared simultaneously across the world's skies at 12pm Eastern Time.

I rejoiced that there was no mention of my robbery being televised, although, like the rest of the world, I wondered what was to derive from this new phenomenon. I used my personal cellular to telephone my wife, who was planted by our sick son's side during his stay at Ottawa's Civic Hospital.

"Hello baby, how's my boy doing?" I enquired.

"He's not doing well today at all, and I'm getting worried that he might---."My wife soberingly responded.

"We have to stay strong for Junior's sake honey! I think that I finally accumulated the proper funds needed for his operation, so tell Doctor McBride that I'll be in to talk to him soon."

"Oh thank the Lord, because I don't know how much more of watching him like this I could take. People around this place are starting to go nuts, I don't know what it is but everyone seems to be in some sort of trance or something."

"So you haven't looked outside all day"?

"Listen I'm with my sick son, so everything is on pause until he's back on his feet. Besides I've been talking with Pastor Lester in Rome, who called to offer up a prayer for Junior."

"Well seeing that Junior is going to be fine, I suggest that you take a walk outside or to the closest window and have a look at the clouds."

"OK I'll take a look, but could you please hurry up and get over here, I think if Junior sees you he'll feel a lot better!"

Chapter 2

At 12:05PM the American Air Force dispatched a surveillance airplane to investigate the cause and origin of the symbols, which was by then well documented by every nationality across the globe. The surveillance airplane was slated to photograph the symbols from different angles and collect specimens of the texture of gas that formed each symbol. The single engine jet that was dispatched to investigating the symbols was approximately a hundred yards from the phenomenon when, as the pilot checked his systems and prepared the aircraft for sample collection, an invisible force grabbed control of his vessel.

The frightened pilot relayed an emergency alert, as he checked his instruments and gauges to decipher why the plane had stopped advancing. "Mayday-mayday, there is something controlling my aircraft, I've lost total control of her! Mayday, Mayday!"

The pilot, who was unable to see the invisible beings around him, was oblivious to the fact there were three angels within the area, who had violently engaged each other. The angel of God who wrote the symbols into the clouds was standing guard by his graffiti work, when two representatives of Satan appeared. The angel of God, who was dressed in their customary white armory, resembled a bright florescent light bulb, while his enemies wore their ordained black war gear, which matched the darkness of their skin. The angels of God, who painted the symbols into the clouds around the globe, were instructed to remain at guard in order to ensure that Satan's hoards didn't erase the signs.

Moments before the surveillance aircraft arrived, Hakeel the angel of God appointed to craft the symbols into the Nevada skies, was attacked by two angels from hell. The representatives of Satan intended on erasing the warning symbols, which were intended to alert humans about the return of their creator, whom the Devil and his allies sought to overthrow. Hakeel had properly installed the symbols and was deep in meditation when his sense of danger alerted him to the approaching foes. The angel of God opened his eyes to the ambush of his nemesis which worked cohesively to attack from opposite sides and bound their opponent. Once the pair of demons secured Hakeel's hands, the confinement duties were passed to one demon while the second whooped on the angel.

"The supposed return of your God has brought the master to abolish this restriction against the religious and offenders of our laws. It's free for all now like it should have always been, which means we are going to annihilate you all." threatened the demonic angel, who held Hakeel's hands secure.

"Your God will never again step foot onto this planet, it was given to my lord to reign over and that's exactly how it's going to remain." the Demonic Angel boasted, while administering furious licks. "Yeah you heard him, never! Mash him up more!" related the demon's accomplice who firmly held Hakeel's arms behind him.

The angel of God, who was well diverse in multiple forms of defensive maneuvers, was placed in a situation where his options of escape were few. With his hands tightly bound, Hakeel thrust his left foot up the crotch of his holder and stumped the demonic-angel in his privates. The cramp that shocked it's way up the demonic angel's intestines, forced the Devil worshiper to release his strangle hold; as the angel of God responded by throwing a straight right punch directly in the face of the unexpecting enforcer. The right punch was thrown with such immense force, that it sent the demonic angel hurling backwards, as the white angel turned his attention to the other combatant behind him. The woozy angel grabbed the shoulder straps of the arch-angel, who had bent forward to alleviate the pain, and began assaulting his enemy with rights and lefts knees to the face. After the third solid connected blow, the demonic angel was knocked completely unconscious as the revived angel spun his attention to his second attacker.

The jet surveillance aircraft was about to fly by the demonic angel who had begun regaining flight control, when the fighting angel from hell, grabbed a hold of the passing aircraft and began twirling the vessel around like a piece of paper.

"Whatever your beliefs are, your God will never again step foot back onto this planet, and if he is ever lucky to, that will be the final decision he ever makes. If we can't have this planet then no one will, we will destroy everything from the clouds to the seas. My lord Lucifer has annulled our arrangements regarding these peasants you and your angels are vowed to protect. We may physically be unable to touch them, but these vessels they fly around in are not a part of the deal. These pesky humans are going to suffer for their treachery, as will the rest of you goons." the demonic angel threatened, as he flung the aircraft directly at a DC600, which had only moments before lifted off from the Nevada International Airport.

The angel who was referred to as a Defender, because of the kind of work he and his allies were sent to the earth to perform, flew off in an attempt to prevent the crash. With the knowledge that hundreds of passengers may be aboard the aircrafts, the angel attempted to reach and grab the surveillance jet before it collided with the passenger plane. The pilot aboard the jet, who caught a glimpse of the demonic angel during the mishandling of his aircraft, dismissed the vision as a mirage and lobbied for assistance from his command centre, as his airplane spun uncontrollably. While the angel of God attempted to save the doomed air travelers, his nemesis who casted the vessel moved to his unconscious friend and quickly escaped. The angel, who flew at full speed, was inches from grabbing the surveillance jet, when it came into contact with its intended target. The cloaked angel was protected from the physical blast of both aircrafts, which resulted in the slaying of everyone aboard.

The air traffic controllers dispatched emergency crews to the coordinates of the crash before contacting their senior supervisors with their reports on what occurred prior to the disaster. While reporting on the disaster, airplanes within the Nevada air space began falling to the ground like dead birds as Satan's demonic angels began carrying out their threats. Within minutes the threat of endangered aircrafts across the world's skies was raised, as other states and countries began reporting that their aircrafts were plunging to the ground. The United States was the first to implement a national grounding of aircrafts, as they suspended all flights.

Vatican City, Rome;

Pastor Craig Lester was a devoted Catholic priest who dreamed of serving the pope while studying for his ministry in Vatican City Rome. The thirty two year old Canadian was raised a Catholic and never deviated away from his faith, even to the point of extensively studying religion throughout his college years. The young pastor sent a formal request to the Vatican to further his studies in the bible, following his graduation from Algonquin College, where he spent three years studying to be a deliverer of God's magnificence. It was on his twenty seventh birthday that his request was accepted, whereby he received an invitation to relocate and further his studies in Rome. Pastor Lester graciously accepted, before departing the St. Andrews parish church, where he served as an alternate Pastor behind Pastor Andrews, who ministered for forty plus years in the parish.

Devon Junior Bryan was three years old when he was diagnosed with a bad kidney and lung problems. At that time Pastor Lester conducted the children's bible studies program at the St. Andrews church, which was Junior's mother place of worship. The young pastor orchestrated several fund raisers to aid the family with the cost of Junior's operations, visited the young lad in the hospital and prayed extensively with the family, which was overwhelmed with the pressures of caring for a sick child. The sole regret Pastor Lester had with leaving Ottawa was that he was unable to obtain the total amount of money desired for Junior's most important operation. During his time abroad, however, the pastor was certain to contact Devon's mother on a daily basis offering prayers and expressing his concerns over the youth whom he'd personally grown to love.

Pastor Lester telephoned Sarah Bryan and spoke exclusively about the status of young Devon Bryan, whose was in dyer need of the transplant, three years after the doctors discovered the problem. The Canadian pastor counseled Sarah on the importance of prayer and her continuous trust in the lord, whom he was convinced would be the one to save young Junior's life. Pastor Lester blessed Sarah's household and instructed her to remain truthful and trusting in her husband, despite his lack of faith. Towards the end of their conversation, the pastor's second phone line beeped in his ear, which indicated that he had an alternate phone call. Pastors Lester's eyes were filled with tears moments after, when an aide summoned him and ushered him outdoors, where the divine symbols brightened up the evening skies. Pope Desmond Arthur, his high priests and every member of their cabinet stood astonished at the revelation, as members of the Vatican heard the translation, though there were few amongst them with the qualifications to actually read the symbols.

"What manner of trickery is this, I bet the Americans are the ones responsible for this false doctrine!" a high priest openly exclaimed.

"His Eminence I personally witnessed an angel drawing such symbols!" an aide revealed.

"Was the angel in the form of an airplane"? another priest mocked.

"I too witnessed this phenomenon and I swear this to be true." a second aide revealed.

"His Eminence I have just spoken with family members in Greece and they too have similar symbols across their skies." a high priest confirmed.

Vatican City had always served as the pope's main platform for delivering his public addresses and masses, thus Christians were accustomed to gathering across St. Peter's Square for various events throughout the year. With the revelation of the symbols came crowds of people, who all flocked to their spiritual grounds for guidance. The pope's aids deliberated at the sight of the gathering, before advising his Eminence of the importance of him addressing and soothing the gathering mob of peasants. The pope himself sought guidance, as the symbols in the sky was never mentioned in the bible or ancient scrolls.

"What am I to tell these people, when I am as blind to the developments as they are?" Pope Arthur demanded of his colleagues.

The senior high priests looked curiously around at each other, as they too were unaware of what lied ahead.

"We ask repentance of them and pray together that the lord will maintain us within his bosom." Pastor Lester exclaimed.

"Very good my son! For your discreet analysis I shall anoint you with the task of writing the sermon I shall deliver to the people. You have twenty minutes to have it completed my son! Go with God." Pope Arthur stated.

While the Pope prepared to deliver his sermon, Pastor Lester returned to his quarters to perform the request demanded of him. A pastor from Spain who had developed a close friendship with Pastor Lester accompanied him, while other members of the clergy ran off to the inner chapel, in order to engage in personal prayers of their own. Within minutes the crowd of thousands which gathered in St. Peter's Square grew to well over a million.

"My dearest friend, the bible warns of these final days yet these are undocumented signs, how are we to comfort and guide the mass when we ourselves don't know what is next to come?" the pastor from Spain reasoned.

"I became a pastor because I believe and trust in our Lord and savior Jesus Christ. This is the only message we have to comfort the people as servants of God. We live and study on the holiest of grounds, Jesus shall not abandon us in this our greatest moment of need. Whatever tomorrow brings is uncertain at this point, but we must remain the truth in whom these people believe." Pastor Lester assured.

The enormous crowd that awaited their beloved Pope, begun chanting his name in expectation of his prayers and guidance. The darkness of night remained interrupted by the brightness of the symbols, which had been lingering about the Roman's skies for nearly forty minutes. Despite the lack of police, the crowd was surprisingly well mannered, as they patiently awaited the head of their Catholic church. The chants for their beloved pope soon changed to the singing of gospel songs, as one Christian female amongst the mass began humming the chorus to 'amazing Grace'. Following the female's introduction, the entire crowd began harmonizing songs which are sung by Christians during worship, as they held hands while staring up at the symbols. There were tears and sorrows on the faces of mothers and fathers, who all nervously wondered about what was to become of their children, and the world, as they knew it.

Fifty minutes after the largest crowd ever assembled in St. Peter's Square formulated, the seventy eight year old Pope Desmond Arthur walked out onto Vatican City's infamous balcony for all to see, with both hands held up towards the sky. The pope's high priests who often accompanied him were by his side where they gracefully stood in submission, while his eminence basked in the glory being attributed to him by the crowd. The crowd below cheered loudly, as if they were at a rock concert and the featured band had took to the stage. After the Pope had finished radiating in the appraisal, one of his confidants handed him the speech that had been written by the young pastor from Canada, who was living his dream as an apprentice to the pope.

"I've never before seen this large amount of Christians gathered in the square". the pope whispered, as the high priest handed him the speech.

There was a chair provided for the pope to sit and deliver his speech, along with a microphone in order for everyone in attendance to clearly hear his words. With Pope Arthur's hands held high, the noise decimal was almost deafening, before he slowly brought the crowd to silence with the descent of his hands. The Pope who had been slightly ill was helped to his seat, as he then fitted his reading glasses and stared at the first sentence of the speech. Before Pope Arthur began reading the pre-written speech, the leader of the Catholic Church looked up at the symbols in the sky and asked everyone to bow their heads in prayer.

"Our most wonderful and loving creator, we humbly come before thee this evening to ----." began the pope.

Chapter 3

It was 5:30pm when Sergeant Keith Lester and member of his First Battalion Princess Patricia Canadian Light Infantry set out on an evening mission to locate and eliminate Taliban Insurgents in the town of Nakhoney Afghanistan. The squad of twenty soldiers left from Kandahar City and travelled southbound, where it had been reported that Insurgents were increasing their attacks across the region. The coalition forces of the United Nations had been battling Al-Qaida forces for several years, and after recent progress that resulted in the foreigners gaining the confidence and trust of the local people, it was imperative that any disruption by the Taliban be addressed with excessive force. The platoon of soldiers left the secured base on foot and walked across treacherous terrain, in an area of Afghanistan, which had proven to be the most volatile regions in the war.

    The soldiers walked through a huge poppy field eight kilometers from the city, where they joked about sewing and reaping such a crop on Canadian soil. The sergeant, who trotted along with the field medical officer, enquired whether or not the fumes from the poppy plants could intoxicate his troops. The medical officer explained that it would be impossible to not be affected by the toxic fumes from the plants, which are used to create powered cocaine. Sergeant Lester warned his troops to simmer down and remain alert, knowing the treacherous habits of their unpredictable foes, whom they had fought for over a decade. The soldiers, who could have utilized the local road that runs around the poppy field, chose the more obscure path through the drug lord's crops, where they suspected there was a less of a chance for hidden Implosive Explosion Devices. The Canadian forces had fought the Insurgents since the beginning of the war, yet even though they'd made drastic progress, not eliminating the key orchestrators of the Taliban had prolonged the fight.

Brigadier General Alex Kozy, a twenty eight year veteran of the Canadian forces, was the supreme commander in Afghanistan. The Brigadier General who was inside the command station in Kandahar, received reports of an ambush plotted against the Nakhoney platoon, which was en-route to the small town. Brigadier General Alex Kozy radioed his troops in the field and instructed them to prepare for the unexpected after receiving the reports from a resident of Nakhoney, who had sided with the coalition forces. Information attained from local villagers has saved the lives of many United Nations soldiers and helped to bridge the trust between both fractions.

With Sergeant Lester at the helm, the Canadian troops carefully pressed on to the town of Nakhoney, which is located in the district of Panjwaii. The winter season was fast approaching and coalition members were well aware of the disappearing tactics of insurgents during the cold season. UN soldiers were also accustomed to the departing memorabilia of terrorism by the Taliban, who've never went into hibernation without some grand gesture of cruelty. It had been almost a week since the last Taliban attack, and analysts were anticipating another.

There were a few soldiers who travelled ahead of Sergeant Lester and the remainder of the platoon. Although these heroic men steamed the point, their duties were purely to locate (IED) Implosive Explosive Devices and report to their commander. Sergeant Lester walked directly behind the metal detector scouts in order to award them fire support should they desire it since they had to pay keen attention to the machine, while carrying their weapons over their shoulders. The soldiers who trailed the scouts paid close attention to were the leaders walked, and made were sure to follow along the same tracks.

As the platoon approached Nakhoney, Sergeant Lester who cautiously trailed the metal detectors unfortunately stepped onto an IED, which made a clicking sound beneath his right foot. The thoughtful sergeant immediately froze in his tracks, before rapidly instructing his troops to move away from his location. With his troops scattering for protection, the sergeant lifted his head to the skies and began praying, while considering his young fiancée and daughter back in Canada. Sergeant Lester looked around to ensure that every one of his soldiers was clear, before valiantly diving towards the brushes left of him.

The Implosive Explosive Device exploded and flung Sergeant Lester almost twenty feet away as the medic and assistant nurse rushed to his aide. The Insurgents who were responsible for the IED had disguised themselves behind walls, houses and other artifacts across the front of the town, and responded to the explosion with automatic gunfire aimed at the vulnerable Canadians. The assistant nurse was shot in the shoulder, while attempting to race to his sergeant's side, while the other Canadian troops began returning fire.

"The nurse is down and the sergeant's probably dead! Boyd, get your ass on that radio and get an immediate E-vac in here!" the second sergeant yelled.

"They're over there!" a patrol member shouted, before launching a grenade over at three bunkered down insurgents. The grenade fell directly in the midst of the militia fighters, who were blown to bits with body parts sent flying.

"Maple Leaf Command this is Patricia Patrol we've been hit by an ambush, Lester got IED and the nurse was shot in the shoulder, we need immediate E-vac. I repeat, we need immediate E-vac!" radioed Specialist Boyd to command.

A huge shootout erupted between the Taliban Militia and the Canadian coalition members. While the ensuing battle raged on, the medical officer attended to the sergeant who had been critically injured by the Implosive Explosive Device. The sergeant's legs had been blown completely off with massive injuries to his entire body. The chief field medical officer first checked the sergeant's vital signs to ensure his colleague hadn't succumbed to his injuries, before administering a morphine injection to help boost the injured soldier metabolism. With Sergeant Lester unable to tend his duties, Second Sergeant Lapoint took command of the unit as he began instructing his troops on where to attack.

"Boyd did you radio in that chopper?" the medic demanded, knowing that every passing moment was valuable in saving the sergeant's life.

"They're on the way"! Specialist Boyd responded, as he withdrew an extra magazine from his pouch and reloaded his riffle.

"I can't feel a thing Claude." Sergeant Lester muffled.

"It's not pretty serge, you're pretty tore up." the medic exclaimed.

Second Sergeant Lapoint could be heard barking orders at his troops, who were beginning to grasp control of the situation. Lapoint ushered orders for his troops to the far right of town, to attack the flank of their foes, who were weakening at their very centre of the ambush. With heavy cover fire being offered by their colleagues, half a dozen troops entered the northern section of the town, which foiled the insurgents' perfect ambush. The Canadians northern attack forced the Taliban to retreat further back into the town, where they fought behind the covers of civilian's homes, while the first battalion pressed their attack.

The Taliban Insurgents refused to surrender the town of Nakhoney, which was a major strategic point in their Kandahar operations. The militia members of Al-Qaida, who were sent to control the town of Nakhoney, were also given decisive orders on how to proceed should the coalition forces mount an assault. The Taliban Insurgents regrouped in the heart of the town, dug deep and held their ground as their Canadian counterparts found cover and engaged in an artillery exchange. The local residents of Nakhoney were forced to lie on the ground inside their homes while the opposing forces warred outside their front door.

While their fellow battalion soldiers pushed the fight away from Sergeant Lester, their field medical officer and his nurse waited for the medical evacuation, which was said to be on route to their coordinates. Sergeant Lester lay flat on his back, while the medical officer and his injured nurse fought to stop the bleeding and keep him alive. The faint sound of a Huey Helicopter could be heard in the distance, as Sergeant Lester looked up over the doctor's shoulder at what he thought was an angel flying in the sky. The perceived imaginary figure of the angel began scrolling symbols across the clouds, which Lester feared disclosing to the medics, with the belief that this meant he was about to cross over into the afterlife. The sergeant immediately reached for his cellular phone in his breast pocket and quickly searched for his brother's programmed number. Believing this to be his final call, Sergeant Lester ignored the doctors toiling over him, as tears ran down the side of this face.

Sergeant Lester was terrified as he watched the angel draw the symbols, before the translation was whispered into his ear. Once the translation was told to him, the sergeant began pointing to the sky, as his contact responded over the phone. The nurse, who meagerly assisted because of the bullet to his shoulder, found the actions of his sergeant strange and turned to look up at the sky. The sight of the symbols in the clouds startled the nurse, who quickly alerted the doctor to the phenomenon. The sight of the bright symbols across the evening's skies fascinated the doctor. However, once the translations were spoken to him, the man stunningly fell back on the seed of his pants.

"Wha-wha-wha-what's all this supposed to mean? Where the hell did those things come?" the nurse nervously enquired.

"How the hell should I know?" the doctor responded.

Sergeant Lester who wished to convey a message to his personal family, knew his fiancée schedule ensured she be a work at those hours, hence the injured soldier chose to call his brother.

"Brother I haven't enough time left; I just accidentally stepped on a land mine. Craig I've just seen the most amazing thing in the sky, they're symbols yet I understand them totally." Sergeant Lester decreed.

"Oh no not you my brother, I pray the lord guides you through to the next life. Is there anything you want me to tell the family"? Pastor Craig Lester enquired.

"Tell everyone I love them and let my little girl know that daddy will always watch over her. I love you brother---." Keith exclaimed as the loud sound of the Huey's engine stifled out the conversation.

The Red Cross rescue helicopter landed a few feet away from the doctors and patient. With the terrain around the medical area cleared of hostiles, the gunners aboard the helicopter ran to the wounded with a stretcher. First Sergeant Lester who had been heavily sedated with medication was scooped up, and his severed limbs collected, before being ushered off towards the helicopter. As the soldiers neared their transport, the injured Lester reached out to the symbols, which brought the account to the attention of the chopper crew. At the sight of the symbols, one of the unwary gunners frightfully released his right grip of the stretcher handle, which narrowly threw Lester to the turf. The gunner quickly corrected his mistake and loaded the injured sergeant on the helicopter before quickly hopping aboard himself. The doctor and his injured nurse were forced to accompany the injured sergeant, who was holding on for dear life.

As the helicopter took to the sky, the clashing forces on the ground soon became aware of the symbols, which brightened up the evening's sky. The exchange of gun fire surprisingly ceased, as the Canadian troops and their Taliban rivals became fascinated with the phenomenon. The majority of fighters from both warring factions became disinterested in the conflict, and walked out into the clear totally hypnotized by the symbols. The historical sight of soldiers dropping and abandoning their arms surprised the residents of Nakhoney, who began slowly emerging from their shelters, once the alert was made professing the symbols. The warning sirens that alerted citizens of various war torn countries of dangers, religious practices and other important traditions; to which residents are urged to seek proper shelter or pay respect, began sounding in areas that used such technology.

Chapter 4

Cassandra Bryan was a nineteen year old college student, who got the opportunity of a lifetime to tour sections of Ghana West Africa, with the students from her Public Relations class. The one week tour was one of spiritual upliftment, where the students were privileged to visit historical sites, while partaking of the natural beauty of the world's first continent. Professor St. Jacque had orchestrated the memorable trip for students for nearly a decade after completing his volunteer service with UNICEF some fifteen years prior. The Ottawa University students were on their fifth day of the tour where they visited the Elmina Castle along the Cape Coast, which was a place where black slaves were imprisoned.

The students made a number of historical visits to places like the home of Yahsantoi the first queen, who was the Ashanti king's wife. Yahsantoi was made famous for her role during the times of slavery, where her infamous phrase, "Ou kum apem, apem bei ba", which means, "if you kill a thousand, a thousand shall come", uplifted and strengthened the black nation. The students also visited the place of Konfu Anachi, who united the Ashanti Clan. Anachi was said to command the Golden Stoll and under that Stoll twelve other small tribes united. The Canadian student learnt about the culture and lives of Africans and also indulged in the National foods like Fufu and Kenki, which they learnt was made from natural corn dough.

While visiting local villages like Abrue, Kumasi, Oboaci and Ewe, the students listened to the African elders, who told stories of ancient and translated famous proverbs like, "The crocodile lives in water, but does not breath water", which in part means, "adaptation is key to survival." Another of Africa's famous proverb learnt by the students dictated that, "If you climb a good tree, someone will always help you." The most intriguing and spiritually enlightened proverb Cassandra believed, was told to her by a young boy begging for spare change, who decreed, "Gie-ayama" after receiving the gratitude, which in translation stated, "Only God!" Cassandra, whose brother had been hospitalized, thought extensively about the beggar's comment as she memorized the phrase to pass on to her mother.

It was 4:00pm in the afternoon and the students were on their tour bus returning from the coast, where they visited local villages like the Ahousa, the Ashanti and spent time with the Ewe tribe, who were said to be a Voodoo obsessed clan. While the students ranted and raved about their experiences that day, the tour bus driver began noticing pedestrians along the roadway, pointing to the skies in utter amazement. With keen interest the driver glared up at the clouds, before frightfully pulling the bus to the soft shoulder of the dirt road. The driver's obvious signs of discontent soon became evident to the students, who were at first confused about the reason for stopping. Professor St. Jacque and the rest of his students dismounted behind the tour-bus driver, whose mouth fell open in amazement the moment he saw the symbols across the African sky.

"Is it only me or did someone just translate the meaning to these signs to the rest of you guys?" Professor St. Jacque enquired.

"I think we need to get our asses back on Canadian soil!" said a classmate named Tenysiah.

"Yeah Professor I think she's right, this is some serious shit." Classmate Jake Ien agreed.

"Everybody get back on the bus, we must go now!" the tour bus driver instructed.

As the students began moving towards the bus, an African observer fascinated with the symbols yelled out in distress, as she witnessed a commercial aircraft tumbling out of the sky. Seconds after the woman screamed out in fright, the troubled aircraft crashed to the ground and explode. The bus driver hurried everyone aboard and continued towards Accra, despite the comments suggesting they assist the victims of the plane crash.

Once it became evident that the driver was not about to waste time in offering aide to the victims of the plane crash, a female student suggested they drove directly to the airport or the Canadian Embassy in Accra. A debate was struck amongst the students, where the notion was made to continue onto the hotel, since a number of the students had left their passport inside their hotel suites. The tour bus driver, who had begun listening to the local radio station for updates, astonished everyone when he uttered, "Oh my God, they just reported that this thing is all over the sky in the world!"

"My God what does all this mean, what is going to happen to us?" argued a terrified student name Melissa Moore.

"I want everyone to relax; now the first thing we're not going to do is panic. We are all going to get back home safely, so stay together and let's support each other." Professor St. Jacque instructed.

"Does this mean that this is the end of the world as we know it?" Vivian Loyal argued.

"Whether it's the end of the world or not, we don't know. All we know is we're still alive and we're going to do whatever it takes to get back home." the professor assured his students.

Despite the professor's reassurance, a number of the students began weeping uncontrollably, as they pondered over what was to become of them. There was a twenty year old male seated in the back of the bus named Alfonso Ford, who was raised in a household of loyal Jehovah's Witnesses. The young man remarkably remained calm as he began professing about issues he'd learnt from a young lad. Nervousness swept through the tour bus like a bad flu, where everyone selfishly thought about their star player.

"The bible has told about these last days forever, its judgment time for everything that is evil on this planet. This is not our war; in fact this is the holiest of wars between the devil and the supreme God. At the end of it all though, we will be judged for our individual sins. That's the way it is, and there is absolutely nothing any of us can do about it." Alfonso stated.

"That's all just a myth, so shut the hell up! You don't know what you're talking about, so stop trying to scare everyone, you asshole!" declared a female student seated in the row of seats across from Alfonso.

"You can believe whatever you want; your stupid grandfather has spent all his days attempting to disclaim the truth in the bible. I already told you God is no laughing matter." Alfonso answered.

"Go to Hell!" the female cursed.

"OK guys enough of that! We have way more pressing issues at hand!" the professor yelled.

While some debated their situation, other students used the time to telephone their parents and loved ones back in Canada in order to update them on their predicament. Despite their religious stance on the issues, Professor St. Jacque was able to calm everyone, as he got them to gather together and pray. The driver of the tour bus watched through his window, as local residents scurried along to reunite with family members, while others found refuge in churches and mosques. The driver was cruising through the city of Accra, when he came across a road block on route to the Royal Cambridge Hotel. The massive car pileup provided nowhere to escape, as people were vacating their vehicles in the middle of the street. After patiently waiting for three minutes, frustrations overtook the driver who abandoned his post and his passengers.

"I'm sorry, I'm sorry, I'm sorry, but I must get home to my family. The hotel is right down this street, you can't miss it. Forgive me but I must go!" the bus driver declared, before collecting his personals and leaving.

"You can't just leave us like this Manuel." the professor argued, before the driver ran off into the crowd.

"Oh God no! What are to do professor?" Jennifer Stebbing a student demanded.

"Listen to me everyone we're going to stay together. Like the driver said the hotel is only a few blocks down this road. I don't wish to loose any of you, so gather your things and let's try to get there in one peace." the professor instructed.

"And then what professor?" Melissa asked from the middle of the bus.

"We'll figure that out after we get to our destination, now get it together and let's go!" the professor stated.

The band of college students abandoned the tour bus, which was jammed between several cars honking their horns. As they exited the tour bus, Cassandra borrowed Vivian's cellular and telephoned her mother, whom she hadn't yet spoken to that day. The telephone rang twice, before a jubilant and relieved Sarah answered the phone. Both mother and daughter were excited to hear each other's voice as they comforted each other.

"Hi mom it's me!"

"Oh honey I'm so happy to hear your voice, are you alright?"

"I'm fine mom, how are Junior and dad doing?"

"We're getting much better honey; your dad finally got the money together for your brother's operations."

"That's terrific news mom, I hope things work out. Have you seen the things in the sky?"

"I'm looking at them as we speak honey. I want you to get home right now before some major things start happening!"

"OK mom I'll try, but give Junior a kiss for me and tell him I love him and to stay strong. Oh-Oh and mom, 'Gie-ayama', it means 'only God'. Love you!"

The group of Canadian college students began scurrying through the capital city, which had become a frantic atmosphere. The chaos amongst Africans, who were scrambling to get home to their families, initially scared the professor who was utterly concerned about his students. Professor St. Jacque was nervous about looters and thieves interfering with his students as they hurried through town, although contrary to his belief, Africans were equally as worried about their survival. The traffic through the city was at a stand-still as commuters abandoned their vehicles. The storeowners and business men along the strip were fast closing their facilities with serious doubt and uncertainty about their future.

Three hundred yards away from the hotel's compound, the students ran by an ally where a police officer had shot and killed two thieves, after they had attempted to rob a local jewelry store. The officer who'd killed both robbers prior to the symbols appearing, has since watched the assembled crowd disappeared, as he awaited the coroner and the crime scene investigative team. The witnesses, who had gathered following the incident, began departing at the sight on the symbols, while the officer, a sincere believer in God, drowned in his sorrows in the wake of his actions. With the belief that he had squandered his chances at salvation, the officer knelt over the deceased bodies and wept while begging for forgiveness. The distraught officer to the surprise of several of the students and other civilians took a machete from one of his two victims and chopped off his right hand, which was the hand that fired the weapon.

Professor St. Jacque, who lead the students had passed the mouth of the ally and therefore missed the officer's radical self-inflicted penalty. However, the frightful screams of a number of his female students, soon brought the lawman's actions to his attention. The professor was forced to attend to a few of his students, who became rather hysterical after witnessing such a gruesome sight. St. Jacque advised everyone to continue at the same pace, as he lingered on behind with the troubled students.

The Canadian students later arrived at their destination, to find the humongous front gate locked without a security guard at his post. The professor ran into the guard station and attempted to telephone the main building, but to no avail. A French student from Quebec named Sylvie Bristol, caught sight of someone running about the grounds and began yelling for assistance, before the remainder of her classmates started hollering as well.

A white male from Belgium who was himself a local guest, noticed the students whom he'd seen around the compound prior, and ran to assist them in gaining entry. The main gate had been latched from the inside for added protection after the security personnel and other staff members chose to abandon their posts and attend to their personal affairs. With the assistance of the Belgium native, the Canadians were able to enter the less stressful environment, where the professor's blood pressure could return to normal.

"Thank you kindly my friend, it's a bit nerve wrecking out there amongst the natives." Professor St. Jacque argued.

"Don't mention it; I'm sure you would have done the same thing for me." answered the Good Samaritan.

"Aren't you going to try to get back home?" the professor enquired.

"There are absolutely no planes leaving the airport. The news has been reporting that all pilots and planes have been grounded until further notice." said the Belgium native.

"What about the different country's embassies, I'm sure they must be doing something to get their citizens abroad back home." the professor argued.

"With all the airplanes that have been falling from the skies today, I don't think too many people want to go aboard one of those things right now!" said the kind hearted man.

"Oh shit we saw one going down only a few miles from us!" the professor said.

"Well according to the news forecast that's been getting televised that's only one out of hundreds since those signs popped up in the sky. Whether we like it or not my friend, we're all stuck here until whatever happens happen!" the man exclaimed.

Chapter 5

NASA Airspace Astronomers received surprising data from Nexus-PX568, which was an exploratory space probe launched in 1980. The Nexus project was intended to locate extraterrestrial life forms in galaxies light years away from earth and relay data about its findings. The Nexus probe, which contained sophisticated state of the art software, was programmed to study planets and life-forms while posing as an ambassador to the earth. Since its launch into orbit the Nexus-PX568 has helped scientists solve a number of anomalies about their solar system, as well as other systems around the universe.

The data sent from the space probe was the last and final transmission posted, hence scientists fought to determine the state of the explorer. The space probe which was light years away from earth, was studying an unchartered planet to determine whether life forms could survive. Scientists speculated that the probe was destroyed by an alien source after it reportedly recorded data describing a plane moving incredibly fast, which was measured at five times the size of the earth. The unconventional report baffled scientists who have never before witnessed a planet travelling at three times the speed of light.

The scientists at NASA airspace analyzed the data and found a startling revelation. The findings by the scientists were so astronomical that the same tests and calculations had to be redone to ensure precision before reporting the data to the highest official. Once the calculations were confirmed, the chief scientist who was responsible for briefing the president immediately contacted the American leader with the report.

The president of the United States, Mr. Ron Flores, received an emergency phone call from the head of NASA Space and Technology, Mrs. Nadine Wright, who telephoned to update the commander in chief about their recent findings and developments. The President, who was being briefed on the report filed by the Air Force, was seated in the Oval Office with aides and advisors who had all gathered to determine exactly what was transpiring around the entire world.

"According to the flight tower engineers the pilot of the weather jet reportedly yelled that there was something grabbing onto the aircraft; before later stating that whatever the thing was is the cause for the airplane slamming into the DC 600." reported Major General Kevin Franks of the U.S Air Force.

The alert phone, which is only used by representatives of critical divisions in times of emergency, rung during the major general's disclosure. The president reached for the phone while his advisers debated the revelations of the major general. After responding to the call, the President placed Mrs. Wright on the intercom for everyone inside the chamber to hear her report, which the President hoped would shed more light on their situation.

"Mrs. Wright the vice president and my presidential advisors are present and may pose questions during your debriefing. With that clarified, you may proceed with your report." advised the President.

"Good afternoon to you all! Mr. President Sir we've received reports from Nexus-PX568 which is an exploratory probe that we launched in 1980. The Nexus Probe has sent us information about an unfamiliar planet that appears to be locked onto a collision course with the earth. We've since triangulated the course of this planet, which is measured at five times the size of the earth, and have confirmed that this data is 99.7% accurate." Ms. Wright stated.

"Do you people have any evidence to connect this planet with the phenomenon that appeared in the skies across this great planet?" the Vice President asked.

"As for both cases we have no immediate evidence to link the spectrums, but our research have clarified that both anomalies are authentic and should be taken extremely seriously." Ms. Wright warned.

"Exactly what's our time-frame before this planet reaches our solar system?" President Flores questioned.

"Mr. President Sir at the speed it's travelling it will reach us in forty six hours and thirty eight minutes, according to our time tracker!" Mrs. Wright exclaimed.

"Mrs. Wright this is General Lloyd Bates, are there any specifics you can send us about the type of planet this is?" the senior general for the United States Army asked.

"General, this planet not only blew by our probe, but also we believe disintegrated Nexus-PX568. The data the probe was able to collect before going off-line gives us a pretty good idea of the type of planet it was, but considering this was no ordinary planet, we believe there is much more than what meets the eyes." Mrs. Wright answered.

"Could you please have your people send me the specifics you were able to gather about this threat?" General Bates enquired.

"No problem general, I'll get my assistant to e-mail you our findings immediately." The NASA scientist stated.

"Mrs. Wright your country applauds you and your division for such swift and diligent work, we ask that you keep us informed should anything arise and thank you once again." The president sighted.

President Flores ended the call before turning his attention to his advisors and strategists. The Vice President Mr. Mark Williams wasted no time as he focused his attention on General Lloyd Bates, the military economist inside the chamber, who was a sixty two year old veteran of the US Army and Major General Kevin Franks, a fifty nine year old Air Force commander. The remaining economists around the table quietly chatted amongst themselves as their increased agitation became evident.

"General Bates, have you anything in your armory capable of destroying such a huge planet?" the Vice President asked.

"I believe we can find something to at least put a crack in it, but it's going to take the efforts of the whole world to break it into unthreatening pieces! We have at our disposal the Ordinance Penetrator bomb, which was designed to destroy the Taliban's tunnel systems in Afghanistan. I'm quite confident that a number of highly modified bombs will knock this sucker out of space!" General Bates calculated.

"I'm in full agreement with my friend Lloyd sir. Our only means of destroying this planet is if every nuclear armed country cohesively launch missile at this thing." Major General Franks added.

"According to the available data, this approaching planet is a beast! I am certain that throwing a few pebbles at it isn't going to solve our problem, so I am on board with these recommendations one hundred percent Sir"! agreed the Secretary of Defense.

"Hit it with all our might at once, brilliant! May just be our best bet." the Vice President reasoned.

"Might just be our only serious means of defense. We have to target our missiles where even if we're unable to destroy the planet, we at lease knock it off course." General Bates argued.

"Should we fail at destroying this planet the earth will be no more, but if we intelligently pursue this, then we stand a chance at surviving this thing." Major General Franks exclaimed.

"General I want you to proceed with this missile strike plan; I'll contact the necessary leaders and bring them on board. Shanice, I want you to get me all the nuclear players around the globe and prepare a public address to the nation. I believe the rest of Americans would like to know their fate and please page the first lady." President Flores instructed.

While General Bates transferred data to the pentagon, the conversation continued amongst the president and his other advisors. The general sought to increase the weight of a conventional thirty thousand pounds bomb, which included three tons of explosives, to a hundred thousand pound bomb, with over ten tons of explosives. The precision-guided bomb would be the biggest conventional bomb the United States has ever fielded, with exceptions to the Atomic Bomb, which lacked the capability to be blasted into outer space. General Bates transmitted the data sent to him from NASA to his engineers at the Pentagon, who deciphered the actual amount of explosives desired to destroy such a massive planet.

"Mr. President Sir, at the expense of sounding stupid, considering the symbols in the skies and everything else we've experienced thus far, what if we're about to shoot at God?" The Attorney General asked.

"Mr. Attorney General, I personally believe we've been threatened and this giant rock heading towards us is the device being used to carry out that threat. Now if indeed this is the lord's work, then he better send another sign fast, because if he doesn't, we're going to blow the hell out of this planet before it blows the hell out of us!" Major General Franks interrupted.

"At ease general, I know you live to blow up stuff, but like those millions of Americans who've ran to churches for repentance because they actually believe in a higher power, I beg to differ against your missile strikes, which, if aren't properly coordinated may just be the devastation we're trying to defend against! Mr. President since these symbols arrived; the weather forecast around the entire globe has been spectacular. In areas where winter should be ravaging the region, the skies are clear and temperatures are record breaking. Here, look at the data! I'm just saying that before we make a critical error, we reanalyze the facts and wait." The Attorney General Pablo Deeds stated.

"Exactly how long do you suggest we wait Mr. Attorney General, before we respond to this threat---?" the Air Force Major General commented.

"General Franks please!" interrupted the president, as he motioned both men to settle the argument. "I'm afraid even though we're gathered to intellectually find a solution to our problem, the general is right Pablo. We simply don't have the time to mess around with this, the risk is far too great."

"At what time do you wish to address the nation sir?" asked the president's secretary.

"Schedule the reporters for the top of the hour; I should be done with the delegates by then." President Flores answered.

Vice President Mark Williams and the President went from the oval office to the conference room, which was equipped with live video conferencing and satellite feeds. The president's secretary had assembled the world's nuclear leaders on a joint conference phone call. While waiting for the videoconference to begin, the leader of the free world and his successor spoke candidly about their duties to the country should their worst fears be realized.

"Protocol dictates that we get transferred to some underground bunker for the survival of the country. But considering all that's at the cost of my family and grandchildren, I don't believe that would be a decision which Merrill and I would accept. No man should outlive his children and grandchildren, and I won't try to be the first to break the trend." the Vice President said.

"We're both lovers and passionate about our families, our country and our God, but given the situation we're facing I know Janet will never vote for secluding ourselves in some secure bunker, while the rest of humanity perishes. Furthermore, should the earth survive this catastrophe, there may not be a single thing to return to anyways, we could find ourselves back in the Ice-Age." the President responded.

"It's understandable that we have the lives of two hundred plus million people to protect, but I sincerely disagree with our approach in doing so." Vice President Williams argued.

"I'm a man of faith and being President means that I as a born Adventist must at times attend church services like the Muslims, Catholics, Jehovah's Witnesses and all others. I'm quite aware of the teachings of Allah or even the Witnesses, who all speak about the return of the Prophet Muhammad, Jesus Christ, Jehovah whoever they pray to. I've even scrolled through their bibles and as such must concur, but in the end, protecting the people of America is our first priority!" President Flores remarked.

"Mister President Sir, the leaders you requested are all on the comp, you may proceed. Gentlemen the President of the United States." introduced the President's secretary.

The president spoke with the forum of leaders, who all faced similar predicaments in their own countries. Foreign leaders of communist countries faced major revolts, as their citizens ignored the orders of their leaders to proceed with their daily routines. There were mixed reaction towards the symbols between True Christians and Atheists across the globe. However, despite their reactions, one thing was assured; which was for the first time in history, the entire world stood in peril. People across the globe were flocking to mosques, synagogs, temples and churches, with the small minority of none religious infidels criticizing those of faith. A grave number of humans who never before entered a building of worship prior to the symbols, sought retributions for their sins as they crammed into worship halls all over the world.

President Flores detailed the findings of his NASA scientists to the none-affiliate leaders of the Outer Space Federation. The President's analysis was confirmed by the Russians, the Chinese and Canadians, who all had space exploration programs of their own. The news of the earth's possible demise wasn't graciously accepted by the leaders of the less predominant countries, who were all eager to learn of the plan to counteract the threat. For the survival of mankind on planet earth, each world leader agreed to the solution suggested by President Flores, where they would coordinate a combined strike at the approaching planet. The major leaders who were all members of the G-20 Summit, knowing that time was of the essence, spent four hours coordinating the timeline at which each country would release their nukes, the transfer arrangements of the Ordinance Penetrator Bombs to countries without similar technology and the designated coordinates for each country.

With an evasive plot secured, the President of the United States embarked on a public address to the nation at 6pm that evening. During his speech, President Flores outlined the severe dangers the entire world faced, as well as the strategy that was being employed to counter the problem. The president warned about the dangers of not acting, as well as the possible aftermath should the protruding planet collide with the earth. There was a measure of despair in the president's voice as he spoke, though he managed to compose himself as he terminated his address by blessing the people of America, as well as those of the entire world.

Chapter 6

For the Almighty so loved the world that he created man to watch over it, while taking care of the beauty he'd perfected. But man was led astray because of the treachery of a serpent, which also attempted to overthrow the creator within his midst. The mutiny attempted by the serpent was the first revolt against a higher regime; hence the serpent and his followers were all cast from the midst of the creator, to live amongst men until the creator's return.

Lucifer AKA the serpent, AKA Satan the Devil, had long sought to rule his own kingdom. Since his eviction from Heaven, the Devil has long known about his day of retribution. Hence, his preparation for the anointed battle begun from the day he was cursed to live amongst the lesser beings of the Almighty's creation. Satan, who had long known the feebleness of the human heart, had long manipulated these subjects of God to perform devastating acts of wickedness, while devoting their prayers to him. The Devil made himself into the perfect puppet master, where he controlled his subjects and toyed with their existence.

In order to maintain a sense of balance on the earth during his absence, the creator assigned a squad of Defender Angels to remain. These angels were to protect God's loyal worshippers and police the entire inhabited earth. Since their projection to the earth, these Defender Angels have engaged in numerous squirmishes with their Arc-Angel nemesis, who are constantly plotting means of bringing forth destruction upon mankind. The Defender Angels of God have prevented countless near-tragedy from occurring since the forming of their division, although such devastation like Hiroshima and 9/11 were catastrophes they failed to prevent. Protecting those true worshipers of God, like Job of ancient times, had always been the priority of the Defenders, although there have been incidents where the Devil's influence have corrupted the minds of the faithful. "The flesh is weak," which is why numerous pastors and men of the cloth have engaged in sinful behaviors, like child molestation and child pornography. There have been those who have embarked on total world domination, like Alexander the Great or Hitler, yet the Defenders have always found means to thwart the plots of such greedy rulers.

Satan, the Devil for his part, has adorned the wicked nature of such men, who he'd personally recruited to serve as soldiers in his dark army after they'd met their timely demise. Lucifer, who was conscious about the predictions documented on ancient scrolls, had long experimented on creating Warlords in order to increase the size of his army of Dark Soldiers. Without the physical capability to inflate oxygen into the lifeless corpses he'd created, the Devil had to find alternate measures of bringing his Dark Forces to life.

In the year 2000, a doctor Heinz Flakiskor of Reykjavik, Iceland, who had been secretly experimenting on a machine to replace the modern day Defibulator, made a breakthrough in medicine when he successfully created a machine which could revive a person hours after they'd stopped breathing. Doctor Flakiskor successfully revived two apes, which were his first test subjects before trying his machine on actual humans. The doctor revived four corpses which had been donated to science, by the donors who sought to advance medicine and help cure diseases. The illegal procedure attempted by Dr. Flakiskor could have landed him behind bars for the remainder of his years, but the success of his dream machine transformed him to celebrity instantly. The successful revival of these corpses proved that Dr. Flakiskor's theoretical machine worked, thus he was able to avert any criminal proceedings. The doctor, later conveyed to an audience of medical experts that critically injured soldiers were his motivation to creating the machine, although he was thrilled that everyone could be saved.

Unlike the Defibulator of ancient, which discharged a controlled degree of electrical shock that jump started the patient's heart, Dr. Flakiskor's machine was a cube, which the corpse was placed comfortably into before the neutrons conveyed by the machine rejuvenated living tissue and resurrected the deceased. For his tireless endeavors, Dr. Flakiskor received the 2000 Medical Award for the greatest invention of the decade, along with countless accolades from his peers. Dr. Flakiskor was dubbed, 'One of the greatest minds of the twenty first century' by the American Journal of medicine, which featured him on the cover of their July 2000 magazine edition. Dr. Flakiskor also graced the covers of the Wall Street Journal, Forbes Health and Fitness, Healthy Living Magazine and numerous newspapers across the globe.

On August 3oth 2000, Dr. Heinz Flakiskor was on a private Leer Jet to Manchester England, where he was scheduled to engage in negotiations with a private contractor who sought to mass-produce the doctor's invention. The Leer Jet, that belonged to the Stebbing Inventors Corporation, was fifty miles off the coast of Iceland during immaculate weather when the aircraft suddenly began experiencing difficulties before if fell off the radar without any reports of danger or malfunction by the pilot.

The private jet was in mid flight when the aircraft flew into a bit of suspected turbulence, which caused the jet to immediately loose altitude. The pilot, who suspected no grave danger, fought to correct the descending aircraft, which eventually crashed and exploded. Unknown to the pilot and crew was the fact that two Demonic Angels had created the air pocket as a diversion before sabotaging and driving the aircraft into the North Atlantic Ocean. The bodies aboard the wrecked Leer Jet were never found, which led to one of the biggest unsolved mysteries of all times. Coast Guard rescuers from both Iceland and the United Kingdom searched the areas around the crash site for ten days before cancelling their search with no inkling as to what became of the plane's infamous cargo.

Doctor Flakiskor, the airplane hostess and their two experienced pilots woke up in a grimy dungeon where the lighting was minimal, the walls were solid rock, and there was only an ancient day pit for a toilet. The awful lighting condition made it impossible to see anything at a distance, although there was constant screaming and moaning by captives being constantly tortured. From inside the adjoining cells came the cries of foreign prisoners, both human and animal. There was a lingering foul stench, which eventually became second nature to the captives after a few hours of confinement. The doctor was the last to regain consciousness, yet the first to begin raising attention to their displeasure as he immediately made his discomfort heard.

"What is the meaning of this? I demand to be released at once, I'm a medical doctor not some would-be criminal. I insist that whoever you are, these bars get opened immediately. Hello, hello can anyone hear me!" Dr. Flakiskor yelled.

While the airhostess felt her way around the grimy cell for an alternate exit, the doctor and the pilots continued their attempt at summoning a caretaker. Regardless of their shared predicament, Dr. Flakiskor was skeptical of the Leer Jet's crew members, whom he secretly believed plotted some kidnapping scheme to extort ransom money. The fear being felt by the doctor was soon experienced by the pilots, who both began yelling in order to raise an alert. After screaming for nearly forty plus minutes, the doctor, who stood closest to the barred door, noticed a faint feature coming at a distance. Doctor Flakiskor removed his glasses from his face and wiped them clean for better visibility before remounting them to his face. While the doctor cleaned his specs, the pilots who also noticed the same figure approaching, began resending to the rear of the cell as the huge creature like figure approached the door.

"Doctor I think you might want to step away from those bars." the air hostess declared.

"What was that love?" Dr. Flakiskor enquired.

The doctor, whose attention was focused on cleaning of his glasses, remounted his second pair of eyes and raised his head. There was a humongous figure standing on the other side of the cell, which was half human, half beast, with folded wings attached to its back. The frightful sight of the black demonic angel who stood outside the bars caused the doctor to fall back on the seat of his pants before scampering to the rear of the cell for safety.

"Holly shit what the Hell is that?" questioned the air hostess as she crawled underneath the right arm of the senior pilot.

Demonic Angels, who've chosen to live underground, were once as white and bright as their ex-siblings from Heaven but centuries of dwelling beneath the ground transformed their appearance to that of their surroundings. Contrary to the angels of God who are replenished by the heat of the sun, the demonic angels of Satan have contorted themselves into lovers of the darkness and adapted to their environment. Hence, dark and grungy are the hearts of this legion of Satan who fled the realm of their creation and devoted themselves to the utter annihilation of their creator.

The humongous beast slightly pushed on the barred door, which the captives had been tirelessly fighting to rattle ajar. The Demon of the Devil, who stood over ten feet tall, was black as night with long black dreads flowing down his back between his wings. The armor across his chest and back was as dark as his complexion, with strings the same color fastening it along his rib cage. The Demonic Angel's humongous hands were like those of a beast; with claw like fingers shrewd enough to rip a man's chest wide open. The pilots, who had been plotting a surprise, looked at each other and signaled with a nod, before attempting to tackle their captor. Despite their close proximity, the pilots were unable to lay a hand on the Demonic Angel, who reactively stumped the senior pilot back into the wall and stopped the co-pilot by grabbing him by the neck and hoisting him off the ground. The senior pilot, who crashed into the wall, uttered a huge groan as he quickly grabbed for his back and cried, 'that his back was broken.' In an attempt to intimidate his captives, the demonic angel displayed his strength and might by holding the co-pilot aloft until he'd just about fell unconscious under the duress. With his audience flabbergasted the demonic angel tossed the co-pilot through the barred door like a rag dog, before loudly roaring at his other captives.

"RARRRRRRRRRRRRRR!" the demonic angel barked, as his captives all screamed out in fear.

The demonic angel stormed out of the cell and slammed the door behind him, before grabbing the co-pilot by the left leg and dragging him along down the darkened corridor. Both creatures of God soon disappeared in the dark as the air hostess ran to the injured pilot's aide.

"Oh my God Marvin, are you alright?" the air hostess demanded, as the doctor knelt down on the other side of the pilot.

"What the hell was that?" the pilot muzzled, with the straining sound in his voice.

"Did you see the size of that thing? It looked human, but I have no idea what that was!" the airhostess conveyed.

Doctor Flakiskor, who was still in a state of shock, examined the chief pilot whose body was completely bent out of shape. The doctor, who'd previously demanded their release, was completely speechless after their first interaction with their captors. Unlike his younger aircraft technicians, Doctor Flakiskor was too old and feeble to disagree or dispute with anyone; hence he did the best possible to sooth the pilot's discomfort.

"What are they going to do to Justin? Oh my God what are they going to do to us?" the terrified air hostess questioned.

"Listen there is no sense panicking until we know what they want from us. Mr. Morris right now you need to remain perfectly still until we're able to move you, because I suspect your spine may be broken or fractured." diagnosed Dr. Flakiskor.

The pilot groaned in pain as the airhostess folded her vest and placed it beneath his head to protect it against the grunge that covered the floor. As the three prisoners patiently waited, the voice of co-pilot Justin Schwartz, could be heard in the distance. The duress under-which the co-pilot was placed magnified the airhostess' fright, thus she cuddled beneath Dr. Flakiskor's arm for protection.

"Never you ugly son of a bitch", first screamed the co-pilot, followed by the ranting expressions of his anguish. "No-No-No-No-please don't, No-Ahhhhhhhhhhhh!"

The screams of the co-pilot continued for three and a half minutes, before only the momentary anguishing sounds of other captives inside the grungy dungeon could be heard once again. Five minutes after the co-pilot went silent, the horrid sight of the demonic creature materialized along the corridor. The giant figure stood on the opposite side of the bars as if choosing its next victim, before strutting into the cell and standing over the cowering prisoners. From its' black sandals which were fastened with straps that wrapped around the demons massive calf to the tip of it's' dreads, the demonic angel was an impressive specimen, which resembled something chiseled out of pure rock. Although the physical appearance of the demon was somewhat scary, the sexy tone of its muscular body calmed the airhostess' frail nerves, to where she actually began looking at the demon sexually. After effectively intimidating his prisoners, the demonic angel moved towards the injured pilot and snatched him up in the exact manner as he did the co-pilot.

Senior pilot Marvin Morris was dragged across the soiled floors of Lucifer's dungeon from his disgusting holding cell through the corridor and into the torture chamber. Pilot Morris screamed throughout the entire ordeal, despite being rudely ignored by his tormentor, who dragged him along like a garbage bag filled with litter. The pilot was strung up with chains, which hoist both his hands and feet in opposite directions. The stench of death, blood and decay filled the room as the pilot looked around and noticed his co-pilot's severed head that had been nonchalantly thrown in a corner. There was a horrid looking creature which resembled a troll, hacking to pieces the remains of his co-pilot corpse with an ax.

"You have only one chance at surviving, and that's if you swear eternal allegiance to the ruler of this world, King Lucifer?" instructed the demonic angel.

"Are you out of your God forsaken mind, never!" the pilot responded resoundedly.

Dr. Flakiskor and the airhostess began praying the instant the pilot was dragged from the cell. As the identical screams of the co-pilot sounded in the distance, both remaining prisoners could feel the other's heartbeat as they nervously clung o each other. The screams of the senior pilot went for a whole minute less than that of the co-pilot, before he too was no longer heard from. Once the pilot went silent the airhostess' eyes filled with tears as she reminisced about her former co-workers. Moments after the pilot ceased yelling the airhostess noticed the demonic figure rematerializing from the shadows of the dark.

"What do you want from us", the woman screamed as the demon drew closer.

The demonic angel opened the gate and pointed directly at the airhostess. The female who didn't wish to be dragged off like her co-workers before her, jumped to her feet and walked towards the demon, who was rather surprised by the female's gesture. The airhostess walked away into the dark ahead of her captor as the doctor slowly watched them disappear from sight.

"I-I know you're probably going to kill me, but I think it may be in your best interest to rethink that decision." the airhostess argued, as she walked towards a glimmer of light at the other end of the corridor.

The female entered the execution chamber to the sight of the troll removing fragments of the pilot from his bondages. The airhostess covered her nose and mouth to prevent herself from both, breathing in the foul stench or screaming at the disgusting display of savagery before her. The female, like her captors before her, was strung up and put through the same interrogation process, although her response drastically differed from those of her co-workers.

"Your only chance at survival is if you swear allegiance to King Lucifer, the ruler of this world"! conveyed the demonic angel.

The female looked fiercely at the executioner holding his weapon of destruction without flinching and said, "If that is all you hunk of men wanted, then all you had to do was just say so? Of course I'll serve the Devil if my life depends on it."

Doctor Heinz Flakiskor sat confused inside the grimy cell no hearing the anticipated screams from the airhostess. The demonic angel returned for the doctor, who followed the airhostess' lead and scurried ahead of the demon instead of being carried by his captor. Not knowing what to expect had Dr. Flakiskor shaking like a leaf as he nervously entered the torture chamber. The sight of the female airhostess alive led the doctor to exhale a huge sigh of relief as his captors attached him to the chains. The humongous captor, who kept the airhostess present as an incentive for the doctor, held the female's arm.

"They won't decapitate you if you agree to their terms!" yelled the air hostess, who hoped the doctor chose life despite the circumstances.

The doctor looked around the room and became fixated at the hideous troll, who was busy assembling the scattered body parts into a bloodied wheel-borrow. The uniforms worn by the pilots told the story of what became of the air plane's chauffeurs, as the demonic angel demanded the question he'd asked of every captive.

"Do you swear eternal allegiance to the ruler of this world, King Lucifer?"

The doctor paused and thought about his response as his predicament dawned on him all at once. The thought that he would never again be reunited with his wife and children brought a momentary tear to his eyes, as he closed them tightly and submissively responded, "Yes."

The demonic angel released Dr. Flakiskor from his bondages as the female ran over to him with open arms. The airhostess had been sobbing continuously after watching as the troll fed the body parts of her friends to what sounded like scavengers beneath the flooring of the chamber. The troll would stack his wheel borrow with slops of meat tossed about the chamber and open a trap gate in the flooring, before tossing the chunks of meat into the den of abomination. The demonic angel instructed the two survivors to follow him as he led the way from the dungeons to the Great Hall of Hell.

There were similar guards armed with spear like weapons at the front entrance of the hall, as the guide who led them pushed open a huge metal door to gain entry. The more time the airhostess spent in the company of the demons, was the less fearsome she grew of them. Hence, by the time they arrived at Lucifer's Grand Hall the female had become fascinated with their captors, who overwhelmed her with their sexually appealing physiques. The temperatures around the Devil's layer was steaming hot, yet still the female's desire to entertain one of his soldiers had her quite aroused. There was a huge insignia of a King Cobra snake on the metal door to Hell's Great Hall and the prisoners walked in behind their guard. Around the chamber were massive guards whose attires were somewhat different from others soldiers around the castle, although the doctor was more interested in the reason for his prototype machine centering the Hall's floor.

Despite the instructions being barked by their guard, Dr. Flakiskor maintained his focus on his machine, which he'd last seen inside his personal lab back in Iceland. "You Infidels are not permitted to gaze up at the King. I want you to keep your heads pointed to the ground, stop when I instruct you to, and fall to your knees in respect! Am I understood?"

Both prisoners shook their heads in acknowledgment as their guide, who instructed them, bowed his head in respect once they reached the foot of the throne. The prisoners, who were motioned by their guide, soon fell to their knees as the Demon presented them to his king. Total darkness surrounded Lucifer who sat upon his Kingly throne as his prisoners tried their hardest to catch a glimpse of the one known as Satan the Devil.

"My Lord your willing subjects." the guard stated, as the doctor and the air hostess presented themselves before Lucifer's throne.

"Today you have been implemented into my household as children of my bosom. You, Doctor Flakiskor, are here to build and increase my Dark Army. Succeed and you will be rewarded beyond your wildest dreams. However, should you fail at my request; I shall have you fed to my pets in the dungeon, as your associates were fed to them!" the Devil ordered.

"How do you know that I can perform the task you seek?" enquired the doctor.

"You would not be here unless, Doctor!" threatened the Devil.

Following their orientation session, the guard escorted the doctor and the air hostess to a huge lab facility where different doctors and scientists captured from around the world were busy fine tuning their individual experiments under the constant watch of Lucifer's Illuminati guards. The laboratory division was controlled by humans who served Lucifer as their Lord and King, choosing to denounce Yahweh as their rightful God and take up arms against the True Creator. Doctor Flakiskor, who was somewhat submissive before entering the laboratory, became flabbergasted at the extraordinary technology being developed inside the lab, as his technological appetite was invoked causing him to enter into a hypnotized state in the presence of the various inventions he gazed upon.

Chapter 7

"The righteous alone shall inherit the earth". Since the creation of mankind, there have been a number of individuals who've devoted their entire lives to the service of God, who resides in Heaven. These great men and women of ancient have stood firm in their faith, even to the point of offering up their lives. Great worshipers of the divine lord such as Job, Abraham, the Virgin Mary and Moses, to name a few, have devoted their lives to the creator of this world. The bloodline of such individuals has been targeted by the Devil since creation, as Lucifer sought to rid the earth of such lovers of righteousness. Satan, the Devil, challenged his creator with the belief that he could transform any of his loyal subjects to serve him. Since such failure the Devil had attempted to vanquish certain historical faithful families, which were keen to the proclamation of God's word.

Terry Duncan was a descendant of Mary the mother to Jesus Christ, who bore other children for her husband Joseph apart from the one sent forth. The thirty eight year old archeologist was a native of Australia, who had completed her studies in England, before returning home to study the ancient relics of her homeland. During her upbringing, Terry discovered something about herself that was rather frightening, before she learnt the essence of her ability. The Australian native was five years of age, when she first alerted anyone of her ability to see and communicate with spirit forces. With the order given by Lucifer to seek out and destroy all humans who possessed *Im*perial blood, the Demon Shaka tracked and found Irene and Norman Duncan, the parents of the gifted Terry.

While preparing her daughter for bed one night, Irene was stunned by her daughter's claims that there was an invisible spirit hovering above. "Look mummy there is a lady dressed in a white dress right there!" Terry exclaimed, as she pointed in the direction of the figure. Terry's initial statement didn't worry Irene, who excused her daughter's wild imagination and continued dressing the child. However, Terry proceeded to engage in a conversation with the spirit, which Irene thought strange and unnatural.

"This is my mommy; she always puts my nittie on for me." The child paused then responded as if she was actually engaged in a conversation. "I know, we can play later, like we did last night!"

Irene, who was stunned by her daughter's revelation, summoned her husband and informed him of their child's physic ability. Norman, who was an Orthodox Jew, grabbed his Old Testament bible and vigorously chanted several Psalms, in an attempt to shun the spirit. Hours later, however, Terry was again engaged with the spirit, proving that Norman's efforts were in vain.

"This is a house of God, so if you can still see this spirit then it must be sent to watch over you by God". Irene speculated as she sought not to worry her child.

Despite her parents concerns, Terry became more and more involved with the spirit, who began following her wherever she went. Terry's teachers found it increasingly challenging to hold her attention due to her imaginary friend. Two weeks after Terry began interacting with the spirit, the demon Shaka visited her home one day while she was at school. Terry's father had left for work and her mom was engaged in her daily chores when Satan's executioner swooped in for a visit. Irene was vacuuming her living room floor while watching her morning television programs when the entire house began shaking as if there was an earthquake erupting. The Imperial bloodline that flowed through Irene's veins had always been protected, despite the female's ability to visually see her protector.

The protective spirits that watched over the family blessed the Duncan's home, hence, it was impossible for certain spirit forces to enter such God anointed domain. However, Shaka the Demon was no mere spirit, thus the rattling of the house was caused by him penetrating the external defenses. The spirit that had always watched over Irene flew to her defense as the demonic angel laid sight on his victim. Irene, who was completely unaware of the paranormal danger inside her home, quickly crawled beneath her dining room table to shield herself should the roof and other serious articles begin tumbling.

The spirit that had always watched over Irene attacked Shaka the Demon, who was far more powerful than any immortal spirit. Shaka grabbed the charging spirit by the neck, which stopped her in her tracks, and began strangling her. The demonic angel from Hell squeezed the protection spirit's life force from its body before tossing the invisible corpse aside. With no one in its path the assassin from Hell moved on to its victim who was crouched beneath the table reciting verses from the bible. The demonic angel proceeded to fly around the room, darkening the interior by closing the available curtains and blinds. The sight of what was occurring inside her home scared Irene to the point of hysteria, where she screamed continuously as the darkness caused her tormentor's vague image to materialize.

Irene eyes became fixated at the demon, which stood hovering in mid air approximately twenty feet in front of the frightened housewife. Once Shaka materialized himself to the female, the black scary looking demon charged at the innerved housewife who thought he was physically about to lunge inside of her. Irene tightly sealed her eyes shut and defensively mounted her hands before her face, while screaming at the top of her lungs, for what to her, seemed like minutes, which, in reality was actually four and a half hours. Irene's neighbor Karen came home at 2:25pm that afternoon and immediately telephoned the police after overhearing the frightened housewife's alert and being unable to gain access to the house.

The Local police arrived some seven minutes after the emergency call was dispatched and quickly forced their way into the house. The inside of the house was in complete disarray, with ornaments and other articles scattered throughout. Emergency representatives quickly attended to Irene, who had a blank stare on her face and fought off assistance, which led officials to believe she'd been raped. Irene's husband and daughter came home to find her sedated and strapped to a gurney. Despite her family's attempt at breaking her mental collapse, Irene never recuperated from her deranged state and was permanently admitted to a psychiatric hospital. Eleven months after Irene was admitted to the Baxter Mental Institute in Sydney Australia, the Duncan family received a tragic call that stated that 'Irene had committed suicide.'

Terry grew up exclusively with her father who was never the same after witnessing his wife's physic episode. Despite her discontent at loosing her mother at such a young age, Terry found comfort in her spirit protector, who assumed the role of a missing mother. The demon, which was responsible for Terry's mother mental collapse, didn't return to claim the daughter's life until Terry's thirty eighth birthdays, which was the day the world experienced the symbols that detailed the coming of the lord.

Present day:

Senior archeologist Dr. Garnet Wallace and his team of relic hunters were behind schedule completing the recovery of a pre-historic dinosaur fossil, believed to be approximately one hundred and fifty million years old. An aboriginal hunter who found several large unfamiliar bones in a remote area and reported the findings to the officials made the discovery of the fossil. Dr. Wallace and his team from the Australian Institute of Archeology were given the task of recovering the fossil in a remote section of Pithara some three hundred miles from the east coast. The team of archeologists had to work late into the night due to funding and scheduling, although Dr. Wallace surprised his prized apprentice at midnight by calling a halt to the work in order to acknowledge her birthday. Under the bright beams casted by spot lights mounted on tall aluminum poles, the archeologists suspended work and began socializing over a bottle of Jack Daniels and classical music from Dr. Richards' disc player. While his relic hunters celebrated their peer's birthday, Dr. Wallace mingled momentarily before heading off to edit a few documents in his personal trailer.

The night sky was clear and slightly humid as the team of five archeologists and seven assistants pranced around the red dirt of the Out-Back and enjoyed themselves. DR. Richards, who was Terry closest confidant, was the first to begin showing signs of intoxication, as he mainly abstained from dancing and drank himself silly. The birthday girl, who hadn't been given the chance to sit since the celebrations began, finally got the opportunity after an hour plus on the dance floor. Terry fell to the dirt beside her intoxicated friend, who immediately threw his arm around her and wished her a happy birthday.

"You're drunk aren't you?" Terry commented, after leaning on her friend for a second.

"Nope I'm not; let's say I just feel immensely overjoyed!" Dr. Richards commented.

"Well I feel great, it's a beautiful night the stars are shinning and I'm going to sleep outside in my sleeping bag tonight."

"You miss terrified of everything wild is going to do what?"

"Stop making fun of me, why don't you go get your sleeping bag and join me?"

"Because I know how scared you are of the wild, I'll join you if you help me up."

Terry rose to her feet and stretched out her hand to Dr. Richards who used her help to get to his feet. Doctor Richards wobbled to his feet and grabbed hold of Terry for stability as they supported each other on their way towards their sleeping quarters. Terry, who was the sole female on the archeological team, had her personal sleeping quarters while the male understudies housed together and the helpers were forced to contend with Mother Nature. DR. Richards was first escorted to the understudies' RV, where Terry left him to collect his apparels before attending to her affairs. While walking to her RV, Terry could overhear Dr. Richards crashing into articles inside the RV, while those already resting yelled and threw things at him.

Terry who took slightly longer inside her chambers, returned to find Dr. Richards comfortably resting beneath the night's sky, while the helpers and two archeologists coupled around a huge fire where they chatted amongst themselves after draining the bottle of Jack Daniels. Dr. Richards was off to Lala Land by the time Terry laid out her sleeping bag and crawled her way inside. The voices around the camp fire soon began rescinding as the two archeologists returned to the comforts of their RV. The single female archeologist looked up at the beautiful stars in the night's sky for a few minutes before peeking at her watch, then turning towards Dr. Richards to sleep.

Before Terry succumbed to fatigue, a sudden rush of air blew across her face, which caused her to awaken instantly. As Terry opened her eyes, there stood floating in mid air before her the spirit which had guarded her since childhood, whom Terry alone was capable of seeing.

"Get up! He is already here." The female spirit declared.

Terry who was a mille second away from Lala Land jumped to her feet and looked around the camp. Across the excavation site, the RV door belonging to Doctor Wallace's' male understudies flew open and Dr. Gales' eyes-less body fell to the ground. The female archeologist shook Dr. Richards who was far too gone to respond to her alert before shaking off her personal afflictions from the liquor and racing towards her RV.

"Everybody get up, get up, I believe we're in terrible danger, get up!" screamed Terry, as she ran across the excavation site.

The two helpers, who were still semi-conscious, rose to their feet and moved towards Terry with curiosity, not knowing from where the threat had originated. Dr. Wallace, who was still awake, soon overheard the screams and stopped his work to investigate. The senior archeologist turned his door knob and peeked outside as something crashed into the side of his RV. A submissive look befell the doctor, who noticed that the thump was caused by a helper who appeared to have been hurled at the RV with massive force. As the doctor surveyed the area fright befell him as he observed a second helper being swung around like a Frisbee before also ending up crashing against an RV. Dr. Wallace froze with disbelief as the aggressor unknowingly began moving towards him. With the body count stacking, Dr. Wallace looked horridly around and noticed other associates lifeless corpses before the faint sound of the single female on his team caught his attention.

"DR. Wallace run"! yelled Terry from the door of her RV.

"What, where, from what"! Dr. Wallace nervously responded.

Terry who respected and adored Dr. Wallace began running towards the good doctor who was totally unaware of what was about to happen to him. The Demon Shaka, who had committed Terry's mother to the mental institute before returning to complete the task, was set on killing his intended target. However, due to the circumstances the demon from Hell was forced to terminate everyone present. The Demon Shaka was a split hair from corralling Doctor Wallace, when Terry's protector stepped in front of the archeologist.

"You puny spirits never learn do you?" insinuated the demon as he grabbed the spirit around her neck.

The Demon Shaka held the spirit around the neck and began squeezing the life force from its body, while Terry grabbed the doctor and ran inside his RV. Seconds before the demon discarded the spirit; a defender angel appeared on the scene and interrupted the proceedings. The angel of God landed behind the demon and shouted out to him: "Shaka, for years I've tracked you while you cause havoc across these lands, but today as sure as this world is about to end, your despicable acts are over."

Shaka the Demon released the spirit from his grasp and turned his attention to his uninvited guest who unlike the lesser spirit, was physically capable of handling the demon. The commotion awoke Dr. Richards who was only a few feet away from the clashing angels. Doctor Richards opened his eyes and glanced over as both angels began materializing, which allowed humans to visually see them. The sight of actual angels with wings startled Dr. Richards, who sobered up immediately without his regularly experienced hangovers. Doctor Richards, although fascinated with the supernatural beings in front of him, observed Terry and Dr. Wallace escaping through the rear window of the doctor's RV and cautiously began reverting towards them.

"What the hell are those things?" Dr. Richards whispered the moment he rendezvous with his associates.

"They are angels doctor." Terry declared.

"But why was that black one attacking us?" Dr. Wallace questioned.

"While they're fighting lets get the hell out of here"! DR. Richards insinuated.

"Steven those things fly around faster than we drive, where do you possibly think we can run to in order to get away from them?" Terry reasoned.

"I'm not about to wait around and have whatever happened to everyone else happen to me!" Doctor Richards declared.

"What we need to do is get whoever is left alive and find some way of frightening that thing." Terry suggested.

"I just watched that thing toss two men around like the wind does the sand around here, I seriously doubt that an army of a million soldiers would worry that thing." Doctor Wallace hinted.

The three archeologists intensely watched the scuffle between the warring angels and moved to their peer's RV once the coast appeared clear. Doctor Gale's eyes-less stare was like looking into a black hole as Dr. Richards removed his Chaps buttoned shirt and covered his associate's face. While his companions searched for their friends, Dr. Wallace maintained a constant visual on both angels, which caused him to linger along as they circled the site.

The angel of God, white and majestic in all his glory, maneuvered his wings allowing for a smooth landing and attacked the Demon Shaka with his glistening sword. The Demon Shaka, who wore his typical black gown with the warring helmet covering his head, pulled out his mystical staff and engaged in battle. The Warring angels fought vigorously as the thunderous sounds from their colliding weapons echoed throughout the campsite.

After realizing that they were the only survivors, Dr. Wallace, Dr. Richards and Terry watched the duel from a distance, as they cheered for God's angel. The gloomy and mystical demonic angel was decisively quick for his appearance as he caught the angel with a tactical maneuver that saw him loose his sword. The cheering section for God's angel went silent with fright as they suspected their brave savior was about to loose. The Demon Shaka tossed the angel's sword nearly twenty yards away and moved in to finish the job. As the demonic creature moved in, the angel timed his movement and cart-wheeled away from danger. With his weapon in sight the angel maneuvered towards it before his opponent began shooting lightening-bolts from his staff at him. The angel was forced to tumble, bob and weave his way to his weapon, before reclaiming his steel and immediately using it to block an incoming lightening-bolt.

The angel from one knee refocused himself, before slowly rising back to both feet. With his sword held firmly at hand, the angel charged his opponent and struck with a series of coordinative moves that kept his foe backpedaling. The angel of God, sighting his advantage, stabbed at the demon, which caused the retreating grim-reaper to protectively swipe down at the sword. Once the black demonic angel attempted to knock the sword to the ground, the attacking angel swung it over-head and chopped down at the demon, who quickly raised his staff to block the strike. With the increased pressure, the demon from Hell began loosing his focus, strength and cunning, which weakened his power as the angel from Heaven severed his staff, with an aggressive chop intended to decapitate the demon. Anticipating his disadvantage, the Grim-reaper from Hell attempted to use his black magic to keep the angel at bay. But the refocused angel cocooned himself inside his wings and swirled in like a tornado with his blade extended, which resulted in the demon receiving several lacerations throughout its body before the removal of its head.

Shaka the Demon after loosing his head fell to the ground and decomposed right before the spectators who all were astonished when the angel from Heaven walked over to them. The angel who had his bow and arrow strapped across its back, removed the weapon and shrunk it to an appropriate size before handing it to Terry as protection. As Terry collected the weapon from the angel's grasp, the skies above became bright as midday as the symbols foretelling God's return materialized.

Chapter 8

"For I say to you this day that you will be with me in paradise." This promise was made by Jesus Christ to a thief who had been strung up beside him and left to die. Since then humans have believed that the day would come when the son of the lord would return to finish the work he'd begun. With the signs suggesting the end of this world is at hand, the devil began his relentless campaign to annihilate the final descendants of God's righteous people. The importance of loyalty is essential to steadfast governing and, with this knowledge; Satan aspired to alter God's plans by eliminating his supporters.

Roland Flores, the only child of America's presidential couple Ron and Janet Flores, attended school at Harvard University in Boston Massachusetts. The president's son was in his second semester at the Ivy League university where he studied for his degree in Criminal Law. Like his father before him, Roland sought to practice law, before moving into politics. At school Roland kept his circle of friends limited due to his status as the president's son, but his security detail made approaching him rather difficult. With twenty-four hour secret service monitoring, students around the university became conscious of the boundaries surrounding the first son. Roland shared his dormitory room with a foreign student from France, whose father was a prominent banker abroad. Due to the fact that both Roland and his roommate, Dejulious Swiss, studied law, both men spent quiet a bit of time together during the semester.

Dejulious, who thought he'd struck gold when he found out he was to be housed with the American president's son, enjoyed the company of his prized American friend, especially the extensive focus attributed to them by Roland's Secret Service guards. During Roland's leisure time at the dormitory, his security detail would ensure the building and surrounding areas were secure. While attending classes, the Secret Service guards would station themselves outside the classroom door and then accompany him at a modest distance while he roamed around inside the building. However, once Roland emerged into the open, his security detail would swarm him like bees and accompany him wherever he went.

The day the symbols materialized across the world's skies, both law students had class from 9:45 till 11:45 that morning. During their class session Dejulious' cellular phone began vibrating inside his pocket. The French student removed the cell phone from his pocket and peeked at the number, before noticing that the caller was in fact his father back home. The law student was astonished by the timing of the call considering his parents were knowledgeable of his daily curriculum. The young man quickly excused himself from the class session at 11:36, and answered the call in the hallway.

"Allo-allo papa, est-tu la? I can't hear you papa, you need to speak up a little louder!" excitedly responded the French student as a loud siren pitch sounded over the phone. "What the hell?" Thought Dejulious to himself, as he removed the phone from his ears and looked down at the device.

Dejulious was about to re-enter the classroom, when he noticed the dean of the university, Dr. Earl Whitenburg hastily walking towards him.

"Mr. Swiss-Mr. Swiss, may I please have a word with you?" the dean enquired.

Dejulious took a few steps towards the dean who appeared to have an urgent message to deliver. Doctor Whitenburg was completely out of breath when he finally caught up with the second year law student. The dean uncharacteristically placed his arm around the young man's shoulder and led him on a short stroll down the hallway as the secret service personnel looked on.

"I'm afraid I have some terrible news from home Dejulious. It's about your parents. I'm sorry but the police have just informed me that there has been a terrible accident involving your mom and dad. I'm sorry son, but they were killed a short time ago!" Dr. Whitenburg declared.

"That's impossible; my father just rang my phone a minute ago!" Dejulious exclaimed.

"I'm sorry son, but arrangements are being made for your swift return." the dean insighted.

Instant tears began running down the French student's face as he slowly walked from the dean's grasp and continued down the hall towards the exit. The devastated student walked directly to his dorm room, while telephoning other family members to collaborate the news. During his walk towards the dorm, Dejulious chatted with his father's brother who expressed his deepest sympathy, before giving his nephew the accounts of what was rumored to have happened to his parents. From his uncle, Dejulious learned that investigative officials who found the couple in a rather precarious state at home were considering his parent's death a homicide. Dejulious' father was found stuffed inside the family's washing machine, while his mother had been strung up with lacerations covering her entire body and had bled to death.

Roland Flores finished his class and immediately became worried about his friend who hadn't returned from his class break. Roland, who sat relatively close to Dejulious, collected his friend's belongings and brought them with him. A female admirer of the president's son tapped him on the shoulder and offered him an invitation to a party being held that weekend before they both exited the building, accompanied by the Secret Service bodyguards. The bold and confident female soon began making explicit propositions at Roland, who found himself in a rather precarious position. Despite his personal afflictions, Roland was quite polite to his admirer, who handed him a piece of paper containing her various contact information.

As both classmates ended their discussion, a female student screamed out aloud as she looked up at the clouds and saw the appearance of the symbols. Roland, the female and every able body person across campus inquisitively looked up to observe what the female was screaming about. While hypnotized by the symbols and the voices that translated the meanings to every individual, Roland's personal cell phone sounded.

"HI mom, you wouldn't believe the weirdest thing that just appeared in the sky!"

"Listen to me Roland, I want you to go directly to the airport without any delays, there is an airplane prepped and waiting for you! Your security detail will get their instructions soon on how to proceed, but I want you to get going and hurry! We don't have much time, so we'll discuss the particulars later. I love you and I'll see you soon."

"O.K mom, see you soon".

The atmosphere across the campus became frantic as students and professors began scrambling in confusion, as if the skies were beginning to fall on their heads. Roland, along with his security detail began towards the dorms where the president's son expected to find his friend. During their scurry towards the dorms, the secret service personnel received their orders that specifically stated "secure the president's son by bringing him to his awaiting plane." The secret agent in charge radioed the vehicle operator and instructed him to bring the car directly in front of the dorm before suggesting to his boss that, "they ignore everything else and get to the plane." The president's son and his bodyguards ran by a large group of students outside the dorm, who were members of the World's Catastrophic Alumni, which was an organization founded by student scientists in the early years of the distinguished university. While others ran about hysterically, these students formed a huge circle, where they lit candles and began chanting amongst themselves, as they celebrated what they perceived to be the end of days.

Roland continued ignoring his bodyguard's appeals as he raced up to the third floor of building G where terrified students were running about confused. It wasn't until the president's son came close to the door, that he silenced his agitated protector by suggesting that if the bodyguard were honorable he wouldn't be suggesting Roland abandon his friend at such a turbulent time.

Dejulious, who had returned to his room, was packing his personal inside his luggage when his room began shaking as if an earthquake was erupting. The vibrations were being caused by another of Satan's grim-reapers who was attempting to break through the force-field which had been installed by the guardian who protected Dejulious. The second year law student, who had been attacked on several occasions, was given instructions on how to survive should a demon attack. Dejulious was given a bow and arrow by one of God's Protectors, who also instructed the carrier of Imperial Blood to find an open area and stand his ground. Due to the fact that Dejulious was capable of visually seeing these demons, being in an open area would provide him precious minutes where he could hold the demon at bay until help arrived.

Having survived such an attack in the past the grieving student was poised at defending himself as he quickly assembled his weapon and armed it. The grim-reaper from Hell began materializing through the wall, while still fighting to bore its way through the exterior force field. Dejulious didn't wait for confirmation of the assailant's identity as he hammered the first arrow into the demon's groin. The black cloaked demon let out a loud roar as the pain from the injury caused him to grimace. Dejulious' second arrow sailed into the grim-reaper's gut, which caused it to scream even louder than previous. The grim-reaper fully materialized inside the room as it fell to one knee and immediately began pulling the arrows out.

Dejulious went to open the door when Roland came blasting in. "Run for your life, there is a demon chasing me!" Dejulious yelled, as he sprinted by his friend.

The curiosity in Roland saw him peeked his head into the room, as the demon pulled the last ancient bullet from its gut. "What in the name of Jesus"! Exclaimed the president's son as he took off running behind his friend.

With their clients racing for their lives like mad-men, the inquisitive agents who sought to solve whatever threat brewed inside the room, busted in with guns drawn and hammers cocked. The sight of the demon scared both agents who began unloading their clips at the grim-reaper. Students emptied the hallways at the explosion of guns as Dejulious and Roland raced down the stairs towards the entrance. The demon, which was down to one knee flew at the agents with such quickness, that both men were unable to escape its detrimental clutches. The grim-reaper smacked the pestilences who disrespected him, leaving both men burnt to a crisp as if they fell from the pot into the fire. The demon from Hell swooped through the hallway after his intended victim, while he maliciously touched everyone he passed, killing them instantly. As the demon flew along the hallway, light bulbs began popping in their sockets as he passed and fire alarms started sounding as his powerful negative energy surged along with him.

There was a secret service agent and two campus security guards running towards the escapees as they raced through the lobby area. The agent, who had already armed himself inquired about his comrades, yet received strict orders by Roland to get back into the vehicle. The campus security continued on to the third floor to investigate the cause of the shootings, as Roland and company ran outside as if the building was collapsing. The two campus employees were on their way up to the first floor when the assassin from Satan came hurling down the stairs. The Grim-Reaper, which had been shot and embarrassed by a puny human, was in a foul mood as it grabbed both men by the throat and flung them aside. Both campus police were left as char boiled as a roasted marshmallow as the demon angrily pressed on in search of his designated victim.

The fleeing entourage mounted the Chevrolet Suburban SUV stationed in front the dorm, with the secret service agent at the wheel, Roland across from him in the passenger seat and Dejulious riding coach. The driver of the SUV sped away with everyone focused on the entrance door to the dorm. The SUV had barely moved when the doors to the dorm blew off their hinges and the Grim-Reaper busted its way from inside the building.

"Step on it Dave, that thing is coming fast!" instructed the president's son.

The driver of the SUV, who still hadn't the slightest idea from what they were running, peeked into his rear view mirror the moment the doors got blown into the street. The black cloaked figure was visible for a few seconds before it completely vanished in the bright light from the outdoors.

"Did you guys just see that? What the hell was that"? the driver of the SUV reasoned.

"Exactly the thing we're running from." Roland answered.

"Go faster, that thing is about to ram us off the road"! Dejulious yelled from the rear.

"What the hell was that thing Jewels and where did it come from"? Roland asked.

"I don't think you would believe me if I told you". Dejulious answered.

"Listen, today I've seen things that I never though possible and by the tone of my parents voice there is much more to these occurrences than the regular citizen suspect, so don't insinuate that you don't think I'll understand". Roland declared.

"O.K since you believe you're grown, they're demons from Hell who're sent here to kill me". Dejulious responded.

The president's son paused for a minute and though about what he'd just heard. "That could make sen—». Began the president's son, before something grabbed the roof of the SUV and completely ripped it off.

Dejulious who had his bow and arrow ready for launch, tracked their attacker's flight movements and fired at the enraged demon. The arrow narrowly missed the grim-reaper and tore through its left extended wing as the demon veered off to the right and circled around for another attack. Dejulious, who was the only person capable of seeing the demon in its cloaked form, pointed out the demon's positioning to his associates, who were both extremely spooked by the demon's latest acquisition of the vehicle's roof. The Grim-Reaper swooped around and began its descent at the fleeing SUV as the occupants of the vehicle lowered themselves into their seats, to avoid being thrown from the vehicle.

With his eyes locked onto the attacking demon, Dejulious expected a much volatile second rush as the grim-reaper closed in on the speeding Suburban. The Demon from Hell was a few feet from shredding the SUV when from out of nowhere came a Defender angel, who shoulder tackled the grim-reaper into the asphalt. Both angels crashed onto the road as the angel from God broke his fall and rolled over onto his massive legs. The occupants of the Suburban didn't wait around to witness who emerged the victor, although Dejulious intently watched the battle as they fled.

The angel of God, who was built like a brick, walked over to his laid out nemesis and lifted him aloft with one hand. The impressively built angel from Heaven brought the battered body of his foe to his ear and whispered to him, "don't you ever mess with my father's children," before flinging the bruised grim-reaper almost two hundred yards down the road into the frame of a parked Dump truck. The Grim-Reaper's body struck the dump truck with such force that it caused a huge dent in the metal frame as the angel turned to watch the SUV vanish from sight. The Grim-Reaper, after colliding with the dump truck was knocked woozy as it slowly wobbled to consciousness before quickly taking its leave to avoid any further altercation with God's Protector.

Following his recent failure, the demon, whose name was Zukai returned home to his master with his field report knowing the punishment awarded to those who've failed. The king of this world, Satan the Devil, was giving one of his aids instructions as the Grim-reaper awaited being summoned.

"—will be their only opportunity to strike a significant blow. Remind them that any one who doesn't abide by my wishes will be tossed into my fiery pit. This war is about to begin and once it has anyone who doesn't present their insignia will be torn apart! Now go and instruct my human subjects, for I alone shall judge their deeds and decided the role they'll play in my kingdom".

The Grim-Reaper fell to both knees after presenting himself before the Devil's throne and began apologizing profuriously, claiming his success was interfered with by the Defender Angel. Despite his pleas for forgiveness Satan the Devil was stern in his judgment as the end of this present world was imminent and failure wasn't an option.

"Bound him in chains and toss him into the eternal fire of damnation!" Satan commanded his elite guards, who immediately moved in and seized the grim-reaper. "Let this serve as a reminder to all; there is no room in my kingdom for failure, nor will there be any failures in my new regime! Let the entire world feel my anger. I order the abominations of my dungeons to be released upon the earth so they will all experience the blunt of my wrath".

Chapter 9

I left my hotel room at 1:30pm, hopped into my Ford F-150 twin cab trunk and drove northeast towards Maloney Boulevard. As I cruised along Fournier Street, the largest group of individuals along the regularly busy strip was assembled outside the Pig Ales adult entertainment club where the club's security personnel were fighting with customers trying to close the venue. The fear brought on by the symbols insighted even strippers to be with their loved ones, although their pervert customers would prefer the show be continued. I continued along my journey with a nervous feeling and the belief that I was being followed despite the tranquility along the roadways. After pulling into the left turning lane at Maloney Boulevard, I looked up at the symbols through the sunroof of my truck as I awaited the appearance of the amber light.

"If your arrival means that my boy will be O.K, then hurry up and come". I thought to myself, as I looked up at the bold symbols across the afternoon's sky.

Bang, sounded a loud thump on the bonnet of my F-150! "The coming of the Lord is here, the coming of the Lord is here------"! yelled a crazy French man in his native tongue, as he crossed the road in front of my truck.

"Hit my truck again and I guarantee you won't live to see the man coming!" I argued after lowering my window.

Once the light changed I drove southbound along Maloney Boulevard towards Provincial interstate 50, entered the west bound section and drove back towards the Ottawa region. I selected a different route than the one I originally took, to avoid any altercation with government officials. There was hardly any traffic along the roadways into the city as the majority of traffic appeared to be diverting from the city's boundaries. I continued along the Quebec coast and snuck into Ottawa over the Maisonneuve Bridge, veered right onto Parkway Drive and cruised to Park Dale Boulevard. The drive along Park Dale Boulevard to Scott Street was terribly uncomfortable, as the crew of road technicians who were repairing the road abandoned the job and went home.

I arrived at the Ottawa Civic Hospital at 1:57pm and was frightened to find so many open parking spaces. The hospital was like a ghost town compared to earlier visits where patients, nurses and doctors ran about throughout the compound. The only patient I passed outside the hospital was a female smoking her cigarette who was very vocal about how she felt about the coming of the lord.

"Do you believe this shit? Six years I've suffered with cancer from smoking and now is the time he chooses to come for this hell-hole. I could have been saved all this radiation, chemo therapy and chronic pain had we gone through this years ago. I curse you Lord for putting me through this life, I don't know why everyone is racing to go worship him, but I couldn't care less". loudly argued the female patient.

The female's arguments were rather disturbing as I walked by her, while harboring the thoughts that 'she should be more appreciative for being alive and furthermore, if cigarettes are the cause of her cancer, then quit smoking them'! As I neared the southwestern entrance of the hospital, I stretched out my hand to open the door, when the female frantically screamed out behind me. I turned around and became dumbstruck at a huge black animal-like creature, which was dinning on the agitated female.

I nervously stumbled through the door frame after clumsily knocking my feet together as the beast looked at me while devouring its meal. I broke my fall before hitting the floor as I immediately began looking around for assistance. The interior of one of Ottawa's busiest business structures was as deserted as Greenland, with no one in sight. I took a second look through the glass door to ensure I wasn't hallucinating, as the abomination continued feeding on the female's diseased body. I ran to the elevator and quickly entered the first door to open before pressing the fifth floor button, which led to the Pediatrician Unit.

As I exited the elevator I looked through a huge glass window at the emergency area, which is typically the busiest section of any health centre. There was an abandoned ambulance parked directly in front the Emergency sliding doors with its emergency lights flashing continuously, although there were no technicians aboard. Across the street, where the hospital's response helicopter parked, the chopper sat grounded with its rotor blades in motion while a creature like the one I had previously seen circled it in search of victims. The sight of a Lincoln LS speeding by along Carling Avenue was quite inspirational as it gave me confidence in knowing that I wasn't the only human dealing the elements.

I ran into the Pediatrician Ward and was surprised to find a small staff of two nurses who both decided to remain with the terminally ill children instead of returning home to their personal families. The nurses were somewhat glued to the television as they watched the local news coverage to learn what was transpiring outside the hospital's walls. The compassionate hearts of these heroines moved me as I pleasantly greeted them while continuing on my way.

"Is there any new news about those symbols in the sky or did anything else happen out there?" one of the nurses asked.

"Ladies all I know is something huge is about to happen. You girl are better off in here right now." I stated as I moved towards my son's room.

I ran into my son's room where I found my wife at his bedside as he sipped orange juice from the paper cup given to him by his nurse. My wife's was elated to see me as her face brightened the moment I walked into the room. I looked over at my son's roommate, who was passed out with a grimacing look on her face, as if she felt pain while she slept.

"Daddy-daddy-daddy!" Devon cried as I went directly to him and hugged him dearly.

"Honey some awful stuff are beginning to happen outside, I just saw a woman got shredded by some creature from out of this world!" I emphasized as I took my wife's hand into mine.

"What are you talking about, what kind of creature?" my wife asked.

I reached for the television remote and turned on the TV set before channel surfing through to the CTV news station. There was a male reporter in centre town Ottawa covering the events around town, which, considering the time of day, was surprisingly deserted. The few patrons who paraded about the streets were Skin Heads and Hippies who boasted that 'they were prepared to enjoy their world as long as it remained in tact.' The reporter who conducted the entire news coverage in front of these radical Hippies, showed footage of the small crowd intoxicating themselves with alcohol, marijuana and other illicit drugs, which on any regular day would have landed them in jail. With the reporter's back towards the celebrating crowd which pranced about to the heavy metal music emitting from their juke box, the technician behind the camera, glimpsed through the corner of his eye a weird creature moving towards the celebrators. The cameraman zoomed in on the reporter and dismissed the image he'd glimpsed as an illusion, as the reporter highlighted the massive transformation the city had gone through in only a few hours.

A shock rushed through the cameraman as he nervously urinated on himself from the devastating skit he observed through his camera lens. The creature that the cameraman neglected as an illusion leapt into the crowd of celebrators and began molding everyone in reach. The camera slowly descended from the technician's face; as his mouth fell wide open from what he was witnessing.

"----as you can see behind me not everyone is squeamishly running for the safety of their homes, as young Canadians aren't about too ----Rob what the hell are you doing? I'm live on the air right now---." commented the reporter, as his technician who was frozen in his stance simply pointed in the direction of the altercation.

The CTV news reporter turned around to the sight of the abomination from Hell tearing apart the celebrators who were beginning to panic. Horrified screams sounded in the distance as the cameraman and his reporter took off racing towards their news van. A number of those being attacked began scattering for safety as the huge creature ripped off limbs and bit through bodies. The news reporter grabbed the camera and began filming through the window as the technician fired up the vehicle and began leaving the scene.

"What the hell was that thing? Did you see where it came from?" the reporter asked.

"Couldn't tell, it just popped up out of the blue!" the technician responded.

The live footage frightened Sarah, who moved closer to my side and grabbed tightly onto my arm. The on-duty nurses inside the children's ICU ward could be overheard frantically reacting to the news highlight, which was scary to say the least. I instructed my wife to prep my son to travel as I moved to the window to check if the coast was clear to depart.

"Honey I'm concerned about Cassandra, how is our baby going to get back to us?" Sarah commented.

"What do you mean, didn't you already tell her to get home now?" I asked.

"I did, but they've cancelled airplanes flights everywhere." Sarah admitted.

"Isn't Cassandra coming home mommy?" Devon enquired.

"As soon as she possibly can sweetie!" Sarah answered.

While staring through the window, a creature walked into view from somewhere around the hospital's compound. I motioned my wife over in order for her to get an official peak at the abomination from Hell, which appeared to be much larger than it appeared on television. Sarah walked over, looked through the window and immediately gasped as she covered her mouth with both hands.

"Holy mother of Jesus, what in God's divine name is that?" Sarah asked.

"I got no clue, but they aren't vegetarians." I answered.

"What are we going to do honey?" Sarah questioned.

"Well for now we're going to keep our asses put until those things leave." I declared.

"Ahhhhhhhhh!" creamed one the nurses from the reception area.

I began walking towards the room door, when one of the hideous creatures ducked its' head under the door frame and peeked into the room. Sarah again gasped loudly as the creature first gazed at Devon, before probing everyone inside the room. The creature caught sight of Devon's sick roommate and fixated its sight on the little girl, who resembled a princess as she slept. With its sleek movement like its ancestors from the wild, the

Yahweh

creature lowered its body and entered the room. With the protection of my family the sole inspiration for my bravery, I moved towards my backpack from along side Junior's bed and quickly removed my Remington Pump Action Riffle from within. As I moved to gain the creature's attention the beast swatted at me with its huge left paw, which forced me to dive across my son's bed to avoid its crushing blow.

I came up firing buckshots at the creature, which had become fixated on the little girl who comfortably slept, despite the arousing events transpiring around her. My first shot struck the creature's left paw and forced the beast off balance, as it tumbled towards my wife. The loud bang startled the little girl, who woke up to a frightening sight. I yanked back the selector and hammered a second shot at the creature's belly, which tore a huge hole inside its belly. The bullets, despite their accumulative effects, angered the creature, which turned and growled at me before it began creeping in my direction.

Realizing that I was being considered as a meal by the creature, I panicked and tried to insert another round into the chamber. My Pump Riffle Jammed and refused to fire, which led me to begin banging the weapon against the wall. The wounded beast limped towards me and trapped me in a corner while everyone inside the room began screaming in anticipation of the beast mauling me to death. I conjured up the strength to charge the creature, which I knew would kill my family had I not been valiant. For all my valiance, after adjusting the weapon like a baseball bat and attacking the beast, I was smacked aside like a piece of rubbish as the creature used its right paw to send me flying half way across he room. With suspended in mid air, I glimpsed a figure through the window, which led me to question if I had been struck in the head.

I believed I saw an Angel taking aim with a bow and arrow, thus I became convinced I was also delusional. Once I smacked into the wall I though something had been broken, as I slowly exercised my limbs to ensure everything was in tact. The idea that I had another round to contend with the beast was very disheartening, as I looked around for my weapon. I began rising to my feet when I heard the window pane shattered and wondered what had been tossed through it. As I looked on, I was surprised to note arrows being lunged into the creature from outdoors which were more effective than my bullets.

The Angel fired three arrows into the creature's body which immediately stopped the beast in its tracks. Once Sarah saw that the beast had been slain, she ran to my side and assisted me to my feet, at which I curiously moved to the window. The hairs on the back of my neck stood at attention as I froze at the sight of the Angel outside the window. I gazed out at this physically altered specimen who made a comment to me, which went unheard as I slowly regained my senses. The brightly glowing Angel was simply hovering in mid air, as I waved everyone over for them to witness and collaborate what I was experiencing. I knew I wasn't imagining things when the faces of my wife and the children lit up like Christmas trees after gazing at the image I was seeing.

"----travel northwest towards the Alexandria Bridge, there is a small island in the middle of the Champlain River called Bates Island; take your family there and stay there until this great war is over! I shall guide your way there, but stop for nothing and take no detours or you all certainly shall die!" the angel advised as he passed me his weapon, which shrunk as it transformed from the supernatural to human. The angel looked at me with a positive stare as if he were anointing me a knight within his army.

"What war are you talking about? When is all this supposed to happen?" I enquired.

The angel advised me about the great war of Armageddon, which he declared was to be fought between the creator of the earth and the present ruler of it. It wasn't until the angel imposed the little girl onto us that I realized that she was the one intentionally being stalked by the creature, which made its way into the chamber on a mission. The angel waved his hand over both my son and his roommate as I immediately began assembling everything in preparation to leave. The little girl who had been terribly ill began removing the needles from her arm, as both children remarkably recuperated from their ailments. After ensuring our safety, the angel withdrew his sword and leapt through the window as the little girl moved towards me and grabbed tightly onto me. I didn't await any further invitation to leave as we gathered everything and exited the room.

As we walked by nurse's station I was relieved to find that neither of the resident nurses had been harmed by the creature; as both nurses emerged from behind the receptionist counter, curious about whether or not the coast was clear. We exited the Children's Intensive Care Unit to a debate between both nurses, who argued whether it would be safe or not to remain inside the hospital. My entourage and I rode the elevator to the ground level where we cautiously emerged to a barren hallway. With my vehicle parked at a distance, I hid my followers behind the main entrance receptionist counter and went to retrieve our ride.

Once I got to the door at the main entrance, I scanned the area for threats while ensuring that all my weapons were properly loaded and ready to fire. With the bow and arrow given to me by the angel at hand, I cautiously moved to my vehicle as the coast appeared clear from present danger. I maintained a three hundred and sixty degree visual around the area by constantly turning and checking as I ran towards the vehicle. As I approached my F-150, I began hearing growling at a distance yet saw no evidence to support my suspicions. I was approximately fifty feet from my vehicle, when I noticed one of the creatures moving to intercept me. I had never before fired a bow and arrow, yet pointed the weapon at the charging beast and released the arrow. The arrow shot from the bow with such force, that it struck the charging beast and flung it backwards; giving me the extra few seconds I needed to safely reach my truck.

I jumped into the F-150 and started the engine as the enraged creature continued its charge towards me. The beast leapt into the air and landed on the bonnet of my four by four as I yanked the gear shifter into reverse and stepped on the gas. The creature's actions frightened me, at which I forgot to check my rear view as the truck rammed into a parked Hybrid vehicle. The sudden crash jolted the creature forwards as it smashed into my front window and sent cracks throughout the glass. I jammed the gear shifter into drive and stepped on the gas before turning towards the hospital. The humongous beast clung to the doorframe with its derrière rubbing along the turf and it hind legs scrapping off the asphalt as the F-150 roared its way from the parking lot.

"How the hell am I going to get rid of this thing?" I thought to myself as I swerved along the roadway to rid myself of the creature.

"Arrrrrrrrrrr!" roared the beast as it fixated its eyes on me while grinding its teeth.

I thought I was coming to the end of my rope, as I turned the corner in the direction of my hidden family. I accelerated the vehicle and jammed on the brakes to shed the creature, but its sharp claws that were driven into the vehicle's bonnet prevented it from detaching. I yanked the pump riffle from my back pack and pointed the weapon in the direction of the creature, which had begun climbing its way onto the vehicle. The angel who assisted us inside the hospital came crashing down from the skies and jammed his sword into the body of the creature. The creature submitted a loud roar as I brought the vehicle to a halt and ran inside the hospital.

I quickly assembled everyone and returned outside to find the angel standing guard by the F-150 with the slain creature disposed of prior to our arrival. The little girl, who I held in my arms across from my son, waved and smiled at the gigantic being, who in return smiled and winked at her. My wife and I quickly loaded the vehicle as the angel took to air and began leading the way to safety. We drove northbound on Parkdale Avenue back to the Parkway, where we turned left and began heading west. The drive along Parkdale Avenue was going smoothly until we began passing underneath the overpass to Interstate 417 where the representatives of Satan stepped up their attacks.

A fire ball smacked into a side column, which supported the overpass and blew out concrete from the wall. Cement debris ricocheted and struck my F-150 as we blew by, which caused no damage to the vehicle yet brought to our attention a demonic angel who was intent on destroying us all. Our guide, who was gliding ahead of the four by four, turned and realized our predicament, before yelling for me to speed onwards while he tackled our antagonist. I instinctively pressed harder on the gas and firmly held the steering wheel as the Ford truck whistled along the roadway.

The angel from Heaven rushed the black demonic angel who was constructing fireballs in the palm of its hand and flinging them at our vehicle. God's Defender angel flew towards the Satan's representative, who altered his fireball throwing to the attacking angel. The sudden change of target caught the angel from Heaven by surprise as he weaved around two fireballs before the third clipped his left wing and sent him spiraling to the ground. The Defender angel crashed to the ground and nearly broke his arm as he tumbled awkwardly. Realizing that he'd momentarily gotten rid of the angel, the demon resumed his chase as he flew off to catch up to our F-150 which was almost to the bridge.

God's Defender angel collected himself and took off running in our direction, while his injured wing slowly healed itself. The Angel, who was assigned to protecting the little girl whom we carried, was racing towards us when an abomination from the Devil's dungeon caught sight of him and began pursuit. The genetically engineered creature chased the angle, whose sole intention was to catch up to our convoy and ensure we arrived safely. With the four legged creature gaining grounds on the speedy angel, the defender sought to deal with the protruding danger without stalling, as he reached for his bow which is typically strapped across his chest. The realization that he'd given me his long range weapon dawned on the angel, who was forced to deal with the menacing creature at his heels. The angle, with the creature gaining pursuit, timed himself as he withdrew his sword and leapt into the air the second the beast lunged at him; which resulted in him pirouetting onto the creature and jamming his sword into its body. God's Defender killed the beast and leapt into the air as he regained usage of his injured wing and soared to the sky.

I was approximately a hundred yards from the bridge when the demon returned and began raining fireballs at our speeding truck. I was forced to swerve along the roadway to avoid being struck as the demon grew ever closer with each fireball launched. It wasn't long before I noticed we had to fend for ourselves without the Defender's support. Thus, I instructed my wife to control the vehicle while I attempted to hinder the menacing creature. Once my wife slid over into the driver's seat, I opened the sunroof and stuck my frame through it. The demonic angel narrowly escaped the point of the arrow, which caused him to employ evasive maneuvers. Realizing the tactical advantages of firing at the demon, I quickly reloaded the bow and continued slugging arrows at the demon.

The Demonic Angel became enraged by our defiance, as he swerved wide right and circled us at a distance before reconvening his fireball launches. Sarah turned onto the Alexandria Bridge as a fireball exploded beside our rear left tire and set it ablaze. Sarah looked through the side window at the flaming rear tire and began reacting hysterically. The Demonic Angel launched another fireball, which forced me to duck inside the front cabin, at it exploded in the rear cabin of the truck.

"Hold it steady or that rear tire might blow out!" I barked at Sarah, while telling the children to lower their heads.

The entire rear end of my Ford truck was engulfed in flames as I became increasingly worried about the survival of my family. At the last minute, the Defender angel reappeared alongside the truck and filled his lungs with fresh air before blowing out the fire with one forceful blow. The Defender then instructed us to divert onto a small island in the middle of the Champlain River, which was a safe haven for certain Canadian animals. There was a protection force field around the small island, which prevented adversaries of God from entering. The Defender Angel, after being humiliated by his nemesis the first time, went at the attacker with an invigorated spirit, which saw the demon refrain from the altercation and vanished.

We came to a halt on the island and remained inside the vehicle, as there was an array of wide animals, reptiles and birds prancing about the grounds. The sight of a pair of polar bears, raccoons, elks and other animals scared both my wife and I, although the children were ecstatic to get out and socialize. We didn't manage to exit the vehicle until the angel returned and instructed us to although the children were convinced we were safe from harm. The children ran towards the wild animals the moment the doors opened, which fascinated Sarah and I because of the reception given them by animals that have never before come into contact with humans. While the children happily played with the animals, Sarah and I spoke with the angel who advised us on the upcoming events. The sight of the previously ill children romping around without needles stuck to their arms was a marvel to Sarah and I as we secretly worried about our daughter abroad and if we would ever see her again.

"----remain here on this island, which has been designated one of my father's holy grounds, for everywhere else shall be perilous!" warned the angel, who went to make his leave before Sarah requested something of him.

"Can you please please somehow have someone watch over my daughter in Africa?" begged Sarah.

"I shall relay the message!" answered the angel before taking to the skies.

Chapter 10

Professor St. Jacque advised his students to contact their families and inform them about their present dilemma. While his students ran off to their various suites, the professor chose for a comfortable seat by the bar where he planned on drinking the evening away. There were no local servers available to assist the guests as the entire staff chose to return home to their families. There was an open bar concept without an attending waiter present, hence scores of various liquor bottles laid atop the bar counter. Patrons were drinking themselves silly, where they partied and staggered about with entire bottles at hand, while behaving as if all were well. There were a few individuals who had drunk themselves to the point where they simply sobbed and wiped away tears as they considered the inevitable.

A small group of Professor St. Jacque's students walked by him and went into the refrigerator where they collected a number of beers and headed out towards the pool area. The professor hailed the students as they walked by before refocusing his attention on his regrets and sorrows at the bottom of his drink. A few Atheists, who cared nothing about the Divine Lord, got overly intoxicated and began behaving unruly as they laughed and teased those with spiritual beliefs, even to the point of cursing God and denouncing his greatness.

"You people are all such idiots; those signs in the sky are made by nothing but some longer lasting foam they're probably experimenting on!" declared an intoxicated American tourist.

"Philosophers discovered years ago that the best way to control humans is by this propaganda they implanted called the bible; and that's why the world is in the state it's in right now!" remarked another Atheist.

A heated argument soon developed between the mocking Atheists and those who considered themselves Christians or worshippers of God. The argument, fueled by alcohol, soon brought the debaters to blows as a Russian Christian threw a beer bottle at one of the offenders. The Serbian male he tossed the bottle at was forced to duck out of the way as the bottle smashed against the wall behind him. As Professor St. Jacque attempted to ignore the quarrels behind his back, the United States president walked onto the podium at the White House to deliver a public address.

"Everyone shut the hell up! Somebody turn the dam television up so we can hear what the US President is saying about this shit!" sternly barked the professor.

The outcry by the Canadian professor abruptly ended the argument, as a mild calm overcame those present and everyone drew closer to the television. The president began by first acknowledging that the events occurring outdoors were no hoax, as many had led themselves to believe. President Flores was definitive in his address as he proceeded to inform the nation about the planetary collision, which he credited Mrs. Wright and the NASA Space Station for discovering. President Flores outlined an international plot to destroy the approaching planet, although he remained reserved about their chances at survival. The leader of the free world, throughout his speech, could find very little with which to encourage his international audience, though he advised Americans at home and those stranded abroad to remain vigilant despite the present hardship.

Following the president's public address the non-religious and skeptical critics openly apologizing for their inconsiderate behavior. The news about the Earth's possible destruction appeared to instantly sober up many of those who had too much to drink. Convulsive fear overtook several guests who sought detailed information on how to survive the impending catastrophe. The vague forecast given by President Flores and his neglect at stipulating an estimated timeline on the collision led many to speculate that the collision was near at hand. The hotel guests, who were already emotionally affected by the developments, began consoling each other while others branched off and returned to their suits.

A sequence of terrified screams sounded in the direction of the pool area as concerned guests raced to offer assistance. Professor St. Jacque with his students' wellbeing at heart responded quickly as he went off in their direction. The frantic professor uncharacteristically shoved people from his path while racing to ensure none of his students were harmed. As the crowd of inquisitive guests neared the end of the cafeteria building, which led towards the pool, three hysterical female and a male ran pass them as if they were being chased by something.

"Run for your lives!" One of the females stated as they ran by the curious professor.

The professor, who was worried about the rest of his students, turned the corner in the direction of the pool and froze as he came across a pair of carnivorous beasts, which were ripping patrons to pieces. Professor St. Jacque abruptly stopped and attempted to retreat, when an out of control spectator bumped into him from behind, shoving him within the reach of the abomination from Hell, which swung its devastating claws and tore open the teacher's abdomen. The liquor consumed by the professor numbed his body as he simply stood and looked down at his hanging intestines, which were touching the dirt on the ground. The Canadian teacher stared at his inner organs for what felt like an eternity, before raising his head to look at the responsible predator, which swung and severed his head from his body.

The creatures proceeded to massacre everyone in reach as they mercilessly preyed on the hotel's guests. The multitude of screams soon transformed to secluded hollers as the grounds were made filthy with corpses and blood. Satan's abominations slaughtered ninety one hotel guests around the compound before sitting down to feast on their victims.

During the massacre, Cassandra Bryan, who shared rooms with a female classmate named Jennifer Campbell, spent time after returning to their suite consoling her nerve shocked friend. After Jennifer calmed down and settled into bed, Cassandra began packing her luggage while attempting to link her mother on the hotel's landline. While awaiting the phone connection, the Canadian student tuned into the BBC World News for coverage on the developments around the world.

The phone rang several times before Sarah responded to the call. "Hi mom it's me, you won't believe the craziness happening here."

"Oh honey I'm so happy you called, where are you?" Sarah asked.

"I'm inside my hotel room, but we have no means of returning to Canada according to the transportation board." Cassandra stated.

"Listen to me carefully, I want you to stay exactly where you are and avoid going outside! There are some kinds of creatures going around killing people over here. I don't know if they're over there but it's better to be safe than sorry."

As they chatted about matters of importance, an eruption of screams could faintly be heard outdoors as the news reports on the television drowned out the noise abrasion. Cassandra, who became accustomed to the loud rackets of overly-zealous celebrators, ignored the outdoor screams as she spoke with both parents who were worried sick about her. During their conversation a couple who was fortunate enough to escape the clutches of the creatures, ran by Cassandra's suite with the female hysterically yelling at the top of her lungs. Curiosity brought Cassandra to the front door where she peeked through the peep-hole and saw nothing of which to raise concerns. The Canadian student walked over to the window and drew aside the curtains before screaming out loud at the disgusting sight outside. Before the horrified student's eyes was one of Satan's abominations ripping the intestines from one of its male victims.

The screams of their daughter frightened both parents on the opposite line as Sarah began yelling for Cassandra to tell her about what was occurring. With her suite located on the second floor of the hotel, Cassandra believed it impossible for the creature to sense her presence. However, the beast turned its attention from its prey and stared directly at the scared female through the window. Once Cassandra realized both the beast and herself were staring at each other, the young student tossed the phone aside and jumped across the bed, while screaming at the top of her lungs. Cassandra leapt over her bed and crashed atop Jennifer, who was comfortably asleep on her twin bed.

"What is wrong with you?" Jennifer crankily stated, as she attempted to push her roommate off her.

Cassandra held tightly onto Jennifer as they both crashed to the floor.

The terrified female jumped to her feet and dragged her friend to her feet before tugging Jennifer along into the bathroom. Fearing the creature would crash through the window, Cassandra retreated to the safest place inside the hotel suite; remaining there with her friend until she was convinced they were safe from harm.

"Why did you drag me in here? What going on?" Jennifer demanded.

"There was some kind of creature outside literally eating a guy! My parents were warning me; oh God my parents must think the worst!" remarked a trembling Cassandra.

Around the grounds of the hotel the slaughter continued as the creatures chased and mutilated anyone caught outside in the open. One of the beasts that snuck its humongous frame into the cafeteria slashed and ripped apart everyone caught in its grasp. While the creature tore apart its victims a Defender Angel appeared on the scene and felt immense grief after observing the decapitated body parts about. The screams of two females inside the cafeteria drew the angel's attention to their plight and the representative of God moved to investigate the problem.

The angel couldn't see the hampered females inside the cafeteria, as he grabbed the creature by the tail and dragged it from inside the building. The beast clawed and scratched to avoid being drawn from the structure, as the angel pulled out half its body before jamming his sword into its belly. The creature released a loud roar as the angel twisted his blade inside its gut, before ripping out its intestines.

"Get out and get yourselves indoors right now!" the angel instructed, as he cleansed his blade by wiping it clean on the creature's fur.

The Defender Angel, who was of dark complexion, resembled a muscle builder from the Mr. Universe competition, with his long-range bow and arrow over his shoulders and his sword shielded by his side. The angel wore long black dread lox that extended to his waist, his chest and back armor, sandals that provided a defense plate over his chin and his prized helmet with the lord's insignia. The terrified ladies inside the cafeteria heeded the instructions of the defender as they nervously ran by the slain creature and continued to their rooms.

With the females safe, the angel, who believed more creatures were about the grounds, went in search of the other slayers. The Defender Angel cautiously looked around the hotel's grounds with his sword at hand should he encounter an unsuspecting attack. The second of the two creatures had made its way to the second floor of the administration building where it indulged in the flesh of an obese woman who was caught attempting to evade creature. The beast went unnoticed by the angel, who expected to find the creatures roaming about ground level in search of victims. The creature halted its feast once it noticed the angel going by before deciding to attack the angel.

The creature leapt on the roof of the building and secretly crept along the northern section as it stalked the angel who believed he was being the predator. The beautiful landscape, abundant with fruit trees made it difficult to locate the Devil's abominations, although the angel remained on guard for anything. As the Defender snuck around a corner, which led to the lawn tennis area, the stalking creature leapt on top of him knocking him to the ground. The angel's sword went sailing as he crashed to the ground with the beast attempting to maul him, while he protectively grabbed the creature by the neck and held it at bay. The Devil's abomination scratched the angel with its deadly claws as the Defender looked around for his weapon. The sharp claws of the beast, which typically decapitated humans, was not effective against the angel's armor, which was built to guard against such blows.

The angel stretched and attempted to grasp his sword, which was slightly out of his reach, as the beast tried to overpower him and rip his head off with its rigid fangs. After realizing he could by no means regain his sword the angel thought of one solution as he held the beast with his left hand and reached for an arrow from his rear pouch. The beast, which had been clawing and scratching, sunk its right claw into the angel skin between his armor and his neck, thus the piercing sensation caused the angel to groan. The Defender Angel withdrew an arrow from his pouch and jammed the beast through its thick skin into its abdomen. The beast reacted to the first stabbing as if it mattered little, which forced the angel to repeatedly stab the beast until it was motionless.

The Defender Angel tossed the beast aside and groggily rose to his feet before collecting his sword and regaining his composure. After collecting his thoughts, the angel again went in search of other creature, to ensure there were no further threats on the compound. The estate resembled a war zone after hundreds had been mutilated and hacked to death. Body parts were scattered across the grounds as vultures swarmed above and prepare to feast, with the stench of death's aroma filling the air.

The Oboaci Tribe

Outside the confines of the compound, the native people of Africa faced the same predicament. The various tribes across the continent dealt with these abominations from Hell as they disrupted and devastated the lives of Africans and others around the world. In Congo South Africa there was a hunting party of fifteen Oboaci Warriors who were returning home after a successful hunt, where they killed a large Giselle and caught several fishes to feed their village. As the hunters jogged home with their prizes, chanting and ramping with each other, the men came across one of Satan's beast in an open field two miles from their village. The creature in the hunters' path had previously devastated a small village where it singlehandedly killed twenty three villagers before roaming off in search of others.

The leader of the hunting party, whose name was Taffy, spotted the beast at a fair distance and motioned his troops to halt. Unsure of what the creature was, Taffy signaled his warriors to scatter for the woods as the beast began charging towards them. The warriors all raced towards the trees with the creature at their heels as they attempted to outrun the creature and gain advantageous grounds. During their race to the trees, the Oboaci Warriors carrying the Giselle realized the creature getting closer and abandoned their bounty. With the speed at which the creature was coming, the warriors to the rear hoped the beast was simply hungry and their offering satisfactory enough for the creature to leave them alone. The creature from Satan's dungeon completely ignored the dead animal and continued chasing the warriors, who were sprinting to reach the trees and climb.

The hunting party was inches from the forest when the beast first struck the slowest warrior in the group. The creature used its huge paw to sweep away the warrior's feet before biting the man's head off his body. The other Oboaci hunters quickly took to the trees and climbed to the highest points possible to avoid the carnivorous beast. Once the hunters realized the creature had an appetite for humans, the men began tactical maneuvers to scare the beast into leaving. The warriors began yelling various sounds aimed at confusing the beast, while others picked fruits and other projectiles from the trees and threw them at the creature. Instead of abandoning the hunters, the beast attempted to climb several trees to get at the men, who realized they had no choice but to kill the beast.

Taffy instructed his warriors without spears to begin carving weapons to strike back at the intrusive beast, which was intent on killing every single one of them. There were a few hunters who were already armed with their spears and intended on firing before Taffy intervened and instructed them on the effectiveness of a combined strike. While the beast roamed the grounds beneath the warriors' feet, the hunters carved spears and threw them to each other, ensuring everyone had at least two spears before the order to fire was given.

While the Oboaci hunters prepared their assault, the beast leapt into one of the trees that protected three of the warriors and gingerly climbed towards one of the men. The beast crawled out onto a branch after a hunter, who became increasingly nervous the closer the creature got. The weight of the beast immediately began bending the branch, as the fear of falling awkwardly forced the hunter to jump from almost twenty five feet to the ground. The Oboaci hunter broke his left leg the instant he struck the turf as he pranced to one leg and hobbled towards the adjacent tree. The creature leap directly onto the hunter and squashed him beneath it before using its powerful jaws to completely rip the man's head off. The sight of the beast tossing their friend's head aside like garbage enraged Taffy, who immediately ordered his warriors to commence firing. The creature was pinned to the ground with spears, as each surviving Oboaci warriors struck the beast with their pinpoint accuracy, killing the beast that mauled their friends.

The Ewe Tribe

There was a tribe of Ewe people whose village was located in the southwest section of the continent. The Ewe people were believed to be practitioners of Voodoo or Black Magic because of their devotion to the underworld and their barbaric sacrificial offerings. The medicine woman for the village, who was worshipped and praised by the villager, received a vision, which she recited to the elders of the tribe. The medicine woman, who was miles from civilization, predicted the coming of Satan's creatures and the upcoming devastation, before the beasts were released to tarnish the earth. Mother Odessa, as she was referred to by her subjects, instructed her people on the preparations required to sustain them through the various destructions.

Mother Odessa ordered her helpers to corral a special cow they'd groomed for years, adorn the animal with the insignia of their master Satan the Devil and prepare the centre of the village for the ceremony. To her personal advisor Mother Odessa gave specific instruction on the specific utensils, bowls and cutlery to be used during the ceremony. The order was given to every Ewe member to attend the ceremony at the designated hour. Mother Odessa commenced the ceremony at 6:00pm, where they all gathered around a huge bonfire and began chanting corals of sacrifice. While the patrons chanted, Mother Odessa danced herself into a trance, where she soon began speaking in the dialect of the spirits whose guidance the elderly Voodoo advisor had always followed. As she telepathically connected to the underworld, Mother Odessa summoned the sacrificial cow, which was led in the circle by her personal advisor. As the ceremony proceeded, various villagers amongst the crowds began falling under the hypnotic forces, which altered and controlled the medicine woman. While everyone gradually succumbed to the hypnotic sensations, Mother Odessa collected the dagger and bucket and instructing her helpers to firmly hold the animal. With the animal settled, the Voodoo woman placed the bucket beneath its neck and proceeded to dance around the animal. The medicine woman spun herself in a circle for nearly three minutes and stopped abruptly while the villagers chanting and beating drums followed her lead. With the entire village quiet like a sauna, the medicine woman stepped to the animal and slashed its throat without any resentment or remorse.

The draining blood poured into the bucket as the elderly woman used the sharp blade to completely sever the animal's head. Mother Odessa instructed the helpers to elevate the rear of the animal in order for the majority of blood to leak into the bucket. Once most of the blood had been collected, the animal's remains were discarded as the medicine woman ordered everyone to form a line for the final portion of the ceremony. The hypnotized villagers walked by the medicine woman who personally nicked a cut on everyone's right index finger, before tipping a small amount of the individual's blood into the bucket with the blood of the cow. With the finalization of the ceremony, everyone was instructed to return to their huts and remain there until summoned.

The Voodoo Queen of the Ewe people took the bucket of blood after everyone had retired and walked around the outskirts of the village pouring the blood around its parameters. Mother Odessa then chopped up the cow into four sections and placed the tail end of the animal to the rear of the village, the right side to the east, the left to the west and the head to the north. After she had completed the task advised to her, Mother Odessa returned to the head of the village where she stood patiently with her eyes closed and staff at hand, and began chanting praises to her master.

As the designated hour drew near, the Voodoo Queen fell deeper and deeper into a trance, until she started shaking uncontrollably with both eyes firmly shut. While uttering the language of the spirits, the monkey's skull atop Mother Odessa staff began glowing a bright red light, which lit up the area like a light bulb. As the Voodoo practitioner continued her séance, one of Satan's lion-like beasts appeared from out of the woods and walked directly towards the Voodoo Queen.

The beast roared and grunted as it walked up to Mother Odessa, before stopping directly in front the elderly woman and lowering its body to the woman's body height. The Voodoo Queen suddenly opened her eyes and engaged in an intense stare down with the carnivorous beast. Mother Odessa's eyes were as red as those of the beast as they both communicated with each other as if she was one of their handlers. After an intense two minutes of staring into the old woman's fiery eyes, the beast refrained and slowly returned to the woods from which it came.

Chapter 11

Pope Desmond Arthur's inspirational speech gave the pilgrims who gathered in St. Peter's Square a divine feeling of solidarity and love. The Christian pilgrims in attendance all held hands, while attentively listening on every word uttered by their pope. The pope advised his audience that: 'it had been written within the scriptures, that their lord and savior Jesus Christ would return to reclaim his earth. Hence be not afraid, for they shall all survive the coming revelation to walk upon this land along side their heavenly father'.

During the pope's speech, Pastor Craig Lester, who was amongst the High Priests and Cardinals gathered inside the waiting chamber, observed a small gathering of seven cardinals who conversed secretly amongst themselves. Pastor Lester, who had been privately mourning the horrid death of his brother, kept fighting back his tears as he reminisced about his beloved sibling. The Spanish Pastor, Gabriel Marciano, who was Pastor Lester's closest confidant, was concerned about his brother's emotional stability as the Canadian apprentice fought to maintain his composure. Despite Pastor Lester's attempt at emotional control, his friend knew something was definitely wrong with him, although he was also aware that Lester would rather die than miss the greatest moment of his Christian career. The priest from Spain, walked over to his friend and gently placed his arm around the pastor's shoulder, consolingly and compassionately.

"Are you OK my brother?" Pastor Marciano asked.

"I'm-I'm-I'll be alright, gracias my friend!" Pastor Lester answered.

Both men stood in each other's arms, as they watched and listened to Pope Arthur whose words were thoughtful and soothing. As the speech progressed, the seven cardinals who whispered secretly amongst themselves soon strolled from the chamber, which was uncharacteristic of anyone during ceremonies by Pope Desmond. Pastor Marciano who keened in on dealings of the Cardinals, found it weird for any of the pope's inner circle to depart during his address and nosily strolled off behind the high priests. Pastor Marciano remained reserved behind the High Priests as they walked through the great hall and down the stairs on route towards the Historical Treasury Building of Vatican City.

Pastor Marciano remained in the shadows along the corridors as he trailed the high priests at a modest distance. The pastor from Spain followed the elders to the infamous vault where some of the earth's greatest treasures were said to reside. Once the cardinals passed through the security checkpoint, which was always safely guarded, Pastor Marciano was forced to abandon his chase since only officials of higher rank were allowed past that point. As Pastor Marciano watched the cardinals disappear from sight, the cause of the priests radical actions during such a perilous time disturbed him. All seven cardinals walked through the most secure sections of Vatican City, access to which required the Pope's personal clearance. The cardinals were ushered through metal detectors without any security check, which was a requirement implemented after it was discovered that valuable artifacts were being stolen from the vault. The overall incident became increasingly bothersome as Pastor Marciano watched the guards abandon their post and accompany the cardinals, leaving their post unattended. Despite the guards' absence, Pastor Marciano was still unable to gain access through the security checkpoint, as the guards left the gates closed and detectors activated.

Due to the abandoned guard station, Pastor Marciano moved closer for a definitive look at what the cardinals were up to, but found his vision obscured after they entered the great vault. The Spaniard was about to return to the ambiance of his brotherhood before noticing something disturbing on the video monitors which covered the grounds of the city. Pastor Marciano covered his mouth in fright as he gazed upon several Satanic Beasts ripping apart the pilgrims, who had gathered for their pope's historical address. The serene scene he'd only recently left had been transformed to pure chaos as the abominations from Hell attacked; ripping off limbs and tearing apart bodies.

Out of the view of the pastor, the High Priests had arranged for a freight trailer to dock at the bay leading to the Treasury Vault. Two chauffeurs, who wore black outfits and black masks, helped the security guards to load the trailer with several priceless artifacts. While their loyalists did the physical labor, the Cardinals stood watch over the proceedings as they debated over what they believed was to occur.

Without hesitation, Pastor Marciano ran up the stairs and down the long hallway, which led to the huge Cathedral Church of Vatican City. The Spanish Minister ran through one of the great halls of the citadel, where huge commemorative pictures and statues aligned the corridor. The sounds of hysterical pilgrims shouting and banging on the church's door caused the pastor to attempt to save those being mutilated. Pastor Marciano slipped after opening the huge brass doors to allow the escaping crowds access, as terrified pilgrims barged into the church in search of reprieve. The wave of fleeing pilgrims began trampling Pastor Marciano, as terrified pilgrims unsuspectingly charged in and stampeded over the generous bible student. The fleeing pilgrims, who were hysterical to say the lease, stampeded into the building and trampled Pastor Marciano to death in the process.

Pope Desmond Arthur was in the middle of his sermon, when three creatures from the Devil's dungeon attacked the massive crowd. The pope's aids, who stood behind him on the fore-lit balcony, quickly ushered their leader indoors once they witnessed the massacre unfolding. The abrupt end to his speech, the eruption of gun fire from the Citadel's personal guards, plus the loud screams from the crowd encouraged the Canadian bible student to look thorough the window where he personally observed the carnage occurring outdoors.

"Oh my Lord in the Heavens, what are those things!" remarked Pastor Lester, as he watched the pope's handlers rushed him off to safety.

Two of God's angels along with their pets, which were humongous saber-tooth tigers, appeared amongst the carnage. The angels behaved as if they were on a specific mission, as they glanced around at the hysteria, while their pets sprung into action against the tormenting beasts. While the angels scanned the scattered crowds, a pair of demonic angels floating about the clouds, sighted them and charged in for an attack. The heavenly angels, who were on the prowl, were conscious of the demons tactful ways, as they cautiously walked about scores of deceased pilgrims.

The shadows of night enhanced the success of the demons, whose dark skin texture made it difficult for pilgrims to see. With the angels' heads constantly rotating to pinpoint their foes, a demon angel swooped down with a dramatic kick to the temple of one of the angels, which knocked him unconscious as he tumbled to the ground. The angel's female companion, after witnessing her partner's demise dove to the ground and rolled to the right as her antagonist crashed to the turf in anticipation of clobbering her from above. The female angel rolled over towards her companion who lay motionless on the cement turf.

"Shyreek are you OK?" the female angel asked while shaking her comrade as she held the demons at bay with her extended sword.

The demonic angels, after their initial attack, laughed as they celebrated before soaring back into the clouds, as they continued their search while their beasts mutilated everything within reach. Two of the three carnivorous beasts, which had been devouring their prey, broke off their attack and went at the charging saber-tooth tigers, in a gruesome battle that had fangs and claws slashing and biting into animals' flesh. The brutal battle that erupted between the creatures awarded a lot of pilgrims the opportunity to safely escape.

The angel of God composed herself and prepared to do battle as she ensured her brethren was safe and extended her wings before soaring to the skies after her antagonists. Several pilgrims viewed the entire incident, but the majority of terrified Christians were more interested in saving their lives, while scattering for safety. The roars of the saber-tooth tigers caught the attention of two of the three creatures, which abandoned their slaughtering in order to prepare for a fight. The two charging saber-tooth tigers rushed their opponents with such force and vigor that once they collided, the animals latched onto each other with deadly claws, which would rip the typical human to shreds. Two of the fighting beasts struggled for minutes, before they separated and faced off with each other, both circling to gain an advantage. The separated beasts then lunged at each other as their claws sunk into the others skin, while they slashed at clawed at each other. The saber-tooth tiger, which was as huge as its opponent ducked underneath one of the creature's strikes and sprung up directly at its opponent neck. The saber-tooth latched onto the creature's neck with its powerful jaws as the beast emitted a loud squeal begging for help from its companions. The third creature, which was busy slashing and mauling pilgrims, heard the appeals of its comrade, abandoned its preys and ran to its sibling's aid.

The combat between the other beasts wasn't as exciting as the second saber-tooth found an opening during their preliminary clash and sunk its fangs into its opponent's neck. The saber-tooth made short order of its opponent, after conniving gaining the advantage at which it ripped the creature's neck apart. After ridding itself of one of Satan's abominations, the saber-tooth looked over to its comrade and noticed the third creature charging at its unsuspecting ally. The saber-tooth rushed to assist its comrade in arms, which received a slashing blow that blinded its right eye from the unsuspecting creature. The slash across the eye caused the saber-tooth to release its opponent, which staggered and gasped for air. After noticing that its comrade had been injured, the second saber-tooth tiger leapt in front of its ally, flexing its muscle and roaring loudly as it challenged the third creature. Despite its injury the wounded saber-tooth sought redemption, as it reactively charged its opponent which was un-intimidated by two challengers. The abomination from Hell refused to back down or surrender as it bravely charged the two saber-tooth tigers, which tore it limb from limb as they dismantled it.

Pastor Lester couldn't merely sit back and watch as the carnage continued as he summoned those willing to help and ran to offer aid. Amongst the scattered crowd of pilgrims was a family of interest to the demons, which sought to illuminate their bloodline from the earth. The Romano family, which consisted of father Andre, mother Alicia, eight year old son Andy and six year old daughter Alison, were targeted by Satan's followers who searched for them before the angels interrupted. The family of four, which was amongst the first to arrive in St. Peter's Square, was only saved thus far due to their positioning in the square. In order for his children to get a proper view of the pope, Andre lifted his son around his neck and held his daughter aloft with the aid of his wife, twenty feet away from the building from which the pope spoke. Once the massive hysteria began where pilgrims scattered and shouted in panic, Andre deciphered from where the dangers originated, before fleeing with the crowds moving in the opposite direction. With his family held tightly, the Romano's found themselves amongst the hysterical crowd banging on the cathedral doors for entry. Fifty feet away from the Romano's position was one of Satan's abominations, quickly gaining grounds as it mauled everyone in its path. The sight of the creature getting closer, forced Andre to reconsider their positioning as they began squeezing their way towards the side of the building. With the creature getting ever closer, Andre's eyes widened as a side door opened from where Pastor Lester and a few priests summoned frightened pilgrims.

The Romanos were a few feet from the door, when a moderate crowd quickly built in front of them. Pastor Lester, who held the door ajar, was knocked to the ground as hysterical pilgrims barged in through the available opening. Alicia Romano broke away from the crowd and moved to help the pastor, who was surprised at the payment he received for his considerate gesture. As scores of people continued pouring in through the emergency exit, a demon appeared above the ajar door and swung the door shut with such force that it completely severed a man's leg and sent the crowd tumbling onto each other, on either sides of the door.

While the demon terrified the crowd, the angel of God battled the second demon as they knocked swords in mid air. The female angel was as skilled as any of her male counterparts as she maneuvered her sword exceptionally well, while dazzling her opponent with her precision strikes. The demon, which perceived defeat, attempted to cheat during the battle as he threw some sort of powder into the female's eyes and backed away before changing his position. Believing the female angel to be completely disorientated, the demon charged from behind and attempted to behead the angel. The female angel, who had calmed herself, collected her thoughts, despite being unable to see, and spun around in time to block the assault before twirling her sword and chopping off the demon's hand holding the sword. After perceiving an assured victory, the demon was shocked at the sight of his hand falling to the ground. The female angel non-hesitantly swung her sword from the hip with one swift motion, which severed the demon's head as its body went tumbling behind its arm.

Across the compound, the second demon caught sight of its primary targets and moved in to execute its orders. With the exit door sealed shut, the Romano family, Pastor Lester and the remainder of survivors began scattering to get away from the threatening demon. Indications that the chapel's doors were opened sounded to the rear of the fleeing family, who found themselves running in the opposite direction. The pastor considerately grabbed Alison from her mother as they all began running away from the demon, which intimidatingly grabbed and smashed several pilgrims against the wall before continuing its pursuit. The angel of God swooped in to assist the Romanos after it became clear that they were the demon's primary reasons for attacking the ceremony. With the demon on the heels of its preys, the Defender Angel did her absolute best to catch up to the Romano entourage, but felt a sense of failure when Andre, who realized the demon gaining grounds, tossed his son to his mother and dived beside a deceased security guard. Andre grabbed the weapon from the guard's hand and pointed it at the charging demon before firing three rounds from the guard's 9mm pistol in hopes of stopping the demon. The bullets all impacted the Demon. However, destroying a force of such magnitude required a lot more than copper bullets.

Instead of stopping the charging demon, the bullets only helped to increase its rage as the assassin from Hell snatched Andre up by the right leg and flung him at a building over fifty yards away. Andre mashed against the wall like a pie to the face as his body simply crumpled once it made contact. Andre's wife, despite her concerns for her children, looked over her left shoulder as they ran from the square and stopped, before launching into hysterical screams at the sight of what happened to her husband.

"Ahhhhhhhhh!" bawled Alicia, as the priest was forced to stop, with consolement being the last thought on his mind.

"If we don't get away from here the same fate is going to become of us! Think about your children and let's go!" insinuated Pastor Lester, as both children picked up where their mother left off and started bawling.

Pastor Lester grabbed Alicia's right hand and dragged her along as the demon looked to soar to the skies after them. The female angel shoulder tackled the demon from behind, which pounded it into the ground as the Romano family got to the main road and turned down the street. The slight tumble after the collision caused the female angel to injure her left arm as she noticeably clutched it against her stomach as both angels faced off.

"Audrey, there is no use trying to come between my king and his destiny." implied the demon named Karma.

"Never say my name out your mouth Karma! You're still a bitch no matter how you look at it, no wonder the humans invented that phase after you. Look at yourself, angels were created bright and glorious to reign about the atmosphere, not cooped away in dark dungeons which after time change your appearance." argued Audrey as she twirled her sword with her effective hand.

"Don't be jealous, my complexion looks better than yours, maybe a tan might help bronze you out a little." answered Karma, as he attacked his nemesis.

"Cling!" sounded the clashes of swords, as both warriors latched their weapons in an exhibition of strength. Audrey held her own despite her injured arm as both fighters pressed up against each other while attempting to out muscle the other. Karma, who believed he should have an advantage due to the angel's injury, was stunned at his nemesis' resolve as he raised his left leg and stumped the female angel to the ground. Once the demon gained a slight separation, it immediately soared after its fleeing targets with knowledge of failure primary on its thoughts. After crashing to the ground, Audrey realized the demon's trickery as she quickly soared after her nemesis.

Alicia, Pastor Lester and the children ran down the main street towards the family's station wagon, which was parked a few blocks away from St. Peter's Square. The small group of people, which ran off alongside the Romanos to escape danger had dwindled to none, as everyone branched off where ever they believed safest to survive. The street along which the family found themselves was totally deserted as Alicia pointed to her vehicle before looking over her shoulder for the assassin.

"Here pastor you drive!" Alicia exclaimed, as she pressed the remote button to open the doors before tossing him the keys.

The children were tossed into the rear seat with instruction to fasten their seat belts as the black demon burst around the corner.

"Oh my God that thing is still coming, go-go!" shouted Alicia.

Pastor Lester started the family's Audi A4 and rammed it into gear before squealing out of the parking spot like an F-1 racing car. Alicia was frantic with worry over her children's safety and the death of her husband, which seemed surreal to her. "Where are we to go to get away from that thing? Why is it attacking my family and me? Why doesn't it just leave us alone?" argued Alicia.

"Hello my name is Craig Lester and I'm a Canada. Since I've been here I've been away from Vatican City twice and both times were with tour guides, so excuse me for interrupting your little hissy fit, but I got no idea where to drive to!" Pastor Lester declared.

Alicia realized her indiscretion and composed herself as she checked back on her children before quickly taking helm of the navigations. "I'm sorry, my name is Alicia Romano and that's Andy and Alison. Their murdered father was Andre. Thank you for helping us, now turn right up here this street is a dead end!"

The pastor, who had been speeding through intersections due to the deserted streets, didn't expect there to be any altercations as he swirled around the corner on a red light. The trailer, which had been loaded with valuable artifacts from Vatican City, was blazing through the intersection as both conductors attempted to maneuver in order to avoid the collision. The trailer struck the rear end of the Audi and sent the car into a twirl as the trailer veered off into a Swiss Bank, which was located on the corner. Both passengers of the semi trailer were instantly killed, as the collision crushed the cabin area of the trailer. The pastor was knocked unconscious as Alicia found herself woozy once the vehicle stopped spinning. With her children's wellbeing at heart, Alicia staggeringly collected both kids and began running down the street towards the only building she believed capable of saving her family. The demon in pursuit witnessed the crash from a few blocks back and smirked to itself as it expected to find its victims laid out on a platter for its dismantling.

Pastor Lester regained modest consciousness as he staggered from the vehicle and looked over at the crashed semi. The right trailer door had been popped open showcasing some of the valuable artifacts, which scattered amongst the wreckage. A priceless painting drawn by Leonardo da Vinci, which Pastor Lester recalled enquiring about during his visit to the vault, caught the priest's attention as he slowly moved to investigate.

The demon assassin landed beside the crashed Audi and immediately went after the family believed to be inside. The towering skeleton of a man who knew it had the vital seconds necessary to kill its victims, ripped off the vehicle's roof in order to get at the remaining family members. Once it became evident that the mother and children had disappeared, the demon quickly scanned the area and noticed his prey racing down the street. With the angel almost at his heels, Karma continued his pursuit with great anticipation of spilling their blood.

Pastor Lester staggered across the street to the crashed semi, which was completely stacked with ancient relics from every corner of the globe. With both drivers of the semi killed, there was no way for the priest to find out the cargo's destination or who authorized such a travesty. After ensuring that the artifacts were indeed original, the astonished priest moved to the chauffeur's cabin, where he found the driver pinned around the steering wheel and his masked partner ejected inside the bank. Pastor Lester began walking towards the rear of the semi, when he truly observed the custom built trailer. The trailer was painted completely black, with black chrome rims and every facet of the interior cabins sporting the same color. There was a purple insignia, which reflected from certain angles imbedded into the dark paint along each section of the semi, which caught Lester's eye as he made his way towards the rear of the trailer. The nerve tingling groan of one of Satan's abominations sounded as the priest neared the tail end of the trailer from which the creature crept. Pastor Lester froze along the side of the trailer as he looked back at the slight distance to the exposed front cabin, before turning back to the sight of the beast staring directly at him. The priest gasped and tightened his eyes shut with expectance of being mauled as the creature simply glanced at the insignia above his head, before prancing off down the road.

Audrey the angel trailed the demon by approximately thirty feet as the Devil's assassin honed in on its targets. With her daughter at hand and son by her side, Alicia ran towards a building where the plaque along the bricks read 'Jehovah's Witnesses'. The horrified family ran along the deserted road for what seemed like an eternity as they neared the facility with the demon fast approaching. While Alicia prayed in desperation that she made it the perceived safe haven, Audrey fought to catch the speeding demon with thoughts of what could be accomplished in a millisecond.

Twenty feet away from the facility, the demon smacked against a force field, which sent it tumbling from the sky. Karma had gotten so absorbed into the chase that he neglected to heed the protected airspace barrier, which was cast around every establishment that housed worshippers of God. After observing what became of the assassin and watching the surviving family members enter a facility of her father's, Audrey abandoned the chase and rushed back to her ailing team members.

Chapter 12

There was a top-secret assembly held in Novosibirsk, which is located a few kilometers northeast of Kazakhstan, in the country of Siberia. Present at this elaborate ceremony were delegates from every super power government across the globe who were all executive members of the prestigious Illuminati Church. The meeting, which was held deep in the Siberian Mountains, was conducted in an area attainable only by helicopter. Hence, the various delegates in attendance were all flown in on private crafts, which featured the insignia for the organization to-which they were bound. The Delegates' chariots brought them to an ancient private compound where the Devil's insignia and that of the Illuminati were posted on the dark colored walls throughout. A gloomy and mythical atmosphere surrounded the compound, which deflects the sun light and radiates darkness year round. The members, who all adorned ankle length black robes with cloaks, walked unified into a gloomy chamber, where only the glares from candles, hung high, offered lighting. The members walked with their hands clasped like monks as they entered behind a priest who chanted hymns, which praised their God and master. After they converged into the chamber, the black cloaked priest continued to an alter in the middle of the hall, while the various members branched off to their individual seats as they remained standing while chanting with their eyes closed.

"Bow in the presence of your Sovereign King!" barked a bass toned voice, as everyone in attendance fell to their knees.

Lucifer, the king of this World, walked into the chamber and sat upon his kingly throne, which was secludely built on a platform a few feet behind the priest's alter. Both the demon who announced the devil's entrance and the second of his guards took to their stations on either sides of his throne as Satan motioned for everything to come to an order.

"You may be seated!" declared the same bass toned voice.

"My loyal subjects, our days of atonement are upon us, and the time has come for you to make your ultimate sacrifice in the defense of our cause. We will not be shown any mercy by this tactful army, so I want everything made ready for a grand welcome. For centuries I have mentioned my divine plan, where your vehicles of war shall be fitted with new defenses. Wherever possible, we shall strike at this army, for this planet is our earth, and that is how it forever will remain!" Satan the Devil instructed.

Every major news broadcaster around the world, from BBC to CNN News Broadcast, began televising footage of the battling angels in Rome, as well as numerous other incidents involving Satan's puppeteers. From the North Pole to Greenland, humans experienced turbulent and treacherous events, which brought the entire world to a perilous standstill. News reporters from every area of the earth instructed their audiences to remain indoors and keep every available entrance locked. With all the heartfelt despair, there were a few triumphant moments where video footage revealed humans actually killing these creatures with which they would pose and showcase their trophy. Social web sites like Face Book and Twitter became most people's personal source for news as individuals across the globe reposted images of the horrors sent to them.

There were thousands of aircrafts already airborne when the order was given to halt all air travel. The aviation sector quickly fell into anarchy as airport information services immediately got bombarded with millions of curious family members in search of details about their loved ones. Almost every airport around the world had stranded passengers, pilots and others, stowed away in areas that offered them shelter from Satan's abominations. Millions of family members, who fought to remain positive that their loved one's plane will arrive, had secretly accepted the unimaginable truth; their loved ones had perished. Hundreds of airplanes were taken down by the Devil's followers, while those able to reach their destinations had to be securely brought into their docking stations under the protection of that nation's armed forces. Military personnel aligned the runways of every major airport, where they used their effective high powered weapons to keep the devil's creatures at bay, in order for domestic and international flights to safely land. Through their onboard communication systems, pilots of uninterrupted aircrafts learnt about the dilemmas facing different countries, as traffic controllers instructed their pilots to cancel signal receptions to the passengers' internet and wireless devices. Travelers on international flights especially had to be kept in the dark regarding the turmoil involving every nation, in attempts to maintain calm and stability on these flights.

Flight 492 left Vancouver's International Airport on route to Shanghai International Airport in China. The flight had been airborne for almost five hours when tragedy struck the passengers and crew. With the plane under the auto-pilot's control while traveling at thirty six thousand feet above international waters, a female passenger alerted the air hostess about something disturbing she noticed through her window. The female passenger fought to compose herself due to the fact there were young children seated in the row across from her as she described the humongous flying creature she noticed flying along side the aircraft.

The airhostess after receiving the woman's claims, sought to inform her pilot, before a second female screamed out in fright after she too noticed the terrifying creature outside the plane. The panic driven passenger rose from her seat and began behaving hysterically, which provoked other passengers who were comfortably resting. The passenger's extravagant behavior prompted the air marshal aboard the plane to get involved and he was forced to subdue her in order to prevent her hysteria from spreading. Despite attempts to discredit the female, passengers on both sides of the aircraft stared through their widows as everyone sought confirmation about her claims.

Passengers aboard Flight 492 began loosing confidence in their flight crew, who all insisted there was nothing abnormal taking place. The chief airhostess went to the pilot's cockpit, where she outlined the developments inside the plane and insisted he regain control by assuring the passengers of their safety. After receiving reports of something weird outside the aircraft, the pilots checked their instruments for other crafts in the area, before grabbing the intercom and advising everyone 'to return to their seats and fasten their seat belts, suggesting that turbulent weather was the cause'.

The senior pilot regained control of the aircraft and began radioing ahead to the Chinese traffic controllers who reported no other airplanes in the immediate vicinity of Flight 492. Traffic controllers scanned the air space around the aircraft and reported nothing abnormal on their radar screens, although they did advise the flight crew of super natural occurrences, by which numerous planes had fallen unexplainably from the skies.

A number of screams erupted inside the airplane cabin as passengers peered through their windows and saw several demons gushing about the night's sky.

"What the hell is that thing doing?" yelled a male passenger, who noticed a demon taking aim at striking the aircraft's wing.

The astonishing statement was followed by a huge bang, as the demon used its fist to punch the left metallic wing off the plane. The aircraft immediately began spiraling towards the earth, sending everyone aloft tumbling throughout the cabin, as the pilots fought to maintain control.

"May-day, may-day, may-day we have an emergency! Our left wing has been struck by an unknown source and we're presently spiraling to the ground! May-day, may-day, lord help us!" exclaimed the pilot, seconds before Flight 492 completely vanished off radar.

With reports collaborating the notion of an international conspiracy against humanity, certain flights, already airborne, were given priority classifications, where fighter jet departed their stations to serve as escorts to these massive birds. Two Chengdu J-10 fighter jets departed the Datong Airbase in the Beijing with direct orders to escort the Chinese President's plane into a hanger. The Chinese premier Foh Chu Mae was returning home from a summit on Climate Control in Brazil when other non-relative incidents persuaded traffic controllers to dispatch the air force. The premier's convoy was amongst the airplanes being tracked by the Beijing Airport Director, who prioritized their leader's aircraft before any other.

"Air Force One, please be advised you've been re-designated to the Datong Air Force Base. Private escorts have been sent to guide you into docking, so please change coordinates to---." informed the air traffic controller.

The pilot aboard the president's aircraft immediately advised his passengers of the precautions being taken to ensure their safety before implementing the strategic measures necessary for their survival. While redirecting the aircraft to the coordinates received, the pilot armed the aircraft's defensive mechanism, which consisted of port and rear side automatic submachine weapons, info-red heat seeking missiles and evasive flares. The pilot descended the airplane from thirty four thousand feet to twenty thousand as directed, before leveling off into the awaiting escorts of two Chengdu Fighter Jets. The leader of the Chengdu squadron Colonial Chan Lee radioed the pilots aboard the presidential aircraft in order for the pilot to update the plane's security systems to accommodate their escort.

Moments after the jets aligned themselves behind the DC 300 that was flying in Chinese airspace, the co-pilot of the aircraft noticed a distressed aircraft spiraling from the clouds towards the main land. The airplane, which was approximately a quarter of a mile northeast of the presidential aircraft, went swooping from the clouds, as the co-pilot began alerting the traffic controller about the incident.

"Mayday, Mayday, Mayday, I just witnessed a plane falling in distress six miles north of the Beijing Airport! Mayday, Mayday!" barked the co-pilot into his headset, as he spoke in Mandarin.

With the threat level raised aboard the presidential aircraft, Foh Chu Mae's personal guards chose to disobey the pilot's 'be seated and fasten seat belts' alert as they scurried aboard the aircraft with weapons drawn, peeking through windows into the night. The sensors, which controlled the submachine weapons aboard the aircraft, detected something along the left side of the aircraft and began firing. Every armed agent aboard the aircraft ran to a window along the left side of the plane in attempts a catching a peek at whatever caused the sensors to fire the weapons. The president's senior pilot immediately advised their escorts of the situation, as the weapon continued firing.

"What is out there, tell me what you see?" the sequestered president demanded of his guards.

"It's dark sir, I can't see a thing!" exclaimed the only guard who wore glasses.

"Well the guns are firing at something, look harder!" Foh Chu Mae insisted.

The demons responsible for the prior plane crash had targeted the presidential airplane and were intent on crashing her to the ground. With the demons closing in uncloaked, the sensors detected their humongous anatomies and spat bullets at them. The attacking demons had to resort to evasive actions in attempts to avoid the spraying bullets as they swerved in every direction to avoid being hit. Colonel Lee, who flew the Chengdu Jet to the left of the Chinese Air Force One, positioned his plane at an angle where he'd be able to visibly see the threatening objects as his instruments failed to detect whatever it was the DC 300 was firing at.

Colonel Chan Lee nearly pissed his G-suit when he saw what it was that the submachine guns aboard Air Force One were firing at. The veteran pilot popped up the visor attached to his helmet and wiped his eyes clean in amazement at what he saw. Instinctively the pilot armed his personal weapons, as he marveled, for some time, at the magnificent specimens diving onto the DC 300. Colonel Lee broke off his escorts and engaged the demons from a surprising angle, which frightened the attacking assassins, causing them to loose focus at the bullets being spat from the presidential aircraft. Submachine shells tore through one of the demons, which went fluttering from the skies as the other assassins broke off the attack.

"Air support one, we have a clear aggression strike at Air Force One, fall into position at 0900 and be advised we're fighting man like flying creatures!" Colonel Lee instructed.

"Say that again colonel, I misunderstood that briefing." said the colonel's partner.

"You heard me Deng; stay on the lookout for black flying man like creatures!" repeated Colonel Lee.

The demons who broke off their attack were not about to surrender to mere mortals, as they converged south of the convoy and plotted another attack. With the faster jets about, the plot was made to expel these fast flying planes before redirecting the attack at their intended target. Once a plan of action was had, the demons separated and went at the convoy from opposing directions as they sought to intercept the planes before they arrived at their destination.

After a few minutes subsided, the members aboard the convoy became confident that their high powered weaponry had driven away their attackers.

Thus, both Chengdu Jets returned to their escort formation behind the presidential aircraft as they flew in unison towards the Datong Air Force Base. Their close encounter brought the involved pilots together where they chatted with each other about what they witnessed, while disclosing to the traffic controller their beliefs for the causes behind the devastating crashes.

The pilot aboard the second Chengdu Jet, who kept checking his instruments for any disturbance, soon felt a slight rattling as if he were flying through a depression. With the thought that his instruments were unable to detect the demons at first, the pilot nervously scanned his surrounding as well as his instruments, which all revealed zero threat. The Colonel, who also nervous about his sensors being unable to detect the flying demons, was looking about the airspace around his vessel when he observed one of the demons crawling along his mate's jet towards the cockpit.

"Deng one of those things is crawling towards your---!" yelled the squadron leader into his intercom, as the demon reached the cockpit.

The assassin from Hell punched his right hand through the glass and gripped the transparent covering that protected the cockpit before ripping the covering off with one hand, while holding tightly with the other. Colonel Lee reactively looped his jet around and came in behind his mate in time to observe Lieutenant Deng ejecting from the cockpit, mille-seconds before the demon grabbed a hold of him. The Chengdu Jet Aircraft, without its pilot, began plummeting to the ground as Colonel Lee coordinated his mate's landing position and transferred the data back to base.

"Air Force One be advised, our problems are far from over. These man like black things just assaulted one of our jets and caused it to crash! My sensors can't seem to detect them and." Colonel Lee reported.

The colonel was interrupted by the automated weapons aboard the Chinese Air Force One, which began spitting bullets from the submachine guns along both sides of the craft. Colonel Lee swooped along the right side of Air Force One and opened fire at the demon, which appeared to relish the excitement of bullets being spat at it. The demon veered off to the left of the plane with Colonel Lee in pursuit, as the enraged pilot sought to rid the skies of one less demon. Without his weapons targeting system available, Colonel Lee simply blasted at the fleeing demon the instant his weapons were pointed at it.

After firing off a few rounds at the evasive demon, the colonel swooped back into position behind Air Force One and continued his duties; while remaining hopeful that they would make the airport before any further altercation. With the silence of Air Force One's submachine guns, Colonel Lee contacted the traffic controller at the Datong Air Force Base and prepared them for their arrival. Unknown to the colonel was the fact that the demon he'd chased brought him on a fool's errand in order for its brethren to easily board the presidential aircraft.

While Colonel Lee remorsefully scanned the airspace around, the activity levels aboard Air Force One had elevated as a demon shrunk itself and boarded the plane. The Demon which entered the plane through an emergency hatch underneath the plane began shredding everyone from the rear of the plane through to the pilot's cockpit as the flares and gun explosions went undetected by the pursuing escort. Satan's assassin used his sword against the guns of men, which were outmatched by the demon's speed and tactical strategies. Everybody aboard Air Force One was sliced up like pork chops as the assassin accomplished its mission before departing the plane.

Colonel Lee, who believed he'd accomplished his mission, circled the base while watching the presidential craft glide in for landing. It wasn't until the colonel overheard the appeals of the traffic controller thru his headphones that he realized the plane had been compromised, as he frightfully watched the plane descend onto the tarmac, where it exploded and burst into flames once impacted. The sight of the presidential plane crashing with its leader aboard brought immediate tears to the colonel eyes as he watched emergency military crews race to the accident.

Chapter 13

The Caribbean islands, like the rest of the world, experienced the dreadful calamities, which uprooted superpower countries as the globe got transformed by the events of the times. Countries like Trinidad & Tobago, St. Lucia and Haiti all witnessed the fury of the devil as the globe continued experiencing the most magnificent climate changes ever recorded. Countries where the frigid winter would normally be causing havoc were as peaceful and serine as a garden filled with roses and birds. Meteorologists and news reporters speculated that this was 'the calm before the storm'. Senekal citizens, who thought the storm was already in full effect, scrutinized their news stations and in some instances boycotted them completely.

Once it was revealed that these massive creatures from Satan's dungeon succumbed to lethal firepower, animal gamers and certain extremists armed their weapons and went out to defend their property. While the majority of humans cowered behind their doors, gang bangers and gunmen worldwide roamed their territories and bravely hunted and ambushed the predators, which had successfully killed many humans.

Gully Side Flankers, Montego Bay Jamaica, the local gunmen around the area who typically coordinate their resources to defend against rivals, maintained a parameter around their neighborhood, where they held Satan's abominations at bay with their weapons. While the guns that kept the carnivorous creatures at bay sounded constantly, a Baptist preacher named Reverend David Anthony conducted a spiritual ceremony to a packed church, where, even from the roof's support beams, salvation seekers hung. Throughout the Reverend's ceremony cannon blasts erupted in the distance, which startled the audience members with every eruption. With the darkness of night, the continued shelling of artillery dissipated as it became increasingly difficult to see the dark colored creatures.

The thugs posted along the eastern section of the barrier, found it increasingly difficult to protect against a creature they could hardly see. The unit of thirty stood firm against six attacking creatures and grew more confident with each beast slain. However, the seventh creature was a bit more tactful in its approach, as it fully utilized the cloak of darkness and crept along the shades of trees to a section that was less guarded because of a fifteen foot wall, which was built with broken bottles cemented along the top ridge. The giant beast from Satan's dungeon ran up to wall and leapt over it, before landing inside the guarded territories. While two or three of the defense members along the barrier fired an occasional shot to defer any future attacker, the majority of thugs joked around, indulging in marijuana and alcohol, while they awaited any further encounter with the creatures.

The abomination from Hell crept through laneways entrenched with zinc fences, as it snarled and drooled for the taste of a human. The creature walked by houses where, through windows, it saw entire family members cuddled, while attempting to strengthen and console each other through the uncertainty. As the creature drew closer to the occasional gun blast along the eastern barrier, it stopped and peeked around the corner at its antagonists, while the preaching chimes of Reverend Anthony sounded faintly. With everyone focused along the opposite end of the barrier, Satan's abomination charged the guarding thugs and began mauling everyone in reach. Ultimate panic erupted as some frightened gunners reached for their weapons and shot at the slashing creature, before either having their guts torn out or heads ripped off by beast. With everyone absorbed with the creature within their midst, a second beast came running uninterruptedly into the camp, which caused the brave-hearted to scatter in every possible direction. Thugs, who found themselves out of the creature's reach, attempted to widen the

Rhoan Flowers

distance as they scurried for safety, while loosely firing to keep the predators at bay.

With one of the carnivorous creatures at their heels, several thugs ran down a laneway away from the beast. Despite wounding the creature several times, the thugs, who had slain many of the creatures, found it difficult to shed their antagonist, which was determined to decapitate them all. It wasn't long before the eleven Garrison Fighters, who had fled the altercation, got trimmed to three, as the creature swept through like a tornado. The three thugs who couldn't find somewhere to hide from the beast decided to run into the church where reverend Anthony was loudly preaching. From the trail of gunfire leading to his congregation doors, Reverend Anthony knew who his newest visitors were. The fleeing thugs bumped into the men standing at the rear of the church and bore through them in order to place some distance between them and the creature. The three surviving thugs kept looking over their shoulders, expecting the creature to blast its way into the church. The calm demeanor of the gentlemen who got bumped into, and the atmosphere inside the church, intrigued the young thugs, who all individually dropped their weapons and stared up at the crucifix behind the preacher as if they'd never before stepped foot inside a church.

"---but fear not said the lord, for you shall be with me in paradise! I say unto you this day, that most of you seekers will not be with us in paradise, so all you murderers and fornicators and adulterers, just go on back through them doors, because mi can't save your soul. The greatest book ever written was constructed with the laws we need live by in order to enter the kingdom of God. For years some of you youths have tormented and disgraced your families with your vile actions. Now look at you, cowering under this system like the rest of Babylon, but you all go burn in the great fire for your sins. All of you who wait till the eleventh hour wait a little too long, you can't come check the man whenever you fell like, for years I teaching about developing that intimate relationship with God, but it too late for all that! God say thou shall do unto others as you'd have them do onto you, but all most of you did was unforgivable things to your neighbors, A Sama Laka….!" preached the Reverent.

"Amen Pastor, burn them with the fire!" yelled one of the congregation's elderly female, who sprung to her feet, as if stricken with the Holy Spirit.

The White House

The President of the United States of America, Mr. Ron Flores, had his military strategic analysts decipher the approximate number of missiles needed to destroy a planet the size of the one on a collision course with the earth. The scientists were given a few hours to deliberate over a matter, although they'd prefer a few days to exercise a few tests before contemplating a definite number. With the gloomiest day in human's history on the horizon, a strategy had to be implemented and executed or the earth was feared lost.

The Russian space program had a probe called Mier V, which was launched into space in January of 1978. The objective of the probe was to allow the Russians the opportunity to be the first to intercept any transmission from Alien Vessels entering our solar system, as well as detect these crafts in advance. The Mier V Probe was launched and sent to the edge of our Galaxy from where it transmitted continuous data back to earth. Throughout the decades, Mier V have attempted to contact several unannounced visitors to our solar system, with no response detected from any of the vessels.

With the daunting prediction cast that the earth will be destroyed, transparency between the different space agencies and governments became essential, as every country sought to find means to combat this impending global disaster. The Russian Air and Space Federation had been in constant contact with Mier V since the threat was discovered, while scientists studied the data received to ascertain exactly how long they had before the collision. The Mier V Probe sent its final report to the Russian Space Institute in Khatanga, along the northern borders of the Federation, at 11pm that evening, at which the vessel reported its attempt at contacting an Alien source. The data sent by the Mire Probe detailed the specifics about the speed, course and dimension of the planet. The Mier V Probe transmitted its data seconds before it was destroyed by an unknown source, which scientists began attributing to the advancing planet. Immediate disclosure of the data collected from Mier V was sent to key members of the United Nations.

The president of the United States of America, who had been surrounded with advisors from every branch of the government since the appearance of the symbols, received the report from scientist that summarized the estimated amount of bombs necessary to destroy the threat. The military specialists of the U.S Pentagon speculated that a collective strike by seventy upgraded Atomic Bombs combined with Ordinance Penetrator Bombs, launched at specific angles, would, if not completely destroy the planet, knock it off course to dampen the impact.' Since the receipt of the report, President Flores had been on the phone with rulers from countries with nuclear capabilities. After short deliberations, President Flores signed the order for twelve Ordinance Penetrator Bombs to be sent to such countries along with the necessary technicians needed to launch each weapon. Countries such as Great Britain, Germany, China, Canada, India, South Korea, Japan, Russia and North Korea, all had bombs that were similar to that of the Americans and thus weren't in need of assistance from the United States.

With the cancelations of flights worldwide due to recent incidents, the president, who was skeptical about the Penetrator Bombs arriving at their destinations, had to be assured of success by his generals, who declared that each convoy would be accompanied by twin F-22 Raptor Jet Aircrafts. The Vice President, whose advice was important to the president, dealt the final convincing argument when he indicated that, 'the earth was doomed unless they acted.'

Mather Air Force Base in California

With the order signed to transfer a dozen Ordinance Penetrators to various countries around the world, measures were implemented to ensure that every single missile arrived at their destination intact. Thus, one of the highest ranked priests of the Illuminati Church, Rev. Wayne Soulless was sequestered to bless each missile and crew before they departed the army base. The brave men who had been chosen to sacrifice their lives if necessary in order to accomplish their mission only attended the private ceremony, which was held inside hanger number four at the base. Rev. Soulless, who was dressed in black, prayed intensely with each missile prior to administering the Illuminati insignia with a colorless marker, which was invisible to human's naked eyes. Following the Reverend's blessings, each

Yahweh

missile was brought out from the hanger and loaded onto towering C-17 Globe Masters, which were the Air Force's biggest combat planes.

The true and accurate data log of Commander Jeffrey Fawcett;

 The base, with the redirection of flights coming in, posted semi-automatic weapons throughout to deter those carnivorous creatures from attacking. Remarkably, the instant the command was received indicating that the base was to serve as the launch pad for a major assault, every weapon silenced as the creatures ceased engaging. The entire squadron received their briefing at 1900 hours Pacific Time for us to deliver twelve Ordinance Penetrators to seven different countries across South America, Asia and Africa. As ranking officer, I was in charge of the three men security detail assigned to deliver two Ordinance Penetrator Missiles to the Government of France. Immediately after receiving our orders, for the first time in my thirty seven year career, we also received some sort of weird blessings and prayers from a priest, who also inexplicably blessed the missiles and the planes with some weird séance. Due to the fact that it was a military mission, the only civilians allowed on board were these intense behaving tech guys, who came along to launch these missiles. My security crew and I, who served our entire careers together, joked about these preprogrammed nerds who walked tight as if they forted they'd explode! While the ground crew loaded the missiles, I walked about the plane and was checking to ensure everything was well, when I observed the priest placing a marking along the rear. As I went by the section of the plane at which I observed the pastor, I personally inspected the exact area and found nothing indicating anything alarming. By the time I boarded the plane, confirmation to take off was already granted and so we were airborne ten minutes later.

 Inside the C-17, which was as huge as a skyscraper, the four missile technicians sat amongst themselves, while my crewmembers gathered along the left side of the plane. Despite the personal escort by two F-22 Raptor Fighter Jets, our importance within the security detail was attributed to the handlings of the C-17 Globe Master's personal onboard weapons system, which featured four Remington Sub-Machine guns. With everyone settling into the flight, I walked up to the cockpit to chat with the pilot Kirk, who was an old and dear friend of mine. Kirk introduced his new co-pilots before proceeding to relate how nervous he was flying an aircraft after being personally told of incidents where other fortunate pilots survived the terrors of crashing. I was gone from the crew for about an hour and a half and returned to find all the technicians and two soldiers under my command soundly asleep. I dove into this novel I'd been reading called 'Informer The Wars of Men' and dozed off some time after, before being awaken by the frantic demands of Captain Kirk, who insisted I get up to the cockpit immediately. I popped up and grabbed my automatic riffle before rushing off to the cockpit, during which I observed the missile technicians fully awoke and alert. I climbed the ladder up to the pilot's cockpit and entered to find Pilot Kirk frantic with worry.

"What's the emergency?" I asked.

"Our personal escorts are gone and Alan reported hearing them yell that something was dragging them from their jets!" emphatically declared Kirk.

"What the hell do you mean they're gone?" I demanded.

"Look for yourself, there is the monitor that highlights the rear of the plane and they're both gone!" continued Kirk.

I needed no further confirmation of an aggression against our convoy as I immediately jumped on the helm and advised my squadron members to, "scramble to their battling posts", while I hustled back to my assignment.

While racing back, it dawned on me that my men didn't confirm my orders, but knew them well enough to believe they'd already manned their weapons. To ensure they had heard me, I again repeated the battle stations alert, while I slid down the ladder into the hanger. I was completely unsuspecting of the technicians as threats, as I raced to get to my personal station along the rear port side of the vessel. I ran into the passengers' lounge to find my squadron members hog tied and faced down against the floor as someone gun butted me from behind, which send me crashing to the floor.

"What are you idiots doing, the world is doomed unless we accomplish our mission?" I argued, as people jumped on top of me and bounded my hands and feet.

"Chill out Commander, humans can't stop the inevitable!" responded one of the technicians.

My team and I became mere spectators at that point, as we watched two of the men grab illuminative messaging boards from their inventory and ran towards the rear of the plane. The two technicians, who remained inside the lounge with us, collected their messaging boards and went to the windows at either side of the aircraft. My team and I concluded that these guys were attempting to steal the missiles as we watched the technicians inside the lounge signal something by reflecting whatever image was drawn to the message board through the windows. All attempts to escape our bondages failed, as we fought to free our hands.

The technicians continued their activities throughout the entire flight as we pondered about their motives and plans. The flight was designated for the Luxeuil Air Force Base in northern France, hence, once we entered the French air space, one of the technicians came about with injections that rendered us all unconscious. We were awakened by the grounds crew, which came aboard to perform their maintenance duties after the missiles had been unloaded and transported to their launch stations. The French maintenance engineers were confident the bombs were on-route to their destinations. After checking the clock, we realized we had been unconscious for nearly three hours and there was no sight of the technicians and the two co-pilots, who also left Pilot Kirk sedated inside the cockpit.

Chapter 14

Second sergeant Pierre Lapoint and several members of the Princess Patricia regiment were unorthodox members of the church; set apart from their devoted Christian servicemen, who abided by the word of God. Following the departure of the Red Cross' Huey Helicopter, thirteen of the twenty well-trained Canadian Light Infantry soldiers decided to abandon the offensive strike against the Taliban and, instead, return to the base in Kandahar City. Second Sergeant Lapoint and the remainder of the Canadian Infantry were confused and disturbed regarding their comrades' decision to allow the murderers of their brethren to escape unchallenged.

"I will see you all court marshaled for deserting the unit! You're traitors of the Canada Sergeant Lester served and loved. I'm disgusted to have had served with you cowards myself, you dam deserters...!" cursed Sergeant Lapoint at the soldiers, who were totally hypnotized by the symbols as they disappeared into the high brushes.

The soldiers, who sought to avenge their fallen commander, regained their chase of the insurgents, who raced down the streets while hollering that the Prophet Mohamed had returned! Despite the eruption of gunfire moments prior, people poured into the streets from their homes, as Muslims worshippers rushed to verify the speculations. The Canadian soldiers, who chased their fleeing enemies, were incapable of disbursing their weapons due to the influx of the local villagers. In an attempt to create an opening to aim at their foes, the Canadian soldiers began screaming for residents to return to their homes as it became increasingly difficult to race through the town.

"The Almighty Allah has returned, the Almighty Allah has returned…!" loudly chanted a female elderly villager, who began going from door to door to alert her people.

Once the residence of the Nakhoney Village began pouring into the streets, it became impossible to clear the dirt roads as even the lame and crippled crawled out to witness the symbols as well as its translation. The entire community of Nakhoney walked in unison as they all went to their local temple to pray and beg for their God's favor. The six remaining Canadian soldiers chased the five surviving Taliban members to the opposite end of town, where the insurgents scattered into the high brushes and disappeared.

"Dam it, dam it they got away!" Sergeant Lapoint recited in French, as they reached the other side of the town.

"You mean we're not going in after them?" questioned one the privates.

"It dark as hell, we don't even have half a platoon and chances are that's exactly what they'd like us to do. Besides, our orders were to rescue and secure the town, so let's get to it. Deschamp, I want you and Taylor to get back to the opposite end of town, secure the area and all those abandoned weapons. Rousseau and Marquette spread out and secure this area, but keep your eyes peeled because these guys will come back! Duhon I want you to raise the command base and inform them about our situation, then get your ass across to the south side and hold the fort. You don't have to play hero, just keep who ever it is at bay until reinforcements arrive, got me? I'll be north of the mosque if anybody needs me. Now remember, stay on the comp everyone, stay alert and prepare for anything." Sergeant Lapoint instructed his battalion.

As the soldiers scampered off to their assignments, the villagers continued swarming their local prayer hall, as both the skeptical and the holiest of worshippers converged to pray. Muslims, like every other form of religious pilgrim across the globe, were sincere worshippers of the divine Lord who created the earth and everything on it. Thus, at the assumed anointed time for God's return, flocks of believers swarmed the Lord's temples and tabernacles in attempts of gaining favors for their sinful souls.

Rhoan Flowers

There was a young twenty one year old male from Nakhoney who wholeheartedly served the Jihad as an insurgent soldier. Young Ibn Ahmad was recruited by the Taliban during one of their recruitment sessions some two years prior, following the bombing of his village by American bombers, which resulted in the deaths of both his parents and two younger siblings. Ibn's grandmother, who was terribly injured in the bombing, suffered an injury to her left leg and permanently lost her vision. Since the incident, Ibn had vowed to killing as many Americans and foreign soldiers as possible, and was amongst the Taliban group responsible for the ambush against the Canadians.

Once the escaped Taliban members began scampering through the village, young Ibn, who was originally from the area, cut through an alleyway between two homes and snuck around to his hut once the coast was clear. Ibn's grandmother was sitting in her favorite chair in the comfortable darkness of her home when her thuggish grandson raced in and hid himself inside the second room, behind the wooden bed. The chants of, "the Almighty Allah has returned", encouraged the old woman to collect her crutch and limp towards the front door in order to experience the excitement brewing in the streets. The old Afghan grandmother, who hadn't seen the desert's sand or anything for two years, opened her eyes to the brightened night's sky and clearly saw the symbols, as a soothing voice translated the meaning to her.

"Oh my Holy Prophet Mohamed, I can see the writings, I hear your words!" loudly declared Grandma Ahmad.

"Hassan, come assist me to carry Grandma Ahmad to the mosque?" declared the old woman's neighbor, who himself was on his way to pray.

"I can see your signs and hear your words Mighty Allah!" Grandma Ahmad continuously repeated, as her kind escorts lifted her and carried her to the mosque.

Ibn was amongst the meager few residents who abstained from attending the mosque, though the young insurgent's reasons differed from everyone else. The Taliban supporter continued hiding until everything had grown quiet. The fury of hatred that burned beneath young Ibn's skin was one of utter deceit; and his grandmother had no idea her grandson was a member of the suppressive militia. Ibn soon crept from his hiding place and snuck to the front door, where he peeked through cracks in the wooden door at the serene streets. The idea of his village permanently falling under the rule of the Afghan Coalition Forces command infuriated the young insurgent, who sought to teach everyone a lesson.

The young insurgent returned to the single attached room, lit a candle and carefully retrieved a suicide vest he'd stored for an attack against the Afghans of Kandahar City. Ibn opened his Koran bible before him on the bed and began chanting verses, as he carefully puts on the vest packed with C-4 Explosives, followed by his regular jacket. With the belief that his grandmother had retired for the night, the young Taliban snuck back from the hut with his Koran at hand, eighteen promised virgins in mind and devious intensions at heart. Ibn Ahmad walked down the street towards the mosque where four hundred and eighty seven citizens of Nakhoney, whom he known since birth, knelt in devoted prayer to their God. The Taliban loyalist chanted scriptures from the Koran as he briskly walked towards the overflowing mosque, where he solemnly intended to show the Nakhoney residents the penalty of treason.

Ibn walked into the packed mosque and moved to the middle of the gathering. "In the name of the most merciful, the one and only Allah, your humble servant comes to you as a sinner---!"

Sergeant Pierre Lapoint was scanning the surroundings through his Night Scope Binoculars when he observed Ibn briskfully walking towards the mosque. It had been nearly half an hour since the streets emptied, and the motions of the Taliban Insurgent was somewhat different from everyone else, who were rather jubilant to pray at the mosque. Curiosity seized the sergeant as he observed the suspect adjust something beneath his jacket seconds before entering the mosque.

"Oh shit, there is a suicide bomber heading into the mosque!" Sergeant Lapoint barked into his intercom, as he jumped to his feet and ran towards the mosque. At the sergeant's alert most of his scattered platoon commenced racing towards the specified coordinates, with each soldier concerned about what would happen should the explosive devise detonate. The soldiers ran briskly towards the mosque with the thoughts of what happened to Sergeant Lester fresh on their minds.

Ibn Ahmad stood in the middle of the Muslim gathering and uttered his speech, with the cord to detonate the bomb firmly at hand. Seconds before completing his speech the worshipper closest to Ibn grabbed him by the leg and tried to drag him to the ground. While tussling with the resident, Ibn's head got pulled around at which his eyes caught those of his grandmother, who looked at him as if she was staring into his soul. Ibn attempted at that point to release the string, but a second worshipper jumping on him caused him to drag it firmly.

"BOOM!" Erupted the bomb attached to the Taliban Insurgent's body, blowing himself and everyone in attendance to bits.

"Oh my God I can't believe it! Don't tell me they're all dead?" Major Private Rousseau enquired once he got close to the destruction.

Sergeant Lapoint who was forced to hit the dirt in order to avoid being hit by flying debris, stood up and demanded to know 'from where this suicide bomber came?' The Canadian soldiers, who have always been commended for offering others aid, were left distort by the incident, as the Nakhoney residents who didn't attend began to gather. Enquiries into what transpired were immediately explained to the gatherers, who fell to the dirt and bawled their eyes out as they mourned their dead.

Down the street from the destroyed Muslim Mosque, Major Private Deschamp and Private Taylor were enjoying the butt end of a Jail Pin Paleco Spliff, laced with the purest Afghan Grade A Cocaine. The two soldiers, who were extremely intoxicated, received a situational briefing from Lapoint who suggested they tighten the formation. Immediately after ending the transmission with Lapoint, the soldiers went right back to arguing about whose hockey team was superior; Ottawa Senators or The Vancouver Canucks.

During the debate, Major Private Deschamp paused and walked over to the huge brushes to relieve himself. While urinating in the bushes, one of Satan's abominations walked out from the bushes and stared at the peeing soldier. Deschamp, who believed he was high out of his mind, turned his penis at the creature and continued urinating while walking towards the beast; confident it was only a fragment of his imagination.

"Here Kitty Kitty, come here you overgrown Kitty Kitty?" Major Private Deschamp professed, while stretching his hand out to caress the perceived mirage.

Just as Deschamp was about to touch the creature, Private Taylor, who became dumbfounded by the physical size of the creature, terrified his brother in arms by implying. "Are you crazy, why the hell are you trying to touch that thing?"

"Uh, what? You can see the stat--?" responded a confused Deschamp, who momentarily takes his eyes off the creature. "RAAAAAARRRRR!" sounded the beast, as it opened its huge jaws and bit Deschamp in half.

"Secure the weapons...", which were orders given by acting Sergeant Lapoint, wasn't even an afterthought as Private Taylor took off running down the centre of the street, while disbursing his weapon at the creature behind him.

The creature's preoccupation with its meal, gave Taylor the opportunity to put some distance between himself and the creature, which appeared to be savoring every bite of the Canadian. The sudden discharge of a weapon placed Lapoint and the rest of the Canadian Light Infantry soldiers on defensive alert, as the sergeant immediately attempted to raise his soldiers over their intercom.

"Deschamp, Taylor what the hell is going on down there?" Sergeant Lapoint demanded.

"Some huge lion just ate Deschamp and, oh shit it's starting to chase me!" screamed Private Taylor into the intercom.

"Are these idiots down there getting high, what the hell did he just say?" sarcastically remarked Sergeant Lapoint, as he shrugs his shoulder at his confused mates. "Did you just say that Private Major Deschamp got eaten?"

The sergeant didn't receive a response; however Private Taylor's weapon continued disbursing, as the chopping sounds of Canadian artillery drew closer to the concerned platoon. Private Taylor gazed over his shoulder and noticed the beast quickly gaining grounds as he began popping the pins from his grenades and tossing them over his shoulder. The explosions from each grenade thrown, coughed up huge clouds of dust into the air, thus the private was unsure of his grenades' effects as he ran as fast as he possibly could to escape.

Sergeant Lapoint would have preferred clearing the streets of its mourners, but neither of the men or women who'd begun sifting through the rubble were about to abandon their quest. Sergeant Lapoint and his troops formed a horizontal line and began moving towards the endangered private, who was still discharging his entire arsenal. The soldiers adjoined their night goggles for improved visibility, as they abandoned the Nakhoney mourners who hopelessly searched for survivors.

Private Taylor became fatigued and slowed his pace as a trembling groan sounded at his heels. The exhausted private bravely spun around at his predator and latched his eyes tightly shut as he squeezed the trigger tightly The already injured creature leapt into the air at its fleeing prey, who managed to spin around and pop several bullets into the creature before it descended on top of him. Despite the creature's injuries, the beast was still strong enough to maul the private, whose eyes never reopened.

Second Sergeant Lapoint and the remainder of the Canadian Princess Patricia Light Infantry showed up to find the creature dinning on Private Taylor. The moment the beast spotted the soldiers, the injured creature attempted to rise and attack the platoon, who all permanently laid it down with their huge automatic rifles. The soldiers, after slaying the creature, cautiously crept up towards the beast to inspect the abomination from Hell, which was something none of them had ever seen before.

"What the hell is that thing Sergeant?" Duhon enquired.

"All I wanna know is where it came from and is there any more of them? Because I still can't believe that thing just ate stinking ass Taylor!" remarked Marquette.

"You see the size of this thing; nobody will ever believe that something like this existed in our times. Duhon toss me your camera; let's take a couple pics of this thing!" Rousseau commented.

"Hey guys this is no time to play around; Duhon I want you to radio command and tell them about this shit. Tell them we need transports to relocate a few people---!" Sergeant Lapoint was still mumbling over the tail end of his instructions, when screams erupted from the Nakhoney mourners.

The Canadian soldiers ran toward the bombed mosque where the mourners were confronted with a similar creature, which was proficiently doing the job for which it was sent forth. The creature attacked the mourners inside the ruined mosque, where it was fairly difficult for most of them to escape. Sergeant Lapoint and his troops reached the destroyed mosque to find the creature slaying the last of its victims. The irritated Canadian, who sought revenge for their slain allies, opened fire at the carnivorous creature, which quickly rescinded its attention from its victims and began charging the soldiers.

"Rrraaaaaarrrrr!" sounded a second creature, whose groans alerted Rousseau, who was positioned to the far end of the squadron.

Rousseau looked off into the distance from where he heard the sound originate and was frightened to see another creature barreling down on them. By the time the flank holder discharged his weapon, the creature had already gotten into striking distance and it slashed its claws against the soldier's protective vest. Rousseau frightfully looked down at his stomach as his entire intestines fell out beneath his vest. The Light Infantry soldier fell to both knees and looked up at the creature, which bit half his body in half. After eliminating Rousseau, the creature slashed Marquette across the face killing him instantly. With the realization of their situation, Sergeant Lapoint grabbed Private Duhon and moved to the first opened door, where they dove into the house and quickly closed the door in hopes that the creatures wouldn't follow. Both Light Infantry soldiers, who felt fortunate to still be alive, remained inside the hut, while the abominations of Satan's dungeon roamed the outdoors.

Chapter 15

The Illuminati Church was a secret society forged by Lucifer the Devil to recruit human soldiers to strengthen his demonic army. Since its existence, the Illuminati Church has fought the laws of righteous doctrines. Hence, to maintain a voice in the decisions of true Christians, imposter priests were planted into the highest spiritual advisement positions in every Christian organization around the globe. The Illuminati order has been around since the beginning of time, with its first member being Cain, the son of Adam and Eve. Lucifer had always visited and spoken with Cain, promising him an important high position in his perceived personal New World. The Devil corrupted his first pupil's mind with promises of riches and power, which became his recruiting slogan. Once Cain committed the first murder of his brother Abel and disrespected Yahweh, he had by then fallen completely out of the favors of God. However, he had already entered into a personal relationship with his new master, Satan the Devil, and thus became the first legal member of the Illuminati.

With the recruitment of Cain, the secret society of the Illuminati was born, with millions becoming members in hopes of acquiring the promised fortune and fame. Thus, many of our ancestors who acquired great feats on this earth, were proud members of the Illuminati Society. Such greatness, however, comes with an extravagant price, as members who are entered into such accords pay the penalties with their very souls.

There are several variations of the Illuminati faculty around the world, where different cultures practice and attribute their worship in various ways. From Africa the motherland, across Europe, Asia, all throughout the Caribbean, The Americas and beyond, worshippers of the Illuminati have been referred by many terminologies, such as Wizards, Black Magic, Obeah, Voodoo, etc. Similar to the Almighty God, Lucifer required continuous expressions of devotion through prayers, which his followers are urged to devote onto him daily.

It has been a well-known fact that it is impossible to accomplish any feat of kindness through the name of Lucifer. Hence, Sorcerers, Practitioners of Black Magic and Spell Casters, have all engaged their devious behaviors through the Lord of darkness, Satan the Devil. People who despised others have contracted these representatives of the Dark Side to inflict some sort of treacherous malice against those whom they hate. The Devil, who ruled the earth until the return of his creator, empowered his human subjects to accomplish miraculous feats, which amazed and fascinated feeble-minded individuals. Every government around the world was subject of Lucifer the king, whose earthly intentions provoked God's Defenders. The sole factors in this world over-which the Devil had absolutely no control were in regards to true Christians of God, who've dedicated their lives to the service of the most high.

BBC News Headquarters

The BBC World News in London England televised an interview with the senior scientist of the United Nations, Dr. David Mais, whose resume included the uncovering of the world's first catastrophic episode, to the theories of Global Warming. Dr. Mais, who resided in Frankfurt Germany, was connected via satellite from his home, which was a territory also under siege by the creatures of Satan's dungeon. With the entire world in turmoil, the scientist's projected theory not only clarified the upcoming cataclysm, but also petrified skeptical viewers.

Following their preliminary introductions, Natalie Withers, the interviewer, dived right into the matters at hand, as she asked the question to-which the entire world sought an answer. "In your professional opinion, from the lessons learnt from to the dinosaurs' episode some one hundred and fifty years ago, what would you say the earth is in store for?"

Dr. Mais who played an important roll in the theoretical creation of an educational video entitled, 'The last days of the Dinosaurs', used inserts from said video to illustrate what happened to the earth millions of years ago, when it was directly struck by an asteroid the size of Mt. Everest. Through the documentary, Dr. Mais plotted the path and speed of this monstrous asteroid, which barreled down to the earth at unimaginable speeds, before crashing in the shallow waters of the Golf of Mexico. The purpose behind Dr. Mais' exhibition was to illustrate the magnitude of destruction caused by said asteroid, which completely wiped out the dinosaurs, and emphasize what a structure millions of times larger would accomplish.

"First of all, millions of years ago, the earth was struck by an asteroid, which was a lot smaller than this planet on a collision course at the moment. This asteroid smacked into the Golf of Mexico and sent sonaristic vibrations, which surged throughout the entire earth. Now, at the point of impact, this asteroid pierced into the earth and shot massive debris thousands of meters into the atmosphere, while spreading its deadly venom in every possible direction. Here you can see this huge ball of rocks and inferno covering the United States in mere seconds after the collision. Thousands of miles away as far as the Middle East, dinosaurs, which resided on this continent immediately felt the tremors, which vibrated directly through the earth's core, creating earthquakes and tremors everywhere.

"British Columbia, which like the rest of the world was saturated with dinosaurs such as the Tyrannosaurus Rex, Triceratops, even Brachiosaurus, felt the fury from the collision within a minute of the crash. Similar to the meteor showers that struck moments before the asteroid; these tremendous rock particles, which exploded into the air, were the dinosaurs' second warning of the coming event, as they were forced to scatter in search of safety. You could say this inferno of fire and rocks came over like a Tsunami, as the entire area got engulfed with toxic gas indulging flames, which baked everything from animals to vegetation. The Pterosaur Dinosaurs who lived at very high elevations, were amongst the first to witness this massive ejector cloud quickly sweeping over the plains, but as they took to the skies to escape, it became impossible to out run the elements that sent them crashing

Yahweh

to the ground. The heat that spread across the surface of the globe killed everything caught out in the open, as only certain mammals which reside underground and dinosaurs lucky enough to hide in cave, survived the first wave of destruction." Dr. Mais exclaimed.

"How far into the earth would you say this asteroid went, and exactly how hot did the temperature rise on the earth's surface?" Natalie enquired.

"This asteroid dug thousands of meters into the earth, to where it interrupted the earth's core and even cracked the ocean's floor. Now, from this development came the after effect, where after the scorching temperatures that rose to at least a thousand degrees Celsius baked everything, things soothed for a few moments as the second wave built. During this time, survivors, that realize their fortune, begin exiting whatever burrows saved them, because remember now, they've been most likely cooped up with some carnivorous enemies of theirs. After the massive ejector cloud passed over with its engulfing flames, the first instincts of these animals were to visit their favorite water hole, in order to rehydrate themselves." Dr. Mais elaborated.

"Now Dr. Mais, please emphasize what you mean by this second wave or after effect?" asked the reporter.

"Well following that torturous oven, dinosaurs along the coast in search of food and water found themselves in a totally opposite yet distinct predicament, as flood water over a hundred feet high consumed everything. You see, these dinosaurs were forced to instinctively find the most notable essentials after this monumental era of their times, and, in doing so, the vegetarians noticed that there was indeed a total food shortage and the carnivorous animals noted how scarce food was. Imagine surviving that inferno and thinking that was the worst, only to find yourself either on the offensive from predators or drowning in paralyzing waters."

"Wow, that's an awful lot to consume!" Natalie declared.

"And that wasn't even the worst of it. Now as I've mentioned about this gigantic mass of rock that struck the outer realm of the earth core, this eventually creates cracks through which dangerous gases escape up into water reserves. Let's say some dinosaurs were indeed lucky to escape all those dangerous elements prior, they make it to their favorite watering hole and lean over for a drink. But before they could drink a sip, they keel over dead from these toxic fumes which eventually turn certain bodies of water into toxic lakes." Dr. Mais commented.

Natalie Withers covered her mouth with her hands and muffled, "Oh my God we're all doomed", which was a professional misjudgment.

Doctor David Mais clearly overheard the reporter's comments and believed it a question, as he proceeded to answer in his professional opinion. "With a planet this huge, there is absolutely no way any of us will be able to survive a collision of such magnitude. The earth herself will shatter like a pane of glass against this unstoppable force and yes, we're all doomed!"

The doctor's comments reverberated through televisions across the globe like an electric shock. Almost immediately telephones inside the television station began ringing with indecisive viewers who also e-mailed and texted their opinions at the comments delivered by the scientist. While many believed Dr. Mais' comments inconsiderate and ignorant, others expressed their gratitude at receiving such honesty, as many believed their governments refrained from publishing definite findings.

In an attempt to neutralize the effects of the chief scientist's to the United Nations comments, President Flores instructed his press secretary to orchestrate a public broadcast from the Oval Office in order to advise the nation about their aggressive plan to counter the threat. With the scientist concluding that the earth was doomed, the possibility of hundreds of lesser-minded individuals committing suicide became real, hence the president insisted they broadcast as soon as possible. The president had received confirmation that all the nuclear missiles sent abroad had safely arrived to their destinations and were assembled and poised for release. Despite the success of military cargos arriving at their destinations, domestic and international airplanes were still crashing like cars during an ice storm, which continually disturbed government officials. The White House had been placed under the protection of the army, with soldiers surrounding the compound in their armored tanks to help keep Satan's abominations at bay.

Once the president was advised that everything was prepared for his Informative Address to the nation, his advisor walked with him to the Oval Office. During their court walk, the Air Force Major General Kevin Franks, who believed the president was about to make a drastic mistake, voiced his concerns for what he believed to be a disclosure of National Security.

"Mr. President Sir, I believe disclosing our intentions will place this mission in jeopardy!" Major General Franks insighted.

"Please elaborate General Franks, I don't possibly see any harm at this point." President Flores argued.

"Sir, there are still all sorts of extremists and radicals out there who I know live to undermine anything government. This is the most sensitive time in our generation and one glitch could interfere with the success of these launches." Major General Franks exclaimed.

"See General Franks, there is where we differ, because I've always believed in responsibility and accountability; and at this moment in our history, to have some scientist kill millions with heart attacks and strokes through fear, is not going to happen on my watch. If I were home with my kids right now I'd be fighting my wife for the bathroom, because after hearing someone tell me no matter what I'm dead, that would immediately give me the runs. Not on my watch general, not on my watch!" advised the president as they walked into the Oval Office.

The president was guided behind his desk, where a technician pinned a microphone underneath his jacket, while a make up artiste ensured he looked his absolute best. President Flores motioned over his secretary, who brought her boss his hand written speech and laid it out before him. With everything in place, the president turned his attention to the director, who motioned his countdown from five to one.

"Good evening ladies and gentlemen, tonight along with the rest of the world, we've set out on a monumental military exercise aimed at protecting our beloved earth. This is a daring attempt at destroying or redirecting this desolate planet, which is still on a direct course with the earth. The United States have sent specially designed nuclear missiles to our allies around the world, along with technician specialists to ensure these missiles get launched at the proper time. Now, I know this is trying times for us. Nobody has any definite answers or solutions, but we, your government, are still hard at work fighting for our survival. I ask that you be vigilant and remain in doors, I pray for all our survival and that of the earth. May God bless you and keep you, may the Lord strengthen you in this our feeblest moment. We will survive, God bless America.

Chapter 16

The three archeologists travelled to Kewdale in Perth, which was where Dr. Garnet Wallace lived and taught at the University of Western Austrailia. The drive south along Interstate 95 was tiring, as the scientists had been toiling under the burning sun, drinking, celebrating and exerting massive energy since the beginning of the work day. The archeologists' fascination throughout the majority of the journey was purely on the symbols across the night's sky which they believed Dr. Wallace was capable of deciphering. The senior archeologist, after being recited the meaning to the symbols, disclosed his knowledge of each symbol to his understudies, who absorbed any information translated by the notable pioneer to Australian archeology. Once they'd gotten in range to access their cell phones, Dr Duncan attempted to inform the local emergency services about their recent episode, only to receive a message stating that the dispatcher had been swamp with excessive amounts of phone calls. With everyone who witnessed the bright symbols across the night's sky calling to report their disbelief, it became impossible to relay the information, as Terry disconnected the call to emergency services.

  A hundred and fifty miles from the city of Perth Australia, Dr. Steven Richards, who was around the steering wheel of their donated Dodge Sprinter CDR multi-van, began dozing off and swerved the vehicle across the vacant highway before refocusing and wiping his eyes as a method to counter fatigue. Dr. Richards looked around at his passengers who were both comfortably asleep, and turned on the radio in search of companionship before adjusted the volume to not obstruct his passengers. Steven pushed the seek button as the radio opened to some sort of Australian traditional channel, which he had no interest in hearing. The numbers on the radio's display flipped once before the hypnotic tone of a male preacher froze him to a station he'd never before heard.

"---have been given our orders, to rise arms against any alien species to set foot on this our planet earth. We have taken over the skies, the land and the oceans around the globe, nothing except our soldiers shall fly amongst the clouds! Within hours, noting except our allies will be allowed to walk upon these lands. There will be no escape from my Lord Lucifer, for he alone is the true king of this earth and his reign will dominate forever. This is to be your only opportunity to join the house of my father King Lucifer. The price of membership, never again to be offered, begins with your falling to your knees and vowing to forever serve King Lucifer. Then, rise again as a reborn soldier, and call the number 1 800 666 and your inauguration will be sealed. ---."

"Ahhhhh! Where are we?" Terry asked.

"Oh ahhhh, couple a miles from Perth!" nervously responded Steven, as he quickly reached and shut off the radio.

"Was that some sort of national emergency advisory you were listening to?" Terry asked.

"Just some Christian quack jawing off about nothing!" Dr. Richards exclaimed.

The daily activities around the Perth region were none existent when the archeologists rolled into town on route to Dr. Wallace's house. The entire city was like a ghost town at a time during the morning when thousands normally commuted to work and other places, which told the story of how seriously folks considered the threat. Steven, who knew exactly where Dr. Wallace resided, turned on Alexander Street, six blocks from the Kewdale community, where he was then supposed turn left onto St. Kilda Road. With the brightness from the sun glistening through the vehicle, Dr. Wallace took the bow and arrow given to Terry and began closely inspected them with his magnifying glass.

Rhoan Flowers

"Ahhhhh, magnificent works of art!" commented Dr. Wallace, who was completely fascinated with the ancient weapons.

Terry, who rode shot gun across from Dr. Richards, turned around and focused her attention at the senior scientist sitting in the rear. "What's gotten you so fascinated doctor?"

"This Bow, why do think it was that that creature handed you th----." began Dr. Wallace.

Boom! sounded the Dodge van, as it smacked into something and spun twice before finally coming to a stop.

Terry spun around and looked through the windshield, before gazing over at the driver, who was shaking the cobwebs from his head. "Are you O.K Steven? What did we hit?"

Dr. Richards who was still unsure of what transpired, looked through the windshield in total disbelief, as he pushed in on the airbag that extracted because of the accident. "Wow! What the hell ran by us?"

With nothing visible ahead of the van, Terry checked in on the Dr. Wallace who was slumped across the rear seat. "Dr. Wallace are you O? Oh my God, Steven start the van, we have to get out of here right now!" Terry yelled with passionate fright.

"What are you screaming ab---? Oh my God, start-start!" Dr. Richards declared, after looking through his driver's side mirror at the humongous beast he had managed to knock off its feet, which was slowly rising onto its four paws.

"You have to start driving with a little more precaution my lad." instructed Dr. Wallace who slowly sat upright on the rear seat.

"It's coming start the van!" Terry yelled, as the senior archeologist looked curiously at them before realizing there must be some impending danger. Following their recent episode that introduced Dr. Wallace to creatures, believed by many in his professional field to be pure mythology, the senior scientist was not again about to surprised, as he spun around to check what terrified his associates.

Doctor Wallace glanced around at the creature, which was walking towards the van. "Oh my dear God, I see our dilemma." commented the senior scientist, as he allowed his body to rescind back onto the seat with fears of the creature feasting on him.

The Dodge van refused to start, as its occupants ensured that every window and door was sealed. The abomination from Hell crept up to the left side of the Dodge Sprinter and lowered its body to the height of the vehicle before staring intently inside at the scared occupants.

"Raaarrrrrrr!" roared the beast, as everyone inside the van screamed in response.

Doctor Richards' girlish scream sounded more feminine than Terry's, as he yelled as if the creature had actually harmed him. While the senior archeologist and his female assistant focused on the crouched creature, which behaved as if it planned on opening the vehicle top like a can of Sardines, Dr. Richards observed a second creature that approached from the east. The mere size and appearance of the creatures gave everyone a sense of what it would have felt like living amongst the dinosaurs some sixty million years ago.

"Guys-guys, I'm afraid our problems just doubled!" Dr. Richards exclaimed.

Terry turned her head slowly to her companion's concerns, which inexplicably increased her heart rate. Both creatures sandwiched the Dodge van as the teeth edging sounds of claws tearing into metal sounded on the top and sides of the vehicle. The long claws of the Devil's abominations punctured through the roof of the van and it became clear that the creatures were about to gain entry. Terry reached for the weapons handed to her and bravely rolled her window down half way before loading an arrow into the bow and launching it directly into the chest area of one of the creatures. The impact of the arrow did far more damage than predicted, as the creature reacted as if a cargo jet struck it.

The trapped scientists inside the Dodge van watched in amazement as the injured creature stopped and staggered away. The creature's paws began noticeably shaking, as the humongous beast suddenly crashed onto three vehicles parked along the roadway. Nobody in the van would have ever phantomed the creature collapsing from one arrow, yet the beast lay dead and motionless. At the sight of its companion collapsing to the ground, the second creature abandoned the vehicle as it began checking the area for what inflicted the blow to its carnivorous sibling.

"Did you just see that, I smoked that thing with one arrow?" Terry celebrated, as she reached for another arrow to reload her bow.

"I don't believe that one little tiny arrow is going to take down a beast like that." Steven argued, as Terry opened the door in order to go after the second creature. "Wait-wait —wait, there must be another angel around here. I say let's wait a minute and make sure before someone seriously gets hurt here!"

"News flash Steven, a few people have already been hurt! Besides, I don't think we are going to get a better chance, so shut up because I'm going!" Terry exclaimed.

The creature walked about sniffing the air around the vehicle, as if attempting to locate a body scent. Doctor Richards could not bare the thought of future stories being told insinuating he was somewhat of a coward for hiding inside a vehicle, while the lone female of his entourage slew two gigantic beasts. In his attempt to prove himself a hero, Steven, who'd momentarily taken his eyes off the creature, believed the beast to be in front of the van and popped from his driver's cabin. Steven's plan was to support Terry in any means necessary, although none of that included physical labor.

Doctor Duncan watched as the beast turned its back to their van and awaited the right moment to exit the vehicle. Doctor Wallace, who kept himself hidden thus far, slightly raised his head and peeked through the window. Steven, who had misjudged the creature's positioning, sought to render-vous with Terry on the other side of the van, and thus precariously walked towards the immanent danger. The primitive creature, which had been sniffing the surroundings to find the slayer of its fallen comrade, caught Steven's body scent and turned its head in the direction from where came the odor. Steven's indecisiveness cost him his life, as he paid little attention to his surroundings while moving towards their female companion.

The abomination from Hell, with its lightening fast reflexes, charged at Steven as he ran around the rear of the van and caught him before he cleared the width of the vehicle. Terry, who had been crawling along the passenger side of the vehicle, reached the tail end of the van and snuck a peek to determine a proper opening to launch an arrow without compromising her position. Doctor Wallace who maintained a close visual on his comrades and Terry, who sought to maim or kill her second predator, were both frightened as they watched the creature devour, with one bite, their friend and associate with whom they'd lived and worked with for months.

Understanding that the creature could track them by their scent, Terry aborted her ambush plot and returned to the sanctity of the van as the creature, after the demolishing of Steven, snuck its head around the very side from which the female archeologist departed. Terry returned to their Dodge van and was surprised to find Dr. Wallace in the driver's seat. After witnessing Dr. Richards' demise, Dr. Wallace, who was uncertain whether any of his apprentices would survive, prepared to fend for himself.

"Oh my God that thing just ate Steven!" Terry mourned, as she disgustingly tossed the bow and arrows to the floor.

"I do know how close you two were and I want you to know that I do know a little something about Christianity. If these are indeed the days spoken of in the bible and past ancient scrolls, then fear not because you will see him again very soon!" Dr. Wallace exclaimed.

Terry sobbed for a few minutes before wiping the tears from her eyes. "Let's get out of here!" she then instructed Dr. Wallace.

The sweetest sound the occupants inside the Dodger Sprinter heard was that of the ignition igniting, as Doctor Wallace then rammed the gear shifter into drive and stepped on the gas. The vehicle sped off with the tires screeching while the creature simply watched the archeologists drive away.

"Have we gotten rid of that thing?" questioned Dr. Wallace after they'd driven two blocks, as he was too nervous to check the rear.

"It appears to be staying still, but I think the most important question here is what the hell is that thing?" Terry remarked.

The Dodge van came to a screeching halt at 328 St. Kilda Street with both occupants keenly focusing their attentions three hundred and sixty degrees around the vehicle, before giving any consideration to dismounting. Terry collected her belongings and armed the bow with thoughts of a relaxing bubble bath to soak her deserving body. With the Dodge's occupants looking nervously around, the passenger's door flew open and frightened Terry, who jumped onto the armrest console between both front seats. Dr. Wallace grabbed the lock handle as he prepared to evacuate if necessary, while Terry sought to follow him at the first sight of danger.

Terry's protective angel, who had to bend to one knee to open the door, materialized by the entrance with instructions for everyone to quickly vacate the vehicle. The angel behaved as if they were about to bombarded with artillery fire, and he quickly rushed everyone indoors. The chief archeologist and his assistant were inches from the front door when a fireball smacked into their abandoned vehicle, causing it to violently explode. The force from the blast knocked the surviving archeologists to the ground, as the angel yelled for them to get indoors. Dr. Duncan, after a lifetime of surviving the horrors sent by the Devil, knew to never argue an angel's orders as she grabbed her mentor's arm and helped him to his feet, before rushing into his house.

Chapter 17

Lucifer's Grand Hall, which was typically empty with the exceptions of his personal honor guards, was filled with Dark Warriors, which were created by the Devil and brought to life by the invention of Dr. Heinz Flakiskor. The Dark Warriors were made in the image of Satan's demons, though they lacked the physical ability, reasoning process, the ability to disappear and they were unable to create fireball which was a trait only bestowed unto angels. The Dark Warriors of Satan were kept in secrecy for decades as Lucifer's ultimate plot was to unveil them against his creator's angels, once the battle for earth's supremacy had begun.

Prior to the remarkable invention by the man who brought Satan's Dark Warriors to life, the Devil had failed to create his perfect assassin soldiers. The creatures, which had been terrorizing the earth, were the results of Satan's foiled experiments at creating his warlords, which he needed since his personal armies of demons were too small to face Jehovah's Universal Army. With Dr. Flakiskor's assistance, Lucifer was able to unify the spirits of his past worshippers with the anatomies of his designed Dark Warriors.

The demon angel Ebak had returned to report his failure at terminating the Romano family, which he and the demon angel Jezkai had been assigned to do. Ebak was the sole survivor of the team sent on the mission, as his fellow demon and primitive creatures were all annihilated by God's defensive force.

Despite his knowledge of the punishment for failure, Ebak believed himself a worthy soldier of whom the devil couldn't dispense. After presenting himself before his king, Ebak fell to his knees before Lucifer's throne and awaited recognition before addressing the earthly king.

"Ebak my loyal assassin, I trust you have accomplished the mission to which I've assigned you?" questioned the devil.

"My Lord, I'm afraid we've had complications! I'm sorry but we have failed." Ebak reported.

"And what of those who accompanied you?" Satan enquired.

"They have all perished my Lord!" remorsefully answered Ebak.

Lucifer pointed across his Grand Hall at a group of demons, who all stood proudly with their arms folded. "Zaka, Uval, Mizka are amongst the successful assassins whom I've sent forth to accomplish my bidding. There is no room for failure in the house of the Universal God. Bind him and toss his worthless body into the eternal furnace of damnation!" grievingly commanded Lucifer.

Ebak pretended as if he were willing to succumb to the orders before unexpectedly pulling his sword and swiping off the hand of the closest guard. The versatile assassin used his off hand to draw his dagger, which he lunged directly up through the armpit of the second guard.

"Seize him at once!" ordered General Cain, who stood by his Lord's right hand as the second in command.

Lucifer, whose most enjoyable means of entertainment was to watch brutal battles between competitors, relaxed on his throne with a slight smirk as the two injured guards waved off others and tended to their wounds before arming themselves in preparation for battle. The honor guard who had his hand chopped off, ripped a leather belt from the chest protector and tied it around the wound. The second guard, who received the blade through the armpit, grabbed the handle and retracted the dagger before tossing the twenty inch blade across the hall's floor.

"Do you wish this to continue Sir?" General Cain asked.

The Devil, whose thirst for conflict and brutality was never quenched, waved his hand signaling his consent as both honor guards charged the assassin. Lucifer considered his personal guards amongst the elite and expected them to show their tenacity at protecting their king and his orders.

Yahweh

With an execution order granted, the Devil expected fireworks from the helm, as the conflict commenced.

"Watch and learn my Dark Warriors, because your time is at hand!" announced the Devil.

The Devil was extremely intrigued in the match up between members of his honor guards and those of his assassins who never trained or sparred against each other. The questions of which division was the greater of the two had long been considered without resolve, hence Satan expected an insight into who might be more proficient on the battlefield? The assassin, after acknowledging his disadvantage, charged both injured guards, who found themselves on the defensive from a single sword wielding maniac. After being forced backwards on the defensive for a few feet, the guards reduced the pressure by blocking the assassin's strike before diving apart from each other to create a wider fighting platform. With both Honor Guards approximately ten feet apart from each other, the assassin soon found himself swinging wildly to keep both attacking guards at length. The retreating assassin, despite his predicament, made an unexpected advancement towards the guard who's had his hand chopped off, as the second guard lunged at him from his position. The sheer artistry and skill with which his soldiers fought excited the Devil, who fully expected God's soldiers to be overwhelmed by his trained armies, should they be lucky enough to feel earth's dirt beneath their feet.

The overwhelmed guard, timed his opponent's strikes and slapped his arm aside, before returning the favor of severing the assassin's hand. The frightened assassin, who stood frozen at the sight of his hand holding his sword, never saw the blade that removed his head as it went rolling along the Hall's floor, before his lifeless body fell to the ground. At the end of the combat, Satan rose to his feet and exited the Grand Hall with his proud generals at his heels.

The dim lightings along the grungy corridors of Hell made it impossible for mortal humans to clearly see fifteen feet ahead, while Satan's Demons, who had become accustomed to the darkness, found the setting quite satisfying. Lucifer led his generals to his strategy chamber where his intent was to assign them their individual task for the upcoming conflict. There was a female demon assembling the strategy chamber, who the Devil instructed to immediately summon Dr. Flakiskor. The strategy chamber was equipped with a single chair, which was placed at the head of a huge conference table on which a map of the entire globe was drawn. There were a number of torches burning around the room, as Lucifer walked to his assigned seat and sat down, while his generals circled the conference table.

"My generals, the planet of Heaven shall arrive in the earth's orbit within a few hours. Arrangements have been made for the humans to lead the first assault, but I'm still not confident that they will succeed at their endeavors. Should the galaxy's enforcers arrive here, we will be prepared to defend what's ours, no matter the cost." instructed the Devil.

"How are we to utilize the humans versus the creator's divine power?" Arch Demon Luzak asked.

"The humans have orchestrated a plan to which King Lucifer has consented. They believe that they might be able to destroy the approaching planet with their long range missiles and at this point any victory will be acceptable!" General Cain explained.

"We will not be caught off guard should these humans fail. Our Dark Warriors have drastically increased our troop levels and they shall serve as our first line of defense. I have kept these warriors a secret for a monumental surprise; they shall hinder our enemies while you crush them! This planet belongs to me, and so shall it remain indefinitely." Lucifer warned.

"There is no way they will be able to withstand the fury and power of our troops. We shall crush them my Lord!" announced Arch Demon Haku.

"Victory will be ours my Lord, we will crush them all!" reasserted Arch Demon Zada.

The Devil looked around at his generals, whom he'd personally chosen to lead his six armies across the six inhabited continents of the world, across which total dominance of the earth would be decided. Each general would command a force of five million plus warriors, which would be complimented with a pack of carnivorous beasts well eager to dominate the battle fields. After centuries of preparation, the definitive moment had arrived to determine earth's final judgment and the Devil was confident of victory. With the thoughts of not only ruling the earth, but the entire galaxy at hand, Satan's optimism glowed from his face as everyone became confident in their perceived victory.

To serenade his generals, the Devil walked over to a mantle bearing liquor and filled seven chalices with Black Wine from his personal vineyard. Each of the six generals walked over to their king and collected their chalice before reconvening around the table, where the Devil proposed a toast before assigning each general his battle ground.

"The next time we raise these cups, you will all be kings over your individual planets. Under my sovereign rule, we will govern over this entire galaxy indefinitely, without any disputes or malice!" Lucifer proposed.

"Hail King Lucifer, the new emperor of the galaxy!" Arch Demon Haku declared.

"Hail King Lucifer, the new emperor of the galaxy!" Arch Demon Luzak declared.

"Hail King Lucifer, the new emperor of the galaxy!" Arch Demon Zada declared.

"Hail King Lucifer, the new emperor of the galaxy!" Arch Demon Bahak declared.

"Hail King Lucifer, the new emperor of the galaxy!" Arch Demon Yezin declared.

"Hail King Lucifer, the new emperor of the galaxy!" Supreme General Cain conveyed.

Each warrior chugged his wine like a binge drinker, before slamming the chalice on the edge of the table. The Earthly King Lucifer then picked up a long ruler from atop the table and began indicating the places on the map each of his generals would be responsible for protecting. Each continent provided its own hazards and challenges and the Devil devoted serious thoughts regarding which general was suited to which continent.

To the frigid continent of North America, the Devil appointed Arch Demon Zada, who was already his personal liaison to the most advanced military continent in the entire world. Arch Demon Zada, who was Hell's Counselor to America, knew every rigid terrain of the land, which stretched from the North Pole to the borders of Mexico. As the Devil's personal ambassador to the United States of America, Arch Demon Zada instructed member of Lucifer's Illuminati Society, who were key members of the government that ruled the nation. The puppeteers of the Devil that were scattered across Alaska, Canada and the United States, were to be summoned to the field of battle in order that every member of Satan's kingdom be included in the battle for the earth. Despite Lucifer's confidence in his soldiers gaining the victory, the Devil ensured he advised each of his generals about his contingency plan, which was for any survivor to flee to the seventh uninhabited continent of Antarctica.

To the oldest civilization of Asia, the Devil appointed Arch Demon Luzak as the leader of his western army. The Devil felt it essential to have knowledgeable representatives of the terrain counter against their enemies on every continent. Arch Demon Luzak had represented his king's interests on one of the world's most war torn continents since Asia's earliest settlers. Even though Lucifer had multiple senior demons across the region, it was Luzak who was favored due to his achievements in communist China. With China emerging as the strongest superpower in the region, Lucifer honored his ambassador with his invitation, which Arch Demon Luzak proudly accepted.

The brutal battle, which was poised to rage over the continent of Africa, was considered by the Devil to be the most significant battle ground. The motherland of the African continent was the birthplace of mankind, and thus a focal point of power to who so ever had it under their control. Africa was scheduled to be the first battleground, as it remained one of the sole terrains where the creator's powers still emanated. With such humongous stakes involved, the Devil was at a dilemma on who to appoint such an important task. After much deliberation, Lucifer handed the reigns to Arch Demon Bahak, whose influence regarding the genocide in Rwanda gained him notoriety to his king. Lucifer, who had demonstrated the penalty for failure, surprised Arch Demon Bahak by suggesting he rendezvous with him in Antarctica should he fail at his appointed duties. The pressures of being the Devil's first representative in the defense of earth was modestly accepted by Arch Demon Bahak, who vowed death before succumbing to the forces of their enemies.

Lucifer appointed his Supreme General Cain to the continent of Europe, which was also the continent to which he assigned the greatest number of demons. The Devil had promised Cain a position of great importance in his army of Dark Warriors once they had defeated Jehovah and his armies from heaven. Cain, who had become the Devil's first human worshipper, was the only ranked ex-human servant dwelling in the house of Lucifer. Those who've toiled over Lucifer's achievements for centuries criticized the Devil's choice as Cain over his other more notable European delegates prior to the actual appointment. However, once the prize had been awarded, every demon under Cain's command had to obey his orders without question. Supreme General Cain was not awarded the luxury as his Arch Demon brethrens, who were told to rendezvous with their master should their armies be defeated. Thus, the general understood that failure would not be tolerated.

To the continent of South America Lucifer assigned Arch Demon Haku, who was said to be the most vicious of all the Devil's Arch Demons. Haku was renowned as Satan's right hand during their foiled attempt at mutiny in Heaven, which cast them from the realm of God. The arch demon became famous during the mutiny battle, where Haku personally recruited the majority of angels, who, in turn, raised arms against their father and creator. Due to the mutual admiration between Lucifer and Haku, the other arch demons across the South American continent never engaged in a competition for power, as they were confident the helm would be passed onto Satan's closest confidant. Arch Demon Haku, who was perturbed by their banishment from Heaven, chose to represent the country of Peru in Lucifer's administration, in order to spend more time in solitude, which he found deep in the jungle of Machu Picchu. The Arch Demon was a monster who controlled, through Satan, a cannibalistic tribe of people called the Canabawi, which dwelled deep in the Peruvian jungle of Machu Picchu. For centuries the tribe of Canabawi had committed despicable acts to humanity in the service of Lucifer, who relished in the glory and tribute awarded him with such brutality against others. While other tribes hunted wild games, the hunters of Canabawi stalked other humans, which were considered a delicacy for the natives who sacrificed vital portions of the offering to the Devil.

The final inhabited continent of Australia was awarded to Arch Demon Yezin, who represented Sydney as Satan's ambassador. The leadership of the continent of Australia required a combat to settle the question of command after preliminary results highlighted a tie between Yezin of Sydney and Arch Demon Kerr of Melbourne. Both demons had to participate in a grappling match where the first to holler in surrender lost the duel. Yezin defeated Kerr after a long and grueling match where he caught his opponent in a bare-naked chokehold and knocked him unconscious, as Kerr refused to surrender despite the applied pressure. Like Arch Demon Bahak before him, Yezin also swore death before dishonor, which were comforting words to Lucifer. Should the other continents get remanded under the control of Jehovah, the Devil sought to mount his final defense on the uninhabited continent of Antarctica, which sat to the far south of the globe. Lucifer reinvigorated the prize of victory as he emphasized what was at stake for them should they defeat the greatest army in the universe.

As the commanders for the Devil's legions of soldiers exited the Strategy Chamber, his assistant returned with an old and fragile Dr. Flakiskor, who walked gingerly with the assistance of a cane. The Devil's assistant opened the huge brass doors to allow the doctor entry, before leaving the two associates to discuss their private business. Lucifer instructed his prized scientist to accompany him as he moved to his personal chamber, which was in the adjoining room. Once inside Lucifer's personal suite, Dr. Flakiskor, who'd spent countless hours with the earthly king, walked over to a table and sat in his personalized chair. King Lucifer walked over to the table and sat across from the doctor who wasted no time as he advanced a pawn on a chessboard, which featured an ongoing game.

"The time of the final battle is upon us my friend. This is where we truly evaluate our creations, at the most pivotal time of lives. All the final preparations are being looked after, I only wish you were still agile to come witness our greatest victory." Lucifer said as he advanced his horse.

"The time for your eternal reign has come my Lord and you will triumph!" Dr. Flakiskor declared as he attempted to decipher his opponent's intentions.

"Fear not my old friend, as I've promised, you shall be amongst those rewarded for this great victory. Even if death manages to claim you, you will be revived and honored for your great deeds." Satan assured.

"I truly thank thee my Lord." Dr. Flakiskor commented.

"I have a few final tasks for you to accomplish yet my friend?" Satan suggested.

"I am here only to serve you my lord." Dr. Flakiskor responded.

Yahweh

"I wish for you to create one final batch of soldiers for me. Inside this vile are the spirits I wish to have implanted into the specimens, which you will find inside your lab. After you've completed the transformations, I want no evidence that those machines ever existed." instructed the Devil.

"You appear apprehensive my Lord, is there anything further?" Dr. Flakiskor asked.

"Here is a remote control, which is the trigger to detonate a barrage of nuclear bombs buried all throughout the planet. Keep this with you at all times, as this is my final command to you; that should my adversaries defeat my armies, you will detonate those bombs which will completely destroy this planet. Am I understood doctor!" Satan ordered.

"Clearly my Lord, your wish is my command!" Dr. Flakiskor acknowledged.

Both associates finished their final chess match, with the Devil winning easily over his favorite opponent. Doctor Flakiskor who'd become totally fascinated and hypnotized by the devil, had completely bought into Satan's dreams of universal conquest and saluted his Fuhrer, before exiting his personal chamber.

Chapter 18

The entire earth was like a ghost planet, with every institution from the private sector to government agencies closed until further notice. Prison Guards around the globe had chosen to lockdown their prison inmates and abandon them, in exchange for spending their final hours with families and friends. As those prisoners in half way houses and minimum security prisons broke out and escaped, the same could not be said for prisons that housed violent criminals. Those who accepted their fate fell to their knees and begged forgiveness, in hopes that God won't abandon them. In facilities where inmates had the privilege to watch television from their cells, every screen was tuned in to the news forecast, as prisoners remained concerned about their futures and those of their families. The wrongdoers of our society, with premonitions of change, suffered pre-catastrophic shock, as they remained confined in twelve by five cubicles with absolutely no contact with their loved ones and outer world.

Major cities as well as the smallest towns were like the barren desert. The emergency wards at hospitals were closed, as only a few doctors and nurses caringly remained to aid their terminally sick patients. Pregnant mothers, whose moments of childbirth had arrived, had to deliver their babies at home as there were no other alternatives. Police officers and fire fighters were few and those who were still on duty were predominantly single individuals who hadn't a family of their own to be with. Die-hearted drug addicts to alcoholics, who had vowed never to resign from their addiction because they're not quitters, drowned their worries and sorrows in the drugs of their choice.

The White House

The first lady of the United States of America held a prayer vigil where she invited a few personal friends, the servants who catered to their daily needs, the entire staff of guards who were unable to be amongst family and the National Defense Staff, which had been at the heels of her husband since the appearance of the symbols. President Flores, who had been extremely busy in deliberations with various governments and agencies, had been too preoccupied to entertain his son, who ached to divulge the specifics on how they narrowly escaped death from an unbelievable source. Roland had brought along his mourning friend who, despite his personal despair, was fascinated with the experience of being around some of the world's most influential people. Once the young men arrived at the White House, Roland immediately related the entire story to his mother, who was eternally thankful they survived such an assault. With the prayer vigil scheduled that evening, the First Lady instructed Roland to show his guest to a suite and find him suitable attire for the evening.

With all her guests present, Mrs. Flores commenced the prayer vigil at 8:00pm inside the prayer hall attached to the White House. Without a designated pastor present, Janet led everyone in hymns, where she chose her favorite tunes from her choir book. After they had sung six renowned Christian hymns, the First Lady, whose main motive behind the prayer vigil was to ease tensions by praising God, spoke to her guests about her faith and beliefs. The American First Lady was three minutes into her emotional address, when notable tears began flowing down her cheeks. Mrs. Flores spoke for another five minutes before the president himself walked up to the alter and relieved his wife. President Ron Flores hugged his wife and handed her his handkerchief before leading her into the awaiting arms of their son.

The president returned to the alter and continued his wife's prayer vigil by expressing his personal feelings about their predicament. President

Flores, who knew he was expected to lead by his actions and demeanor, showed resolve and strength as he spoke candidly about God's mercies in his life and the reason why he believed the earth would survive. The President barely spoke for three minutes before his associate barged into the room and whispered something into his right ear. At the end of his associate's disclosure, the President abruptly concluded his motivational talk and motioned his Vice President's wife to the alter. The President, who was forced to attend to more presiding matters, galloped from the prayer hall with his Vice President and advisors giving chase.

While the prayer vigil continued, the President and his chief advisors returned to the conference room where the chief scientist of NASA Airspace and Technology, Dr. Nadine Wright, awaited with late developments about the approaching planet. The President and his panel of decision makers took to their seats, as his assistant connected the live video feed. An image appeared on the fifty inch television screen, which showed scientists rushing about, as the chief scientist appeared before the panel.

"Mr. President Sir, we are now able to watch this massive planet through the Hubble Space Telescope, which is the most powerful spyware on this planet!" reported Dr. Wright.

"So then we should have a more precise time to the collision?" President Flores asked.

"Yes we do Sir and at its current speed, this bowling ball is going to hit us in six hours and eighteen minutes!" Dr. Wright declared.

The President's assistant, who stood beside the video conference equipment, was forced to sit in the closest available chair, as his knees buckled beneath him after hearing a definite timeline to the collision.

"How-how is this even possible, where did this planet come from?" asked the stunned Vice President.

"We can't say for sure at this point Sir; this is completely irrational from what we've learned about planets in the universe. We have never before recorded anything above asteroid level travelling at such velocity, so this is as puzzling to us as it is you." commented Dr. Wright.

With thoughts on the prayer vigil they'd just attended, the lives of everyone inside the White House, those throughout America and the rest of the world, President Flores was desperate to have some soothing news

Yahweh

as he asked more questions about the approaching dilemma. "According to your data, has this planet swayed off course or anything since the first projections?"

"I'm afraid not Sir; this planet has taken dead aim at the earth, and there is absolutely nothing in space to come to our rescue and knock it off course." exclaimed Dr. Wright.

The President slowly wiped his hands across his face and brought them to rest beneath his chin. "Have these reports been shared with the Pentagon and our allies?" President Flores asked.

"Yes they have Sir, along with the specific trajectory point of impact, which is somewhere in Africa." Dr. Wright answered.

"General Bates have your people calculated our launch times yet?" President Flores promptly asked.

"I'm on the line with them as we speak Mr. President!" answered the Army General.

"Mr. President Sir, I know this may seem unsubstantial at the moment, but we have four astronauts at the international space station who are requesting to come home. These guys were scheduled back to earth with the next shuttle ride in three weeks. After witnessing what became of the different probes this approaching planet passed, no one wishes to try their luck." stated Dr. Wright.

"Technically speaking, are we capable of such a rescue with the timeline we have now? demanded the President.

"None of our shuttles are mission ready Sir; therefore a rescue of such magnitude won't be possible!" Dr. Wright exclaimed.

"Haven't those guys seen the catastrophes we're facing down here? I think if I had the opportunity to survive what the rest of humanity couldn't, I'd be sad to see everyone go, but happy that I'm still breathing. Then again I'm not any of them; so have a video link arranged in order for us to give these guys our best regards. They may be all that's left of humanity after all this is said and done!" dictated the President, as he tossed his pen to the conference table.

"I'll have our technician adjust the equipment to the proper video feed, which will take a few minutes, them you'll be able to talk with them Mr. President." Dr. Wright answered.

"Mrs. Wright I'd like for you to keep me informed should any changes arise with this planet. This is a very fragile moment in our history and this administration wishes to know we made the right decisions." President Flores ordered.

"You'll be the first to know Sir!" Dr. Wright assured.

The picture on the television screen went out before the signal connected with the Space Station's systems. The video feed allowed the astronauts to conversing with the American President, whose space program had two Americans aboard. Despite their Russian and Canadian origins, the non American astronauts were as eager to hear the verdict about their return, as they floated about the capsule in front of the camera. Once the connection was made clear, the single female and three men crew shouted hello in there individual languages.

"Good evening to you lady and gentlemen. I would first like to commend you all on the wonderful work you've bone, you've all been a shining light to your individual countries and we here all salute you. I'm afraid we won't be able to bring you folks back before this devastating collision. As I understand it, most of you would rather be back here on earth, but I think we here are all jealous of the position you've found yourselves in. Our future is still doubtful, but there is a bigger chance you'll all survive to carry on the human civilization and that in itself is monumental. From a very thankful nation, we again salute you, may God bless and keep you and may you live to advance the human civilization. Thanks for your dedication and service, good bye and good luck!" President Flores dictated.

The President signaled his assistant to disconnect the video link, as he dishearteningly looked around the chamber at his advisors. The nervous tension around the room was clearly evident as Vice President Williams slowly shook his head in disbelief, while General Bates packed his secret documents into his attaché case and prepared to depart.

"Mr. President with your permission I'll be returning to the Pentagon to command this missile strike. I have my personal escorts awaiting me at the front door, so if there nothing further at this point, I'll keep you up to date on our progress once I've arrived at base." Gen. Bates declared.

"General, as it appears we are the earth's last chance of survival. Should we fail, the lives of our families, friends and enemies all perish, and the earth will be no more. I would hate for this to be the last time I see you Lloyd, I'm betting my last dollar on you." President Flores acknowledged.

"I'm not much of a betting man Sir, but if I was to bet, I'd put my life savings on our technology. With the tools at our arsenal, I'm quite confident we'll blow that rock right out of the sky!" insisted a confident General Bates.

General Bates went around the room shaking the hands of his peers, whom he'd had the honor of serving with. Major General Franks of the Air Force, who had known the army general for decades, respectfully hugged his compatriot. President Flores firmly shook General Bates' hand, which was the sole picture captured of the moment, by the President's assistant on his Android phone.

"The nation prays for your success in the effectiveness of those bombs. May God bless our integrity to acquire this resolve, may he guide and protect you and may he strengthen your technicians. Our lives are in your hands, good luck!" President Flores serenaded.

The Vice President, Mark Williams, threw his arm around General Bates' shoulder and offered to walk him to the front door. With the transfer of power passed onto General Bates, the president, who felt as helpless as a lamb, walked his delegates back to the Prayer Hall where the prayer vigil was still proceeding. There were four soldiers dressed in black ops outfits with masks and helmets covering their faces and huge automatic riffles at hand standing in waiting by the door. The Vice President, who had been whispering in the General's ear during their walk through the hall, released him into the protection of the soldiers, who all surrounded him and ushered him into the centre vehicle between two well armored Hummer trucks.

The Vice President watched as the guards helped the general into his transport, before branching off to their individual assignments. The vehicles were as black as the outfits the soldiers wore, with the imbedded Illuminati Insignia painted into sections of the vehicle. The headlights on the vehicles were all purple and reflected actual figures of the Illuminati's Insignia, while the rear lights reflected the same, once the driver stepped on the brakes. Vice President Williams appeared pleased at the sight of the Hummers departing as he closed the front door and went to rejoin everyone else inside the Prayer Hall.

President Flores, who was unexpectedly interrupted during his prayer earlier, was back at the alter delivering his second address. "Our most heavenly father in the heights, tonight we come before you to beg for your strength during this treacherous point in our lives. We pray that you guide our bombs to be effective, so they may destroy this planet before it annihilates this wonderful planet, which you've created. Tonight the world is at a stand still, as no one knows whether we'll be here tomorrow, which is already never promised. We pray for the people of America, may you grant them your strength and courage to make it through our coming predicament. To my family and friends who are gathered here tonight, should we never witness another full day, I pray you hold them to your bosom and keep them safe dear Lord. Heavenly father, we leave our lives and those of the world in your hands, as we beg for your continued mercies, Amen!"

"Amen!" exclaimed everyone around the room.

First Lady Janet Flores reopened her hymnbook and led in the singing of three more songs, before they ended the prayer vigil with everyone embracing and encouraging each other. The servants went to the kitchen and brought out pastries and beverages before rejoining the gathering, as the first family insisted everyone casually enjoy themselves. The President, for the first time since his son came home, sat down with the youngster, who after introducing his roommate, went directly into the details of what happened on campus. The remarkable story fascinated the president, who was extremely relieved that they survived such a scare. Once Roland told his father about his friend's tragic loss, the President simply embraced the young mourner and advised him to be strong. The overall warmth inside the room kept everyone preoccupied and distracted, as the minutes ticked off the clock.

The President's alert beeper sounded at 12:20am, which startled everyone in the room who had relaxed and succumbed to the instrumental music playing over the stereo, the warmth from the wooden furnace and admirable company. After checking the alert, the President motioned at his Vice President and his personal assistant before instructing everyone else to continue their socializing. The three men walked to the oval office, where the President's assistant connected both leaders with General Bates at the Pentagon over a live video feed.

General Bates had arrived at his command post at the Pentagon, where his team of twenty trained engineers monitored their computer screens, which reflected the various countries contributing to the global defense. With the planet predicted to strike at the heart of Africa, the eastern countries were scheduled to release their missiles at precisely 1am, with their western allies individually launching at various specific times after. General Bates' technical engineers had calculated the various launch times for each of the twelve other participants combining to save mother earth and her children. The technicians awarded the tasks of launching the missiles were briefed on the importance of timing.

The President and Vice President sat with prayers of hope, as they listened to General Bates usher the order to commence the countdown to launch. Once the countdown began, the men inside the Oval Office felt their heart rate increase as they clinched their fists and listened for confirmation of a successful launch. The countdown was to twenty-five when the second alert phone inside the Oval Office sounded with Dr. Wright of the NASA Space Station on the line. The President quickly grabbed for the phone and answered, as a bewildered expression fell over his face.

"Mr. President Sir, it's the most magnificent thing I've ever seen, the planet appears to be dramatically slowing down!" reported Mrs. Wright.

"I need specifics Mrs. Wright, slowing down as in stopping or just enough to eradicate mankind?" President Flores demanded.

"Sir the planet just began reducing speed and is still loosing velocity. We believe it may stop short of a collision." Dr. Wright insinuated.

An insinuation made earlier by one of his advisors, who was ridiculed for suggesting, 'that maybe this planet was home to God', dawned on the President who uttered, "holy shit", as he attempted to avert the disaster he'd aspired to avoid. The president who could still hear the faint sound of the countdown, attempted to call a halt to the proceedings with seven ticks left to launch. "General Bates abort the missile launch, abort the missile launch!" Yelled the President into the Pentagon's intercom, as the connection unexplainably severed and the line went dead.

Chapter 19

A coalition of fourteen countries launched sixty-nine total nuclear missiles at the planet Heaven, as the planet approached the earth like an airplane descending for landing. The missiles launched went as followed; Canada launched five missiles, America launched nine, Japan launched four, China launched eight, Russia launched five, Germany launched seven, India launched five, Pakistan launched two, Israel launched two, France launched four, Spain launched three, North Korea launched three, South Korea launched four and England launched eight missiles, all with the intentions of destroying the presumed potential threat. Every country involved in the coordinative assault launched their missiles from different strategic points across the world to ensure some success. Scientists at the NASA Airspace and Technologies Centre, space telescope explorers and observation towers used by astrologers around the world, all watched as an impressive display of nuclear missiles ascended towards the invading planet.

The Planet Heaven was as beautiful as a garden covered with the most wonderful flowers and plants throughout. The vegetation was luscious, green and productive for all the inhabitants of Heaven. There were animals of different species and various creatures, which all lived in cohesiveness with the heavenly beings of the planet. Unlike the planet earth, which after creation was maintained and cultivated through the forces relayed by the sun and the moon, Heaven generated its magnificent powers of existence from the most powerful being in the universe. Heaven, was home to the most unique creatures in the universe, even its oceans were vast and plentiful with abundant species of fishes. There were multiple flying birds and creatures of the skies, which all obeyed the calling of the angels who governed over the planet.

The most diverse planet in the galaxy was home to Yahweh, who is the Supreme Being that created the Earth and everything that dwells upon the Earth. Yahweh, who created the Earth with vast similarities to his home planet, intended for this planet to be as perfect as Heaven, where every living organism lived in harmony. The humans that Yahweh created were technically designed from the blue prints of his angels, who were created as vessels to toil over his magnificent creations. The Planet Earth, unlike Heaven, was infested with the impurities of violence, sickness, famine, disease and death, which came through the disobedience of mankind and their desire to be Godly.

As Heaven approached the Earth, Yahweh who sat on his throne in the presence of his Heavenly Tribunal, was in the midst of their final preparations when one of the Lord's Defender Spies telepathically contacted with him from Earth. The Almighty closed his eyes while his delegates continued chatting amongst themselves as his Defender Angel instantly materialized before his minds eyes.

"I welcome thee back my father, but I have horrid news as the humans and demons have collaborated to launch destructive missiles at our home." briefed the Defender Angel.

Yahweh, after receiving the report, waved his hand across the flooring of his Grand Palace, which opened like a television screen highlighting outer space and the approaching missiles. The members of Yahweh's Tribunal were outraged at the gesture, as they rose to their feet and stared at the video footage in disgust. Every member of God's Heavenly Tribunal fell silent, as they closed their eyes and meditated, while Yahweh rose to his feet and stretched out both hands towards the screen across the floor. The Almighty's hands miraculously extended from the planet Heaven itself, as they expanded in outer space; capable of encompassing the missiles forthcoming. The gigantic hands of the Lord enclosed all sixty-nine missiles into both palms, where he subdued them tightly, before they exploded without any vibrations or disturbance to the surrounding stars. The multitude of telescope observers across the Earth were dumbstruck by the magnificence of what they'd witnessed, as Yahweh brushed the residue from both palms and retracted his hands.

The Devine Creator, who was foretold to return to earth at an undisclosed date, was considered absent for millions of centuries. However, in retrospect, Yahweh was merely gone for a short period of time, as a day in the life of the Eternal Father was equivalent to a thousand human days. During the Lord's temporary absence, Yahweh appointed his spies tasks and sought regular briefing on the activities of Lucifer and his demons. In order for his Defenders to provide the information, Yahweh built a time portal in the midst of the Bermuda Triangle through which his angels transported from one dimension to the next in seconds. There have been multiple incidents over the years where aircrafts and ships have entered the Bermuda Triangle and vanished, never again to be seen or heard from.

"How dare these earthly peasants disrespect their Sovereign Lord? Summon my chief generals to my palace at once!" dictated Yahweh.

The Creator was displeased, as he sat back on his throne and awaited recommendations from his Tribunal on how to proceed, before rashly condemning the humans in anger. The Heavenly Tribunal, which had arrived at a number of sanctions prior to the missiles incident, changed the methods of their engagement plots and implemented tougher penalties, which were to commence immediately. The previous strategy that presented more diplomatic solutions with the handling of Earth's affairs was totally discarded in exchange for more rigorous disciplinary actions.

With a high definition view of the Earth through the flooring, Yahweh refrained from striking the planet first and chose to begin his exploits in outer space, as he feasted his eyes on the International Space Station. The Creator interpreted the existence of the Space Station as an example of the humans' desire to live amongst the Gods of the stars, which was prohibited for man, whose feet were made to trod the dirt on the Earth's surface. Yahweh simply made a gesture as if clinching a fist, which caused the multi billion dollar Space Station to crumple like lined paper. The pressures and gases on the International Space Station soon caused the module to rupture and explode, as fractions of debris blew off into outer space. After eliminating the Space Station, Yahweh turned his attention to the array of probes and satellites orbiting the Earth and began pitching his finger at each of them, which sent a direct lightening bolt from Heaven; striking each device and destroying it.

Once Yahweh had ridden space of the probes and satellites, the Creator turned his attention to Earth, from which all the impurities originated. At the snap of his fingers, the marvelous temperatures, which the entire Earth had been experiencing, drastically changed to the most unpleasant weather systems ever recorded across the globe. Three of the world's largest volcanoes, the Paricutin in Mexico, Mount Tambora of Indonesia and the 10,924 feet Mount Etna in Sicily, were the first of eight devastating volcanoes to blow their tops, spewing deadly lava and ashes thousands of meters into the atmosphere. Huge hurricanes began forming in the Caribbean and other oceans, as thunderstorms, tornados, massive snow blizzards, destructive landslides, typhoons and earthquakes began pounding the entire planet. The view from Heaven of the land and seas on Planet Earth quickly became obscured as clouds of ash from each volcano merged to block the light from the sun and the moon.

The divine palace of the most powerful entity in the universe was the most spectacular fabricated dwelling across the Heavenly plains, considering it was built to accommodate the ultimate king of kings. The palace was built as a staple of the planet, with bright glorious gold and white colors throughout; decorative assortments and all the amenities desirable for the comforts of the Creator. The Hallways and breathtaking chambers were exquisitely designed, with unique furniture samples and glamorous masterpieces covering fractions of the walls. The Grand Hall was surrounded with golden windows, which provided a clear spectacular view in either direction; through which the Creator was able to glance out at the beauty he created. There were absolutely no centurions on guard throughout the entire palace, as the Almighty had no need for one on a planet where everyone lived in peace and serenity.

The generals, whom Yahweh summoned, reported to their divine king and honored the great one by kneeling in his presence. The genetically perfect angels, who bowed before their creator, were the ultimate specimen of physicality, with muscular physiques, strikingly handsome good looks, and beards and moustaches complimented by luscious long flowing hair.

"Father you requested us?" insighted the Supreme Commander of Yahweh's elite army.

"Have the final preparations been handled?" questioned Yahweh.

"They have my Lord." answered the Supreme Commander.

"And what of the troops, are they prepared?" Yahweh enquired.

"They are my Lord, and they also patiently await your blessings and approval." the Supreme Commander assured.

The Heavenly Father arose from his throne and walked down towards his generals before guiding them to their feet and directing them towards a section across the hall. Yahweh walked over to one of his many observation points, where he stopped and stared through the glass at his kingdom. The magnificent view that presented a world of peace, love, kindness, respect, serenity and oneness, was shared amongst the immortal beings, which were Yahweh's intentions for all his creation across the Galaxy.

"My sons, this had always been my intentions for every creature of the universe with which I've created. My wishes have been no different from any loving father's desires for his children, which is that they live in peace, love and harmony. My children on the Earth shall adapt the principles by which we abide, without hesitation or quarrel. The time has come for this illusion to end, and let these undisciplined humans know who their true sovereign God is. Have the troops returned home to partake of the love and warmth of their mates and children, for I shall be amongst you all once the final warrior's heart has been filled with gladness and content." Yahweh indicated.

"At once my father!" Supreme Commander Michael responded.

The Supreme Commander and his supporting general walked out onto the entry platform, which was a wide solid surface used by angels to land and ascend. Michael and his supporting General, named Lecouvie, flew across miles of the most breathtaking terrain before arriving at the training facility for God's Universal Soldiers. The training facility, which more resembled an exclusive spa with immaculate service, provided first class training in the arts of weaponry, as well as defense and offensive maneuvers. The Supreme Commander and General Lecouvie landed on the balcony, which led to Michael's strategy chamber, as their wings folded in place the instant they touched down. The two commanders stood on the balcony that overlooked a large open field where millions of angels trained to perfect their fighting craft.

The angels fought as one cohesive unit and thus trained telepathically, while assimilating possible battle challenges. However, during individual sessions, such as archery and fire ball tossing, individuals challenged their counterparts to determine the absolute best. The majority of challenges made on the archery practice field ended up as draws, as each contender would repeatedly split their opponent's arrows directly down the middle. The friendly wagers made were in good fun as Heaven was a socialist planet where no one begrudged their brethrens for anything.

The Universal Armies of Heaven were successful on the battle field because they attacked and defended in unison, where each fighter fought telepathically connected to a network. Through the network every warrior could simulate their brethren's technique, as they envisioned the enemy and reacted to any offensive strike. The weaponry, armor and defensive shield were complimentary assets to the manner with which an angel fought, as every dimension of a warrior angel was detailed and concise. The angels fought with an assortment of weapons, such as their traditional sword, spear, bow and arrows and knives. Their shields were made from Zyclynx, which was an indestructible transparent material, found on a tiny star at the far end of the galaxy.

The Supreme Commander removed a small whistle from a pouch on his belt and used it to summon the troops. Once the legions of God's angels fell into formation, Michael went down before them and addressed them. "Your Lord and father have advised me to send you all home to be with your families until your hearts' content. Upon your return, the selected few shall be chosen to represent our divine Lord and reclaim the Earth. Now go and enjoy the love of your mates and children, for they shall miss you when you're gone."

The customary cheers after hearing the words 'go home', were absent from the angels celebrations, as they merely bid their brethrens good bye and took to the skies. Although they were appreciative of the gesture suggesting they pass time with their loved ones, the warriors were more focused on the battle at hand and a bit eager to get on with the proceedings. After the warriors had departed, the Supreme Commander himself took to the skies and flew home to enjoy the company of his family.

Michael returned home to his personal palace where his wife and children were ecstatic to have him home. The Commander affectionately greeted each of his children as they removed his sandals and apparels, while his wife prepared his bath. Michael was bathed and massaged, as his wife thoroughly cleansed and oiled her husband's solid frame with the most delectable of body oils. After the soothing bath, the Supreme Commander was treated to a meal fit for a king, as his entire family dinned with him and enjoyed his company, before ushering him off to another planet. God's Supreme Commander embraced the affections of his lovely wife, as they passionately romanced each other, before peacefully resting his body before the rigorousness of war. Once Michael's heart was content, the Supreme Commander expressed his heartfelt affections to every member of his household, before then returning to the training facility.

Once Michael arrived at the facility, the commander went directly to his Strategy Chamber, where he focused on the detailed charts of the Earth. With their journey scheduled to carry them through the most treacherous terrain across every continent, Michael visually surveyed their course and highlighted areas of concern at which possible attacks could emanate. God's Supreme Commander was never complacent in believing that Lucifer's Demonic forces were simply going to surrender each continent of the Earth without conflict. Hence, Michael prepared for every sort of trickery from an opponent he'd expected nothing less from. For a bit more insight into his opponent's secret plot, Michael telepathically connected the spy Clyde, who was one of their absolute best.

"Clyde my brother, it's Michael." announced Heaven's Supreme Commander.

"I am here my Commander, how may I be of service?" Clyde responded.

"I feel Lucifer has something defyably instored for us. I want you to seek out his secret plan and report back to me." Michael instructed.

"I shall acquire whatever knowledge possible my Commander." telepathically responded the spy.

After both angels disconnected the telepathic link, Michael went back to studying the map of the Earth, while concluding his final preparations. Before long, General Lecouvie entered the chamber with his report on the troops, who had all returned from their time spent with their families. The General had also received word that their Divine Creator was on route to bless and commemorate his warriors, who were prepared to begin the ordeal of reclaiming the Earth.

While the Heavenly Father's generals deliberated over matters of importance, the warriors who'd returned from their brief vacation were busy packing their desired accessories and readying their weaponry. With all the participants finalizing their preparations, the traditional summoning of the angel's companions was given the green light. An angel used a conch shell to summon the great beasts that had fought alongside the Universal Warriors of Heaven since the beginning of time from the forest surrounding the facility. The angels trained the resourceful animals, which live freely amongst an assortment of creatures on the planet. A pair of Tyrannosaurus Rex, which fought alongside the Supreme Commander, led a cavalry Saber Tooth Tigers into the training facility minutes after the conch shell sounded. The wild creatures were welcomed into camp by their angel comrades, who childishly played around with the animals.

The commanders soon materialized onto the training grounds to personally inspect their troops before the arrival of the Divine Lord, who was said to be en route to the facility. As Michael walked out onto the field, his pair of Tyrannosaurus Rex Dinosaurs excitedly charged at him, to which he fondled and played around with them before attending to the business at hand. Once the alarm signaling the Almighty's approach sounded, Michael ensured that every one was properly aligned and prepared for inspection, as even the great beasts from the wild subdued themselves. With the Heavenly Legion all unified and standing at attention, the flying chariot of the Lord swooped by overhead before gently coming in for a landing on the strip.

Despite his long grey beard, mustache and white flowing lox, Yahweh was physically capable of manhandling any warrior on his legion squad. With everyone kneeling in respect, the Creator stepped from his chariot with his Scepter of Ruler-ship at hand as he walked to the helm of the hundred and forty four thousand representatives of Heaven slated to battle the Devil's forces on Earth. The Scepter of Ruler-ship, which was crafted with gold and platinum, was engulfed in diamonds and priceless artifacts, which matched the glamours of his kingly crown. Yahweh stood aloft before the rows of Universal Warriors as he surveyed those chosen to cleanse the Earth and shook his head in approval. With his consent granted, the angels before him received their confirmation telepathically as they all stood at attention before being serenaded by their Creator.

"My children of this universe, the time has come for us to reclaim this planet, which is mother to the human's that I've created to govern over her. You my children are accustomed to the levity that I've aspire to offer to provide ever living being of my creation. We all live in peace and love with respect for our brothers, sister, families and friends, which is one of the primary laws of the universe. Every inhabited planet survives through the Inter-Planetary balance, which is the simple basis for gaining immortality. I wish for none of you to think of this war as an angel versus angel battle, for you alone are the true defenders of everything which is right and truthful throughout this universe. Allow no human or self absorbed creature to distract you from the mission at hand, for they are the threat to everything you hold sacred and cherish. You are all my children, we have all drank from the same chalice, ate from the same plate, fought on the same field, as I've always been with you, I shall always be with you. What we are and who we are, is the force that brings our rivals to their knees, because as we destroy and demolish, so too do we construct and create. I now send you forth my Warriors of the Universe, to right the wrong which had been wronged by evil, may your swords be fierce, the arrows from your bows direct, protect your brother as he will protect you, and dominate!" Yahweh insighted.

"Dominate-dominate-dominate----!" the Warriors of Heaven continuously repeated.

Yahweh raised his scepter above the heads of his warriors and animals, which groaned and roared, while the angels chanted and physiqued themselves up for the challenge. The Creator twirled his scepter over the heads of his army and a humongous bubble encircled those slated for Earth. With deep concentration at such an important task, Yahweh closed his eyes and guided the bubble up through the atmosphere of Heaven and through the midst of space. The entire continent of Africa was being decimated by thunder storms, when the sun struck a bright beam through the dark clouds directly onto the soil once known as The Garden of Eden. The Majestic One safely transported his Warriors of the Universe through the equator of the Earth, and down to the soil of the planet, where everywhere across the globe was being ravaged by treacherous weather.

Chapter 20

The Angel Clyde flew to the Fiji Island where he glided along its southern shores, before casting out to a small island called Totowa, in the Coral Sea. The weather across the globe was continually dreadful as sever thunderstorms pounded the Fiji islands through the thick mist of ash that covered the skies. There was a specific section on the Island of Totowa where the local residents placed a permanent restriction on anybody visiting after it was reported that evil demons frequented the area. Entire teams of foreign scientists have disappeared without traces after attempting to solve the mysteries behind what they believed to be an 'old wife's tale'. A local fisherman, who went insane after his fishing boat drifted off course, mentioned seeing black angels bathing in the beach attached to the restricted area, before committing suicide by hanging himself with his fishing line.

There was a cave twenty feet from the sea which had never before been explored. Clyde was awaited in the bushes, where his superior vision allowed him to watch the on duty guard, who appeared bored. The objectives given to the spy demanded he attained a notable observation point from where he could learn more about Lucifer's scheme. Hence, Clyde surveyed the entire area as he sought alternative means of entry, of which there were none.

Clyde snuck along the ridge of the forest until he came to the point closest to the cave's mouth. The Spy Angel was aware of the fact that Satan's Demons also telepathically communicated, suggesting a linkage between the guard and his commander. The guard's fatigued demeanor played into the hands of the spy, as he waited until the guard nodded off for an instant before he snuck up and choked the centurion to death. The Spy Angel dragged his victim into the ocean and tied the body to the ocean floor. While returning to the cave, Clyde hid their tracks to the ocean by blowing horizontally at the sand, which caused the imprints to disappear.

The Investigative Angel snuck into the most secretive place on Earth, a place hidden from spy satellites from space, a place that sailors referred to as 'Pirate's Cove' due to the amounts of sea vessels sunk in the water surrounding the cave. The cave's opening offered the only means into Hell, which was the domain or palace of King Lucifer, the Ruler of Planet Earth. While it is true that spirits can pass through walls, there a specified dimensional width through which they can transcend. The depths to which Hell was submerged into the core of the Earth made it impossible for any spirits to simply transport itself into and survive.

The pathway to the Devil's Layer was long, winding and grimy, with moist walls and the pitter-patter sounds of dripping water. There was an occasional torch burning every twenty feet, which made visibility poor for any human, while the corridors lit up like a florescent light bulb through the eyes of an angel. Along the journey, Clyde noticed several crevices and dead end trails, which he ensured were empty to avoid any surprises. Two miles into the Earth's belly, Clyde could literally feel the ground beneath his feet rumbling, as he sensed a thunderous array of warriors trampling towards him.

With only a split second to conceal himself, Clyde decided to take his chances by engaging a tactical maneuver practiced in training but never executed against the immense number of warriors forthcoming. In order for the maneuver to be effective, Clyde would have to find a secured spot and place himself in a lifeless trance, where his enemies could not detect his life force. The Spy Angel retreated to a dead end tunnel, which he believed capable of shielding his body, while the enemy warriors scurried by. Once he found his safe spot, Clyde quickly crouched and brought his breathing and body functions to a halt, as he disappeared into the darkness of the tunnel.

A minute after the spy vanished off his enemies' radar, the Devil's convoy of fighters, en route to war, ran by the tunnel's opening as they ascended to the terrains of the Earth. The Spy Angel remained in the lifeless trance for an impressive two and a half hours as the warriors of Satan's armies continued pouring by. The trance-like state that the spy utilized was clinically calculated to be effective up to one hundred and seventy minutes before the subject began convulsion and was forced to gasp for oxygen. Although invisible, Clyde utilized his sense of hearing to decipher the number of passing demons. With the expiration time on his evasive state fast approaching, Clyde fought to maintain control of his faculties, as signs of the last demons to exit the layer reinvigorated his efforts. After concealing himself for nearly one hundred and sixty eight minutes, Clyde forcibly had to materialize, as he'd begun experiencing the effects of suffocation. One of the Devil's higher ranked soldiers was lagging behind his unit when he felt the powers from the spy regaining his life force as he trotted by the tunnel.

Once Clyde completely materialized, the curious warrior detected his scent and hid. With the belief that his enemies had all passed without suspicion, Clyde snuck to the mouth of the tunnel and peeked in the direction to where they went. The echoes reverberating from the armies' thunderous march continued fading, which convinced the spy that he hadn't been detected. Clyde turned in the direction of the layer and reconvened his journey, with added confidence knowing such a massive army would not be toiling around his destination. As the Spy Angel walked by the first crevice, the suspecting demon who had hid within the creases of the rock, lunged out at him and caught him off guard with a sword plunge to the stomach.

"You dare invade my master's layer!" argued the Demon, who had managed to bore his sword completely through the Angel's stomach, pinning him against the wall.

The injured Angel, who was held helpless by the sword, reached over his shoulder and withdrew an arrow from its pouch. Before the Demon was given the chance to react, the Angel plunged the arrow's point directly into its right eye before quickly retracting it and jamming it permanently into the Demon's left eye. The Demon released the sword handle and uttered a huge sigh, as he bent forward and grabbed onto the arrow before yanking it from his eye socket. Clyde gathered up the strength to grab hold of the sword and pull it from his stomach, as he fell to one knee, while applying pressure to the area.

The blinded Demon withdrew his knife and began swinging erratically all about. With the thoughts of his demise at hand, the Demon attempted to telepathically link his brethrens. The thick rock between the Demons momentarily blocked the communication attempt, but, through perseverance, the link statically connected, as the Demon fought to alert his allies. Within seconds, Clyde, who was down to one knee had recuperated enough, and utilized the Demon's sword to aid him back to his feet. The Angel was vexed at himself, as he swooped in and used the Demon's own sword to sever his knife wheeling hand before twirling in the opposite direction and removing his head. The Demon's corpse disappeared within seconds after hitting the ground, as the Angel began racing towards the beach.

Clyde, who was displeased with himself for allowing the Demon enough time to alert its allies, was confident his mission had been compromised, and thus, desired to inform his commander of the information he'd uncovered. The Angel raced through the corridors in hopes of confronting his enemies on the beach instead of the cramped corridors that surrounded him. As Clyde rapidly climbed, the thoughts of having the Demons release their abominations into the tunnels invaded his mind, as he concentrated on connecting with his Supreme Commander who was in the midst of being transported to Earth under the magnificent powers of Jehovah. As he approached the surface, the spy connected with Supreme Commander Michael, whose transparent bubble was smoothly descending through the furnace within the Earth's Equator.

"My Supreme Commander my field report is prepared!" emphatically stated Clyde the Spy.

"I feel your enthusiasm my brother, report." Michael, who through their telepathic link, became aware of the spy's predicament, declared.

"My Commander, Lucifer has invented some sort of puppet soldiers to strengthen his folds by millions. Your divine army may have to face up to five million enemy soldiers across every battle field." Clyde conveyed.

"You need not concern yourself with such meaningless theatrics right now, as it appears you have greater problems ahead of you. I wish I could be by your side my brother. Be vigilant for we will reunite back in the stars!" compassionately declared Michael, as he emphatically pounded his fist into his palm.

"For the creations of our father God!" Clyde announced.

"For the creations of our father God!" Michael conveyed, as their telepathic connection severed.

As Clyde neared the mouth of the cave, the Demons that awaited him on the beach grew impatient of his refusal to materialize and released two of Satan's lion-like beasts into the cave. As they released the creatures, Clyde could over hear the cynical remarks being made by the Demons, who seemed hesitant to flush the Angel out themselves. With the creatures racing towards the cave, Clyde jammed the Demon's sword into the ground and bent to one knee, before removing two arrows from his pouch and arming his bow. The pair of carnivorous beasts blazed into the cave like starving dogs, with the Angel's scent attained. Clyde tugged back on his ancient trigger, as both creatures lunged into the cave, before the arrows repelled them back out onto the beach in front of their caretakers. The surprised Demons looked down at their pets before raising their heads to the sight of the Angel standing at the mouth of the cave.

"I was hoping that it would be you my cousin." implied one the dozen Demons, who stood awaiting on the beach.

"You are no cousin of mine, in fact I am of no relations to any of you traitors!" Clyde Responded.

"Be as it may, today you shall regret not joining my Lord Lucifer's rebellion!" the Demon threatened.

"When I cease to breathe my father in Heaven shall comfort and nurture me back to life. But when your Earthly breath gets taken, you will never again be spoken of or remembered." the Angel assured.

"Your Father like you shall be no more!" the Demon warned.

"Our Father will exist for eternity, you insolent swine. Enough talk, come get some!" the Angel argued.

The Angel focused his mind to the task at hand, as the heavy doses of rain ran down his face. With both swords held firmly at hand, the Angel charged into the midst of the twelve Demons, like a Samurai Ninja, without fear or respect for his enemies' fighting abilities. The Angel's cousin and three other Demons initially back away from the conflict, as they allowed the eight engineered Dark Warriors to take the lead. Sparks gashed as steel collided with steel, as Clyde both attacked and defended himself against

Lucifer's great hopes. Lucifer's Dark Warriors, which lacked the ability to reason for themselves, fought like preprogrammed robots whose defaults were exposed by the injured Angel.

During the conflict, one of the observers along the sidelines noticed evidence of the Angel's prior injury and highlighted the concealment to its mates. Despite his weakened state, the Spy Angel completely outclassed his foes, as his fighting techniques was vastly superior, his speed much faster, agility and weapons handling impressive even to those watching. Clyde easily dispensed of the first four Dark Warriors without breaking a sweat as he'd perceived the Demons plot being for him to tire, which would drastically increase their victory ratio.

The Angel intelligently used the Dark Warriors' over aggression against them, as he bated them in with a feigned injury to his left leg, before subsequently somersaulting over their heads and relieving two heads before landing firmly on both feet. Clyde proved he had plenty of reserved energy, as he gazed over his right shoulder to pinpoint the Dark Warrior and lunging his sword into its lower back and slicing upwards till the blade reached his armpit. Frustrations mounted on the side of the awaiting Demons, as an angry demeanor appeared across their faces once the angel reduced their puppets to a lone soldier. The Angel gazed over at the awaiting Demons as the last Dark Warrior turned around to find its surviving brethren sliced in half and the inflictor of the injury standing insultingly with his back to it. The Dark Warrior gripped its sword with both hands above its head and charged at the blatantly disrespectful Angel. With an assured confidence of success, the Dark Warrior approached its target and came within striking distance before the Angel fell to one knee, spun around into its attacker and sliced completely through the Warrior's midsection.

The enraged Demons surged at Clyde from the air and sand, as the spy fended them off while backpedalling towards the ocean. With no time allowed to rest after he'd disposed of the Devil's flunkies, Clyde for the first time found himself heavily pressured as all four remaining Demons simultaneously attacked. The Angel had to quicken his tactics against the Demons, who were similar to him in traits, but lacked his advanced tactical portfolio. Jehovah's Angels were the undisputed champions of the Universe, with some fighting secrets known to Satan's Demons, although the modern Angel had vastly improved the assault techniques since the Devil and company were hurled down to Earth.

Although the Angel allowed the Demons to believe his regression was due to their immense pressure, his every action was planned, as he sought to neutralize his enemies' quickness. Clyde backpedaled into the ocean and stopped as the water rose to his thighs, before uniquely changing his defensive counter actions, which forced his attackers to take their first steps backwards. The Angel suddenly stuck both his swords into the sand, crossed both hands across his stomach while retracting a series of blades from his utility belt, as the Demons looked at each other. Clyde withdrew eight piercing blades from both sides and flung them at the two hovering Demons, which managed to block a few. The blades that escaped each Demon's defensive efforts sailed directly into intended paralyzing nerves throughout their wings, before gravity brought them crashing to the sand.

"Enough of this, we'll deal with this lover of Yahweh the old fashion way!" instructed one the Demons, who motioned his mates to begin circling the Angel. "You can't run or hide from us Angel!" threatened the same Demon, while yanking the blades from its retracted wings.

"I'm a soldier of God, we don't run and we certainly never hide!" Clyde stated proudly.

With his nemesis spreading out to circle him, Clyde retracted his blades from the sand and backpedaled into the ocean, until the water rose to his waist level. The Angel, who had duly noted that he was slightly taller than his opponents, stopped at a depth in the ocean that allowed him to maneuver freely as the shorter Demons who sought to encircle him, were forced to abandon that idea. With the ocean level beyond the Angel's position rising to chest levels for the shorter Demons, to achieve a maneuverable platform on which to fight, Clyde had no problems viewing his attackers, who scattered out a hundred and sixty degrees ahead of him.

The Angel, who had memorized the various attack strategies of each of his opponents during their earlier confrontation, calculated and ascertained which Demon was the strongest of the bunch. Once the Angel reached his conclusion, Clyde sunk his pivot foot into the sand and measured his enemies' distance by waving his swords at them, which also kept them at blade's length. The Demons, which sought to kill the Angel at all cost, behaved defiantly against his outstretched swords by slapping at them with their own swords, as they attempted to get closer to their prey.

The 'chings' from clashing swords again sounded, as Clyde maneuvered his swords to fend off the pressing attacks of his enemies. The skillful Angel fought with vigor and strength, as his resolve angered his opponents, who were held at bay despite their numbers. The Demons, after realizing they stood no chance at gaining any grounds, backed away from the conflict and telepathically linked each other, as they devised a possible plot to succeed against their nemesis.

The Demons improvised their plan, which was intended to have the warriors to the far end of the confrontation both press the Angel, while a third Demon approached from the air and the fourth attacked from underwater. To offset his enemies strike formation, the Angel, after recognizing their intents, charged the Demon to his right with a barrage of chops and stabs, while its comrades trailed closely behind. The stunned Demon, who went from an attacking posture to a defensive one, could barely fend off the mounting blows, as it bumped its heel and tumbled backwards onto the water. Once the Demon struck the water its sword fell from its grasp, which gave the Angel the opening it sought. With its enemy at his mercy, the Angel leapt like a cat and descended directly with his sword piercing through the Demon's chest. The Demon yelled out in pain, as its underwater brethren snuck his blade through the Angel's left thigh, before his aerial brethren in pursuit severed the Clyde's head. The Angel, who had humbled himself to the acceptance of his fate, ensured he had slain one of Satan's faithful before collapsing into the ocean.

Chapter 21

"My Lord, the festivities celebrating your grand return to the Planet Ashton have begun. Your beloved servants of great integrity have sent their humblest greetings to wish you a safe journey during your travels there." briefed the Ambassador to Planet Ashton.

"Upon your return to Ashton, advise the people that I look forward to the visit and will be present at the appointed time." Yahweh declared.

"Thank you, your exact words shall be transferred my Lord." exclaimed the Ambassador, who bowed in respect to the king, before humbly departing.

With matters relevant to the governing of Universal Issues handled, the Heavenly Tribunal turned their attention to the presiding issues of cleansing the Earth. Yahweh once again waved his hand across his Grand Hall's flooring, at which opened the viewing screen highlighting the entire Earth. The Heavenly King pointed his index finger at Africa, which caused the screen to begin zooming in on the area where Michael and his Universal Army had settled. With the torrential deadly weather persisting across the globe, Michael, a number of ranked Angels and General Lecouvie meditated in memory of their fallen soldier, while their fellow brethrens around camp also paid their respects. Yahweh telepathically linked with Michael, which disrupted his meditation session, as those around him continued glorifying the existence of their slain comrade.

"My son!" Yahweh appealed.

"I am here my Father!" Michael exclaimed.

"The Tribunal seeks an accord. Go to the top of the nearest mountain, so we may converse." Yahweh instructed.

"At once my Father!" Michael responded.

The Supreme Commander of God's army stepped from the tent into the darkened exterior. Michael took a few steps before quickening his pace as his wings spread as he leapt into the air. Michael flew to the top of the closest mountain and landed safely, inches away from a warm and cozy fire that burned from a tree in the midst of treacherous downpours. The Supreme Commander of God's elite Universal Army walked up and crouched by the warm fire as he telepathically linked with his father, while staring into the blaze of fire. As if connected by a live video conferencing feed, the Sovereign Lord's facial image appeared in the ball of fire and they conversed about matters of importance.

"My Father I am here." Michael announced.

"My son, Heavenly praises have been bestowed onto you from the Tribunal, which have longed for this coming resolution. Shortly we shall begin administering punishments to these human subjects of Lucifer who have disrespect their Creator when they should have celebrated and glorified my anointed return. In time I shall call to those long deceased, who will hear my voice and awaken, for they too are slated to be judge. To those who have wasted their prayer by acknowledging false Gods and idols, we shall burn forever in Hades, as there have never been, nor will there ever be anyone as great as I! Throughout the many lands my laws have gone discarded; hence, we shall teach them the penalties of disobedience." Yahweh declared.

"My Lord, your Guardian Forces from across these plains have assembled and await their commands during this historical war?" Michael conveyed.

"The Earth's Great Defenders shall serve as our demolition forces across the entire inhabited Earth. Instruct them to demolish these skyscraper towers reaching into the skies and leave nothing standing above the height of the Arc. Wipe away clean these weapons of destruction under ground, as well as those kept for various measures above. Finally, at the time of the awakening they shall serve as my bounty hunters to all who attempt to disobey my calling." Yahweh instructed.

"I have acquired news of Lucifer's grand scheme my Lord. Our spy has reported that he has created warriors in their likeness, which has drastically increased their numbers." Michael exclaimed.

The images of Yahweh through the blazing fire highlighted him reaching forward, as he fanned his hand to separate a section of the thick ash cloud covering Africa, which revealed Lucifer's grand army as they marched across Somalia on route to engaging God's Angels. While continuing his discussion with Michael on one section of the screen, Yahweh and his Heavenly Tribunal gazed in curiosity at Lucifer's puppeteers at another section. The Heavenly Tribunal and their king were rather impressed at their former comrade's valiant attempt against Heaven's undefeated warriors, as they had assumed something of epic defiance from Lucifer the Tyrant.

"What are those things; are they human?" commented one Tribunal member.

"Outstanding, they should if anything at least provide a challenge!" confidently added a second, as the Tribunal Members chatted amongst themselves.

"Five million one hundred and three in total. As we've discussed my son, your opponent will not operate conventionally, thus, prepare for the trickery and cunning of your ex-sibling. Go now and finalize your endeavors, for your enemies approach to accomplish the deeds of their master." Yahweh instructed his Commander.

"Understood my Lord." Michael humbly answered.

The Supreme Commander rose from his crouched position and turned his back to the fire, at which the flames extinguished and total darkness befell the mountain top. Michael ran to the edge of the mountain and leapt over the side, as his wings extracted and caught a gust of wind, on which he glided down into their camp. General Lecouvie greeted Michael the instant he touched down with information from their surveillance team, which divulged everything about Satan's approaching army, from their time of arrival to their weapons count. Once the Supreme Commander landed, he went directly to the Defender's tent, where his fellow protectors of the Earth had gathered and awaited their assignments. The long ritual of anointing Clyde the Spy Angel to the Natural Mystics Realm of Heaven had only recently ended, which was a process in which every Angel participated.

Michael nonchalantly dejected the salutes of his peers, who bowed at his entrance, as he entered the tent and requested everyone's attention.

"My brothers of Heaven, I bring the admirations of your families and most importantly, the gratitude of your Father!" Michael stated vigorously.

"Yeahhhh!" cheered the gathered Defenders.

"Your Father has not forgotten you during this historic war, as he had bestowed onto me your desired contributions. At this junction in time our deeds and success are trivial to the freedom from oppression these humans dwell under. We live in a free society, which was our father's desires for all his creation. These humans have longed for such harmony and we are going to ensure they get just that. As I would graciously have you all fight by my side, there are essential chores that require your expertise. Hence, Our Heavenly Creator has instructed that you scout ahead and scour every terrain across this continent, and demolish every dwelling above three stories, eradicate these humans' weapons of destruction and corral the spirits of yesteryear, slated to awaken at the call of our Father's voice. We have awaited this day for a while, Lucifer as you know believes he is prepared for our invasion, but there is not a single army across this universe capable of matching wits with us. Whether they come screaming or mute, their day of atonement has arrived." While Michael spoke, the sun materialized outdoors and shun so brightly that the entire tent brightened. "Now go forth, and as the Father has instructed us, dominate!"

"Dominate-dominate-dominate, yeahhhh!" cheered the Earthly Defenders.

Following the Heavenly Tribunal's judgment regarding the continent of Africa, Yahweh, whose army was about to battle over the birthplace of mankind, casted a series of plagues that affected every human across its territories. Yahweh after receiving the punishment from his Tribunal Advisors, closed his eyes and concentrated on the assigned task before snapping his fingers at which the plagues were administered. At the snap of the Lord's fingers, oceans surrounding Africa such as sections of the Southern Ocean, Northern Atlantic Ocean, Mediterranean Sea, Golf of Guinea, Golf of Aden; rivers, lakes, pools and every water source throughout the continent, became red like blood. Significantly, heavy volume of rain continued falling across the continent, as the very drops of rain turned red once they struck the grounds. Yahweh cleared the skies above Eden, where the conflict between his soldiers and Lucifer's was set to occur, while the second plague casted resulted in the deaths all lives stock across the continent. Goats, cows, sheep and every eatable source of meat began tumbling to the ground, as citizens who owned such animals watched in fear and amazement. The Heavenly Father invoked a third plague, which affected every sort of vegetation causing rapid began rotting and spoiling.

After casting the various plagues across Africa, the Heavenly Father, who sent orders for his Defender Angels to remand and police the resurrected spirits, called out to such spirits forces and awakened them from their various places. Yahweh formed a funnel with his left hand and aimed it towards the globe across his flooring, before placing his mouth at the top end and talking through it like a loud speaker.

"Hear my voice and awaken all you insolent souls who've defied the glory of the cycle of life." the Heavenly Creator lamented, as a sonic voice wave heard only by the ears of spirits, transmitted through every crevice of the Earth. At Yahweh's summons, every spirit force who has failed to register at their appointment following death, arose, from their places of deceit, with the fear of knowing that judgment day was at hand.

Since the dawn of time there has been countless humans who've lost their lives in scenarios from-which they fully expected to survive. At the moment when the body dies, the spirit of that person has to accept their fate and transcend into the afterworld, which is determined by the manner by which he or she lived. For those who've lived by the laws of the Lord, a divine bright light illuminates to guide such souls to God's covenant, while the darkness of the underworld is opened to consume servants of Satan to Hell. There have been those who've refrained from the acceptance that they've passed on and thus continue to probe the earth as ghosts, jinns or duppy, depending on the views of said culture.

At the summoning of the Lord, spirit forces that were capable of ignoring other appeals, found themselves vacating their most secretive of hiding places, which exposed them to other spirits. Lucifer, who had a significant amount of defiant spirits, immediately dispatched his Grim Reapers in order to capture such spirits.

Satan's largest Collectors of Souls or Grim Reapers were, remarkably, sent to the small island of Jamaica, which possessed the greatest amount of treacherous souls throughout the entire planet. The deserters that hovered across the island were renowned to the locals as 'Badman Duppy', because these ghosts would regularly torment the living. While some spirits revered the concept of the coming judgment, others, like the Madison brothers Sean and Wayne, along with their gunmen mates Keith Day aka Stylist, Carlos Willis aka Crazy and O'Neil Dunn aka Moon, who were referred to as the Insane Boys, aspired for that historical day. With none of these Ghetto Thugs living to embrace adulthood, their preconceived notion that the Lord would grant them pardon, was a belief they truly attained.

These five young men were made infamous by one specific incident, despite their lengthy criminal careers. The Montegonian youths, who were the product of neglect and poverty, formed a community click from a young age after they experienced the need to provide for themselves. Without the daily requirements provided by parents, the youths began collecting enough bottles to sell and acquire goods like floor or rice. These Ghetto youths, who were resourceful, soon escalated their hustle after acquiring arms from older gangsters, who realized the benefits of having children perform their vile deals. These so called good intentions O.Gs, would eventually introduce these kids to addictive drugs, which altered their already flawed personality, sinking them into an abyss of no return. By the time these growing uneducated thugs reach the age of twelve, they are evicting grown folks from the area through threats or force, murdering for cynical reasons, raping females of all ages, robbing whatever they desired and terrorizing the neighbor hood and shooting whoever protested.

December 15, 1994

On the day in question, these five thugs were between the ages of fourteen and sixteen when they plotted the hijacking of a tourist bus filled with vacationers out on a tour of the city. The five men staked out a JUTA Tourist bus that brought shoppers to the Craft Market in downtown Montego Bay, which was filled with vacationers who spent an hour shopping. The young men, who had all disguised themselves as some sort of salesman, approached the reboarding tourists offering to sell their goods of peanuts, bottle water, face rags etc, before forcing their way onto the bus while intimidating everyone by exposing their concealed weapons. After successfully hijacking the bus filled with tourist from various countries, the boys instructed the bus driver to drive into the Anchovy Hills where they embarked on a dirt road that led to an old shack a few meters in. Once they arrived at the wooden shack, the young thugs had everyone lay face down on the ground beside the bus before walking on top of people and shooting every male in the back of the head.

The boys then ordered the females to remove their clothing, which they collected and piled inside he wooden shack. The survivors were all terrified, as their captors, despite the midday hour, behaved as if they had an eternity to do their filth. The young men ignored the naked females for half an hour, as they joked amongst themselves while snorting cocaine and drinking liquor. The young men seemed uninterested in a profit, as they began sexually assaulting and sodomizing the woman by fondling them in some cases while forcing hem o lay on the backs of the dead men. The horrific episode continued into the late hours of the night before the thugs retired from fatigue, while their victims who suffered the tragedy wept and consoled each other.

After raping the many females that ranged from the ages fourteen to eighty eight, the young thugs exited the tour bus, which encouraged several women to begin thinking about over powering their captors with their sheer numbers. Although the multitude of women were apprehensively, the decision to attempt a rush at the opportune time was decided upon. While the female aboard the tour bus plotted, the five young thugs outside painted themselves with white paint while elevating their intoxication, before arming themselves each with full length machetes. Once they had prepared themselves, the young thugs rushed back onto the tour bus and began slashing everyone within their path, as heads, hands and every body fraction of females got hacked to pieces by the butchers.

The Young Thugs bragged about their achievements, while stacking the fragments of body parts inside the abandoned hut, which they later burned to the ground. Instead of torching the bus, the young geniuses decided to sell it to Chino's chop shop on King Street back in town. After cleansing themselves of the paint and blood, sixteen year old Sean Madison took the steering wheel and drove the bus out onto the main road before turning back towards the city. Sean's driving experiences had been limited and he fought to maneuver the huge coach along Montego Bay's country roads. It wasn't long before impatient motorists began sounding their horns as the bus crawled along the main road.

Three constables in a police squad car, which was caught in the line behind the crawling JUTA Tours bus, became concerned at the rate the bus travelled and threw their siren on. At the sound of the police's siren, Sean, who knew he was incapable of out running the squad car, decided to pull over to the soft shoulder and have his gunners ambush and kill the constables. Three constables assigned to the Barnet Street Police Division occupied the squad car, which pulled up behind the stopped bus and ran the plate information. Once the police realized that the JUTA Tours bus had been placed on a nation wide missing alert, the constables radioed for assistance as they attempted to take up a more commanding positions around the bus. The gunners, who hid throughout the bus, began peppering the constables with bullets as Sean stepped on the gas and brought the vehicle up to its most impressive speed thus far of fifty-five miles per hour, as the coppers raced back to their vehicle and began pursuit.

Shots rang out along the busy main road as the young thugs fired bullets at the pursuing constables. The officer, who rode shotgun returned fire with his SLR Automatic Riffle, which shattered the bus' rear glass and forced the youngsters to duck for cover. The young thugs attempted to trade bullets with the constables, while oblivious to the fact there was a roadblock assembled ahead. Sean came around a corner on the Old Bog Road at speeds exceeding sixty miles per hour when his eyes widened at the sight of the road block with heavily armed constables standing at the ready. At the sight of the bus, the officers who were instructed to simply disable the motor-vehicle opened fire at the engine and wheels, to which Sean swayed the bus off the road into a sugarcane plantation. A slew of Jamaican Constables rushed into the rows of sugarcane after the bus, which overturned and slid to a halt. Despite the excitement, not a single shot was fired until the police deciphered that the missing tourists were not amongst the thieves. Once it was noted that the thugs were alone, a significant amount of gunfire was traded between both parties, before the single pop of the thugs' hand pistols totally subsided.

Chapter 22

Defender Angels took to the skies in every direction, as they branched off towards the various tasks assigned them across the continent of Africa. Since the dawn of violence on the Earth, the time that elapsed since Yahweh destroyed the advantageous missiles had been the longest streak at which humans across the entire globe had ever experienced utter peace. Despite the frightful roars of thunder and lightning that mainly terrified the youngsters of African households, families across the continent suffered an uneasy nervousness from waiting for the unknown. The worries of the entire African nation were, however, short lived, as God's Defenders swooped into territories with precise instructions, bombing of cities from South Africa to Libya, where Angels demolished infrastructures belonging to governments and the private sector. Every facility of importance located in small towns, villages and rural areas were also struck; although the major cities with their huge skyscrapers and fashionable buildings were far more devastated.

The military facilities across the continent were given priority, as well as industries that manufacture any sort of destructive devices. Every government facility, including missile silos, electrical grids, financial institutes and spy agencies were all destroyed. Defender Angels went about cities unchallenged as they leveled everything above three stories. Oil fields and mines from which precious gems are retrieved were targeted and destroyed; although the most significant losses came through the crumbling of inhabited buildings, both residential and commercial. In order for God's people to fully conquer the globe, it was imperative for such monumental structures, through which governments have gained power, be demolished. The Governments of the world had always been the invisible force through which the Devil reigned over this planet and Yahweh's divine plot included the eradication of such facilities.

Under the miserably dark skies of ash caused by the erupted volcanoes and a constant beat of rain, cities throughout Africa went up in flames, as electrical transformers and gas lines that lead into buildings exploded, causing huge fires. People lucky enough to escape the crumbling buildings, had mixed emotions, as they either stood outdoors amazed under the drops of red rain, or scattered for safety against the perceived to be creatures of Satan. Every weapon of destruction, from hand pistols to explosive devices, were sought out and eradicated from the Earth, as toxic chemicals and gas plants were bombarded with firebombs. The Defender Angels struck targets and disrupted global communications, which were already dismal after the Creator annihilated the various satellites orbiting the Earth.

Cassandra Bryan and her classmate Jennifer Stebbing remained hidden for hours before Jennifer grew weary of not knowing what was developing outdoors and snuck from the confines of the bathroom, while Cassandra dozed off in the bathtub. The touring Canadian student crept out into the hotel suite and gingerly walked over towards the window where she peeked through cracks in the curtain. The mutilated bodies of tourists who had been bludgeoned and shredded to death lay across the hotel grounds and the frightened female covered her mouth to prevent her screams from being heard. The drops of rain made the disfigured bodies appear far worst, as it seemed as if blood was still draining from the corpses. The female, who had been concerned about her family back in Canada, searched about and located her purse with her cellular phone inside. The television that had been left operating had grains across the screen, as if the channel had ceased broadcasting. Once Jennifer activated her cell, the signal indicating low battery immediately flashed, as she ignored the appeal and dialed her parent's number. After a few seconds of patiently awaiting a ring tone, Jennifer looked at her phone to determine the reason for the lack of connection. Once it became evident that her phone had zero signal strength, the concerned female moved to the landline phone assigned to the suite.

At the realization that their communication devices were out of service, Jennifer raced to the bathroom in order to inform her roommate. The female student, who had become slightly hysterical, alerted her classmate with her information as she entered to find her friend sitting up in the tub.

"Cassandra, Cassandra the phones and television don't work! And the rain is some weird color!" Jennifer yelled.

"What did you say? Why didn't you wake me up before you snuck out of the bathroom?" Cassandra questioned.

"I had to call my parents, but all the phones and television aren't working! And outside all those people dead, what are we going to do?" Jennifer cried as tears flowed down her face.

Cassandra arose from her tub bed and went into the suite, where she thoroughly checked the phones to ensure they were out of service. From the view of outside, both females decided to acquire some information of what was transpiring as they decided to check with their friends down the hall. Despite her mother advice to remain indoors, Cassandra, like her roommate, could not simply wait around without knowledge of what exactly was developing around the world. With their purses at hand, both females snuck to the front door and peeked out, before Jennifer turned and ran into the bathroom, where she grabbed her hair blow dryer to use as protection.

"And what purpose is that going to serve against those things?" Cassandra sarcastically enquired.

"Listen, a girl can't be too careful in these places." Jennifer joked, as she snagged onto Cassandra's back.

The door to the young ladies suite crept open as Cassandra timidly snuck her head out and checked if the coast was clear. Their girlfriends' suite was slightly down the hall as they kept their backs to the wall while maneuvering to ensure nothing crept up on them. To abstain from creating any noise that could possible alert the creatures, the females placed a rag at the point where they knocked on the door and slightly tapped to gain access. After a few minutes of gradually tapping without any response, Jennifer, who suffered from claustrophobia, began pounding on the door as she became suffering from the symptoms of her sickness. Cassandra, who had personally observed the viciousness of the creatures from which they hid, was at first disturbed by her roommate's actions, before nervously joining the pounding.

"Dam Melissa I told you to carry your room pass." sounded a female's voice on the opposite end of the door, as she approached the entrance.

The door to the suite barely cracked before the two students came barging into the room. Jennifer, who was to the rear, quickly locked the door behind them as Cassandra shoved Tenysiah to the ground.

"What the Hell is wrong with you guys; dam you drunk or something?" Tenysiah argued.

"Is the hotel's phone in here or your cell working?" Cassandra questioned, while moving towards the phone on the night stand.

"Were you sleeping? How could anyone possibly sleep at a time like this?" Jennifer argued.

"Where is Melisa? Oh my Lord their phone doesn't work either!" Cassandra implied.

"What's with the twenty questions, as if the professor sent you guys up here to question me?" Tenysiah argued from inside the bathroom.

"What have you been doing all this time?" Cassandra asked, as she walked towards the bathroom.

"Getting my beauty rest of course what else, with all this end of world talk I had to get some rest. Melisa and a bunch of others went out drinking but I wasn't up for it." Tenysiah declared.

"Well Miss Canada, while you were getting your beauty rest, people have been getting torn to shreds by some sort of creature outside." Cassandra stated.

"Oh God are you guys serious? Melisa has been gone for hours; you don't think she could have been?" Tenysiah insinuated.

"Didn't you hear all that screaming outside earlier?" Jennifer questioned.

"You tell me when there isn't someone drunk and screaming around here?" Tenysiah reasoned.

"Come on guys arguing isn't going to solve anything. We need to go find Professor St. Jacque and the rest of the gang, so at least find out what is going on." Cassandra suggested.

"You gotta be kidding me? You want us to go back outside where whatever those things are that's been eating everyone is waiting? Besides, for all we know they could all be dead. Those chopped up bodies outside were no joke; this is real life so count me out." Jennifer lamented.

"If people are getting killed outside, then maybe it would be best if we wait in here---." Tenysiah suggested.

"Until what? Until someone comes and save us. Listen, whether we like it or not this world is about to end, now staying locked up in some hotel room not knowing what's going on isn't going to save our soul." Cassandra argued.

"Neither is having some creature eat us for breakfast!" Jennifer countered.

"Whatever, you girls can stay here locked up not knowing what's going on if you want to, but I'm going to find our schoolmates and locate a church, where we should have gone in the first place." Cassandra declared.

The young lady walked over to the bed and grabbed her purse before walking towards the entrance. Cassandra gradually pulled the door open and carefully snuck her head outside, as she cautiously checked both sides of the hallway to ensure the coast was clear. While Cassandra gazed through the door, Tenysiah, who had decided to accompany her, walked up unexpectedly and placed her hand on her classmate's shoulder, which startled Cassandra nearly to death.

After noticeably scaring Cassandra, Tenysiah joked about startling her friend. "As scared as you are, you better wait for me!"

There was no way Jennifer was about to get abandoned, whether her friends were headed towards certain doom or not; so she rearmed herself with her blow dryer and caught up to them in the hallway. Cassandra had to point out the importance of discretion to her friends, who soon began complaining about their discolored shoes. The three Canadian students snuck their way through the hallways towards the stairs and down towards the reception area. The young ladies checked every suite their classmates occupied along their way to the ground level, where the first evidence of the carnivorous incidents was revealed. At the sight of a deceased female, whose anatomy had been ripped apart, and a number of separate body parts scattered about the lawn, Tenysiah, vomited over the floor.

The miserable weather disguised the elegance of a predicted glorious morning where the bright sunlight typically illuminated across the skies of Africa. The Canadian students cautiously stepped over scattered body parts as they made their way towards the reception area, where they hoped to find some sort of assistance. Though none of the girls chose to admit it, they believed everybody to be dead. Evidence supporting their theories expanded the closer they got to the recreations area, which was littered with corpses. Once the girls arrived at the primary reception and recreation area, the dreadful sight of corpses covering the entire flooring brought everyone to tears, as evidence of a number of their companions' demise surfaced. A left leg severed at the thigh, which was dressed with a white Polo ankle sock and a blue and white Nike Air Force sneaker, was all the remains necessary to inform the girls that the creatures had victimized their professor.

Tenysiah who had become disenchanted from the excruciating sight of deceased bodies scattered about, wondered off in search of her roommate, whose remains had not yet been found. There was a grieving female crouched with her deceased husband's decapitated body in her arms, who Tenysiah felt sorrow for, but declined approaching. Tenysiah, en route to finding her roommate, became fascinated at the sight of one of the slain abominations from Lucifer's dungeon, which had half its body squeezed into the cafeteria room. While speechlessly staring at the creature responsible for the trauma, Cassandra walked over to Tenysiah and placed her arm around her shoulder as both females sobbed at the thought-provoking realization related to the deaths.

"I'm sorry girlfriend, but that thing also killed Melisa and the others." Cassandra whispered into Tenysiah's ear.

"No Lord, not Melisa!" Tenysiah cried.

Jennifer walked over to her classmates and joined the hug fest seconds before the building closest to the swimming pool imploded and crumbled to the ground. The curious females ran out onto the lawn to obtain a better view but were dumbstruck by what they witnessed instead. The Defender Angel credited for demolishing the building was as visible as penny dollar, as he hovered above the building while drenching it with fireballs after he had sabotaged the structural posts that caused it to collapse. The Canadian students stood nervously by and watched the Angel nonchalantly dismantle the entire building, before their housing unit also imploded and caved in. The three friends tightened their grip on each other as explosions began sounding rampant throughout the entire city.

Chapter 23

Michael walked to the helm of his father's Universal Army, as they awaited their opponents, who marched to rid the planet of God's servants. Although the demons that represented the Devil were still beyond visible range the Angels could feel their immense forces as the demons stumped the ground. As Michael passed his personal assistant Shyreek, the Supreme Commander collected his helmet and protective shield before toying with his twin dinosaurs for an instant. The dinosaur's master, with whom they smudged up against like puppies, named his Tyrannosaurus Rex Dinosaurs Hax and Zow. Both Dinosaurs had been fitted with their battle gear, which included sharp blades attached to the tail, to fend off rear attacks, plus an array of other defensive toys. After toying with his dinosaurs for a few seconds, Michael released them in order for them to take their position ahead of Heaven's beastly warriors, who roared and growled at the stench of their approaching opponents.

The Supreme Commander, who, like his father, was never short on enthusiastic speeches, spoke to his brothers in life and arms, as they savored the calm before the storm. Despite the drastic difference in numbers, the confident Angels of Heaven were anxious to engage their enemies in the ultimate battle that had been prophesied for centuries. God's divine army of Angels, which amounted to a hundred and forty four thousand warriors, lined up across the plains outside of the infamous Garden of Eden, fully suited and prepped for battle.

"My brothers, the Universal God our father, have long been disrespected by these proclaimers aspiring to be rulers who have been allowed to govern over these lands by the rightful owner. The sole title of Universal God belongs to one everlasting entity. Those who chose to oppose us are knowledgeable of that fact, yet it has fallen on us to remind them of all that is, was and always will be! To those who may hesitate because the face before you was once family, the relations between us has long been severed and there is no existence throughout this universe for us both. We are here to eradicate all that is evil from this world, and today it begins with these peasants, who've been sent by he whom we will destroy!" During the Supreme Commander's address, Satan's multitude of warriors arrived and became engaged in a stare down competition versus the angels. "I am almost insulted by these theatrics, mere smoke screens to prolong the inevitable. But they shall serve as our first example, which will transcend the message of who we are. For we are the champions of this Universe, there are no equals to us. As they are about to learn, as their peers will find out, we are the warriors of Heaven and we shall forever, dominate!"

"Dominate-dominate-dominate----!" chanted the Universal Warriors of Heaven.

With the Angels and Demons sizing up each other, the abominations of the Devil's dungeon and Heaven's animals focused their attentions on the impending confrontation. The four-legged creatures showed less restraint, as they immediately clashed on their separate battlefield, where claws and fangs were sunken into hinds, while they fought like the primitive scavengers their species were known as. Similar to their Angel counterparts, the animals of Heaven were also drastically outnumbered by the creatures from Hell. However, the pair of vicious Tyrannosaurus Rex Dinosaurs equalized the battlefield as they used their powerful jaws to snap the Devil's carnivores in halves, and defensive weaponry to fend off cheaters.

The Supreme Commander walked into the midst of Heaven's Universal Soldiers and disappeared into the formation with which the warriors were aligned. Michael moved to the rear of the army, where he swooped into the air and recovered his position at the Commander's Station alongside General Lecouvie and a squad of elite Angels. The Universal Warriors of Heaven, whose shields played an important roll in their attack and defensive formations, began walking towards the astonished Demons who expected to be the aggressors. Each Angel's shield was six inches wider than its owner's body frame and a third of his body length when contracted. Each Angel's shield was six inches wider than its owner's body frame and a quarter of his body length when contracted. The shield's versatility gave the Universal Warriors an advantage in protection, as its rectangular shape with perfectly straight sides, assembled like a puzzle that created an impenetrable wall, which could not be breached. The shields versatility also gave them the ability to extend to triple times their close combat length, which offered each Angel's entire body full protection without compromising the strength of the material. Even though the lengthier shield resembled a thin pane of glass, its' durability was just as efficient once retracted. With puncture holes that were crafted into the shields located at different areas depending on the length, it was imperative every Angel be aware of the strike zones from which to launch.

At the sight of the Angels advancement, General Bahak, who was awarded the helm of the African Demon Army, deliberated with comrades of similar rank, who overwhelmingly suggested sending forth their archers. With the much larger army at his command, which featured a thousand mutineers who sided with the Devil during their revolt in Heaven, and over four million Dark Warriors engineered for God's war, General Bahak, who felt disrespected by the Angels' advancement, called an all out attack. With the belief that his overwhelming number of fighters would easily overpower their enemies, General Bahak went against the opinions of his peers, who all waited while the lowest ranked Dark Warriors engaged.

"Attack, attack you fools, kill them all, attack, attack!" General Bahak barked.

The Demons from Hell watched the Angels during their advancement and were puzzled by their continued shift in formation, which was not a technique invented or implemented during their lives in Heaven. The entire third row of angels, while advancing, swooped into the air above the soldiers along the front line as another row of Angels joined in behind them. At the completion of their assembly, the Angels had created an impenetrable cocoon as their extended shields fitted together to form the transparent shell. Although several of his peers believed General Bahak should recall the dispatched Dark Warriors, the undeterred General was confident in gaining a victory.

A number of Satan's attackers threw their spears at the approaching targets, which gave the Demons their first inkling of the type defense they were about to face. Despite watching their weapons ricochet off the Angel's shields, which should have served as a lesson causing them to retreat, the brainless fabricated soldiers of Lucifer pressed forward. The Dark Warriors charged profuriously into the impenetrable barrier with their weapons smashing against the Angel's defense. The Universal Warriors responded to their aggression by dispersing and retracting their blades through the secret slots built into the shields, as bodies all along the frontline began crumbling to the ground. Within the protective layer of the cocoon, Angels worked in unison, as some held the structure of the shield, while others slaughtered everything outside.

The Demon's view from their strategic standpoint was somewhat obscured at the beginning of the battle, as the belief was had that their Dark Warriors had broken through the Angels from Heaven barricade. It wasn't until the Angels had begun massacring a significant amount of Dark Warriors, allowing room to advance by stepping on those they had killed, that General Bahak began questioning his decision to call an all out attack. Once the Universal Warriors deciphered the manner with which their foes fought, dismembering them became mere child's play, as they mowed through them like weeds.

The formation of Dark Warriors relentlessly progressed forward, despite their realization of the profligated manner in which their mates were being eliminated. The pictures along the battle-lines were horrendous, as they featured the mutilated corpses of Dark Warriors who had been slaughtered by grand masters. General Bahak watched in disgust as the Universal Warriors decimated their troops, which were terribly outclassed across the field of battle. The level at which their troops were being reduced prompted Bahak to attempt some form of interjection before their entire Dark Warriors unit was wiped out. The General instructed his Army of Demons to take to the sky and distract the focused Angels by launching a barrage of arrows from their position.

At their commander's order, the Demons extended their wings and soared into the sky, where they armed their bows and aimed at specific targets. It was already evident that the Angel's transparent shields were indestructible, thus the Demons from Hell aimed at the sole point they believed vulnerable. A shower of arrows was fired at the protected Angels who were fully engaged against the Dark Warrior. The majority of arrows fired at the Angels missed their target. However, for those which crept through the tiny windows of opportunity, allowed by way of the strike holes built into their shields, the shots were extraordinary, given the distance fired from. Thirteen Angels beneath their protective cocoon were struck with none life-threatening injuries as General Bahak's plot to disrupt the Angel's progression succeeded.

The Commander of the Universal Warriors was not at all pleased with the scrupulous actions of Satan's goons as he flew to the aide of his brethrens. The steady advance of the Angels had temporarily stalled, as those who'd been struck were removed from the formation. Michael and his band of specialists swooped in front of the second onslaught of arrows, to which the Prince of Peace simply waved his hand, causing the arrows to tumble to the ground. Such divine powers was only awarded to the one who holds the staff of command in whom the Heavenly Counsel had favored. Thus, once awarded this prestigious honor, Yahweh himself would then anoint the recipient with mortal powers, which gave him the ability to do supernatural deeds. With the conventional battle strategies tossed out the window, General Bahak and his Demon allies withdrew their swords and prepared for combat as Michael and his strike force honed in on them.

Across from the Angel's battlefield, the savage creatures continued mauling each other with the definite advantage tipping in favor of the animals from Heaven. The two Tyrannosaurus Rex Dinosaurs were the dominators of their battle grounds, and they ensured a level battlefield, where any Saber-tooth Tiger caught in compromising positions could expect help. The first Saber-tooth Tiger killed was ambushed by three carnivorous creatures from Hell, who secluded the animal away from the engaged dinosaurs, before collectively mauling it. Hax, while disfiguring one of the abominations from Hell, caught sight of the ambushed tiger and rushed to his aid, but got there seconds after the decisive blow was struck. The saddened dinosaur immediately retaliated to avenge his fallen ally, as he grabbed the first creature with such force that he immediately broke its spine before tossing it motionlessly to the side. While disfiguring the creature, Hax glimpsed an opportunist rushing towards its leg, to which he used the sharp blades attached to its tail and slaughtered it.

Hax grabbed the second creature responsible for the killing by its right leg as it attempted to scamper away from the dinosaur's clutches. The pressurized force, with which the dinosaur's jaws slammed shut, shattered every bone in the creature's leg, as Hax whipped the creature from side to side until its body tore away from the limb. The creature, after crashing to the ground, uttered a loud groan from the pain, as the Saber-tooth closest grabbed it by the neck and finished the job. Hex whipped his head around to face the third creature, which had been sizing up the dinosaur with intentions of attacking. Before the creature could act on its impulse, a separate saber-tooth blindsided it and latched onto its neck with a detrimental grip, which sent the creature crashing to the ground.

With the abominations from Hell wisely declining to challenge the dinosaurs, the great animals could survey the field, after dismissing their victims, allowing them to locate those in trouble and assist. Hex sited an incident developing where one of their ally was overpowering two creatures, before a third pounced on its back and changed the tide. The shrewd animal took off running towards the skirmish before being interrupted by a creature that had been clawed across the face. Although their encounter was purely coincidental, the injured creature that found itself in the path of the dinosaur had ceased rationalizing whom to tackle, and charged the great animal.

Hex had other immediate concerns, but the challenge before him had to be rectified before any other encounter. With his sibling fully engaged with a crowd around him, the un-intimidated Hex met the disrupter half way as they charged at each other. The irate creature leapt into the air at the dinosaur, which caught it mid air and bit a chunk from its belly, killing the disrespectful beast instantly. With Hex's priority being the wellbeing of his ally, the dinosaur again took off running across the battlefield as scores of conflicts raged around him.

Although the Saber-tooth had shaken off the demon from its back, the odds of success had drastically tipped into the creatures favor; though the saber-tooth showed great courage in refusing to submit. By the time Hex reconvened his journey, the Saber-tooth had fallen in a compromising position, where it firmly latched onto one of the creature's neck, while the second creature sunk its fangs into the Saber-tooth's hind leg. The third creature was intensely circling the battle, as it sought the perfect opening at which to inflict its deadly grip. With the Saver-tooth Tiger continuously turning in its attempt to rid itself of the creature latched onto its leg, the third beast found it difficult to join the engagement.

Hex ran up to the encounter and used his tough head to knock free the creature hanging on, despite previous attempts by the Saber-tooth. The Saber-tooth, after realizing that aid had arrived, released the creature from its jaws, as the beast fell lifelessly to the ground. The Saber-tooth attempted to stand aloft on all four hooves before it was sent crumbling to the ground as a result of its injured hind leg. Hex looked over at his injured ally, who fought desperately to stand on its hooves. Once it was realized that the Saber-tooth's injuries were too severe for it to participate, Hex charged the two responsible culprits, who separated in opposite directions. The dinosaur chased and caught the creature that actually caused the injury, while the second of the two circled back around and unknowingly attacked the injured Saber-tooth.

Once Hex had finished dealing with the creature, the dinosaur sought to attend to the injured Saber-tooth Tiger. At the sight of the illusive creature that escaped its clutches prior, sinking its fangs into the injured Saber-tooth's neck, the dinosaur went berserk and charged at the carnivorous creature. Once the abomination from Hell realized that the dinosaur was again giving chase, the creature sprung to its hooves and took off running across the battlefield. The creature ran frantically around the war zone chased by the dinosaur that refused to quit. Despite all attempts by the creature from Hell to escape, the dinosaur eventually caught up with it and ripped out its intestines.

The Universal Warriors that formed the cocoon reconvened their attack, with a steady march through the menacing Dark Warriors. Those who had been seriously injured during the onslaught of arrows launched by the Demons, emerged from the rear of the cocoon as their mates progressed forward. The Angels rebounded despite having lost eight of their finest warriors. Those inside the cocoon revamped the durability of their protection before proceeding to add additional carnage to the already dispersed field.

The pause in motion by the Angels had given most of the Dark Warriors confidence, as they poured to the frontline craving to spill the blood of their inherited foes. For all their efforts at striking against the indestructible shields of the Angels, the Dark Warriors' only payment was excruciating death by the piercing blades of their enemies. Although the Dark Warriors were extremely valiant in their endeavors, the Angels proved they were in a separate class, as they terrorized the forces of Satan's army.

The Supreme Commander and his band of angels attacked the commanding general of Lucifer's army and his squad of Demons in mid air. At the clash of the most powerful entities on the battlefield, swords echoed in the distance as they collided with each other. Unlike their Dark Warriors siblings, who weren't awarded shields, the Demons carried five feet circular shields, which were constructed from dark metal and had a rigid surface across the front. The battle between the airborne Angels and Demons went fascinatingly different from their allies that fought on the ground, as they individually partnered up and dueled to the death.

The centuries of separation was illustrated by the manner with which both sides fought, as they individually brought different styles of fighting to the conflict. The Angels from Heaven fought like mere images of themselves as they utilized their telepathic capabilities to support each other. Through their telepathic link, each Angel while fighting used the vision of those in the immediate vicinity to serve as their third eye against danger. Thus, while engaged with other opponents, Angels would occasionally move abruptly, at which they would always escape the trauma from some sort of harmful device. The techniques with which the Demons fought were drastically inferior to the opponents, despite the fact they provided more challenge than their Dark Warriors siblings.

The gruesome battle between both sides persisted for another three hours, as the battle between Satan's abominations and Heaven's animals was the first to conclude. At the termination of the first conflict, two Saber-tooth Tigers laid dead with a dozen others injured with deep scratches and bite wounds. Three of the dozen Saber-tooth injured were life threatening injuries, hence the animals rested on the turf to preserve their strength. A number of the animals were compassionate to the point where they actually shed tears over those lost and injured.

The protective cocoon of the Angels was the second victor on the battlefield. The manner with which the Universal Protectors fought was absolute poetry, as their enemies were absolutely confused and disoriented during the attack. Despite their uncertainty, the Dark Warriors never wavered from their attack, as they continuously washed up against the Angels' defense like waves of the ocean. The Universal Defenders' defenses offered them the convenience of striking at their foes; hence, the line of corpses left by the Angels resembled a butcher shop with meat on display. Following the injuries inflicted by the arrow attack, the Angels rebounded and mowed through the entire squad of Dark Warrior without any further injury. After their victory, the majority of Heavenly Warriors stood by watching the air dynamics of their brethrens, who were casting Demons from the air at an incredible rate. Michael and his band of specialists who entered the battle out numbered, had flipped the ratio difference drastically, to where a number of Angels had even become spectators of the battle they'd begun.

The Supreme Commander, after eliminating two Demons, found himself with General Bahak at the tip of his sword. Both Angels personally knew each other, as they'd once spent countless hours joking around as youngsters. Yet, Michael refrained from conversing with the convicted traitors. The Supreme Commander pressed the attack against Satan's General, as he used his skills and agility to overpower the Demon. After being forced on a constant retreat, General Bahak locked swords with Michael and attempted to use the rigid edges of his shield to injure the Commander. Michael blocked the attempt with his shield and managed to knock away the Demon's circular protection at the cost of loosing his shield also. With only their swords at hand, both Angels backed away from each other, as General Bahak surveyed the field of dead Dark Warriors. Satan's first leader tightly gripped his sword with both hands before bravely charging at the Supreme Commander, who patiently timed his attack and sidestepped him before chopping off both hands gripping the sword.

Fearing he was about to be killed, General Bahak hovered stunned while staring at the nubs created by the Supreme Commander. The concept of his massive army being defeated had begun sinking in, as he slowly lifted his head and stared at Michael. The Supreme Commander moved in with his blade held low, as General Bahak vividly inhaled his assumed final breath on Earth. Michael grabbed the trembling General Bahak by the armor and yanked him close to his face, as he stared in the eyes of Satan's commander.

"Fear not Bahak, for I shall not terminate you on this day, in order that you shall be the one to announce to all your master's armies the result of what you've witnessed here today. Let all your master's armies know that the army of their true God is coming, and woo be unto anyone caught across the battlefield from us, for there shall be no others granted mercy. Then finally, take the message to your master himself, and advise him that we'll be along soon!" Michael instructed.

After the Supreme Commander finished dealing with General Bahak, a huge cheer sounded from the victorious Universal Defenders, as Michael immediately saw to the healing of those injured during the battle. The Prince of Peace saw to those severely injured first, as he'd simply place his hand over the wound, close his eyes and concentrate, as his healing powers cured their ails. The Supreme Commander treated Angels and animals, before the army of Heaven began their march towards their next conquest.

Chapter 24

The weather system across the continent of Europe was treacherous, with each separate country, from Iceland to Turkey, all experiencing astronomical events. The entire planet was as dark as if we neglected to pay our hydro bill to which the services had been interrupted. Great Britain received an unprecedented eight feet of snow during the worst blizzard ever recorded in their civilized history. The entire country that had already been under serious duress from the abominations of the Devil, found itself completely buried in snow, as patrons cling to transistor radios for news, while others maintained their constant prayer vigils. With the destructions of satellites out in space, communications and news broadcastings had been interrupted across the globe.

Russia, to the far north, received tennis ball sized hail throughout its European territories. The remarkable phenomenon pulverized vehicle, smashed through windows and glasses and killed several spectators. The pounding of hail against certain roofs and building structures terrified and killed several elders with weaker hearts, as they struck like mini bombs. Several residents, whose roofs had collapsed under the immense pressure, were forced to find alternative shelter beneath durable structures as the hail pelted everything. The powerful hail devastated the affected sections of Russia as it knocked out power transistors and electrical grids that eventually disrupted electricity throughout Moscow and other regions. The force of the hail not only shattered the windows of vehicles, but also pounded huge dents into their frame works. Russians of faith, like Christians around the world, gathered or worshipped privately, as only said humans were confident that the Almighty God had returned.

Ukraine was struck with a 10.3 magnitude earthquake, which was felt as far away east as Paris and as far west as Asia. The biggest earthquake to ever hit the region sent tremors that destroyed ancient and fragile structures, opened huge sink holes along certain streets that swallowed up vehicles, broke dams and reservoirs that initiated flooding and claimed the lives of an undisclosed amount of Ukraine citizens who perished. The magnitude of the earthquake was so powerful, that it destroyed buildings in the surrounding countries of Romania, Belarus, Slovak, Russia and Poland. The devastation forced capable citizens from their homes, despite their fears of being mauled by the abominations of the Devil. Ukrainians who rushed from unstable structures ensured they were fully armed and prepared for the unexpected, as every male and the majority of women who eventually participated in the search for those buried alive, did so with their weapons strapped to their bodies. Throughout the streets of Ukraine, despair and sadness marked the faces of mourners, as God praising worshipers began gathering in groups, where they conducted prayers and mourned.

The Supreme Commander and the rest of his father's army travelled north to Morocco, where they sought to cross over the Mediterranean Sea into Europe. The Heavenly Lord, who watched over his Universal Defenders with the remainder of the Tribunal, waved his hand over their Three Dimensional viewing screen through the floor, which calmed the rough stretch of ocean between Spain and Morocco. With the calm of the Mediterranean, Yahweh also laid out a firm path on which his Angels could walk in order to cross the sea.

While his army crossed the Mediterranean Sea into Europe, the Almighty God in Heaven peered down at the insubordinate humans across the continent, as the Tribunal deliberated over the sort of punishment to be administered. Once a unanimous decision was reached, Yahweh who was given the sanctions pointed his index finger at the screen, before twirling his finger in circles. Everyone on the continent of Europe became mute and deaf, as even the babies were unable to utter a sound to indicate their discontent.

Without the ability to hear or speak for the first time, even the strongest of males broke down to tears, unaccompanied by sound. A second strain of plague was also casted across Europe, as trillions of Cockroaches began flying into cities, towns and villages. The invading insects raided homes and occupied places of humans, as they lurched into cupboards, refrigerators, bedrooms, bathrooms and every areas of human's dwellings. The Cockroaches invaded the food supplies of Europeans, where they contaminated everything possible with infectious diseases. The curse of plagues administered by Yahweh sent a realization of the seriousness of the times.

The underground agents who've devoted themselves to the succession of their Lord Lucifer's Empire, gazed over the annihilation of military and governmental influences throughout Africa, and vowed to protect Europe's weapons of mass destruction from being eradicated. Representatives of the Illuminati Masons, who served the Armed Forces of their countries across Europe, were placed on alert and posted at missile launchers and submachine weapons throughout the various army bases. The soldiers were inserted prior to the infliction of plagues, as news about the wide spread destruction across Africa prompted a different tactic. General Bahak, who's army of five million plus experienced defeat within hours, did as instructed by the Supreme Commander, as he flew to the different continents and delivered the message.

The news of his first line of defense getting defeated was not graciously accepted by the Devil, who received the highlights via courier. Lucifer, who plotted a separate reception for his Heavenly guests on the European continent, asked the spy a number of details. The Devil, after receiving the report, sent commandments to his human alliance and Demonic Forces across Europe indicating the manner with which to engage their enemies.

The moment the Universal Warriors stepped foot on the shores of Spain, their brethrens commenced their raids throughout the countries of Europe. Humans of yesteryear would have considered the events on the island of Great Britain the works of Sorcerers and Black Magic, as, despite the wintery weather, countless Cockroaches ascended on the entire country. Many angry Brits, who found themselves staring through the window after realizing they had been stricken with disability, ran for safety as the already darkened skies became black due to the swarm of Cockroaches.

The surge of Defenders into cities like Manchester, London etc., set off huge explosions that doused each city's skies with thick black smoke rendering certain cities completely dark. The Defenders struck the already paralyzed Great Britain like a demolition ball, as they demolished government infrastructures and leveled skyscrapers across the island. Monuments that served as historic emblems which have existed for centuries; such as Buckingham Palace, where the queen resided, crumbled like condemned buildings slated for demolition as the Defenders sabotaged the support beams before dousing the structures with fireballs. Murals and statues built to commemorate certain individual's achievements were leveled along with infamous structures throughout the island.

One of the world's military superpowers surrendered their dominance without any resistance, as the weather gave the advantage to the Angels. God's protective forces swooped into military bases across the island of Great Britain where they dismantled jet aircrafts, war tanks and every piece of destructive device found throughout. The Angels sought out Missile Silos and underground military facilities that stored and produced chemical and biohazard materials, which they completely destroyed. Police Agencies, Spy Agencies and Private Government Agencies were also destroyed, as the Angels ensure the success of the different phases of transformation.

The country of France, which experienced a deluge of rain, was devastated by severe mudslides and flooding that occurred throughout the region. The mudslides completely wiped out a number of homes and businesses, while the floodings dumped enough water to fill subways stations with levels of water climbing to eight feet in some areas. The Defenders invaded France like gangbusters, as they sought out their assignments and commenced the bombardments. Like every other city visited thus far, edifices from three stories, to the outlandish skyscrapers, crumbled to the ground, as the demolition crews abided the instructions of their creator. Infrastructures like the Eifel Tower were melted to the ground by Angel Defenders who hovered above and dowsed it with fireballs.

A pair of Angels, by the names of Rico and David, was assigned the Luxeuil Air Force Base, located in the northern region, which was an imperative base for the Illuminati placed under the command of one Brigadier General Christophe Maxim. The base was secretively built on top of the Illuminati's command post, from which military and civilian operations are sketched out and assigned. The Illuminati personnel were awarded six Dark Warriors to aid in maintaining the property of their underworld society. Brigadier General Maxim's scheme was to have the Dark Warriors serve as spotters for his six manned sub-machine weapons, which were loaded with bullets specially designed by Hell's engineers. The high powered weapons were then welded onto trailer beds and covered over with camouflage sheeting, to conceal them from the Angels.

Prior to the launch of the Heavenly plagues, the French soldiers were confident in their ability to retain control over the base with the support of their added allies. However, confusion sat in once the first plague took effect, as Brigadier General Maxim found himself unable to command his forces. The commander, who was stationed inside the flight tower along with four other officers, used sign language to communicate, but there was no means of conveying his orders to the troops around the base. Indecisiveness caused Brigadier General Maxim to react stupidly, as he activated the compound's emergency warning system, which caused the red emergency lights to flash while sounding the compound's loud horns.

The technician around the monitors jumped to her feet and pointed directly up to the clouds, which had become black with the gathering of cockroaches. At the sight of the dark skies filled with insects, the commander ran over to a glass casing that housed the gas masks, shattered the glass and quickly fitted one to his face before passing out the others. Everyone inside the air traffic tower paused and awaited the effects of the swarm of cockroaches, as the rain continued to fall heavily across the region. At the sight of several cockroaches sticking to the exterior of the tower glass, the sole female inside the tower began convulsing as if she suffered from some sort of phobia. The Brigadier General and staff members began intently checking around to ensure that the little critters didn't find an entrance point that might have invited them into the closed tower. One of the male technicians ran over to a tiny hole in the floor where a cockroach was squeezing its way through and stumped the critter before it made its way inside. While the technician attempted to clog the hole, others searched patiently before it was pointed out that there was a liberated insect flying freely about the tower.

"Find the hole it came through, I'll try to kill it!" said the Brigadier General to another technician. Within seconds the single cockroach had multiplied, as the little critters found entry into the shell of the tower before emerging through section of the aviation monitors.

The soldiers, who manned the submachine weapons around the base, were comfortably awaiting the Demolition Angels when the flashing lights of the compound's alarm placed them on high alert. In each of the gunner's cases, the soldiers only began aware of their disability when they realized they were incapable of hearing the loud sirens. The "call to duty" nature of these soldiers saw them ignore their personal emotions and prepared for conflict.

As determined as the soldiers were despite their lack of hearing or speech, the invasion of the cockroaches placed them in a different mind state. The Dark Warriors, who were so huge they had to sit alongside the trailer beds, were by no way bothered by the insects, which crawled underneath the clothing of soldiers and disrupted them. The pestering insects caused four of the six soldiers to pounce from their seats, as they swarmed the camouflaged tents and everything inside. Some of the shooters attempted to rid themselves of the insects, which were pitching on people and crawling all over them.

The Fifty Caliber Submachine weapon to the northeast of the compound began rapidly disbursing, as the Dark Warrior spotted the approaching Angels and pointed them out to his shooter. The Angels, who were approximately a quarter of a mile away from the compound, swerved through the streams of oncoming bullets, as they made their way towards the Air Force Base. When they neared the fence, a second weapon to the north opened fire from its camouflaged position, which informed the Defenders to be weary of the portable huts positioned at certain junctions around the base. Both Defenders separated and branched off with reservations, while other weapons around the compound blasted at them continuously.

The lightening quick Angels moved with such agility, that the sharp shooters of the Brigadier General could not follow the pace to which they maneuvered. The Dark Warriors that were assigned to serve as the gunners' spotters grew frustrated with their sharp shooters' incapability to hit the targets, which they alone had the ability to see. Rico, who had swerved off to the left, came up under the scope of the northeastern weapon, which was the radar that announced their approachment. The Angel who had been developing a fire ball in the palm of his right hand, maneuvered through bullets that appeared to be travelling at speed far slower than that of Angels. After developing an adequate platform from which to fire, Rico launched his intended fire ball at the camouflaged structure from which a Dark Warrior took off running before the impending destruction.

Rico telepathically linked David and advised him about their unexpected guests. With the knowledge that aid was being awarded to the humans, both Defenders elevated their tactical schemes and became more aggression in their attacks. The idea of a more challenging competition stimulated the Angels' competitive spirit, as they wagered against each other on who would "take out" the most opponents. With Rico's advanced score calculated, David, who had positioned himself to annihilate the northern Fifty Caliber Submachine Weapon, tossed a pair of fireballs at the bullet-spitting contraption. The fireballs struck the camouflaged trailer bed and sat the gunner on fire, as the Dark Warrior who assisted the burning soldier callously walked away. David began moving to confront the Dark Warrior, when the Fifty Caliber Weapon to the southwest that had been spitting bullets at him, pieced his right wing with a shot. The wound sent a pain through David since each Angel's wings are an extension of their bodies.

"Are you alright my brother?" Rico asked, sensing something wrong through their telepathic link.

"I will be as soon as we've destroyed of this place." David reported, as he charged at his second weapon.

The injured Angel challenged the shooter aboard the submachine weapon, as he dodged and weaved through the spitting bullets, while quickly closing the distance between them. David rushed his nemesis with such agility that by the time the spotter recognized his intentions; the Angel had decimated the gunner with a humongous fireball and was inches from severing its head. David the Defender disposed of the southwest defense and believed that his latest conquest had gained him the edge over Rico in their friendly wager.

"That's two my way youngster, looks like you need to catch up!" David boasted.

"Only two son; I thought you were keeping up with your elders?" Rico declared.

"Don't tell me that?" David commented.

"That's right baby, three down to your two! I believe you need to play catch up!" Rico joked.

By the time David got to the last Fifty Caliber Submachine gun, the operators of the weapon were busy popping bullets at his co-combatant. With all the attention being paid to Rico, David found time to survey the base, while formulating the fireball necessary to destroy his enemies. Once the fireball in the palm of his hands grew to a sizable dimension, David flung it at the camouflaged trailer bed, which exploded upon impact. The gunner aboard the submachine weapon was killed instantly and his partner staggered away dazed and engulfed in flames. Without knowledge on procedures to extinguish flames, the Dark Warrior burnt to death as it staggered about fanning the fire from its burning fresh.

The Angels, after ridding the base of all its security, went about demolishing the buildings, hangers and equipments of war as ordered. Commander Jeffrey Fawcett and his flight crew were still grounded with their aircraft commandeered inside Hanger E, which was on the Angel's list for destroying. Following their hijacking ordeal, which the French officials dismissed with claims they received their missiles, hence 'no harm no foul'; the American flight crew received one unexpected delay after the other. The destruction of Intelligence Satellites in outer space had interrupted communications between Commander Fawcett's Purolator Team and their command station in the U.S. The Americans' problems were then compounded by the eruptions of some of the world's deadliest volcanoes, plus the most disastrous weather systems ever simultaneously experienced worldwide, which resulted in their flight privileges being cancelled.

Following their ordeal, the Americans remained aboard their aircraft, which was the only place either of the men felt comfortable. Hence, the curse of the plagues caught them in a celebrative mood, as they were confident that the missile concept had destroyed the threatening planet. In the spirit of celebrating the Americans popped out a deck of cards and began enjoying a game of Poker, before they realized that they had been strickened with multiple disabilities. At the realization that they were incapable of speaking or hearing, the Americans faulted the French, whom they assumed to be responsible for their newly acquired handicap. Fearing the worst, Commander Fawcett moved to the closest window and peeked out into the empty hanger, where the only thing operational was an emergency siren attached to the wall. Jeffrey motioned over the remainder of the crew in order to get their impressions, which led to a decision to revolt and take off without permission.

The commander and another soldier snuck from the C-17 Globe Master armed and prepared to kill should anyone attempt to halt their intentions. Pilot Osborn, who was skeptical about the plane being able to generate enough thrust to lift off because of the water levels outside had begun firing up the engines in preparation for flight. The water level inside the hanger was high enough to rattle loose the holding planks, which was used block the tires of the aircraft. The water was up to the soldier's calves as they cautiously looked around, while moving to the remote opener against the wall. Fawcett stood guard, while his companion edged his way over to the controls, while the Defender David, on the opposite side of the door, concocted the fireballs required for demolition. The humongous hanger door rose to the soldier's thighs, at which a huge ball of fire blew into the hanger and struck one of the right engines of the Globe Master. Although the Air Force Base sounded like a war zone, where bombs were exploding randomly, the disabled Americans were incapable of hearing any of it, as other fireballs struck the structure at other sections. The C-17 Globe Master exploded, at which everyone aboard was instantly killed and both soldiers blasted out onto the tarmac. Commander Fawcett was crippled by the by blast, which also terribly injured his companion.

Rome looked like a decimated city after the clouds opened up and drenched its territories with acid rain. The phenomenon was never before witnessed throughout the European Continent, as residents were amazed to see the hazardous chemicals falling from the skies. The chemical rain horribly scorched a number of Romans as they inquisitively snuck their hands out beneath the rainfall to test its effects against the skin. Such daredevils all sustained second degree burns, which scorched away their skin. The catastrophic rainfall killed an unprecedented amount of animals, birds, humans and other living creatures, which were dissolved to nothing by the toxic fluid. The massive destruction brought on by the rainfall left the region crippled without hydropower, drinking water and every natural resource necessary for the survival of mankind.

Pastor Lester, who had made his way back to the Vatican, had reported his findings to the Pope by presenting him with a few priceless truncates from the crashed trailer. The Canadian pastor, with all the killings occurring around the city, made a calculated gamble and adorned one of the uniforms being worn by the trailer's occupants, which aided him in returning to the Vatican. The Pope, who was already saddened by the massacre that occurred, dropped the items to the ground and brought both hands to his face in disgust, and he wept profoundly. At the sight of the Pope's gesture, the High Priests responsible for the treachery gathered together and exited the room, as Pastor Lester bowed to his Eminence and walked to the Cathedral to pray and assist those who needed help. While assisting the injured pilgrims inside the Cathedral, Pastor Lester was humbled at the sight of the Pope and his entourage, who attended to help strengthen those who were in despair.

During Pope Desmond Author's sermon, the Heavenly plagues descended on the continent and immediately interrupted his address, as the disability caused everyone inside the church to begin looking around confused. Everyone inside the church dropped to their knees, whether they were at the alter or seated comfortably, once the realization of what transpired sunk in. The abominations from Hell had long departed and the acid rain rescinded, as the cockroaches began invading Rome and all her territories.

The Defender Angels of Heaven swooped into the historic city of Rome with their demolition orders in hand. As they had done since stepping foot on the shores of Italy, the Defenders proceeded to dismantle government and privately owned buildings, Iconic Statues, murals, skyscrapers and defensive infrastructures. The Defenders leveled the airports, financials institutes, government agencies, gas stations and a number of other facilities. Both the clergy members and their pilgrim worshipers huddled inside the St. Peter's Cathedral perished, as the huge walls caved in from the fireballs of Defenders. The Roman army, which was incapable of mounting any sort of defense, faced the same judgment as Great Britain, which had its entire armed forces completely decimated by the servants of God.

Chapter 25

General Bahak, after completing the assignment awarded him by Arch Angel Michael, reconvened with his profoundly outraged master, who had relocated his forces to Antarctica. The armless General flew into Lucifer's camp, which was busy with Demon and Dark Warriors scurrying about aimlessly. The snow beneath General Bahak's feet was soft and powdery, which was the last thing he observed before being placed under guards. The two guards, who advised General Bahak he was being held under Lucifer's orders, directed him towards their master's tent, which was the most extravagant and lavished dwelling throughout camp. Every servant of Satan they passed along the way turned their head aside in disgust, as word had spread about the defeated General's treachery. The guards brought General Bahak into their king's royal domain, where they tossed him to the ground in the middle of the tent.

"I have failed you my king! I beg your forgiveness as I've underestimated the --." insighted General Bahak, who fought to maneuver himself onto his knees.

"Silence! You have more than failed me Bahak, to the point of disgrace. I instructed you to return should you fail; yet you've chosen to do the task of a mailman. If fear was the motivation behind your actions, then let me remind you exactly how revered I am." Lucifer threatened, as he waved his hand, signaling his goons to confine the General.

General Bahak, who refused to be disposed of like garbage, pounced to his feet and stumped the closest guard in the chest, who approached from the right. Despite his recent handicap, the General proved his vigor for fighting hadn't diminished as he swung around and kicked the second guard across the face. Both guards went tumbling, as Bahak generated enough strength in his legs to thrust himself off the ground and into the air. In order to escape the shell of the tent, General Bahak made himself invisible, at which he was able to pass through the barrier. At the sight of his condemned commander escaping, Lucifer grabbed a whip that hung from the side of his chair and lassoed the General around the right ankle after Bahak had cleared through the shell and was well on his way to escaping. With one hand holding the whip sturdy, Lucifer dragged the General back down to Earth, where he crashed down in the very same spot from which he'd departed.

With the opportunity to disrupt the Natural Balance of the Universe and alter the prophecies of his demise, Lucifer, over the centuries, had elevated his combat skills to the plateau of being invincible amongst his peers. The Devil illustrated his astonishing quickness as he withdrew his sword and removed the General's head from his shoulders. After disposing of the General, Lucifer twirled his sword around impressively, before cramming it into its holster. General Bahak's body vanquished like the invisible air before Satan returned to his high chair and calmly sat down.

Lucifer's entire Demonic forces across Europe gathered in Austria, where the second battle in the War of Revelations was marked to unfold. A number of the Devil's abominations from his dungeons were killed in different sections of Europe, such as Italy, where Lightening strikes physically destroyed power plants; ignited oil reserves stations etc. and Germany, which was the only European country that experienced stones the size of Golf ball drenched in Solphuric Acid falling like rain. The mortality rate in certain countries was significantly higher than others, as the severity of the attacks varied. The skies over Austria were lit up like fire works caused by sever thunder prior to the arrival of God's angels, where the temperatures surrounding the battlefield transformed to a more suitable climate. The destructive weather that struck certain areas made the Defender's tasks rather easy, as they simply swooped in and exterminated what else remained standing.

The soldiers from Hell, particularly the Dark Warriors, had to battle through the elements as they marched towards the battlefields, while the trail ahead of the Universal Warriors continually lightened prior to them passing through. Through all their turmoil along the journey, the forces of Satan still posed the more impressive display across the battlefield, as the Universal Army resembled a small flock in comparison to the much larger herd. The Militant Warriors across the different lines of Hell's army were eager to engage their enemies, as Dark Warriors were fearless zombie fighters. Once the Universal Defenders got in range of Satan's abominations discrete sense of smell, the creatures became irritated and began pacing about the grounds, as they roared and growled impatiently.

The Supreme General Kane, who was the highest ranked soldier in Lucifer's army, was awarded the honor of defending the continent of Europe. Despite having at his disposal a quarry of heartless mercenaries who weren't hesitant to tackle or brawl, the Demons who used their puppeteers to strengthen their forces and disguise their tactics, were extremely nervous after learning about General Bahak's defeat. To avoid falling under the same fate as General Bahak, Supreme General Kane separated his command into five sections, where he entrusted a million Dark Warriors to four of his fiercest Demons. Kane also evenly divided the Demons entrusted to him, as he arranged the different armies in front of his personal command, which remained in reserves to the rear.

At the sight of Supreme General Kane's attempt to diversify his troops, Michael smirked to himself, as both armies engaged in their customary stare-down. Michael who at one time may have challenged the Devil's entire regiment with only a hand full of Jehovah's Angels, was confident in his father's legions as he summoned four of his highest ranked brothers. The Angels who received the summons immediately presented themselves to their Commander, who sought to prepare for his opponent's battle strategy.

"Someone should really go over there and tell those guys that they are really scary looking all spread out like that!" Commander Rhovon joked.

"Shut up you fool!" Commander Jahvon remarked.

"I vote we throw Rhovon over there so he can go tell them!" Commander Shakeem injected.

"Can't you imbeciles stop playing around for once, business is on the table." Commander Lecouvie stated.

"I see no reason for us to disappoint our friends, so let's incorporate their style and defeat them with it." Michael dictated.

"Hail!" cheered all the Commanders, who appeared thrilled at the disclosure.

Michael the Arch Angel instructed his Commanders on their alignment across the battlefield before reclining to the rear of battle to simulate his opponent's commander. The sight of an entire army separating without loud barking instructions or an organizer showing everyone where to move was marvelous to behold, as the Angels used their telepathic communications to instruct their personnel where to go. The maze of confusion that developed while the Angels reorganized their entire forces was abrupt, as their bewildered foes across the battlefield pondered the attacking. At the end of their coordinated shuffle, the Universal Defenders had properly matched up against the rivals, as they had created five separate armies to counter the Devil's forces.

"My brothers of Heaven, the Universal Creator our father has led us here to continue our march towards expelling these evil forces from this planet. As we have made an example of their allies before them, so shall they also realize that we alone are the undisputed champions of this Universe. No other being across this vast Universe is subjected to the submissive laws that Lucifer has enslaved these humans with. Look there, in front of you at the great lengths this wanna be God has gone to, to ensure victory in order that everything remains as they are. These fighting Zombies are an insult to us all, because none of them deserve the privilege to stand against the absolute best that this Galaxy has to offer. We alone are the true defenders of this Universe, our compassion and love for all the creatures our father has created is why we are here; they shall forever be wiped out, as we will dominate!" Michael dictated to his troops, who stood poised while facing their nemesis.

"Dominate-dominate-dominate---!" repeatedly shouted the Universal soldiers, whose continued chants heightened their fighting spirits.

The animals from Heaven remained vigilant, heeding the words of the Supreme Commander, who was almost a mile away. While the dinosaur led pact of tigers savored the inspirational deliverance of the Supreme Commander, their carnivorous opponents growled and paced the grounds beneath their paws, as they eagerly awaited the battle horn. At the loud utterance of the Angels, a creature from amongst Satan's carnivores set off the clash as it went charging at a section of Saber Tooth Tigers. Seeing the creature's charge, a Saber Tooth from the midst rushed at the beast and they collided in a heap of rage.

At the clash of the dueling creatures, their companions eagerly engaged and the carnage that occurred on the first battlefield got resumed. The huge creatures that began the ordeal met violently as they leapt at each other, before crashing to the ground fully engulfed with deadly claws tearing into each other. While both creatures attempted to sink their fangs into the other, the Saber Tooth's lengthy front fangs caused more damage, and they ripped its opponent at every twist. It became impossible for either creature to release the other, as they'd both sunken their claws to depths that made it difficult to extract. The creature from Satan's abyss grabbed at the Saber Tooth's neck, although its mediocre grip was quickly broken as the Saber Tooth jiggled its neck from the creature's clutches. Freeing its neck from the creature's grip came at a price, as the Saber Tooth felt the agony of having skin ripped from its neck. The Saber Tooth retaliated by sinking its fangs into the creature, which immediately became submissive by the paralyzing grip.

The Saber Tooth Tiger clutched onto the creature's neck until every breath of life exited its body. Once the animal was confident that its opponent was deceased, it then released its pressure jaws and dropped the beast to the ground. Almost instantly another beast pounced onto the weakened Saber Tooth and latched its powerful jaws around the animal's neck. The injured animal let out a loud sigh, as the creature controlled it with the same detrimental grip it used to kill its prior opponent. As the breath of life squeezed from the Saber Tooth's body, the animal hazily noticed something huge rushing towards it, as unconsciousness crept in.

Zoe the Dinosaur interrupted the creature's trophy kill, as it witnessed the tragedy about to unfold and raced in to alter the events. The Dinosaur attacked from the creature's blind side, where it used the blades along its powerful tail to slice the creature across the face. The sharp jolt of pain that Satan's abomination felt, caused it to immediately release the animal from its jaws, as it went staggering into another creature that was lodged in a chokehold. After slicing off a fraction of the creature's face, Zoe was confident that his first strike had done the job, as it began surveying the area to ensure there were no lingering threats. The concerned dinosaur was about to tend to its injured ally, when through its right peripheral it sighted a creature lunging at the immobilized Saber-Tooth. Zoe swung its humongous body around with its tail aimed directly at the attacking creature's trousseau, which resulted in the beast getting both its forelegs completely severed by the blades attached to the dinosaur tail. The Heavenly animals had grown accustomed to the conniving tactics of their scavenging opponents, who sought any means to expunge the life force of their adversaries.

The huge disparity in numbers overwhelmed the second of the Devil's commanders. With his forces divided equally across the battlefield, the Supreme General Kane instructed his second officer to sound the battle trumpets, at which the four armies before him began their engagement. The inspiration soldiers obtain from psyching themselves up with a colossal chant before jumping into battle was a mental motivational tool the Dark Warriors lacked in their arsenal due to their incapability to speak. Hence, the thundering stomping of their feet shook the ground and replaced their volatile war chant with Earth tremors.

With the Dark Warriors rushing in, the Supreme Commander gave the orders for his troops to commence launching arrows over at the attackers, which maintained their formations. The Angels of the fifth battalion began hurling arrows over the heads of their colleagues, which resulted in the elimination of several Dark Warriors. With their different battle formations formed, the Universal Warriors patiently awaited their approaching enemies. The Zyclynx Shields of the Angels, which awarded them adequate protection, were fastened like a welded gate, while their sharp blades stood ready to pierce armor.

The four Commanders who were awarded the task of leading the different platoons, all began communicating with their individuals platoon members. The surgical precision with which the Angels fought required keen concentration and dynamic skill. The dark shadow that was Lucifer's army crept up on the well-structured Angels like nightfall before the loud sounds of a violent collision occurred. The diverse complexity of Hell's army, which was mixed with an assortment of Dark Warriors and Demons, had the Demons entangled amongst the Dark Warriors from the fourth rows to the rear of each army.

At the initial clash, the defense of the Angels again proved its durability, as the Dark Warriors that smacked into the wall expressed a look of surprise once they realized the impenetrability of the wall they had ran into. The Dark Warriors smacked up against the Angel's Zyclynx shields as if they had ran into a brick wall, as their different lines of fighters kept adding to the confusion. The Angels remained unfazed by the mounting pressures until they had accumulated up to five lines of soldiers pressing against their shields. With their foes pressed up against them, the Angels flexed their muscles and sent everyone on the opposite side of their shields flying.

The Angels across the field, who were tucked inside their protective huts, began unexpectedly launching arrows at their opponents through the visors in their shields. Although fired from close range, the impact of the arrows lifted and tossed the Dark Warriors across the front lines into the arms of their colleagues, who tossed them aside and again rushed their opponents. Instead of the same defensive stance, the Angels began carving up their foes like butchers, as their marquee fighting techniques began to dominate the battlefield. The Angels' tactical compositions, which were built around solid defense, had personnel maneuvering inside the shell who kept their offense unconventional with abrupt launches of arrows and other methods.

Although the Devil's Demons offered up more competition than their Dark Warriors allies, they also proved no match for their ex-siblings, who removed the heads of every Demon they battled. Within the first hour of the battle, Supreme General Kane had lost his confidence and became enraged at the rate his armies were being dismantled. Despite their being triumphed over by a more sophisticated army, the fearless Dark Warriors continued advancing against their foes, who were poised and energized to eradicate every single member of their opponents' team.

The battle between the Heavenly animals and the creatures of Satan's dungeons was in full flight as the savagery that transpired across their field complimented the brutality on the battlefield of the Angels. The sight of exposed intestines scattered across the red dirt fields on which they fought, demonstrated that the once equally matched conflict drastically, favored the dominating dinosaur led pact. Zoe, who refused to abandon the critically injured Saber Tooth Tiger, had fought and protected the weakened tiger throughout the carnage, as other creatures sought to finish the expiring animal. The dinosaur had to prance to the aid of the injured animal several times as Satan's carnivorous creatures sought an easy prey. Thanks to Zoe the Saber Tooth actually survived the ordeal, despite being mauled several times by a number of creatures.

The intensity in each battle waged was as deadly as the previous, as the creatures, unlike their colleagues, fought like scavengers. The vast amount of Heavenly animals injured during the battle, were wounded by third party affiliates. There were instances where Satan's atrocities were confronted with Saber Tooth Tigers and abandoned their opponent to attack an alternate foe, which had its back to the creature as it concentrated on the challenge before it. Thus, it appeared every creature involved in the beast battle was integrated into a massive brawl, where any creature without its rear protected was a potential target. The creatures of Satan's abyss proved their worth in battle, utilizing every treachery known to sway the results in their favor; yet at the end of the conflict their entire pact laid decimated about the grounds.

The Universal Defender's Supreme Commander and his band of specialists took to the air and flew towards Satan's European Commander. Michael and his associates landed approximately twenty feet from the fifth and final European regime, where they formed their famous cocoon before reconvening their attack. Although the projections across the Angelic battlefield pointed to a second victory for the invaders from Heaven, Kane was delighted to see Michael's command pursuing his band, as he knew the rewards of eliminating God's chosen leader. Michael immediately became the objective, as Supreme General Kane confirmed his desire in eradicating the platoon and killing Jehovah's son.

"Advise your friends to target their attention at their leader, while these nuisances of ours distract everybody else!" Kane informed his second in command, whom he expected to telepathically relay the message.

"Attack you fools!" the Supreme General barked at the Dark Warriors under his command, who responded by charging at the Angels.

With the shields of the Angels being clear, maintaining a visibility on the Supreme Commander proved not to be a problem, although Michael made the task much easier by fighting along the front line. The Supreme Commander, who led his specialists, was the first to thrust his spear in a Dark Warrior's stomach as the final European battle raged on. The knowledge that Michael's death would count as a modest victory for their furor flamed the fighting spirit of the fifth army, which had lost all passion for conflict after watching their allies get conquered.

The Angels, like their colleagues across the battlefield, wasted no time at shredding the less experienced Dark Warriors, as they persistently advanced without fear. The specialists, with whom Michael fought, were equally up to the task of slaying Demons, as they relished their work and the purpose it represented. After ridding himself of his first two Dark Warriors, Michael, who had noticed the Demons infiltrating the battles around the firth rows, was astonished to find a Demon attacking him as early as the third row. The fearless Prince of Peace fought nothing but Demons from them on, as Satan's worshippers lined up to challenge the most powerful being on the battlefield. Once the remainder of his colleagues began tackling other Demons, evidence of their progression began to be obvious before Michael found, at his blade's tip, the commander for the troops of whom they fought. The Angels maintained their fighting formations until they had diminished their opponents to a small number then they broke formation and individually tackled those who remained.

The Supreme Commander, who used his finesse and cunning instead of raw power to gain his victory, dominated General Kane, who was physically less strong than the other leaders of Lucifer's armies. Michael met blades with the first human who befell Satan's cunning misconceptions of wealth and power, as the two commanders came together and exchanged unpleasant greetings before the actual contest. Kane stared in the eyes of Jehovah's anointed son and said, "this world will not be taken from my master", as Michael assured him that his 'master will be none existent as he will', before shoving him aside. Following the momentary separation, Michael rushed General Kane with a series of chops aimed at disarming him, before connecting with a surprising blow that sliced a long cut in the General's thigh. The pain from the cut caused Supreme General Kane to loose focus on the contest, which was all Michael needed as he swooped in and removed his head.

Once every Demon was eliminated from the field of battle, a triumphant roar sounded between the fields of Angels and animals. Almost immediately the sense of hurt from those injured befell onto the Supreme Commander, who went around and administered healing to those in need. The Angels, who were on a mission to eradicate every Demon from the face of the Earth, suffered minor wounds during the battle, which they dominated before pressing on to Asia.

Chapter 26

The continent of Asia was devastated by the crippling weather that struck across its territories, leaving many in disarray, frightened and unsure about their survival. With the different bodies of water, such as the Bering Sea, The Sea of Japan, The Pacific Ocean, The Indian Ocean, The Persian Gulf and The Red Sea all rumbling to treacherous levels, islands like the Philippines, Taiwan, Japan and others became susceptible to Tsunami type waves. Evidence of the chaos succumbed to by the entire Earth, was visible by the destroyed boats and marinas along the seashores, as even tankers and larger vessels out at sea were overturned by the rumbling ocean.

One of the oldest civilizations on Earth, the People's Republic of China was bombarded by five hours of scorching lava balls at the commencement of the treacherous weather, followed by a steady drizzle of light rain. The skies resembled a magnificent fire works display as the scorching Lava Balls fell. The unprecedented event that occurred throughout the biggest communist country in the world, devastated cities from Qiqihar down to Tibet, and killed every abomination of Satan's dungeons which had been terrorizing the Chinese people throughout. Despite the soothing rains that followed the lava showers, the burning particles that fell from the skies remained for hours after crashing to the ground; hence scores of infrastructures were destroyed within the first few hours of the Lava Balls Showers. A plan to secure one of the world's largest military surpluses by

Illuminati worshipers was thwarted by the unexpected Lava Ball flurries, which engulfed everything beneath China's dark skies. Explosions erupted at several facilities that stored chemical and biological agents, gas stations and ammunition depots, as entire cities were transformed into deserted ghost towns.

The skies over Saudi Arabia were as dark as midnight, while freezing rain and winter-like conditions engulfed the entire region. At a time during the day when the sun was typically bright in the centre of the sky, the people of Saudi Arabia wondered if things would ever return to normal, as they gathered together around fires to keep warm. Their neighbors in Yemen and the surrounding Arab Nations, which weren't accustomed to such temperatures, endured freezing climates as the thermostat dropped to record lows. The Saudis, who were mainly people of faith, were imprisoned in their own homes by the carnivorous creatures from Hell, which would also attack lives stock like camels and sheep. A large number of Arabs, who were inherently passionate about their camels and horses, were either killed by the Devil's abominations or the blasphemous freezing weather, as they did whatever possible to save the lives of their valued animals. While the majority of Arabs throughout the region flocked to their burning fires and blankets, others devoted their time to praying to Allah for his will to be done, which they perceived would free them from their eminent punishment.

The Country of India, with all its natural resources, impoverished slums and large population, was crippled by the fury of an Ice Storm, where hail the size of tennis balls smashed to the Earth. The height, from which the ice balls fell, caused them to crash to the ground like mini bombs, as they immediately knocked out and killed anyone caught within the fury. The dangerously hurling ice balls slayed several of Satan's creatures, which were caught within the region after the hail had began falling. Amongst the Asian nations, India surrendered the most victims to Satan's abominations, which found easy pickings throughout the slums where malnourished and homeless individuals lay weakened about the streets. Indians who were tucked inside their homes, prayed diligently to their various Gods as they gathered together to accumulate body heat. The -45 Degree Celsius temperatures that accompanied the ice ball storm, was so frigid that the majority of elderly and the young died within the first fifteen minutes. The frigid cold that encompassed the country reached perilous degrees that had never been experienced by most North American wintery countries. Hence, even though the very wealthy within the region suffered tremendously, it was the impoverished Indians who felt the blunt of the storm.

Countries that promoted the worship of idols witnessed excruciating weather systems, which destroyed infrastructures and killed millions of people. Residents along the eastern shores of the Island of Japan were riveted by torrential tidal waves, which destroyed the entire coastline. The second largest economic country in the world experienced cosmic tidal waves that gushed in from the Pacific Ocean with fifty foot high waves that bashed the island continuously. While the oceans grumbled, the dark skies above electrified with lightening strikes, which caused several disastrous episodes to unfold on the ground. Lightening strikes struck imperative facilities like power plants, oil reserve plants and defensive missile silos, which all exploded and expanded the devastation. The bomb dropped by the United States on Hiroshima was a simple cut wound in comparison to the devastation brought on by Mother Nature. Japan, like every other nation affected thus far, resembled only a shell of itself, as its survivors prayed to their individual Gods for mercy.

With the Creator's demolition forces of Defenders screeching into Asia followed by his Universal Police, Yahweh waved his hand over the high definition floor viewing, which brought the distort continent onto the screen. The Heavenly Tribunal was thus far pleased with the manner with which the invasion had unfolded, as they acknowledged video clips of the ravaged Earth, while deliberating over the sorts of punishments to implement upon the people of Asia. While the panel deliberated, Yahweh looked about the continent at the creatures of Satan's army, which emerged from the different bodies of oceans prior to reuniting with the remainder of their allies.

Yahweh opened two other screens like television sets, which highlighted the perils being endured by humans of the continents already reclaimed. The people of Africa battled turbulent climates, as the red flowing waters formed monstrous streams where entire communities were ravaged with floodwaters. Areas in Africa, such as the Deserts of Congo, Kenya and other places where wintery climates unleashed their venom, exhibited animals and other creatures crumbling to the ground, as their source of nourishments was covered with snow, their water holes frozen with the poisonous red liquid and temperatures way below sustainable levels. The people of the African Nations were scavenging for food in their different places as people, watched the fruits on their trees wither away before their very eyes. Mothers, who were accustomed to breast-feeding their infants, were astonished to find white powdery substance seeping from their breast instead of the desired milk, as babies began dying of starvation and thirst. Despite the perils being endured by humans across the many countries, Yahweh was pleased to observe God fearing worshipers still congregated either in churches, private homes or public forums. Throughout the territories, the only thing evident on the faces of humans, regardless of creed, race or class, was their heartfelt pain and regret for not adhering to the warning signs that foretold Jehovah's return.

The people of Europe faired no different from those in neighboring Africa, as the nation's agony persisted. The swirling winds off the shores of Italy and Greece created tornado systems along the Mediterranean coastline, which eradicated everything along their path. The swirling high winds from the Mediterranean Sea, combined with the unstable systems on the Ionian Sea and the Tyrrhenian Sea, propelled detrimental tornados across Italy, where cities like Ragusa, Catania, Marsala, Trapani and others throughout the country, were devastated by huge funnel clouds swirling dangerous winds. The same horrific systems caused the country of Greece great despair, as cities like Pygos, Pireas, Vlore, Glyfada, Volos and Kalamata were ravaged. The Holy Monasteries, where only monks are allowed to dwell along the coast of Athina, were all destroyed by tornados, which removed the very foundations on which such proclaimed tabernacles of the Lord were built. The different calamities throughout the individual cities, along with the provocation of the plagues, proved humbling even for the anarchists of God's Government, who bowed and prayed for the Lord's retribution to end. Despite the global plea by humans for mercy, Yahweh ignored the cries of even his most devout worshipers, as the father continued scolding his children.

Once the Heavenly Tribunal arrived at their decision, the sanctions against Asia were passed onto the Devine Lord who simply pointed his index finger at the continent and swirled it around six times. At the casting of the Asian plagues, people across its territories began experiencing huge boils growing on their skins, which made basic tasks like sitting, laying down or even standing painful. The boils infected people from their hair scalps to the soles of their feet, and increased in dimension until they eventually burst and transformed into huge soars, leaving citizens already in despair utterly traumatized. Trillions of Dragonflies, accompanied by similar amounts of Blue and Golden Poison Dart Frogs, which are considered amongst the world's venomous reptiles, ascended onto the entire continent. Swarms of Dragonflies swooped down from the clouds, though in most cases the forceful wind simply carried them to their destinations, where they aggravated citizens across the continent by landing directly on their newly acquired lacerations. The Poison Dart Frogs brought a different element to the bewildered people, most of whom had never encountered such venomous reptiles. Honored guests and those stranded in elaborate hotels like The Burj Al Arab, located on the edge of the Persian Gulf, witnessed actual frogs falling from the skies, which attached themselves to window panes and other building materials while seeking entry. Once the Poison Dart Frogs gained entry into the ravaged homes, citizens found themselves at the mercy of the reptiles, which appeared intent on attacking humans. Eruptions of gunfire sounded across the territories as patrons fought to keep the venomous reptiles at bay.

With nearly the entire world set ablaze, clouds of smoke shot up into the atmosphere over every horizon, as it became difficult to breathe in overpopulated cities where the air circulation was minimal. The deadly gasses that escaped from hazardous refineries across the nations added to the mortality rate, which climbed globally by the second. The vast amount of Defenders assigned to Russia swept across the dual continent from Europe into Asia with the continuation of their eradication orders. As vast as the lands of Russia, so too were the many complex targets that the Defenders were assigned to destroy.

The people of Chokurdah, which is a small town built five miles from one of the world's largest Nuclear Power Plant, were annihilated when the Russian plant was destroyed by the Defenders assigned to the task.

Their individual government had cautiously shut down other Nuclear Power Plants across the invaded continents, but attempts to shut down the Chokurdah Nuclear Power failed after increased activities from other reactors going off line caused the reactor to reach dangerous radiation levels and refused to cool. At the eruption of the nuclear power plant, massive nuclear radiations spread into the atmosphere and infected Russians for hundreds of miles with radiation poisoning. With the destruction of the Republic of Sakha's Nuclear Power Plant, the entire zone became pitch black, as a deluge of smoke blackened the region for miles. The unexpected colossal explosion simplified the Defenders assignments as their targets were destroyed by the nuclear type eruption. The oxygen levels dropped dangerously low, as the high altitude of Russia's landscape reduced the already minimal air supply. Hundreds of thousand of people were instantly killed, as neighbors who dwelled miles from the disaster area experienced the aftermath where the earth shook from the explosion.

In every country across Asia, where the dark forces of the Illuminati had orchestrated ambushes for those assigned the task of demolition, the erratic weather had foiled their schemes, except for Ulaanbaatar Mongolia where the ice storm and frigid temperatures, weren't obstacles to deter the ambushers. There were two others ambushes foiled in Asia. First, lava storms across China interrupted the Illuminati's plot to secure one of the world's largest weapons depots in Changsha, and, second, in Kazakhstan, which was the only Asian nation to get struck by fire and brimstones which decimated the entire region. The Illuminati worshippers in Mongolia built a special weapon called the A-X Eruptor, which they mounted around their Kachin Army Base, where the nation's entire weapons inventory was kept. The specially designed weapon, which fired an Electronic Plasma Beam at its targets, was capable of destroying two simultaneous armored tanks with one beam, with the only drawback being that the weapon needed three minutes to recharge before another beam could be fired. The Mongolians, like every other nation that sought to defend their master's honor, were awarded half a dozen Dark Warriors to assist the inferior humans in their struggles.

The Defenders, who brought their fury into Mongolia, were well aware of the treachery executed by their human nemesis, as the results from the altercation in Europe were made public. Hence, the Angels assigned to the army base approached with caution, as they knew there was always the chance of retaliation. The specially built A-X Eruptor provided the Illuminati worshipers the opportunity to defend themselves in bunkers, which were designed to hinder anything from entering. The specially designed Plasma Beams prevented the infectious reptiles from penetrating the soldiers' hives from which they sought to protect their weapons of mass destruction. Despite the Illuminati soldiers being struck with boils from the plague administered by Yahweh, their fighting spirits never wavered, as they opened fire at the first glance of an Angel.

Even though the pair of Angels assigned to the Kachin Army Base approached with precaution, the Plasma Beams that were fired at the Angels propelled with such velocity, that one of the Defenders got his right wing completely severed. The wounded Angel pivoted several times in mid air in order to regain his balance before landing harshly on both feet. The Dark Warrior aboard the A-X Eruptor that struck the pivotal blow could see the vexed Angel stumping towards the recharging weapon, as they waited for the weapon to recharge. The Illuminati shooter, who was completely unaware of the approaching Angel, became concerned when his Angel spotter began behaving erratically. The Dark Warrior aboard the A-X Eruptor sought to dismount the weapon before the Defender got within reach, although such a maneuver would compromise the mission by exposing his shooter to the approaching enemy.

The second of the two Angels glided about the army base as he used his remarkable vision to pinpoint the other weapons' positions, before descending to deal with the problem. Each A-X Eruptor was attached to a mainframe generator that powered the weapons from a central source of energy, which was powerful enough to operate a nuclear submarine. The weapons were, therefore positioned underground where its four feet by thirty inches long nozzle was all that stuck out from the ground. While the Dark Warrior aboard the first A-X Eruptor attempted to rise from its seated position, the Illuminati shooter grabbed onto the warrior's immense arm and emphasized the importance of its continued assistance.

"You can't leave me like this, you're ordered to assists me till death you Dumb Ox!" the Illuminati soldier exclaimed.

The Dark Warrior paused and looked down at the little man, with an intense stare that caused the shooter to removing his hand. Before the Dark Warrior could rise to his feet, a thundering punch came smashing through metallic frame that supported the canon, puncturing the hull and knocking out the gunner's spotter. The invisible Angel, whom the shooter was incapable of seeing, was as visible as an eclipse, as his humongous fist was withdrawn from the A-X Eruptor's operations quarters. The weapon's operator cringed in his seat, as the red light that indicated the machine's readiness flashed on the console. The A-X Eruptor's operator was surprised when after approximately ten second nothing further occurred, but the Angel turned and walked away towards the next Plasma Beam.

"You forgot about me you Dumb Ox." whispered the shooter to himself, as he aimed the weapon at the Angel's back.

"Not at all you Dumb Ox, fear not for your soul shall fry in the abyss!" casually said the Angel, whose supernatural hearing could detect everything within miles.

Unknown to the operator of the A-X Eruptor was the fact that once the Angel withdrew his hand several Dragon Flies and Poison Dart Frogs immediately invaded the operator's chamber, where they wasted no time in latching themselves to the locals. With the Angel aligned on the weapon's trajectory screen, the operator went to fire the Plasma Beam and froze up as his limbs succumbed to the paralytic effects of the Poison Dart's venom. With the weapon's indicator beeping to alert its readiness, the Angel, after walking a few paces turned and tossed a fire ball directly at the A-X Eruptor, which exploded and sent a backlash through the system that also destroyed the mainframe generator. The lack of power to the individual Plasma Beams foiled the defense plans for Mongolia, as the Angels destroyed the A-X Eruptors along with everything else related to the governments of Mongolia.

The people of Vietnam were rocked by an 11.7 magnitude earthquake, which also caused havoc along the southern shores of Asia in countries like Cambodia, Laos, Myanmar and China. The earthquake opened huge crevices in the ground, busted underground water pipes, brought down light posts, trees, buildings and other infrastructures, while leaving nearly ninety five percent of the population homeless. A large amount of

Vietnamese were crushed in the rubbles, as the debris that toppled kept victims submerged, while others fought to rescue trapped loved ones. With a total communications failure across the western hemisphere due to the crippling assaults by God's Angels on satellite towers and radio stations, those who were fortunate enough to survive the dilemma, felt helpless.

The terrible ordeals experienced by the Vietnamese people culminated with Yahweh's casted plagues, which basically added insults to the already devastated. Once the boils began growing on people's skin, only the God fearing faithfuls remained mentally composed, confident that the book of Revelations was being revealed. The unleashing of the Dragon Flies and the Poison Dart Frogs brought a whole different reality to the surviving sufferers, who realized for the first time there was no escaping Yahweh's judgment. By the time God's Demolition Crew moved into Vietnam, resistance was non-existent, as the country was like an old deserted western town where almost everyone was deceased. As Defenders began their bombardment of assigned targets, the bewildered people of Vietnam were rattled with an aftermath surge from the earthquake, which measured 5.9 on the Richter scale and lasted another fifteen seconds.

Almost everyone who survived the Lava Balls Showers in China were residents of major cities such as Beijing, Shanghai, Hong Kong etc., where the opportunities to escape the skin dissolving Lava Balls was more prevalent. The Chinese Government's decision to transform their country into a modern day oasis, where they confiscated the lands of poor people, bulldozed their shack houses and rebuilt poorly constructed skyscrapers, temporarily saved thousands from the Lava Balls deluge. Regardless of the time that elapsed since the actual Lava Balls Showers, many buildings still burnt uncontrollably, as survivors moved out into wide open areas to avoid the flames. Once it became safe for everyone to abandon their homes after the Lava Balls Showers ended, patrons went directly to report the travesties to their local fire departments, which were, in some cases, engulfed in flames.

When the plagues began infecting the Chinese people, skeptical citizens who believed it to be an airborne virus, ran back into damaged burning buildings against the advice of professionals. While the decision proved life saving for some, others perished inside such dwellings, as many dwellings caved in. Those lucky enough to choose a sturdy edifice temporarily avoided the descent of the insects and reptiles plagues, which brought their separate horrors onto China. The least likely culture to have its citizens behaved hysterical about flies and frogs had everyone screaming as the Dragon Flies and Poison Dart Frogs began descending.

Despite the immense destruction caused by the Lava Balls Storm, the Defenders still had an array of targets across China to be destroyed. China's famous landmarks such as the one hundred and one story World Financial Center, The Oriental Pearl TV Tower and other supersized structures throughout the country, were included on the Angel's hit list. Every facet was government was destroyed, as their Communist Regime was wiped out, the transportation sector depleted and the military dismantled, as Defenders pounded the country with firebombs. To all who ever heard the phrase 'God's Armageddon', there were no arguing the facts the Supreme Lord had returned, as humans could only attest to the worldwide catastrophes from stories recited in bibles.

Chapter 27

After hours of hiding out in the town of Makhoney Afghanistan, due to the carnivorous abominations from Hell, followed by hours of hail at which golf balls size frozen lumps of rain fell, Second Sergeant Pierre Lapoint and Private Duhon emerged from their place of solitude. Without the availability of the searchlight attached to the nozzle of both men's automatic riffles, the soldiers would have been practically blind, as it was as incredibly dark with thick ash clouds covering the skies. The symbols attesting the Creator's return had vanished, as the soldiers looked up at the skies with grave concerns. The Canadian soldiers did a mediocre search around the village for survivors, before deciding to hike it back to their command base in Kandahar. The First Battalion Princess Patricia Canadian Light Infantry soldiers had gone several hours without an actual base contact due to fact that they hadd lost their communications equipment. Hence, both soldiers were adamant about surviving and disclosing what transpired in Makhoney.

Half way back to their Kandahar Base, the symptoms brought on by the Lord's atrocious plagues began affecting the two soldiers. Private Duhon, who thought of himself as somewhat of a pretty boy, was the first to notice the tiny pimples growing, as they expanded in size rather rapidly. By the time the bumps grew to the size of warts, they transformed into lacerations that resembled the Leprosy disease. Both men were forced to halt their travels in order to shed a few garments, as the boils covering places like their feet burst and turned into aching soars. The soldiers' determination to return to their base, where they believed medical aid for their ailments would be available, saw them shed their all-terrain boots and they supported each other as they limped across the rocky and rugged terrain. The day's sun should have had the entire terrain lit bright; yet the skies were as dark as night, which obscured the soldiers from seeing the intrusive Dragon Flies arrive. The Poison Dart Frogs however, immediately impacted the soldiers, as they tumbled from the skies onto the heads and shoulders of both men. The soldiers had lightened their load by shedding their utility belts and backpacks that carried additional gear and weight they could no longer struggle with, but were forced to keep their helmets as protection from the falling reptiles.

The Canadian Soldiers had climbed a ridge and began descending into the valley, which was along the trail with which they had traveled. As they descended down the hillside, both men froze in astonishment, which caused a Poison Dart Frog to sting Private Duhon. In the plains of the valley, stood General Luzak along with his legions of Devil supporters, who were standing across the field from the Arch Angel Michael and the Heaven's Universal Army. The Supreme Commander was in the midst of encouraging his soldiers for the impending battle, when the venom infected Private Duhon slipped and sent pebbles of rocks tumbling down the hillside. The rumbling noise created by the pebbles interrupted Michael, who turned his attention towards the two soldiers who had begun scampering in search of somewhere to hide. The Arch Angel pointed both his middle fingers at the frightened soldiers, who were both frozen and made into statues, as they became pillars of salt.

"-----let us not become complacent, although we are aware of who the superior fighters are. They battle in vein because they fight for something that was never given to them, nor will it ever be handed to them. As I look across this field at our foes, all I see is jealousy and envy for the privileged lives we live, which is exactly what we're here to return to these lands. They have disgraced the house of our father, as their aspiration is to serve a spirit of equal attributes, strength and vigor. Thus I say to you, for these reasons they are an insult to the frames that house their life forces. Look at them, they are mere shells of their former selves! Angels aren't meant to be as black as the realms of outer space, but rather the contrary. To our father, who has created these lands and countless others throughout these galaxies, praises and appreciations should be bestowed, but these worshippers of envy crave such devotion. Hence we will wipe them off the face of this planet and this world will know who its true master is! For we are?" Michael insighted, after freezing the Canadian soldiers like manikins.

"The Defenders of the Universe!" responded the legions of Angels.

"And we've been appointed to?" Michael lamented.

"Dominate-dominate-dominate---!" chanted the Angels.

With all the preliminaries out of the way, the two armies prepared to engage each other in battle. The Universal Defenders, who thus far defeated two of Lucifer's grand armies, were unimpressed with yet another of their challenge, as they awaited the larger army to reveal their attack strategy. The Commanding General for the Demons pointed at a specific platoon, where five rows of Dark Warriors, each containing five hundred fighters began marching towards the Angels.

"They advance twenty five hundred fighters against an army which defeated ten million plus of their peers; there must be some trickery to this display." thought Michael to himself, after observing the squadron being sent.

"Commander, it appears as if their general wishes to see a preview of what's to come?" telepathically declared General Lecouvie.

"We certainly are abridged to illustrate. Lecouvie, counter with two hundred." Arch Angel Michael telepathically instructed.

"Thanks for the workout brother." General Lecouvie responded, as he signaled the amount to accompany him to the company of Angels.

General Lecouvie and two hundred Universal Defenders began moving towards the advancing Dark Warriors, as the remaining armies stood by as spectators. Michael aimed at illustrating exactly how such a small amount of Universal Warriors were capable of defeating armies many times larger. Thus his decision to dispatch only two hundred Angels vexed the opposing general who aspired to catch a least a thousand Angels in his sprouted web. General Luzak's face brindled with rage, as his expectations fell short on a plot he knew would never succeed a second time, and was totally irreversible once the wheels had sat in motion.

General Luzak's plan, should he not be capable of defeating the Universal Army from Heaven, was to significantly decrease the number of Angels advancing to battle his master. Hence, the twenty five hundred Dark Warriors were actually a platoon of suicide bombers, who were dispatched with a specifically engineered bomb designed to mutilate any angel caught in its rage. Satan's tricksters cleverly disguised their scheme, as the bombs were attached to the warriors that centered the platoon to hinder the Angels from detecting the concealed canisters.

The conflict between the animals from Heaven and the creatures from Hell was already in well under way. The treacherous weather systems across the Asian Continent had severely reduced the number of Satan's carnivorous beasts the Heavenly animals had grown accustomed to tackling. Lucifer's creatures, which had outnumbered the Heavenly animals by almost twenty five percent in Africa, had been reduced to three quarters that amount; hence the battlefield was much more even regarding numbers. However, the pair of Tyrannosaurus Rex Dinosaurs dramatically shifted the betting odds in favor of the naturally born animals, although the abominations from Hell weren't concerned with betting pools.

The pair of Tyrannosaurus Rex Dinosaurs led the charge, as tigers leapt at tigers in a spectacular show of power and agility, while attempting to rip each other's heads completely off. After two remarkable victories on two separate continents, the Heavenly creatures had almost perfected their art of killing, as they had grown accustomed to the tactical and evasive maneuvers of their opponents. Following Africa and Europe, the Heavenly creatures optimized a system with which to fight, plus a separate for assisting an ally in danger. The Heavenly animals fought more in pacts and listened for each other's call for assistance.

There was no limit to the vicious tyranny of General Luzak, who also planted an explosive canister on one of the creatures of his master's dungeon. The General thought about tagging more of the Devil's creatures, but feared some tragic accident where the creatures might unintentionally blow themselves up. Hence, General Luzak tagged a specifically trained beast, which was instructed to eliminate the most destructive force on the creatures' field of battle. With such instructions, the creature waited and watched as its comrades clashed with their nemesis, while trying to determine the most proficient killer on the field.

Yahweh

A Saber Tooth Tigress called Darah fought two intense battles at which she defeated two of Satan's lion-like beasts. The Tigress used her versatility and power to gain an advantage before striking at her opponent's most vital pressure points, causing instant paralysis prior to a suffocating death. Against the first beast, the Saber Tooth and its opponent fought on their hind legs, as they scratched and clawed at each other while suspended in the air. While pawing at each other, Darah received a wound across the face, to which she returned a powerful smack that knocked her unbalanced competitor onto its side. The Saber Tooth wasted no time as it jumped at the recovering beast and slashed at its throat with its long and powerful claws. The sharp claws of the Saber Tooth Tigress ripped open the creature's neck and punctured an artery, which sent the beast staggering back to the ground.

The second of the two beasts jumped onto the rear of the Saber Tooth Tigress and bit her above the tail. The Saber Tooth flung her massive body around while kicking her hind legs at the creature and they came face to face with each other. Darah's opponent charged at her possessed, as if she had killed the creature's partner, before jumping in the air at the tigress that remained poised under pressure. Instead of meeting her competitor at the height of its jump, the Saber Tooth positioned herself and undercut the descending beast, catching it in a throat death grip. A groansome roar omitted from the entrapped creature, which clawed at its predator momentarily, before surrendering its final breath of life.

While draining the life force from its opponent, Darah observed the tagged stalker whose opportune moment had arrived, where the two dinosaurs that had fought at separate ends of the battlefield were relatively close enough to detonate its bomb. The Saber Tooth Tigress noticed the canister object, attached to a rubber ball stretched across the creature's mouth, which was the actual detonator for the bomb. Darah was unsure of the creature's intensions; however its direct path towards the most dominating factors on their battlefield was a definite sign something was foul about the situation. Once the creature began its charge at the unsuspecting dinosaurs, it unknowingly became Darah's prey, as the stalker became the one being stalked. As the suicidal creature drew closer to the dinosaurs with the expectations of detonating its package, Darah intercepted the beast about fifty five feet from both Tyrannosaurus Rex, who were occupied with other opponents. The surprise attack startled the creature, which accidentally bit onto the plastic ball that triggered the explosive mechanism.

"Boom"! Erupted the explosive device, which was so powerful that it blew both the bomb carrier, Darah and others within close proximity to bits. Despite their slight distance from the actual bomb, Hax, Zoe, their opponents and others were thrown clear, as the force of the blast left them with minor injuries. The explosion that killed five Saber Tooth Tigers and six creatures from Satan's Abyss, only served as a temporary interruption in the fighting, as the beasts were back at it as soon as they'd regained their balance.

The Angelic altercation had already begun, with General Lecouvie's troops slashing through the walls of Dark Warriors before them. Although the larger platoon of Dark Warriors cast a shadow over the lesser Universal Warriors like a swarm of bees, the Arch Angel and his company weren't in the least bit concerned, as their confidence in two hundred eliminating twenty five hundred was assured. The eruption of the bomb attached to the suicide bomber on the beast battlefield brought to light the engineered plot of General Luzak, whose face grimaced at the sound of the explosion. The Arch Angel leapt into the sky and hovered above his troops as he stared intently at the battle being waged between his troops and Lucifer's. Through the superhuman vision awarded him, Michael could clearly visualized the canisters of explosives hidden beneath the clothing of several Dark Warriors, which were scattered amongst their engaging opponents.

"My brothers get out of th---!" the Arch Angel Michael began telepathically warning, just as the second and largest explosion erupted.

"Noooooo"! yelled the army of Universal Soldiers, as they brought their weapons to the ready in preparation of the attack chant.

The canisters that were meant to kill at least a thousand Angels didn't quite reach it quota, but did manage to slaughter every Dark Warrior and Angel that participated in the scrimmage. The severance of the telepathic connection shared between Michael, General Lecouvie and all who perished, was a link also shared amongst the remaining Angels, who all embraced the heartfelt loss of their brethrens. At the sight of his vanquished brothers, Michael became overwhelmed with rage, as he slowly hovered towards General Luzak and company, with both hands calmly by his side.

"Archers, fire you fools, fire!" General Luzak commanded, at the sight of the floating Arch Angel hovering across towards them.

At the sight of the archery regiment moving in position, Michael waved his left hand causing the grounds to soften like quick sand, where General Luzak's entire army sank to their knees before the grounds hardened like cement. Once the grounds hardened with their feet submerged, neither Dark Warrior nor Demons could escape, as Michael operated with a power far beyond their comprehension. With his superhuman vision that awarded him the opportunity to see as far as the Hubble telescope, Michael observed several other Suicide Dark Warrior Bombers who were being reserved for a third suicidal attempt. The Arch Angel extended his ten fingers and used each of them to detach ten bombs from ten different Suicide Bombers. Michael then aligned the bombs at their most effective positions between General Luzak's army, turned and casually glided away.

"This is not the way the righteous fight, what of the honor and respect towards your enemies?" General Luzak shouted.

"None shall be given, because you deserve none!" Michael answered, as he snapped his fingers and caused the bombs to explode before going off to attend to the injured animals.

While their Arch Angel attended to the injured, the remorseful army of angels all gathered together and began commemorating their fallen brethrens. For the first time since the Universal Army began their invasion, they were forced to temporarily halt their advancement due to the fact that the death of Universal Soldiers was a historical event, which demanded a celebration of joy as the deceased ascent to the Covenant of Heaven. The band of Angels all held hands and bowed their heads while telepathically linked with their fallen comrades in a ceremony where adorning sentiments are ushered onto the deceased while they made the journey to Heaven's Reincarnation System. Unlike the Angels who will be revived, their Demon counterparts, who had their Heavenly privileges revoked from God's Covenant, could no longer be revived without the powers of Heaven.

Chapter 28

The northern coastline of Austrailia was submerged under water, as the torrentially deadly Tsunami waters of the Pacific Ocean swallowed up smaller islands throughout the Philippines, Indonesia, all the way south to New Zealand. The Island of Guinea, which was eighty percent submerged under water, protected most of Australia's northern coastline, as the island's citizens who failed to reach the highest elevations all perished. Fleets of the Great White sharks feasted on the bodies of those washed away by the Tsunami. Despite the large amount of drowned bodies sinking to the bottom of the ocean, the frivolous sharks that traversed the waters that submerged the Guinean Island still attacked victims battling to survive the life-threatening catastrophe. The volatile ocean demolished the impurities that were assigned the Defenders on a number of islands, where the forces of Mother Nature propelled ships into objects, swooped up everything in its path and crumbled buildings to the ground.

Terry and her personal mentor, Dr. Wallace, were nervously sipping coffee inside the Doctor's living room, when the temperatures began to dramatically fall. With the unavailability of the internet, phones and every other communications devices, the scientists were left powerless against the forces of God. Doctor Wallace, who lived an illustrious life where he travelled abroad regularly, had several items of winter apparels, which they adorned to kept themselves warm around a wooden fire. Almost six hours had elapsed since the final underground radio station went off the air, at which the disc jockey, who claimed to be a priest, warned everyone about God's apocalyptic vengeance. Following the disc jockey's testimonial, Terry revealed her personal history to Dr. Wallace, which was a story she had never revealed to anyone prior. Terry began by talking about her parents and the strain that Demonic episode had on her family. Talking about her mother's insanity and father's impending alcoholism was painful for the young scientist, who broke down several times during the story, which completely fascinated the doctor. Hadn't Dr. Wallace had similar experienced regarding the spirits of whom Terry spoke? His interest in her past would have been obsolete, but the doctor believed Terry held some important information in regards to stopping the catastrophes transpiring around the world.

Despite the mounting frigid temperatures, Dr. Wallace and his companion remained quite upbeat, until the faint echo of an explosion sounded. The electrical lights went out suddenly, as the faint explosion heard by the archeologists was actually a transformer at the electrical grid erupting. Dr. Wallace, who had gathered some emergency apparels turned on a flashlight, as both scientists again heard what sounded like an uncontrolled dump truck rumbling down a rocky slope. As the rumbling noise drew closer, Dr. Wallace grabbed Terry's hand and raced to the section of the house furthest from the tremors, which the doctor suspected to be some sort of plane crash. Outside the doctor's home, the rising ocean levels contributed to a surplus of water, which formed eight-foot level walls of water capable of washing away automobiles and damaging buildings. The surging waters crashed into the doctor's house with such fury, that the whole house shook as if it was about to get carried away by the frothing waters.

Dr. Wallace and Terry didn't have to go very far to find out what happened, as flood waters rushed around both sides of the house, seconds before a twenty foot boat crashed into the western portion of the house. The boat ripped a huge hole in the left side of the house as floodwaters began pouring in, which forced the occupants to exit the damaged structure or suffer the consequence. With the ravaging floodwaters whipping by every lower exit at treacherous levels, Dr. Wallace decided that the roof was their only option for escape. The obstinate elder scientist, instead of moving towards the stairs, concluded that he needed his life vest that was stored inside the basement. Terry was half way up the stairs before she realized the doctor had made a detour, as the light being offered by the flashlight disappeared.

"Dr. Wallace where are you?" Terry hesitantly called.

"I'm going downstairs to get my life vest." Dr. Wallace answered.

"Forget it Dr. Wallace we're almost out of time, we must get out of here!" Terry argued.

Terry felt her way in the dark towards the sound of the doctor's voice and stood at the top platform, while Dr. Wallace stepped into the water that had begun flooding the basement. After watching the doctor sink to where the water level reached his calves, Terry became concerned about what would happen if he didn't return. Following the numerous disastrous episodes where death was narrowly averted, watching the doctor disappear into the abyss jolted the fear inside the young apprentice, as she prayed that her mentor safely returned. Dr. Wallace mingled around for a few minutes, during which Terry held her breath in suspense, before signs of his safety became apparent by the glares of light reflecting off the walls. Once the doctor came back into focus, Terry ran down the steps and assisted him from the rising waters, as they both climbed the stairs and went up to the third floor. With the forceful waters threatening to break through several windows of the home, the urgency to climb to the roof was clear. The scientists used a ladder inside Dr. Wallace's closet to climb up to the attic, from where they climbed out onto the roof and gained their first full view of Australia's pending disaster.

The sight of an already ravaged country brought tears to the eyes of Dr. Wallace, who was born and raised in Perth, Australia. After a few minutes of watching the destructive powers of the floodwaters, which lifted several homes off their sturdy foundations and relocated them, the scientists became doubtful the foundation beneath their feet would remain intact. Both scientists watched in horror, while entire houses floated by with families hysterically pleading for assistance within, overturned ships and tankers crashing into buildings as the water current maneuvered them along, plus an occasional victim fighting to survive by clinging to some object. With each fading moment the scientists' dyer situation worsened, as the thoughts of there being no rescue attempts brought a sense of hopelessness.

While the Creator's grand army made their way to the Continent of Australia through countries like Singapore and Indonesia, and his Heavenly Tribunal deciphered the type plagues to be administered to the peasants of Australia, Yahweh viewed the island of Australia through his 3D High Definition Screen that highlighted every corner and crevice of the Earth. Through his floor view screen Yahweh could see the Lava cracks beneath the ocean's floor, which had been slowly reconstructing the Earth, the factories disbursing Toxic Gases that destroy the Ozone Layer around the planet, the prohibited Nuclear Radiation dump sites that had been slowly polluting the Earth, the killing zones where animals such as dolphins are cornered and slain for meat and countless other destructive government facilities where the deplorable experiments are labeled Top Secret. The Creator was somewhat fascinated by the aboriginal people of Australia who, like some tribes in Africa, had maintained their ancestral ways of living, while the modern world, with its robots and computers, continuously advance. The Aboriginals of Australia who, like every other Native Indian Tribe across the globe, had been murdered and tortured for their lands, because it was determined by others that "savages" were not entitled to such amenities. Yahweh, who had watched the total extinction of several tribes across the pulverized continents, was knowledgeable about many of their satanic practices, where cannibalism and various Black Magic crafts are performed.

The Aboriginal elders of Australia maintained their ancestral ways of living because it was beneficial to their continued survival. Through their inherited physic abilities, the aboriginal people were able to foretell God's Armageddon War before it began. Hence, instead of fleeing an inescapable force, the entire tribe retired to their homes and bravely awaited their faith. Unlike their modern counterparts, who did everything within their powers to survive the catalectic episodes, Aboriginal Natives knew the times would only become more deplorable before the final end came, where Jehovah's judgment would be rendered unto all.

Despite the global cries of suffering humans across the Earth, Yahweh, the merciful and caring God wasn't about to become soft hearted and save the rod from the behinds of his children who neglected and disrespected him for centuries. Immediately after the two hundred Universal Warriors were ambushed by Satan's trickery, Yahweh summoned reinforcements from the training academy, as fraudulent tactics were deemed unacceptable regarding the reinforcing by the Tribunal. While gazing at the Australian Continent, Yahweh's special assistant presented her beautiful self before the grand court to present the arrival of the Universal Defenders' reinforcements. The spectacle of Earthly lights that reflected through the 3D Imagery of the Lord's view screen, radiated the assistant's beauty as she began presenting the requested two hundred warriors before the Lord suspended his viewing screens by waving his hand horizontally.

"My Lord, I present the warriors you've requested!" the assistant introduced, as the replacements marched into the hall.

Yahweh stepped from his divine throne and descended the stairs onto his palace floor, where he strutted about the replacements who stood bravely at attention. The Heavenly Creator returned to the front of the platoon after his inspection, at which time he climbed the stairs to his throne and stood mightily with an appeasing look on his face.

"Your aspirations of partaking in this Great War have been granted. Despite your late addition to the team, we are a divine force, which means wherever your brother engage in battle, so do you engage in battle. The free and joyous society under which we live is the right of every creative being throughout this Universe, with the sole exception being this planet. Lucifer and his followers who have corrupted this planet, have once before attempted to influence their ideals of slavery onto our free society. Their desires to become rulers have tarnished their judgments, to where they even mutinied against the very soul who've created them. The genuine love we extend to each other and to every living organism throughout this galaxy, will be experienced by those judged worthy to inhabit this planet, those who have devoted themselves to a life of righteousness. With my everlasting blessings I now send you to assist your brothers in the fulfillment of reclaiming this planet. You are all my children, unique in your individual ways, yet your hearts beat at the same tone, and your compassion towards each other will never waver. You are members of the sole undefeated defenders of this Universe, forget not what your enemies have done to your brothers and this planet, for I unleash you to support your brothers and dominate!" Yahweh dictated.

"Dominate-dominate-dominate-----!" the Replacement Warriors chanted.

The Creator of the Universe stretched forth his Staff of Rule, which created a huge transparent bubble that encased the warriors on the place floor. With his warriors safely inside the bubble, the Almighty God used his unoccupied hand to wave across the floor, which transformed the solid ground into a jell-like substance. Yahweh's eyes were tightly closed as he concentrated on the task at hand, where the bubble that encased his Angels descended through the solid floor and flew through the atmosphere of the planet into outer space. The Replacement Angels were transported from Heaven gently down to the ground, despite the turbulent weather systems throughout the region. The spectacular view of the Replacement Angels descent to Earth, featured a gigantic Funnel Cloud, usually associated with Tornados, through which the Angels descended as if in an elevator. With his Universal Army in transit through Palembang, Yahweh sought not to disrupt their travel arrangements and thus lowered the Replacements in the city of Malang, which was in the direct path of his army.

With the reinforcements to his Universal Army safely on the dirt of the planet, Yahweh sought to proceed with Heaven's National Security matters, as his Tribunal's spokesman declared that they had finalized their judicial ruling. Yahweh brought back into focus his multiple screens, as if he'd pressed the button to feature different sections of the earth on his remote controller. Through the central screen, Yahweh could clearly watch the different facets of his Australian invasion intertwine, as the Earthly Defenders were pouring into Australia to begin their demolition proceedings, while the main army's reunion with their reinforcement colleagues was set to occur. After receiving the plagues to be accessed the people Australia, Yahweh pointed his index finger at the continent and twirled it around in a circle. The sufferers on the continent, already devastated by the harsh weather, were all struck with Chronic Internal Pain, which shocked nerve systems from the brain throughout the entire body and sent victims curling in anguish to the ground. Residents, who were lucky enough to store certain pain medications at home, were enraged to find that no medication created by humans could douse to effects of the pain, as the usage of any curing remedies brought about excruciating diarrhea and abdominal pain. Yahweh's plagues also turned loose the dangerous reptiles such as alligators and crocodiles onto the nation, as the different levels of floodwaters across the island made it easier for the reptiles to maneuver around.

The Angels' reunion in Malang;

Regardless of the Heavenly Tribunal's decision whether or not to restock their national army, the Universal Defenders were confident in their ability to defeat any army they came across, and thus had no concerns during their travels. Although the Arch Angel Michael was made aware of their reinforcements, once the actual meet occurred, it became an emotional affair with the demise of their associates. While the Universal Army broke formation and hugged their new arrivals, Michael moved to the commander of the new unite, who welcomed him with open arms.

"I see Dad has finally allowed you to venture out of the crib!" the Supreme Commander joked.

"Very funny big brother, I know you're pleased to have the greatest talent in all of Heaven fighting by your side." General Timothy commented.

"Still got that lazy left hook?" Michael teased as they embraced each other.

"I got it up to lightning speed now." General Timothy declared.

With the floodwaters up 98.5 percent on the side of Dr. Wallace's house, the scientists' acknowledged their doom and were seated on the roof, when the plagues from Heaven struck. Both archeologists cringed in pain and curdled up like babies in incubators once the acute pain sat in. The Scientists were cramped in pain, when a Good Samaritan passing by with his wife and children offered refuge on his ten-foot motor powered boat. Despite the immense pain, the man was able to glide the boat along the side of the house, enabling the female scientist the opportunity to climb aboard. Despite the stomach pain, the human's resolve to surviving was what motivated the scientists to rise from the roof and climb into the boat. Dr. Wallace, who had to be motivated by his companion, hoisted himself onto the boat and was in the process of being helped into the boat, when a crocodile lashed up from the water and bit off his left foot. The Doctor yelled out in pain, while crashing onto the deck, as Terry removed her belt from her pants-waist and wrapped it around the wound.

The Earthly Defenders scattered across the continent of Australia like a swarm of bees, as they broke away to their individual targets. Organized strikes against government and private infrastructures were made by the Defenders, who destroyed buildings of parliament, statues and Muriels, factories of all sorts, military equipments and weaponry, high rise buildings, banks and economic facilities, chemical and biological plants along with a whole array of other corporations. There was no planned defensive counter by the Auzzies, who would have found performances of their duties rather difficult with the body cramping effects sent on by the plague. The weather crippled Australia, whose skies were light grey and dark, but significantly brighter than the northern Asian countries, where the skies were completely dark. Despite the majority of their targets being attacked across the larger continents, the Defenders still had a significant amount of their targets on smaller islands, some of which had been buried under water, where the Angels went to accomplish the missions. Australia, like its surrounding neighbors of Indonesia and New Zealand, went up in smoke from the demolished facilities, which exploded and burnt despite the ravaged floods.

Chapter 29

While the destruction persisted around them, the Universal Army pleasantly made their way through Penengaham, where the Arch Angel Michael used his Godly powers to calm the treacherous waters that connected the Java Seas to the Indian Ocean. Michael step forth and outstretched his right hand to the rumbling waters, which brought about an immediate calm and laid a track on which walkers could cross over into Bojonergara. The Universal Defenders met up with their replacement comrades in Malang Indonesia, where they spent a brief moment consoling and enlightening each other, before continuing their journey to Australia.

After reinforcing with their comrades from Heaven in Malang, the Universal Army proceeded to Nusapenida, where they crossed a second body of water over to Mataram; then from Pringgabaya over to Nusa Tenggara Barat, from Nusa Tenggara where they crossed the Savu Sea over to Pulau Padar; then finally the Timor Sea, where they crossed from Timor Leste into the water siege city of Darwin Australia. With their opponents awaiting them in Alice Springs, which is located in the heart of Australia, the Universal Army made their way south to participate in the battle for the continent.

Yahweh who had watched the progression of the Universal Army, visually inspected the troops provided by the opposing commander, who had proved their willingness to recede to immoral tactics in order to gain a victory. The Almighty Father, who was displeased with the fraudulent efforts of their Asian opponents, knew proper precautions should have been taken since deceitful practices were to be expected. With a quick glance at Satan's representatives, Yahweh determined there was no threat of illegal materials being used by the army, which stood ready to defend their master's claims. Every member of the Lord's Tribunal sat upright in their seats as the grand champions of Heaven arrived on the battlefield to confront Lucifer's fourth army. Heaven's Grandest Hall was like an elaborate movie theatre, where the visibility and sound made it appear as if they were actually ringside watching the event.

The weather system around the battlefield was remarkably soothing, contrary to the blizzard type system rumbling outdoors. Michael stepped in front of the reinvigorated Universal Army with his patented rallying speech, as their opponents ruffled amongst themselves like a pact of wolves eager to attack. The commander for the Australian Rebels, General Yezin, who had been patiently awaiting his opponents, was as eager as his troops to begin the dance. Hence, the honor of allowing your opponent the opportunity to properly prepare was not awarded by the Demons, who attacked moments into Michael's speech.

Unlike the twitching Demons that aspired to hear the attack horn sounded, their beastly counterparts weren't as patient, as they clashed with the Heavenly animals the instant they faced off against their enemies. The Australian pact of carnivorous creatures from Hell's Dungeon was the largest force the animals faced since Africa, as the creature's ability to survive beneath the ocean and certain frigid temperature aided them against the rugged Australian climates. The generic components of Lucifer's abominations enabled the creatures the ability to survive under water, which was how they managed to migrate to different countries around the globe.

There was an added fierceness to the creatures defending Australia, who went charging at the Heavenly animals with malicious intents. Disenchanted by the naive bravery of the lion-like creatures, the dinosaur lead animals countered by also charging, as the two entities violently clashed in their War Den. With a width of nearly two hundred feet, the colossal field on which the beasts fought was cramped due to the large amount of participants. At no point along the field of battle was there any sign of compassion, as both pacts mangled the other with pure hatred. The significantly larger coalition of creatures in Australia allowed the malicious beasts the opportunity to divert many at the larger dinosaurs and both found themselves circled by at least seven creatures. There appeared to be a more structural basis to the Australian creatures, which isolated both dinosaurs before demonstrating their strength. Several of the Heavenly animals that observed the creature's tactics fought with greater aggression, as they sought to quickly eliminate their opponent and assist their leaders.

Hex knew he couldn't deal with his six challengers at once, yet he knew that as long as he sustained help would eventually appear. By his opponents' gestures and formation, the dinosaur deciphered that the creatures desired to rid the Heavenly conquerors of their most dominating factors. The heavily armored dinosaur rushed the creatures ahead of it and grabbed its first victim before simply grinding its pressurized jaws into the carcass and hurling it aside. Hex lashed its powerful head around and clobbered the attacking creature to its left, as three creatures from the right leap onto its back. The Dinosaur used the blades attached to its tail to void any rear attack, as the sharp blades ripped through the stalking creature's hinds. While whipping its huge body around to shed its attackers, Hex caught sight of its third victim, which it grabbed by a foreleg, as its powerful jaws snapped right through the cartilage. Two of the three opponents aboard his back had their claws sunken so deep into the dinosaur's flesh that it became impossible to shake them loose. The third of the three back riders fell from saddle, as the gyrating dinosaur swung its powerful tail around and pounded the beast into the ground. The sharp blades sliced straight through the monstrosity's carcass, leaving it lifeless and spewing fluids from different areas.

The two creatures on top of Hex's back sank their fangs into the dinosaur's back, in an attempt to bring down the historical animal. The fourth surviving creature, which had been looping around the dinosaur in an attempt to locate an adequate striking point, believed it found a solid opening and went to take advantage. Hex, who had almost been immobilized by the weight of the creatures aboard his back, began straining once the third creature leapt onboard. The endangered dinosaur swung his head around and grabbed the beast closest in a detrimental grip, which viciously ripped a fraction of its stomach open, at which the beast's intestines poured out onto the soil. Hex, in an attempt to rid itself of the other free-riders, leapt into the air and landed on both feet, at which one of the creatures was throw to the ground. Before the creature could regain its balance and pounce back upright, Hex ran over to the satanic beast, lifted his huge left leg into the air and stumped the beast into the ground.

The closest Saber Tooth Tiger to rid itself of its opponents went racing to the dinosaur's rescue, leaped at the latched on creatures aboard its colleague's back and dragged the beast to the ground. The velocity at which the Saber Tooth knocked the creature to the ground, shattered bones throughout the beast's body as it lay impaired and incapable to retaliate. The weakened dinosaur, who had been bitten several times, felt it necessary to relax for a minute, with no immediate threat within the vicinity. While rejuvenating Hex heard the desperate squeals of its sibling, which was in dire need of assistance. The injured dinosaur, which understood the fate of any creature perceived injured, rolled over onto its massive trunks and charged directly at its sibling's altercation, transacting at the other end of the spectrum. Hex barraged through the middle of several combats, where it swirled its head and slashed his tail at the challengers and aided its allies en route to helping its sibling.

Zoe was not intimidated by the seven creatures, who managed to isolate him from his colleagues. The growling creatures around the dinosaur continued circling in order to confuse the fiercer predator, which was poised to dismantle the entire bunch. Zoe, who felt the presence of a rear attacker, swirled his powerful tail around and caught his first victim attempting to leap on his back. The sharp blades attached to the dinosaur's tail, pierced through the belly of the creature and held it aloft, before its lifeless carcass was flung across the Den. The Dinosaur was fiercer and more intelligent than its opponents, which lacked the war experience of a veteran like Zoe, who knew the importance of not remaining stagnant and thus charged at the creatures before him. The dinosaur used its tough battering-ram head to knock three creatures to the ground, before gripping onto the hind leg of the creature closest to him and hoisting it across the field. Zoe caught the second creature staggering to stand upright by the neck, and released it after a mere three seconds with its neck broken.

The Dinosaur whipped its huge body around and faced off against the remaining creatures, which seemed unimpressed by Zoe's show of strength. Before Zoe could revitalize his lungs with a breath of fresh air, the Devil's abominations were sprinting towards him with yet another attack. Zoe poised himself for the rush and waited until the correct moment to whip his tail around and slashed at his opponents. The dinosaur was successful at eliminating two of the four attacking creatures, which were slashed open by his blunt blades. The two surviving creatures leapt at dinosaur and fastened themselves with their claws sunken into Zoe's skin, as they fought to bite into his tough skin. While attempting to respond to the aggressions against him, the creature that Zoe had knocked aside before eliminating its allies, bit into his right leg and ripped out a chunk of flesh. The sharp pain caused the dinosaur to retaliate at the inflictor, whose bones shattered between his pressurized jaws.

The abomination, from Lucifer's dungeon that was closest to the encounter, overheard the wounded appeal of the dinosaur and abandoned its unbalanced conflict to aide its comrades. Zoe, who was staggering to shed the extra weight of the two creatures, soon found his burdens heavier as the third creature leapt onto his back. With Zoe's agility drastically reduced, the creatures sought to bring down their first dinosaur trophy, who was steadily loosing his maneuverability. Zoe caught another of Satan's abomination running in by the throat, which allowed another creature the opportunity to rush in and sink its teeth into the dinosaur's stomach. The dinosaur made quick work of its prey, during which the toils of the other creatures weakened and brought the great beast staggering to the ground. Zoe growled for help with its last burst of energy, during which one of the creatures pinned its head to the ground and scared his face with its claws.

Zoe believed the last thing he was about to see was the creature gouging its left eye out, while laying motionless as the scavengers mauled away at his immobilized body. After enduring the savagery being imposed by his opponents, the dinosaur's eyes began closing as his life force drained. Zoe's eyelids were almost closed, when the mauling creature atop his head was grabbed by the throat, at which its head got completely severed from its body. Zoe was confident his sibling had rushed to his aide, as he closed his eyes to conserve his energy. The weighty pressures that held the dinosaur pinned to the ground, voluntarily retreated, although the animal's critical health refrained it from moving. After Hex eliminated those responsible for his sibling's injuries, he returned to Zoe's side and compassionately used his tongue to lick away some the blood, as the extent of Zoe's injuries became obvious.

"Revenge is not a part of our mission, but we will fight with our fallen brothers at heart. The mission that has fallen on our shoulders will be completed and we will make them all proud. We live by and practice nothing but love, yet we will allow them no compassion, for they shall offer us none in return. Our mission is to eradicate these Demons from this planet and regardless the deceptions they…" The horn to release the Dark Warriors sounded in the middle of the Arch Angel's speech, prompting Michael to halt and revert back to his command position.

Contrary to every army encountered thus far, the Australian Demons proved less coordinated, with their unorthodox gang rush intended to confuse the Angels. At the revelation of the Demon's attack strategy, the Commanding General telepathically instructed his command, 'to enclose their shields, while archers fire freely.' The shields of the Angels banged against each other, as they interlocked and created the Universal Warriors' indestructible force field. With the Angel's infamous war machine in operation, arrows were launched high into the atmosphere, as well as directly through the visors in their shields. The velocity, with which the directly fired arrows are launched, repelled victims struck onto their comrades. The mastery with which the Angels fired their arrows was a sight of beauty, considering the cramped quarters from which they operated.

General Yezin and his Demonic colleagues reserved themselves for the grand finale, while the lesser- experienced Dark Warriors took up the charge. By the time the Dark Warriors neared the defenses of the Angels, their forces had been trimmed by thousands, after their opponents' sharp shooters pitched target practice. The well-oiled killing machine of the Angels appeared as if they hadn't missed a beat with the incorporation of their new allies, who performed as veterans amongst Heaven's finest warriors. With their defense properly intact, the Angels operated effectively behind their huge shields, which enabled them to dominate the battle.

The inability to reason proved fatal for the Dark Warriors, who were unable to ascertain a solution to their opponents' defense. Hence, the conflict soon resembled a farmer's plantation during harvesting, where huge farming equipment plows through fields of vegetation. At the sight of his entire reserves being depleted, General Yezin instructed his archers to commence dousing the preoccupied Angles with arrows in hopes of catching them off guard. The Supreme Commander was quick to instruct his fighters to 'mass protect', which called for them to form a cocoon that couldn't be penetrated from above.

At their Commander's request, the circular defense that protected the Angels thus far began receiving modifications, as a sea of glass popped above the Angels' heads and fastened into positions like a puzzle. By the time the Demons launched their arrows, the Angels had already installed their indestructible roof, despite the continued rush from Dark Warriors. A member of the playful bunch of Angels who stood alongside the Arch Angel, yelled out 'patriot', which was an archery game played by show-boaters in Heaven. The objective of the game was to split directly down the middle, any arrow fired by your challenger, with the lowest tallied points considered the looser. Michael who was assured his warriors on the battlefield were adequately prepared against any threat, allowed his reserves to compete amongst themselves instead of rushing to attack General Yezin and his repugnant troops. The Arch Angel also knew that the friendly competition would benefit the troops on the battlefield, as he'd observed several episodes between challengers, where simultaneous arrows were being shredded.

The sharp shooters, to compete in the challenge, armed their bows and selected their targets, as a swarm of arrows got launched from the Demons' command post. Although a large amount of arrows were successful in crashing against the Angels' shields, the spectacle of watching arrows shred other arrows while in flight was like watching the American Patriot Missile in action. The Demons looked confused before sending a second wave of arrows at their enemies, which received the same treatment.

"If today we should fall to these weaklings, let us give them Hell for that is where we represent!" General Yezin declared, as he withdrew his sword and prepared to combat the Angels of Heaven.

The Arch Angel withdrew his sword and ascended to the skies with his platoon of fighters, as General Yezin and his troops flocked to the skies. While Heaven's main army dissected, the persistent Dark Warriors, their Supreme Commander and his band of specialists clashed with their former siblings. There was an absence of greetings or salutations between the Demons and Angels, some of whom were close family members of the same household. The Civil War that caused the separation between the Angels was one which could only be rectified with the extinction of one party, as there is only one divine God worthy of praise.

General Yezin and the thousand Demons assigned to his detail clashed swords with their adversaries, who abandoned their shields, which would have slowed them drastically against the much quicker opponent. Michael brought approximately four fifth the amount of Demons to the dance, where the collision between forces was unlike any of the battles fought on the ground. Being outnumbered didn't bother the Angels in the slightest, as their superior techniques compensated for any blemishes they encountered on the battlefield.

Angels and Demons scattered the skies, as their enormous wingspan demanded much room for dueling. A number of Angels fought with spears, which demanded greater balance from the handler while suspended in mid air. One such spear handler was Karl Hanson from the Southern Territories of Heaven, which had been pronounced the Embassy of the Finest Females in the Universe. The Warrior Angel fought a splendid match versus two Demons, who both came at him fanatically with all sorts of strike variations. The initial surge of the Demons forced the Angel backwards, before the fast counters of the masterful tactician reversed the polarity against him. Once Karl transferred the momentum in his favor, the Demons became hesitant to tackle their opponent. With his enemies caught in reverse, the Angel increased the pressure and kept his challengers on the defensive, which created more areas to strike. As the battle progressed, the Demons inherited more wounds throughout their bodies, as the blades attached to the tips of the Angel's spear slashed and punctured with surgical precision. Karl weakened his opponents until he had created the proper opening, where he wasn't hesitant to remove his challenger's heads.

After dispersing of the pair of Demons, Karl found time to survey the battlefield, which had begun indicating a Heavenly victory. The Arch Angel, who had been dueling General Yezin and an alternate Demon, had only recently eliminated the lesser-ranked soldier and appeared to be in total control of the conflict. As Karl looked away from his Commander, the Angel caught sight of an unsuspecting assassin who had been crouching ever closer towards the Arch Angel, who was preoccupied with his back to the assassin. With the assassin almost in striking rage, Karl had to react immediately, and he drew back the spear like a javelin and launched it at the Demon. Without adequate time to properly aim at his target, the spear luckily pieced through the assassin, yet was incapable of stopping the Demon. The Arch Angel, who was completely unaware of the assassin, overheard the huge sigh once the spear pierced through the assassin's stomach, and glanced over his shoulder in time to avoid the striking Demon.

With the injured assassin pointing his sword at Michael, the Arch Angel spun around and used his short knife to knock aside the sword, before swinging his sword around and relieving the Demon of his head. The Arch Angel, while dealing with the unexpected assassin, was mind-sensed of his primary opponent, who believed the perfect moment to switch the momentum had arrived. General Yezin brought an overhead chop down at the Arch Angel, who blocked the sword with his short knife and chopped off the General's striking hand. With one continued fluent motion, Michael whipped his sword around in the palm of his hand and sliced off the General's head as if he'd drawn up the blue print for the maneuver in his mind.

Immediately after eliminating the General, the Arch Angel, who felt immense sorrows around the battlefield, attended to those wounded during the conflict. Michael saw to the most critically injured, before dealing with injuries of a lesser caliber. By that point, Zoe the dinosaur had fallen unconscious to where the animals that surrounded the ailing leaders, believed he'd expired from his wounds. Michael landed and knelt alongside the injured dinosaurs before placing both hands on his protectors, with his head bowed and eyes closed. As the healing powers of the Supreme Commander surged through the injured dinosaurs, Hex popped his head up and stared at his sibling with impatience from wanting to see his brother revived. Zoe's eyes remained closed and body motionless, as the Arch Angel moved to the head of the dinosaur and covered its blinded eye with his right hand. After a few seconds, Michael removed his hand and moved on to the next patient, leaving the spectators around the unconscious dinosaur in suspense.

Chapter 30

My family and I were instructed by the Guardian Angel to remain amongst the animals on the tiny Bate Island, located off the Champlain Bridge between Quebec and Ontario, in the middle of the Ottawa River. The Guardian Angel, who has protected us since our encounter at the Ottawa Civic Hospital, had been absent for hours, leaving us with more questions than answers. We took shelter inside an abandoned structure that used to be a prominent restaurant, which was the only building on the island. While both children slept amongst the warmth of the furry creatures inhabiting the island, Sarah and I stood guard by the door, while we discussed our present predicament and pondered over what had became of our daughter Cassandra.

My wife Sarah and I spoke about our critically ill child, which eventually brought the conversation back to the fate of the entire world. While discussing Junior and God's obvious return to reclaim this planet, my beautiful wife convinced me that there was absolutely nothing that any doctor or physician could do to save our son at that point, considering the world was about to receive a face lift. My spiritual faith had never been as strong as my Christian wife, who had devoted her life to the service of God. However, after witnessing the events over the past few hours, my faith had definitely been rejuvenated.

Following Sarah's convincing argument, the backpack loaded with stolen money and weapons felt like we were carrying the sins of the world, which led Sarah and I to the edge of the island, where I intended to toss the bag into the river. There was rain drizzling outside the single story building, with a thick fog bordering the entire island that prevented a clear view beyond the river's edge. According to the time on my watch, outdoors should have been as bright as a spotlight, although it seemed like ages since we last saw the glares of the sun. As we walked towards the river we began noticing a blurry view of Quebec's mainland, which, unknown to us, was being pulverized with Acid Rain. A loud explosion sounded in the distance, which terrified Sarah and caused her to grab a tight hold of my hand as I tossed the backpack into the river and scurried back to the shelter.

"Honey I think there are terrible things happening around the world that we're being shielded from." Sarah indicated as we entered the abandoned facility.

"Why would we be getting any special treatment?" I argued.

"That little girl, remember back at the hospital the way that creature ignored us and went directly for her. I think we are being protected because of that little girl." Sarah suggested.

"Taejah mom, her name is Taejah." Junior disclosed, as he rolled over and stretched out both hands to his parents.

I walked over to lift my son into my arms and was flabbergasted by the sight of the sleeping beauty, who had Polar Bears, wolves, raccoons and other rodents all snuggled around while she slept. Junior jumped up into my arms and gave me a huge kiss on the cheek, as I hugged my family tightly with tears flowing down my face while worrying about my daughter and our unknown future.

The weather system across Canada was deplorable, as every province received it share of turbulence. The torrential biohazard infected the drinking water supply from Yukon to Labrador and elevated the Canadian Government's Security Alert Status from serious to dire. Schools of dead fishes began popping up from every body of water throughout the nation, while the deluge affected every outdoor animal. Nowhere throughout the skies was there a flying creature, after the acid rain disfellowshiped every species from the clouds. The squirrels, chipmunks and other rodents of the trees, along with the crawling reptiles and mammals of the ground faced similar judgments, as the Toxic Rain killed them all.

The great aboriginal descendants of native Nunavik, all experienced the same horrors as the multi national provinces that shape Canada. The proud Inuit people were as helpless against the trials of Mother Nature as every other Canadian who had been confined to the perimeters of their homes. The mighty polar bear, buffalos, wolves, etc., all lay wasted across the frontier as the Chemical Rain brought its showers of impurity. To the west of the country, in provinces like Manitoba and Alberta, the Acid Rain sparked huge fires on oil refineries, which burnt uncontrollably without the caretakers who constructed such massive oil refineries around to extinguish the flames. The dried bushes throughout British Columbia's acres of forest land also sat ablaze, which eventually extended to homes and businesses, killing a great number of occupants and animals.

The skies over Alaska, which were already dark, appeared a fraction darker with the added smoke generated from the Russian nuclear explosion. The Eskimos of Alaska to the extreme north of Canada had experienced every sort of wintery climate imaginable. However, the elders themselves, who could not recount hearing tails from their ancestors about the epic hail that fell from the clouds, described the dangerous tumbling balls of ice, as 'the tears of God'. At the appearance of the symbols in the sky, which marked the coming of the Lord, most Eskimos who believed themselves separate from the ways of the world, expected to be excluded from the judgment to be attributed to every other nationality across the globe. Hence, a large amount of Eskimos continued about their routine affairs, undeterred by the warning signs written in the skies. Had the suspected planet crashed into the Earth, a number of tribes, like some underdeveloped Eskimos villages, would have been wiped out without anyone aware to the fact, considering many tribes lacked proper access to modern technology. Those who believed themselves to be true worshipers of God, retreated to their homes or safe havens of worship and remained there, during which time the living conditions outdoors only got worst.

Lucifer's abominations, which travelled to every inhabited continent on the face of the Earth, stalked and killed many Aboriginal Inuits and Eskimos out on the plains, as those stubborn enough to ignore the seriousness of the times surrendered their lives. The resourceful hunters of the Inuit people killed several of Satan's creatures, although in each case the beast was credited for slaying more humans. While most humans chose to lock themselves behind their doors and await the inevitable, many chose to fight to avoid being mauled and eaten. Thus, in many regions throughout the North American continent, gang bangers, soldiers, police officers and armed citizens who refused to surrender their turf to Satan's creatures, battled against these carnivorous abominations.

The United States of America was one of the countries that received the most destructive weather phenomenon on the planet. The President, his family, their honored guests, servants and security personnel, all engaged in prayer vigil during the launches of their missiles against the impending planet. Following their insolent attempt at destroying the Planet Heaven, President Flores developed a sense of embarrassment and self pity, by which he went off into his studies and sobbed in private. The White House's entire household had been glued to CNN Newscast throughout the entire ordeal, as the news provider broadcasted video of the abominations from Hell which had been tormenting citizens around the world. Every gruesome footage shown of Satan's creatures in action disgusted the audience, as even the news anchor was caught vomiting in the garbage pale, at the sight of people being eaten by these creatures. Live video footage of the interception of the missiles by the hand of God was made by the Galaxy Planetary Observer Probe, which was destroyed shortly after the feed was transmitted back to Earth.

The entire Earth became as serene as a sleeping baby, before practically all Hell broke loose, as Yahweh commenced illustrating his disappointment in his children by transforming the Earth's entire weather systems. While everyone present inside the White House gazed around nervously at each other, the meteorologist for the news station discussed a breaking news bulletin about a volcano eruption in Mexico. The video footage, which had been chopped midway through due to transmission interruption, was replaced by a video feed taken from the CNN News Tower's video cam, which showed what appeared to be flaming stones falling from the clouds. The news anchors, who had been informing everyone to remain indoors, were at first speechless at the revelation.

"Oh my dear God, it's raining fire and brimstones!" the Meteorologist declared seconds before the thundering flaming rocks smashed the camera.

The White House roof began sounding as if the kids from the neighborhood were pelting it with rocks, as Janet, the First Lady, went to peek out the window at the disturbance. The First Lady released a huge sigh at the sight of the light show occurring outdoors, where the forecasted brimstones lit up the cloudy skies. Members of the security detail went to the front door for an adequate view of the phenomenon only known through bible stories. The Security Chief instructed his crewmembers to be precautious, as it quickly became evident by the burning grass that the burning stones were to be taken seriously. While watching the brimstones crash to the Earth, the fire alarm began sounding on the upper tier, which brought the President racing from his private suite in suspense.

"What is going on out here? What the Hell is that?" the President said in amazement at the sight of the falling brimstones.

Two members of the security crew, who went to check out the reason for the fire alarm sounding, raced back down the stairs and informed everyone that the roof of the house had been set on fire. Chief of Security Terrence Gibson took control of the situation and instructed everyone to gather together in order to evacuate the building. While everyone was advised to abandon everything, First Lady Flores ran into the television room in order to fetch her beloved puddle, which was basking by the warmth from the fireplace. While guards chased behind the First Lady to ensure her safety, Roland took off after his friend Julius up the stairs, who went to collect his personal effects from his assigned suite.

"Get back down here a-sap misters!" shouted the Chief at both men, who disobeyed his orders.

"We'll be right back Chief; we just gotta get something important for my friend's survival!" Roland stated.

The aspiring lawyers raced down the hallway to Julius' suite where they barged inside to a spreading furnace of fire running across the ceiling. Julius was about to recklessly charge into the burning room when common sense got the better of Roland, who reached out and grabbed a hold of his friend. The foreign exchange student was dragged back by the collar seconds before the ceiling fan that hung above the bed inside the room came crashing down.

"Wow, thank you my friend!" Julius declared.

"I think at this stage you can do without your weapons, don't you?" Roland argued.

"It is not my weapons that I am concerned about; it is the photos of my parents." Julius answered.

The young man ran into the suite and collected his bag, which contained the items he sought, before quickly exiting the burning room. The Law students were the last to join the others with the President standing at the foot of the stairs waiting patiently. Julius nodded his head at the President in appreciation, as the Commander and Chief pointed to Chief Gibson, indicating they were properly ready to proceed. While everyone ran along behind most of the guards, President Flores, who remained behind to savor one final look at the castle of his Presidency, expectedly found himself with two Secret Service personnel. President Ron Flores took one final three hundred and sixty degrees turn around one of the grandest monuments in the world, acknowledging everything from the ornaments to the historic photos of past presidents.

For the majority of citizens in District of Columbia and around America, escape from the furnace of their homes was impossible. However, for members of the most prestigious house in Washington, there were many preparations in case of emergencies. Chief Gibson and his unit directed the President's entourage to the security passages beneath the White House, were they acquired gas masks and other survival supplies before proceeding to a safe spot built to protect and house the President. With enough living supplies to survive for years underground, the group of influential politicians, employees and friends gathered together and prayed for those above grounds, who were obviously being tortured.

The Fire and Brimstone storm fell for five hours before a moment's pause came where the sounds of rocks clashing ceased. By the time the falling flaming rocks stopped, the skies were as dark as midnight with the ashes from the volcanoes blocking out the sunlight. The President, and everyone with him, were impatient to return above ground and assess the damage. Within ten minutes of the Fire and Brimstone finalization, a slight rain drizzle began falling, which hardly affected the enflamed particles.

The President and his entourage returned above ground after six hours of isolation in one of the only facilities equipped to survive such calamities.

Yahweh

The group of survivors came up through a secret entrance built at the George Washington Monument, where the sight of the destruction was too much for some of group's members to absorb. The entire city for miles was in ruins, as even the monument from which they surfaced had been badly damaged. The Vice President and his loving wife fell to their knees, while being careful to avoid coming into contact with the scattered fires about the grounds. While sobbing in sorrow with the belief that no one could possibly survive such a travesty, Vice President Williams gazed in the distance and saw four images crossing the main street.

"I see survivors over there, they're not all dead!" Vice President Williams screamed.

At that point everyone took off running to locate other endangered survivors amongst the ruins. More survivors began popping out of weird places, through which they were able to survive the cataleptic event. There were many individuals who had been terribly burnt by the flaming rocks, who were attended to by someone who cared to help, as the President's entourage used the stored medication to assist those suffering. A medical station was formed by the President's entourage, which luckily consisted of a licensed doctor, who supervised the various treatments handed out. While some of the men went out in search of survivors, others remained behind to assist at the clinic as they began forming an emergency response team. Despite the travesty, the survivors encouraged each other until every capable individual unexpectedly crumbled to the ground; stricken with the North American plagues casted by Yahweh.

Chapter 31

While the Universal Army travelled along the east coast of Asia towards Russia's north eastern region, the Heavenly Creator featured Antarctica on his main screen, which was Lucifer's hideout while his armies fought over the over six continents. Yahweh's face exhibited a firm stare, as he inspected the forces of the sole Angel to coordinate a mutiny revolt against his government. The Heavenly Father, who enjoyed stroking his lengthy beard, leaned forward and gazed into the tent of the self appointed King of the World. Lucifer was in the midst of plotting a mission and had four Demons around his strategic table while instructing them on how to proceed. Although Yahweh missed most of what was discussed, the Creator did manage to catch a glimpse of the area for which the plot was intended, as Lucifer pointed at the crossing between Russia and Alaska.

The Heavenly Tribunal reached their decisions regarding the plagues to be administered to the North and Central American Continent, which was one of the regions to launch a significant amount of missiles against Heaven. Yahweh appeared incensed by the sight of Lucifer, before his attention was requested by members of his cabinet. The spokesperson for the Tribunal spoke and delivered their assessment of what forms of punishment were to be administered, to which Yahweh consented and twirled his index finger, which brought about the plagues. Every living human being on the continent of North America became crippled from the neck down, which sent citizens uncontrollably crashing to the ground. Rodents such as squirrels, rats, etc. began infesting the dwelling of humans, where they attacked citizens and prolonged their agony.

Lucifer had spent centuries preparing for this epic war, and he invested in an array of scientific weapons, intended to terminate his nemesis. These inventions of the Devil were transported to several different war vessels to be used by humans, who represented a small fraction of Lucifer's regime. The American USS Ronald Regan Aircraft Carrier and The USS Abraham Lincoln Aircraft Carrier, The Spanish Principe-de- Asturias Aircraft Carrier, The British HMS Invincible Aircraft Carrier, The Canadian HMCS Halifax Battleship and several other battle ships all tussled about the hostile waters of the North Pacific Ocean, while launching squadrons of war aircrafts. There were F-22 Raptor Fighter Jets being launched, F-18 Stealth Bombers, F-16 Fighter Jets, F-14 Tomcats, F-117 Nighthawks and even several unmanned Drones. Every manned fighter jet had been equipped with sensors that highlight Angels, along with missiles and bullets specially designed to slay God's representatives. The Captains and a majority of the crew members, especially the pilots, were members of the Global Illuminati Secret Fraternity who had been commandeered to fight the battles of their master.

Unlike the incoherent Dark Warrior spotters assigned to the airport big guns, Demons who shrunk themselves to human size took on the appearance of men and instructed the captains of each vessel on how to proceed. Beneath the waters of the Pacific Ocean, the Bering Sea and Arctic Ocean, there were two Type 093 Chinese Nuclear Powered Submarines, The USS Kentucky and two other American Nuclear Submarines, two Soviet Union Nuclear Submarines, one Japanese Nuclear Submarine and a Canadian Sub. Illuminati members, who aspired to have their master return to his former glory as the King of Planet Earth, captained all the Nuclear Submarines. Neither the sailors beneath the oceans nor those floating above were affected by the plagues on the land since they were well off shore and away from the quarantined area.

Prior to the fighter jets being deployed, a Blackhawk spotter helicopter was air lifted off the HMCS Fredericton Canadian Battleship, which was located in the Golf of Alaska fifty miles off the Yukon coast. Due to the sensitive components aboard the aircrafts deployed to sabotage the Universal Army, parameters were established to avoid pilots flying into the Ash Clouds, which would interfere with the plane's computer and cause crashes. The task of the Blackhawk Helicopter that took off from the Canadian battle ship was to locate the exact crossing point of the Universal Army, and lock their specially designed tracking beam on them in order for the long range missiles to be launch from the ships at sea and hone in on their targets. Despite their physical agility and training, the mission commanders didn't wish to have their jet fighters engage the Angels personally. However, should their initial plot fail, the jet aircrafts were the human's last resort.

During their travels through Russia, Yahweh telepathically linked his Supreme Commander and instructed him about the Devil's planned ambush. Through the eyes of space you could literally see the players on the battlefield, with the humans and their war vessels positioned at strategic points across the North Pacific, while their targets travelled north towards the awaiting ambush. Once the Universal Army got to the Bering Sea, the Arch Angel again stretched out his right hand at the ocean, which brought the rumbling seas to a calm and provided a platform on which walkers could cross. The pilots aboard the Blackhawk spotter helicopter were instructed to remain at a lengthy distance and allow their equipment to locate the Angels for whom they searched. However, the helicopter's sensors malfunctioned due to the bad weather, which forced the Blackhawk's crew within seventy miles of their target.

The Arch Angel Michael casually led the Universal Defenders across the Bering Sea, while ignoring the Earthlings. The reports brought back to Heaven by Earthly Defenders over the centuries gave the Supreme Commander an insight into the war tactics of humans, who, like every other race, employed certain weapons into their arsenal. Michael soon stopped and allowed his mates to proceed, while assessing the situation from his perspective and telepathically summoning a number of his brothers.

"Anthony, Timothy, Ramus, Rhovon, Jahvon, Shakeem, Shamar; you warriors care to have a little fun?" Michael implied.

Once everyone summoned had gathered, the Arch Angel and his sequestered gang sprung their wings and ascended to the skies. Michael's first task was to place a shield over the entire path on which the Universal

Army crossed, which would protect them from any forms of attack. The Supreme Commander's extraordinary vision allowed him to see the Blackhawk helicopter hovering over the Alaskan plains seventy five miles away, with its tracking beam aimed at his colleagues. Michael pointed his left hand in the helicopter's direction and crimpled his fingers as if attempting to open a bottle before turning his hand at an angle, which also caused the helicopter to turn. The Blackhawk Helicopter's pilot fought the controls to realign the chopper, which repositioned itself and began targeting The Principe-de-Asturias Aircraft Carrier from Spain, which was north of the Polynesian Islands in the Pacific Ocean. Regardless of what the pilots aboard the Blackhawk Helicopter tried, the tracking beam switch refused to deactivate and the controls remained frozen towards the battleship.

The incentive to kill an Angel caused an Illuminati pilot to disobey orders, as he broke formation and attacked the Angels prior to the missile strike. "Command centre my instruments indicate that there are a number of unfriendlies ascending to the clouds, I'm engaging pursuit as ordered!" reported the pilot of an F-22 Raptor that originated from the USS Ronald Regan.

"Who is that? Stand down pilot, I repeat stand down, the missiles are on route to the target, so stand down!" the Missions Commander aboard the USS Ronald Regan barked into the microphone.

The airplane pilot continued disobeying orders and launched one of his specially engineered missiles at the ascending Angels. Pilots aboard the F-22 Raptor were accustomed to firing a missile from miles away, turn back home and ignore the laser guided bomb, which would incidentally destroy its target. The missile fired by the pilot travelled much slower than an Angel's average speed, thus it was highly unlikely that the humans would succeed at their endeavors. The F-22 pilot surveyed the missile until it exploded and believed he's succeeded at annihilating the Angels, yet his instruments still indicated the targets were unfazed. At the Mac two speeds with which the Raptor pilot swooped around the skies, he believed himself uncatchable and thus sought to curl around and unleash his Gatlin Guns at the Angels. Rhovon, who was considered one of Heaven's best Javelin throwers, hovered forward and timed his throw perfectly spearing the plane directly through its computer circuitry. The plane exploded instantly without the pilot having an opportunity to exit, as the squadrons of aircrafts began swirling around to attack.

Through the mist of thick fog burst a significant amount of missiles, which were all aimed at the army of Angels crossing the Bering Sea. Missiles launched from submarines submerged deep in the ocean could be seen with the Angel's extraordinary vision beneath the ocean, as they glided their way towards their target. Through the eyes of the angels the speed with which the travelled was as slow as watching a turtle cross the street, which gave the Angels ample time to alter the effects, though none of that would be necessary. The missiles smacked into the force field that Michael placed around the Universal Army, which brought a huge cheer from the pilots aboard the planes circling the parameter.

"Command Centre we have a direct strike!" the American Squadron Leader reported, which also brought a huge cheer from the sailors aboard the different vessels.

"It's impossible I can't believe my eye, they're still there." declared a British pilot.

The amount of bombs that detonated were enough to level a city, yet still the intended targets appeared unfazed. The pilots aboard the different jets were stunned, as the only explosion relevant thus far was the one that killed the American pilot. After being awed thus far by the magnificence of God's Angels, the Illuminati pilots weren't as eager to tangle with the mystical Angels. The hesitant fly boys circled around until the commanders ordered them to launch an all out attack, at which the servants of Satan activated their weapons and began launching missiles, bullets and every form of weapons at their disposal.

The Arch Angel responded to the pilots' aggression by unleashing his warriors at the insolent humans who dared to involve themselves in Heavenly matters. A number of secondary missiles fired at the Angels were re-coordinated towards the Principe-de- Asturias Aircraft Carrier stationed around the Polynesian Islands hundreds of miles away. The Spanish Warship was the first sunk by Angels, as the ship's emergency defense systems were overwhelmed with the amount of incoming missiles. The Blackhawk spotter helicopter, after guiding the destructive missiles towards the sunken Spanish ship, began transferring its guidance systems towards the Canadian HMCS Fredericton Battleship. The Captain aboard the Canadian vessel was not about to allow the same tragedy to befall his crew, hence, once advised about the situation, the captain made a judgment call and ordered the chopper be shot down.

The Fredericton Battleship's weapons guidance systems were repositioned as even warplanes from the Canadian regime were placed on alert. The occupants aboard the helicopter were advised to evacuate, with several weapons targeting them and ready to fire. Long range missiles were launched from the battleship at the Blackhawk, while Canadian Jets over the Bering Sea launched short range missiles in support. All occupants aboard the Blackhawk helicopter successfully evacuated, without any inkling as to whether they could get rescued.

"Rico my brother, I wish for you to assemble a strike force and scour the oceans, rivers and streams for these metallic vessels of man, which operate above and below. Seek them all out and destroy these vessels, for they have no place in the future of this Earth." telepathically instructed Michael, as he spoke with a member of the Earthly Defenders.

"It will be done my brother." Rico telepathically responded.

While the Supreme Commander returned to guide the Universal Defenders across the Bering Sea, his appointed enforcers pounced into action against the technologically modified warplanes. The engineered Angel locator worked perfectly on each of the installed aircrafts. However, getting the targets to remain still in order to be targeted was another issue. With the Angels zipping about the guidance screens aboard the aircrafts, pilots became confused which resulted in two separate mid air collisions. The introduction of fireballs into the scenario added definite fear to the hearts of the Illuminati pilots, who had arrived at the realization that they were totally outclassed.

The elusive angels toyed with the humans and their expensive war machines, by landing on the aircrafts while they flew at Mack speeds, and either damaging the planes or evicting the controller. There were planes crashing into the ocean at an alarming rate, while others just appeared to malfunction during flight and exploded. After watching several jets unexplainably crash into the ocean or shattered, a Chinese pilot aboard his country's replica of the F-22 Raptor, observed Anthony the Angel ripping one of the jet thrusters off an ally's aircraft and simply open fire at the F-16 jet. The Angel, who didn't believe it possible for colleagues to assault their brethrens, was shot directly through the right shoulder, rib and thigh, as bullets tore off the wing of the F-16 and sent the Angel spiraling to the sea. The Illuminati pilot watched the Angel fall to the ocean and believed he had slain an enemy of his master, before Anthony disappointed him by extending his wings and catching a gust of wind before hitting the water. Anthony, while flying, flipped over on his back and constructed a fireball in the palm of his hand, while the Chinese pilot, after observing that he had angered the Angel, boosted his airplane's speed to Mack four in order to escape. The Jet Aircraft took off like a rocket with the fireball giving chase, yet the Angel's missile caught up to the jet and blew the plane to bits.

A squadron of five American F-18 Stealth Bombers flew north across Alaska and out into the Arctic Ocean, before circling back to launch an attack against the Universal Army. The Arch Angel, while travelling with his peers, received notification from his Father, who continued to supervise over the battlefield. After being notified of the Stealth Bombers, which were being piloted by suicidal pilots whose plane were rigged with explosives, Michael stepped to the forefront and raised both his hands to the skies with his fingers spread apart. Currents of lightening bolts emanated from the clouds the instant the Stealth Bombers came into focus, as the lightening strikes were precisely aimed at the aircrafts flying below. The pilots in the cockpits of the F-18 aircrafts didn't see what hit them, as the lightening strikes either, split the planes in half, short circuited the onboard computer or ruptured the fuel tanks that caused the plane to explode.

The Arch Angel's enforcers eliminated every single aircraft from the skies and reinforced the 'flight restrictions', which were already in effect. Once the Demons aboard the sailing vessels of humans realized their master's scheme had failed, they all abandoned their Illuminati worshippers and travelled south to Antarctica to rejoin their king. The automated weapons systems aboard the battleships at sea began firing once they detected the Angels approaching, but the quick and evasive Defenders evaded the particles fired at them and fatally damaged the vessels. The huge protective weapons aboard the Aircraft Carriers and Battleships weren't enough to deter the

Defenders from attacking and sinking the metal warriors of the ocean, while condemning the submarines that hover beneath the waters to the depths of the sea. The explosions that erupted and burnt before the ships sunk to the ocean's floor made sections of the ocean look as if they were engulfed with bonfires, while the sailors aboard struggled to launch the flotation devices and escape.

The Defenders also sunk the thousands of pleasure vessels, like The Oasis of the Sea, The Discovery, Carnival Cruise Line, Norwegian and every other tour ship that operated on water. The largest ocean dredger ship, the Cristobal Colon that holds forty six thousand cubic meters of sand, was found with zero survivors aboard prior to the Angels destroying it, as the crew had fallen prey to one of Satan's carnivorous creatures. The beast, which climbed aboard on one of the robotic arms, through which the sand is vacuumed into the storage container, tormented and killed the entire crew. The Defenders were much more cautious in their handling of ships like oil tankers, which were drained of their oil reserves before being sunk and destroyed. God's Angels, who have witnessed the ecological disasters caused by human's oil spills over the centuries, were more environmentally cautious knowing the havoc such chemicals reeked on the creatures of the ocean and the wildlife along the coast lines. The biggest water vessels to survive the annihilation of ships were fishing boats and smaller crafts, considering that all vessel larger than ten feet, were burnt and sunken. The Universal Army's march on the Americas never wavered or yielded, despite the interruption of ungodly humans attempting to defend their master's dishonor. After eliminating the members of the Illuminati across the North Pacific, the Universal Army was again on track in its North American conquest.

Chapter 32

Yahweh was incredibly pleased with the manner in which his army had progressed, as he gazed down at the next continent to be reclaimed. Although the Heavenly Creator's plans for the Earth included the demolition of nearly sixty five percent of the structures built by man, Yahweh, after inspecting the inventions of humans, was quite fascinated with the advancements his subjects had made. With respects to the houses they have built for shelter; the cars, trains, boats and airplanes they have built for transportation; the cellular phones, computers and radios they built for communications and the clothes and other materials they invented to protect, cover and shield themselves against the elements, the Lord was undoubtedly pleased. While Jehovah's admirations for the accomplishments of mankind grew, there were several issues that displeased the Creator; the foremost being the manner with which humans have treated the Earth; their lack of compassion for the creatures with which they have shared the planet and their continued disobedience towards the laws that he had implemented for a morally clean lifestyle. Like any parent who established the rules for their household, so too had the Sovereign Creator expected his laws to be upheld.

The plagues assigned to the citizens of the North American Continent foiled plans by the Illuminati Society across Canada and America. Members of the Illuminati, who adorned specially, fabricated garments designed to keep Lucifer's abominations at bay, were the only human-beings on Earth allowed to operate during the attacks across the globe. Thus, the ambushers used such opportunity to prepare their Angel traps, which were all left severely damaged after the horrid weather. Hence, the Defenders of Heaven were able to freely swoop into the North American Continent's grandest cities, which saw some of the world's most infamous buildings, statues, murals and technologies vanquished. Historical structures crumbled across the continent, as staple structures like the CN Tower in Toronto, the Sheraton Wall Centre in Vancouver BC, the Statue of Liberty in New York, the carved faces on Mount Rushmore and many others were destroyed by God's Defenders. Millions of people lost their lives in the demolition of sky scrapers, Government facilities, as well as other institutions where workers resided. Technologically invented engineering like Wind Turbines were ignored, while oil refineries on and off shore and mines of all sorts were destroyed. The Tsunami Floods that leveled Japan and a number of smaller islands throughout the Pacific Ocean crashed against the western shores of North America and brought a sea of destruction along the coastline from Mexico to British Columbia. The furious mountains of water extinguished entire neighborhoods and killed millions, as the weather system continued reeking havoc across the globe.

To harm the very people that the Defenders had protected during centuries of sentry work appeared inhumane, however the Defenders were ignorant towards the cries of their dying associates because they knew the glorified life that awaited those who qualified. The worshippers of Satan, who had their ambushed plots unearthed by the Defenders, were all slain without malice after the Defenders observed the types of weapons devised to be used against them. Furthermore, to disrespect the Supreme Creator was a punishable offense, to which absolutely nobody was immune, especially the primary Demon whom Heaven's grace had returned to abolish from the Earth.

Yahweh watched with interest as his Defenders destroyed the multitudes of honorary artifacts bestowed to humans of historical feats. Structures such as the Pyramids in Africa, to the Monuments carved into Mount Rushmore, showed the Heavenly Father the depths of infidelity and greed humans employed to illustrate their Godly powers. Through his 3D screen, Yahweh had an exquisite view of several of the statues built to commemorate people of different statures, which the Defenders melted into piles of scrap metal.

Unlike their northern global powerhouse neighbors, whose cities resembled Sulfur Pits where steam and deadly gases evaporated into the atmosphere, Mexico and the other Central American countries received their thrashing of wintery weather, which buried the countries in avalanches of snow and frigid temperatures. The temperatures throughout the Central American countries fell so low that patrons actually froze to death in their unheated homes, while others burnt everything possible to acquire a bit of heat. Stern yet passionate was the Heavenly Tribunal in their deliberations over the type of plagues to be administered on the Americas, as the Central Spanish speaking colonies were struck with blindness. The venomous snakes and centipedes of the outdoors were released against humans, where they infested the dwellings of citizens and attacked. Every human being on the planet felt the wrath and judgment of Yahweh, as the Heavenly Creator continued scolding his children with deplorable catastrophes.

Sarah, who was well schooled in the bible, was the one to calm me down after we had been struck by the crippled plague. The realization of not being able to move my arms and legs for the first time was a bit overwhelming, as I responded by screaming at the top of my lungs, to which Sarah's soothing voice calmed my fears. I willed myself to turn in the children's direction, to sooth them both after creating an unnecessary stir, only to find both kids laughing their heads off at my childish behavior. After watching the kids laugh at my reaction, I also had to giggle to myself at the thought of my frantic scream.

"Honey what's going to happen to us?" I enquired of my wife.

"I don't know dear, in the bible the plagues casted against Job saw him struck with Leprosy, but the Egyptians received some different sorts of plagues when Moses was trying to get the Israelites out of Egypt. This time I believe the stakes are a little higher, so nobody have any idea what to expect." Sarah declared.

"How about Cassandra, you think she is experiencing the same problems in Africa?" I asked.

"I just pray she is OK and we get her back soon. Lord I beg of you to protect her" Sarah exclaimed.

The animals, reptiles, rodents and insects that migrated to the tiny Bates Island in the middle of the Ottawa River between Quebec and Ontario, were specially chosen to succeed their clan and advance their species. All the animals on the island were therefore calm and domestic towards humans, which was fortunate for us as rodents were molesting humans across Canada. My family members, little Taejah and I snuggled together and coupled up, with the animals around us generating heat.

A blind patch covered the gouged out opening where Zoe the dinosaur lost his right eye. There was an abnormal demeanor about the Dinosaur, which despised its opponents across the battlefield for being related to the ones that caused its injury. The animals of Heaven had taken to the battlefield across from their North American opponents, which, like their predecessor were eager to tangle with Heaven's animals. Hax had taken up its regular position at the opposite end of the battlefield, although the dinosaur had sought to fight alongside its sibling. After narrowly escaping death on the battlefield in Australia, Zoe was actually more anxious to re-engage their rivals than any of Heaven's animals, as the dinosaur stood poised to attack.

Lucifer's North American defense, which was led by General Zada, met their challengers on a clear field northwest of the Great Lakes, on the border between Canada and the United States. With the desire to get the maximum usage out of the lesser skilled Dark Warriors, General Zada had the thousand Demons awarded to his regime adequately divided amongst the Dark Warrior forces and lead their individual platoon against the Angels. The Dark Warriors were appointed to each Demon's squad days before the actual confrontation between the Angels in order to allow the leader of each team time to develop their personal chemistry. General Zada himself had his legion of Dark Warriors instead of the usual protective Demons to his rear, as he adhered to his commander's proposition.

General Zada's attack strategy resembled a bunch of untrained delinquents, due to the manner with which they were scattered across the battlefield. With each one of the Demons individually standing with their five thousand Dark Warrior platoon, the Angels were confused as to what to expect, but confident in their abilities to defeat anyone. In order to avoid any complications, the commanders ranked below the Arch Angel were instructed to divide the Universal Army, in order to create more of a balance against their foes. Although the Universal Soldiers had defeated a few of the Demons' armies, the lessons learnt from their Asian encounter proved valuable in understanding the treachery of the enemy.

A slight drizzle of rain fell from the clouds, as Michael and the Universal Defenders stood poised to battle the representatives of Satan. The Supreme Commander, from the helm of the Universal Defenders, spoke to his brothers in arms, as they prepared to clash against General Zada and his Dark Warrior command. "Regardless of how you feel about these engineered combatants that Lucifer constructed to antagonize you, they are still who we have to go through to reclaim this planet. Let nothing they do be of a surprise to you, their tactics and skills are minimal yet remain vigilant and never become complacent. The work of our Father is half done, which means after all the battles that waged we're still as committed and hungry to free these humans from the unjust tyranny of Lucifer. Our Father created a paradise for these humans to live a perfect life, where everyone was immune to sickness and shortage of breath. These humans were meant to live and breath through the existence of time as we do, yet were robbed the magnificent privilege awarded by our Father. We are on the verge to regain such privileges to humans worth of such honor, and neither they nor their myriads of associates shall stop us from accomplishing that feat. Inferior or not, I wish for you to wipe this battlefield with their anatomies, we were sent here to conquer and dominate these battles, hence dominate!"

"Dominate-dominate-dominate----!" cheered the reformed army of the Universal Defenders.

Zoe the Dinosaur came out of the gate puffing like an angry dragon, while the army of Saber Tooth Tigers followed suit. The dinosaur used its' sole eye to quickly locate the more aggressive of its foes, before using them as examples to illustrate what was in stored for their mates. Zoe grabbed its' first victim and raised the creature to its absolute height, before crashing the beast to the ground with such force that the creature literally split in half. With the dinosaur's friends lunging at their opponents, Zoe got the opportunity to freely select its' next victim, which was actually trying to avoid the fierce raging animal. The creature was immediately crippled by the dinosaur's grasp, as its spine was crushed under the pressure. Zoe behaved like a dinosaur possessed as it went ballistic and snatched an opponent from atop a Saber Tooth Tiger and flung the creature some sixty feet into the air before prancing onto its next victim. The beast crashed to the ground hard and got the wind knocked out of it, before a scavenging Saber Tooth latched onto its throat and strangled it to death.

Hex paused from its affairs to look over at its sibling, who was dominating the fight in the den versus their combatants at the other end of their battlefield. The realization that its sibling was back to normal was pleasing, as Hex watched Zoe used its sharp razor edge tooth to rip the head completely off one of their adversaries. The concerned dinosaur soon realized that it needed to quicken its killing pace, considering that Zoe was eliminating an opponent every fifteen seconds. Hex, although elated that its sibling was performing up to its ability, secretly wanted to boast about owning the record for the most opponents killed. Hence, the dinosaur became enraged and used the blade attached to its tail to puncture the stomach of an opponent that was tackling a separate Saber Tooth. The inspired dinosaur lunged at its opponents and, as if recharged, began thrashing its enemies across the den, while narrowing the killing gap between both dinosaurs.

The Saber Tooth Tigers had tangled with enough of the Devil's creatures to the point where they had become accustomed to the fighting tactics of their opponents. While their dinosaur leaders led by example, the Heavenly tigers followed the charge and fought with vigor and finesse. Nowhere across the huge beast fighting grounds, was there a Saber Tooth under siege by Satan's abominations. The contrasting styles between the more agile Saber Tooth Tigers and the brutality of the Dinosaurs proved insurmountable for the creatures from Hell, which were lucky enough to inflict a few malignant injuries.

The war between the masters of such primitive animals was in full flight as the different platoons of General Zada's army advanced against the awaiting Angels. With the frail confidence of each Demon at the helm of the various platoons, the Dark Warriors through the lack of strength from their superiors were doomed before the conflict even began. Regardless of the Demon's fighting talents, the thought of the multitudes of the Devil's refugees slain by their opponents was enough to occupy and bother the unfocused minds of Lucifer's North American Demons.

The main army from Heaven was separated into five sections, with a hundred and twenty thousand Angels organized in field platoons and the final twenty four thousand standing alongside the Supreme Commander. The Angels organized themselves in their patented cocoon shell, where the joining of their shields made their defenses vertically impenetrable. The battle formations, with which the Angels fought, had their platoons resembling military tanks, as they shuffled across the battlefield, eliminating their foes with an array of assaults. It didn't take very long before General Zada found himself questioning his tactics, after realizing that, regardless the Demon training, his warriors were simply out matched.

There were several platoons defending Lucifer's dishonor, which fought with shields manufactured from raw steel developed on Earth. Unlike the Angles' indestructible shields and swords, which were both carved from Zyclynx, the Universe's toughest metal, the protection awarded to Satan's followers was useless against quality weaponry. The powerful Angels were able to easily pierce or chop through their opponents' defenses with the Zyclynx metal, which also proved resistant to the furious strikes being inflicted by their challengers.

Commander Timothy, before leading his platoon into battle against Lucifer's defenders, looked across the battlefield at the commanding general and realized it to be someone he had clashed against during the mutiny plotted by the Devil to overthrow Yahweh. The altercation left an awful taste in the Angel's mouth, due to the fact that he was almost killed by General Zada, the traitor, before a friend intervened and saved him from certain death.. The thought that had haunted his dreams for centuries manifested and fueled his drive to plow through the myriads of Dark Warriors and settle their unfinished affairs. With General Zada as his motivation, Timothy led one fifth of the Universal Warriors against Lucifer's goons, through which his platoon plowed like a field of tall grass. At the sight of his younger sibling's platoon, Michael, who was knowledgeable of the incident between Timothy and Zada, smirked to himself at the thought of his brother's intent.

Timothy was not to be denied redeeming his personal status and conscience. After centuries of simulating different clashes involving General Zada in his dreams, the opportunity to finally implement his theories was not one he was about to pass on. While overseeing the battle as it unfolded, Timothy's platoon became relevant in the eyes of General Zada, who soon marked the key reason for the platoon's speedy advancement. At the sight of Timothy leading the charge, General Zada's blood boiled to where he constructed a fireball in the midst of his hand, before flinging it at the protruding Angels. The fireball smashed and extinguished against the Angels' shields, as the two Angels' eyes fastened onto each other.

With the challenge made between the two contestants, General Zada simply pointed his hand, which gave his Dark Warriors the order to attack, while he went aside to settle the personal grudge against Commander Timothy. While General Zada and Commander Timothy reacquainted themselves, their platoon members fought to the death, as the Dark Warriors knew no surrender or retreat.

"I will finish the job I started back in Heaven today." General Zada threatened.

"There is one problem with that you traitor." Timothy declared.

"The only problem is that I should have killed you centuries ago." General Zada stated.

"No, your problem is that I'm not the same person I was then." Timothy indicated, as they clashed swords for the first time.

Both the Demon and the Angel fought without shields, which would have hampered their fluid movements and award the more lucrative fighter, the victory. Commander Timothy drew his sword before progressing with a series of blows that kept General Zada reversing, while struggling to block the strikes from connecting. With his opponent in a defensive posture, Timothy chopped down at the blocking sword until the feeble metal broke, to which General Zada attempted to utilize his karate skills to keep his opponent at bay. Once Zada realized his sword had broken, the Demon kicked at the Angel who spun away from the contact and chopped off the kicking leg. The Demon's eyes widened with surprise at the sight of its leg lying on the floor, as Commander Timothy wisped his sword across the General's body twice, before nonchalantly walking away. General Zada's head remained in place for a moment before it came sliding off his shoulders, as his body also separated and split in half.

Chapter 33

Lucifer summoned one of his messengers and sent him to deliver a message to Dr. Flakiskor back at their main headquarters. With the Universal Army from Heaven on the verge of defeating the armies he had sent forth to defend his many continents, Lucifer was intent on having some comfort should his former siblings do fulfill their mission. With fresh news circulating about the defeat his North American combatants suffered, Lucifer was by no means about to leave anything to chance, as he would prefer to destroy the Earth than surrender it to its rightful owner. The messenger was given specifics regarding when Lucifer wanted his grand finale unveiled, as he expected to ambush some important clientele in the wake of his suicidal aspirations. Should Lucifer loose control of the Earth, the sole Demon to challenge the Most High God was aware of the ceremony to follow, and the persons scheduled to be in attendance at such a ceremony, therefore, there would never be a more opportune time to unveil his masterpiece.

Doctor Flakiskor confided the assignment given him by Lucifer in Andrene, who was never totally committed to Satan's cause and thus rejected the idea. The former airhostess thought the idea of destroying the Earth was cruel and unjust, although the doctor was totally committed to fulfilling the Devil's instructions. Once the Demons vacated Hell, their captives, who had been abiding by the rules provided, transgressed against their Illuminati guards and won; celebrating their victory by falling to their knees and praying to their God in the Heavens for forgiveness. The messenger sent by Lucifer, who had to dive deep underwater to locate the entrance to the Lair, arrived in Hell to find their abandoned home in disarray, as the former slaves had revolted against their masters and were disobeying the primary law of praying to a foreign God. The Demon who was never totally fond of humans, withdrew his sword and slayed every kneeling worshipper in sight, before storming through the rest of their lair in search of the doctor.

The Demon found the doctor inside his quarters, where the plague condemned to the Australian continent had both he and the airhostess curled up on the bed in pain. The Messenger marched over to the female, placed his humongous hands around her neck and hoisted her upright.

"Are you with those traitors?" the Demon demanded of the frightened airhostess, who knew that he could snap her neck like a twig should he choose to.

"What is the meaning of this? Unhand her at once!" Dr. Flakiskor conjured up the strength to utter, despite his continued discomfort.

The Demon held Andrene until she was almost unconscious, before releasing her as she crashed on the floor and gasped for oxygen. Dr. Flakiskor, who could not physically assist the female, rolled to the edge of the bed and looked down at his personal assistant. The intimidating Demon knelt down towards the doctor, who was nervous and unsure about the Demon's intentions, before being informed of the message from Lucifer.

"Your Master wishes to inform you that come the seventh day, before your will has expired ignite the detonator." the Demon instructed, before whisking around and charging form the quarters.

The Caribbean Islands of Jamaica, Cuba, Haiti, Trinidad and Tobago, St. Lucia, St. Vincent, Grenada, Dominica, Antigua, St. Kitts, Barbados, Puerto Rico, Dominican Republic, Bahamas and Nassau all experienced some of the most volatile hurricanes ever witnessed. The El Nina type system triangulation, responsible for creating that many hurricanes, was never before recorded in the region, where a dozen hurricanes were created within days. None of the tropical Caribbean countries were spared the blunt fury of a hurricane, as every country had at least two hurricanes make landfall. Once the true monsters of the ocean came ashore on these tropical islands, the destruction became extensive and the death toll staggering. Despite the horrid temperatures, God fearing patriots of the Caribbean still stacked churches and religious facilities after days of prayer ceremonies, fasting and preaching from their pastors and others clergy members. A number of the weakened shacks, under which religious patrons gathered to glorify God, were swept away by turbulent hurricanes. People, livestock, artifacts such as cars, boats, trucks, roofs, houses, trees and even stuff anchored securely, could be seen flying away in the stiff winds, which were categorized as high as level five. The Central American symptoms derived from the Heavenly Plagues also cursed the islands of the Caribbean, and everyone was left blinded, before being molested by some sort of rodent or insect.

South America

The South American country of Brazil in all its beauty, was hosting a World Cup Soccer qualifying match between their national team and Argentina's National Team at the time of the Symbol's appearance. The soccer match was being held at the Agricola Paes Barros Dome in Cuiaba, which is located in central Brazil. Due to the dome covering, the audience in attendance was unable to see the symbols, as they loudly cheered on their superstars in a 1-1 contest. At the kickoff of the second half of the match, the officials got word that there was, "a phenomenon of God happening outside", which led to their postponing the match. However, after looking around the stadium at the soccer enthusiasms, the referee who didn't wish himself or his crew members harmed by some lunatic craving a victory, reversed the decision to stop the match. The referee, who was an atheist, decided that anything of major importance can wait an additional forty five minutes, as he deliberately refused to call off the match.

The news about the symbols was never transmitted over the Dome's PA system, as the match played on till its conclusion. However, had many soccer loyalists inside the dome answered their cellular phones, checked their E-Mails or text messages, many more lives would have been spared. The soccer match was decided during regulation time, with a victory to Brazil determined by an offside goal that the linesman failed to properly call. The Referee, who suspected the linesman didn't wish to prolong the match into overtime, allowed the goal to stand, despite objections from the visiting team and coaches in the eighty eighth minute of the match. Once the Argentinean strikers kicked off the ball to continue play, the referee, who didn't once check his watch, terminated the contest and signaled his linesmen to the locker. With the Brazilian fanatics going coo-coo over the victory, the referee and his linesmen associates ran from the field with a slew of Argentinean players and coaches giving chase. The local officers assigned to the dome had to intervene to protect the game officials, as the situation quickly escalated into violence, where the Argentineans sought justice after being robbed a critical three points. A barrage of un-pleasantries and insults were leveled by the Argentineans, who seemed poised to charge the soccer officials, had not the police stood between both parties.

The soccer referees, who were in a haste to exit the hostile atmosphere that had developed in the Agricola Paes Barros Dome, aspired to safely mount their tour bus stationed in the parking lot. With the Argentineans cursing, the referees protectively made their way out into the parking area, were the attention spans of celebrators had completely been altered. The noise disparity between those inside the dome and the celebrators pouring from inside the building was acute, as everyone who exited went from drastically loud to tragically silent. Once the referees and their angered entourage stepped from the dome, the arguments immediately ceased and curiosity overtook citizens, some of whom went to their vehicles in attempts to get away.

The players from the victorious Brazilian team continued celebrating on the field with their multitudes of fans, the majority of whom stuck around to celebrate their national World Cup hopefuls. The celebrations for the Brazilian team qualifying for the world's largest sporting spectacle, waged on for almost another hour as fans celebrated as if their team had won the actual event. At the arrival of Satan's abominations, soccer enthusiasts were pouring out from the Dome to the realization of the horrors the rest of the world had been experiencing. The roars of fans inside the Dome excited the creatures, which immediately attacked and mauled everyone in sight. Tailgaters from both countries and spectators attempting to leave the premises were forced to hide inside their vehicles or rush back into the building, as the creatures struck with reckless abandon. Fans, which had left the Dome celebrating, began creating exit blockages as they collided with spectators seeking to exit.

Frightened spectators fighting to escape the clutches of the gruesome creatures, who were shredding the limbs off individuals, shattered the huge twenty-foot entrance glass doors. With the damage to the entrance doors, the creatures that typically abstained from attacking people behind barriers, waltzed directly into the high ceiling facility, where they could freely operate and maneuver. With such a loud and festive atmosphere, those who were unaware of the invading creatures believed those tormented to be overzealous celebrators, the typical reference to soccer lovers. It wasn't until one of the creatures walked from the Dome's tunnel with a policeman's dangling from its mouth, that everyone else took note of the danger and began frantically scattering for safety.

The Abomination from Hell released the screaming male from its mouth with a definitive fascination for the magnificently engineered structure, not to mention the scores of prey scattering about. The beast used its powerful hind leg to stump the severely injured male beneath it directly in the throat, breaking the man's neck like a twig. Other people up in the stands began screaming as a second creature walked into the bleachers with its face soaked and dripping blood. The police officers around the playing field withdrew their weapons for protection, while heeding common sense first and retreating in search of safety. Those lucky enough to find areas where they could safely seal doors behind themselves were lucky enough to survive the creatures' assaults, but found they had trapped themselves during a critical era for mankind.

The South American Continent, like the rest of the world got pounded along the coastlines. The unusually high waters wiped out boat marinas, vanquished the tourists resorts along the beachfronts and annihilated local villages built along the shores. Once Yahweh uprooted the weather climates around the globe, the South American Continent began experiencing terrible tornadoes, where hundreds of destructive wind funnels decimated the entire continent from Venezuela to Argentina. Every tornado created collectively sat out on a mission of terror where every major city and small village was struck with a fury never before witnessed by Mankind.

Soccer coaches, players, referees and spectators who survived the

Brazilian Dome's attacks, were scattered across the stadium in chambers that offered them sanctuary from Lucifer's beasts, when a volatile tornado swept through the area. The monster tornado, handled the securely built dome like it was a piece of scrap paper, as it ravaged and uprooted cement pillars with its hundred and eighty miles per hour wind gust. Those inside the Dome, who weren't swept away by the funnel cloud, were crushed underneath crumbling debris, as the tornado passed overhead and severely damaged the structure.

Chapter 34

Earth's entire human population suffered from some sort of ailment as a result of God's plagues. Throughout the six inhabited continents of the globe, survivors of different creed were engaged in some sort of religious activity, which saw the majority of humans kneel in submission to the Lord. The severity of the times had dawned in the minds of survivors, forcing even Atheist to their knees with the conclusion that God had indeed returned to do as the bible foretold. Hence, despite the unbearable torture experienced by true God-fearing individuals, such devoted worshipers continued praising the Father, knowing that eventually Jehovah would transform the Earth into a peaceful paradise.

The Sovereign Lord and his Heavenly Tribunal veered down at the burning planet, which had almost been totally transformed and cleansed of Lucifer's influence. As the observers of Heaven surveyed the planet, the sight of the Devil's ex-worshippers denouncing his kingdom and attempting to redeem their condemned souls was wide spread across the globe. With all the pleas for forgiveness by human sufferers, the Creator was insulted to observe patrons actually praying to false idols and statues, which they were convinced, were Spiritual Gods. Cultures like the Tibetan Buddhist who pray to Buddha, the Indians who pray to statues and many others, prompted Yahweh to complete the mission.

After surveying the reclaimed territories, Yahweh was again ready to advance their operation, as he inquired about the punitive decision to be awarded South America. The spokesperson, for the Heavenly Tribunal, addressed the Creator and advised him of their decision, to which Yahweh unhesitently pointed his index finger at the continent and twirled it in a circle, which launched the final plagues. The Spanish speaking Continent of South America was struck with a diverse plague, where no two individuals in the same radius spoke the same language. With millions of citizens across the continent carried away in tornados, the few survivors found it impossible to understand each other. The second wave of the plagues saw an influx of poisonous reptiles such as snakes and centipedes, invading the private places of South Americans who, like the rest of the world, suffered tremendously.

The Demolition Squad sent by the Lord swooped into the South American countries, which were all left in terrible ruins. The destruction caused by the hundreds of tornados across the continent simplified the Angels' duties, although there remained significant work to be done. As in every country visited thus far, the military programs were priority as they proposed both chemical and biological hazards, not to mention defense systems such as missile silos and aerobatic machinery. The Angels had to see to the destruction of millions of war tanks, aircrafts, weaponry and other dangerous materials built by man, which were strictly forbidden in the new world. The Angels also had the different agencies of governments with which to contend, which provided their individual challenges considering the fact that South America owned a significant amount of the world's oil reserves. Therefore, the Angels had to clog the shafts through which oil is pumped and seal the wells both on and off shore.

Through the powers of Yahweh, despite the continued suffering of the citizens across South America, a clearing was prepared to enable both armies the opportunity to duel. The severe tornados reduced the Devil's beast army by hundreds, as many were caught in open areas where there were swept away. The Prince of Peace, who had never been immuned to delivering inspirational speeches, stood before Heaven's Universal Warriors and addressed his brothers, with whom he had fought to help abolish the Devil's tyranny. With the look of confidence gleaming through his brethrens' eyes, Michael was assured that he need not engage in a lengthy speech, as his brothers were eager to accommodate their opponents.

"This Historical Mission of which we have almost accomplished has been foretold. Knowing what was expected of you never wavered your judgment, as you maintained your focus through each of our battles and proved why you are the best this galaxy has to offer! We have lost brethrens, yet we continue to prevail; our enemies cheat in battle, yet we shall not be defeated. The presence of us standing here, now, scares the life force from their hollow shells! For we are"? insighted the Supreme Commander.

"The Defenders of the Universe"! hollered the warriors from Heaven.

"And on this field we shall"? Michael lamented.

"Dominate-dominate-dominate---"! the Universal Warriors shouted.

The cheers of the Angels fueled their animals' drive to attack, as the Dinosaur led pact of Saber Tooth Tigers busted out against the Devil's monstrosities. The Creatures from Hell, which had out numbered Heaven's animals on several occasions, still had a modest edge despite the visual similarities. The pair of powerhouse dinosaurs, which anchored the Saber Tooth team, balanced whatever numeric advantage the demons claimed. Despite their losses throughout the previous battles, the Saber Tooth Tigers were quicker to initiate their attack than the dinosaurs that sparked the initial charge. The Dinosaurs, while encouraged by the Saber Tooth Tigers' herculean initiative, were never to be outshined on the battlefield, and they roared in with the blades attached to their tails slashing the enemy and jaws ripping into flesh.

The group of Saber Tooth that raced by their leaders, clashed with the abominations created by Lucifer's scientists, in yet another epic scrimmage of claws gouging and fangs piercing by both pacts. The animals from Heaven, which had fought against numerous of Satan's creatures, were more accustomed to the tactics of their foes than their foes were of theirs. Hence, having battled their foes on several continents, Heaven's animals had no reason to expect anything different from graduates of the same Dojo Academy. To the animals from Heaven, Satan's monstrosities fought like mere reflections of each other, which allowed them the ability to read their opponent's maneuvers and adjust accordingly.

With beast lunging at each other from all angles, it wasn't long before the gruesome sight of hanging intestines and fractured limbs became common in the den of the beasts. The manner with which both packs fought was utterly different, as the creatures from Hell were mere savages that fought selfishly, while their opponents aided and protected each other.

The scuffles between the animals and creatures would have been the ideal betting pool for game enthusiasts, though animal rights activists would go ballistic at the brutality. The largest creature of Lucifer's South American scavengers was casted in a showdown versus a lesser-experienced Saber Tooth Tiger. The undeterred animal from Heaven circled its opponent, stalking, with the expectation of using youth and flexibility to defeat its challenger. Both creature growled and taunted each other, expressing their deep animosity. At the end of the taunting session, both creatures charged at each other and collided with such force that the more robust of the two knocked the lesser to the ground. The Monstrosity from Hell was quick to jump on its victim and grabbed the Saber Tooth by the neck and sunk it fangs into the animal's throat.

The Devil's abomination held the Saber Tooth sedated for ten long seconds, at which point the animal began fading into unconsciousness. The thrill of a kill relaxed the creature, who crouched down to savor the final breath exhaling the Saber Tooth's lungs, and neglected to hinder the ground thumping stumps graduating towards him. Hex grabbed the creature inflicting the harm by the back of the neck, at which the fright and blunt force from the dinosaur's rigid tooth prompted the creature to release its victim from its jaws. The Dinosaur threw the creature high into the air while maintaining a firm grip, which caused the beast's neck to snap under the pressure, before Hex began swinging it violently from side to side. Hex flung the creature across the battlegrounds where it landed motionless as the dinosaur stood by and guarded its injured ally.

There was not a single victory attained where the animals from Heaven weren't thoroughly tested, as their opponents only lacked cohesiveness, which summed up the reason for their demise. The pair of dinosaurs played a dramatic role in balancing the field of battle, considering that the abominations from Hell outnumbered Heaven's animals by a significant margin on every continent. As Hex looked over the millions of scattered caucuses across the field, the sense that all their conflicts would soon end seemed surreal, as the dinosaur nudged the injured Saber Tooth to assure it that help was forthcoming.

General Haku and his legions of fighters stood poised to attack their nemesis on the opposite end of the divine battleground. Unlike their nervous allies that appeared hesitant to charge their foes, the obtuse Dark Warriors behaved like glutinous dogs eager to be released, as they were programmed simply to attack and destroy. General Haku chose to advance his troops in conventional means, as he moved to the helm of the Devil South American army and led the charge. Contrary to the other Generals, who remained at bay until the main body of the army had been defeated, General Haku, who had dreaded betraying his Creator, sought his personal retribution at the end of an Angel's sword.

At the sight of General Haku's noble gesture, the Supreme Commander utilized his Godly vision to ensure foul play was not affiliated, before following suit in leading his command. The Angels formed their impenetrable defense, where their shields locked in place and allowed for no penetration, as they proceeded to meet their advancing foes. The spectacular eclipse created by the clash of both entities was nothing short of magnificent, where the influx of Demons resembled a swarm of Monarch Butterflies descending onto a plain of flowers after months of hibernation. The Angels countered by thrusting arrows through the slots in their shields, which decreased the numbers of their enemies, yet failed to dampen or break their thirst for battle. Michael, who observed General Haku being slaughtered after crashing into the Angel's defense and receiving a spear to the stomach; believed something was peculiar about the General's suicide, as he continued eradicating his enemies.

With the main army of Angels preoccupied with the deluge of Dark Warriors, it wasn't long before Arch Angel Michael became concerned about the lack of other Demons, which were supposed to be entrenched amongst their allies.

"Tighten the shields; they're planning to rain a Fire Cloud! Archers, take out those in the clearing and Rhovon, Jahvon get your squad together and take out those in hiding!" telepathically instructed the Supreme Commander, as he could clearly see the Demons around them putting their energies into the creation of the Fire Cloud.

All the Demons assigned to General Haku's army had broken from their formations and redeployed to distance positions around the battle to orchestrate their grandest ambush plot, which if execute correctly was expected to eliminate everyone affected. A Fire Cloud could be created with no less than a thousand Angels cohesively building a giant fire ball, which once released, poured to the ground like hot lava reservoirs. Each Demon that broke away from the regiment had taken up a position around the warriors, where they channeled their fire creative energies into creating the monster Fire Cloud. The Demons knew that they risked loosing their entire reserves of Dark Warriors. However, such a scheme had to be implemented for the desperate puppets attempting to save their master's kingdom.

The Angels realigned their shields so that they resembled a bowl hat, as they continued slaying the ever-advancing Dark Warriors. Flashes of light sparked from the army of Angels in different directions, where the assassin Angels broke formation to execute the Demon extremists plotting their Fire Cloud. While Michael's commanders sat out to defend against the hostiles plotting terrorism, his sharp shooters selected specially designed long ranged arrows, which they loaded and took aim. With the attentions of Demons in open areas focused on the task of building their giant Fire Cloud, pinpoint accuracy on such gigantic frames was child's play for the archers. The eyes of Angels watched their arrows strike the targets at pivotal areas, which instantly knocked over and killed their victims.

With the Demons building the Fire Cloud dropping like flies, the plasma of fire became jittery and began spilling onto everyone beneath. For the first time since the Angels knocked swords with Satan's Dark Warriors, they actually saw fear in the eyes of their foes, once the scorching inferno poured onto their skins. The attacking Dark Warriors became confused, not knowing where to find safety from the scorching lava rain falling from above. The Indestructible Zyclynx Shields of the Angels protected them from the raining inferno of lava. At the end of the deluge of fire, a number of Angels received treatable burns and two Saber Tooth Tigers, too close to the downpour, got accidentally killed. The Assassin Angels sent forth, engaged their plotting nemesis in a number of different ways, as some struck with their swords, while others lanced Dart Blades, which are the Angel's version of the Ninja's Star. Both parties clashed in mid air, where the angels who customarily fought with discipline showed no respect for their treacherous opponents. Those responsible for the Fire Cloud were all killed by Heaven's Universal Warriors, who neglected to celebrate their victory with Lucifer still at large.

Chapter 35

Human Governments here on Earth have hunted some of the most vicious mass murderers over the centuries, though none as prolific and high classed as the Master of Evil, Satan the Devil. Had it not been for Lucifer, the catastrophic episodes caused by vindictive men such as Hitler and Ben Laden, to name a few, would never had come to pass, as the world would have known only love and nothing but love. Humans have much to thank the Devil for, though some would rather to curse the Lord in their time of ailment, even though Satan is the reason we are all cursed with sin. Hence, the operation to cleanse the Earth of the parasite known as Lucifer became the biggest military campaign ever launched on this planet.

Yahweh telepathically linked his son and instructed him to travel to the tallest mountain in Australia, where he sought to have an accord with Heaven's Universal Army Supreme Commander. Michael travelled to the top of the Andes Mountain, where the warmth of the burning tree soothed the chilling wind that huffed about the mountaintop. The Arch Angel landed gently on the rocky surface and folded his wings while walking over to the flaming tree. Michael, who chose to stand while conversing, could visibly see his Father's face in the flames, as he bowed his head in respect to the Creator and stood at ease.

"All hail King Michael for his continued success, Hip-Hip!" cheered a Tribunal member.

"Hurray!" remarked the rest of the Tribunal Committee.

"Your work has thus far been exemplary my son, I know that the troops must be eager to finalize the mission and return home for a well deserved vacation." Yahweh complimented.

"They are more determined than ever to complete the mission my Father; for far too long these humans have suffered, we will grant them peace." Michael responded.

"Remain vigilant against the Slithery Serpent, for he is always conspiring evil against others. I sense there is something of great importance as I enter Lucifer's orb, yet exactly what, remains a mystery for the Mind Probe. Have the Earth Defenders travel to the most hideous corners of this planet and capture the noncompliant spirits and these disloyal Demons, as I shall awaken those in trance throughout, for the time of judgment is near at hand." Yahweh highlighted.

"I shall have someone thoroughly check his lair after we've dealt with Lucifer My Lord. We now march to Antarctica to arraign this insolent traitor, have you any further instructions?" Michael asked.

"Remind them who is the Supreme God!" Yahweh indicated.

As Michael turned away and spread his wings to return to the Universal Army, the burning bush instantly extinguished, as the thunder that barked through the clouds cemented the facts that Yahweh had begun to follow up his wishes. The thunder that erupted shook the Earth to its core and widened the lava cracks beneath the ocean's floor, which brought about massive earthquakes across the globe, erupting volcanoes and cresting the ocean levels to their absolute peak. The tremors brought about by Yahweh's voice intensified the terrible weather phenomenons happening around the world, as tornados, hurricanes, snow blizzards, ice storms, acid rain, tsunamis, monsoons, red poisonous rain, fire and brimstones, massive floodings, landslides and rock storms began to intensify.

"You insubordinate spirits, who have disobeyed the Cycle of Life, listen and heed the commandments of the one who have created you. Come out from your desolate places and prepare to be judged for your transgressions! Awaken you deceivers, for Yahweh your true God has returned to cleanse the Earth, and with it all who have disobeyed the commandments I have bestowed!" Yahweh ordered.

At the appeal of the Lord, myriads of spirits began returning to the soils of the Earth, the majority of which were displeased to hear the actual announcement. There were schools of people killed at sea, which began walking onto the shores of continents around the globe. The coffins, pine boxes, tombs and every sorts of grave ever awarded by humans, began releasing the spirits of their dead, in order for everyone to be judged. While the majority spirits heeded Yahweh's summons, there were those who were too ashamed of their crimes against humanity to simply surrender, regardless of the fact that resistance was useless.

The Prince of Peace returned and rejoined the Universal Army, which rested in waiting in the desolated city of Las Leas, Argentina. The Supreme Commander returned to find the Angels in a festive mood, after vanquishing six seventh of Lucifer's army, and were on the verge of settling their affairs with the number one fugitive on their wanted list. Michael summoned the Earth Defenders, who had completely demolished the structures and items assigned them and awaited further orders. The Arch Angel first congratulated the Defenders for their immense contributions to the invasion, which had thus far gone according to plan. Michael then proceeded to assign the Defenders their final task, which came directly from the Sovereign Lord. The brothers in arms parted ways for the final time, as the Defenders began branching off towards their individual tasks around the globe.

With sections of Argentina's coastline under water, Michael and the Universal Army proceeded to Ushuaia, Southern Argentina, where the Supreme Commander outstretched his hand to the violent ocean, and brought the raging waters to a calm. Through the high raging ocean a straight valley was formed, where twenty-foot barrier walls aligned both sides of the corridor that led directly to Antarctica. The Supreme Commander led the army of Angels across the parting of the two largest oceans, which provided the Angels one of the most spectacular views they had ever seen. The ocean provided the Angels the most spectacular view through the walls of water, as the creatures of the sea swam to the borders for a look at God's first creations.

King Lucifer was not about to surrender centuries of dominant ruler-ship without bloodshed, regardless of the fact that his enemies had annihilated his entire reserves across the continents. The greed that propelled many communist rulers to their eventual demise, corrupted the worship crazed Demon Leader, whose entire existence was dependent on being glorified and worshipped. The Angels did not have to travel very far to find the Serpent himself, as Lucifer was present to greet his challengers at the highest elevation point, which was at the refueling station in Fossil Bluff. The Devil, who stood at the helm of his army, was adorned with a lengthy black robe, exquisite diamond neck piece with blemish-less jewelry on his fingers and wrists, a bejeweled throne that sparkled even in the haze and a specially built golden body armor suit, which differed from the ones worn by the warriors of his command. At the sight of Lucifer's attire, Michael smirked to himself, knowing the Devil's intention was merely to boast about his Earthly kingdom.

The entire island of Antarctica had been vacated, as the penguins, walruses and other wintery mammals took to the ocean in search of protection from the calamities forthcoming. Despite the suffering endured by humans globally; animals, birds and every Earthly creature experienced the hardships that came from the turmoil being unraveled around the world. The forest fires that were sparked on several continents, plus the destructive weather climates, eradicated the homes of God's creatures and killed numerous, who were unable to escape the fury. Across the great forests, deserts and plains lay countless animals, mammals and other slain creatures, which also paid the price for human's sinful existence.

Once the Angels marched to a halt across the wide-open frozen plains from their primary target, the Universal Warriors all feasted their eyes on King Lucifer, as if there were no one else accompanying him. The blatant stares by the Angels emphasized their personal impressions of the Demon who once sought to disrupt their entire philosophy of life by assassinating the Creator of all living things. As Lucifer himself gazed across the faces of the fraternity of Angels from which he was outcast, their anger and rage towards him was clearly evident by the intense screw-faces focused at him.

"Am I not my brothers' keeper? Ha-ha-ha-ha, you fools are forever nothing but puppets serving a puppet. You all truly envy me; deep down you know you envy me! I am the one who went for what I wanted and took it, these lands I have ruled over all these centuries and always will! I shall have my justice, with you all present to witness. For I am King Lucifer, the rightful ruler of this planet." Lucifer announced.

At the end of Lucifer's gibberish, the Supreme Commander, who noted the moral booster such an arrogant statement proved to be for his brethrens, neglected to respond to the Devil's speech and addressed his troops.

"Universal Warriors, battle formations!" Michael declared, which brought the Angels to interlock their shields and prepare for combat. Once their defenses had been aligned, the Arch Angel who had waited on their opponents to attack on other occasions, gave the order to advance after their fugitive. "Let's get him!"

The beautiful, predominantly white fur of the Heavenly animals caused them to blend in adequately, with the heavy snow from the blizzard that descended upon the island. Lucifer spared no expenses at coordinating a strong resistance force to dominate the battle between the creatures, considering there were nearly twice as many monstrosities to deal with than the previous encounter. Regardless the difficulty, the animals were poised for the challenge, although neither of the Saber Tooth Tigers was as eager to take the helm. Before leading the charge against the flock of creatures, both dinosaurs gazed back at their followers with taunting gestures, aimed at mocking those that failed to behave noble during their last altercation.

The dynamics to gaining a victory over the much larger pack of creatures, dictated that the animals fight intelligently to avoid a large casualty rate. The Monstrosities from Hell were overzealous and thus attacked like bucking bulls against a more subdued Heaven's squad. At the point of their collision, the Tyrannosaurus Rex Dinosaurs simply grabbed and hurdled creatures back into the litter of Saber Tooth Tigers, where it became as if they drowned in the sea of white. Both Hex and Zoe raced directly through the army of beasts, crushing and knocking aside their opponents, which once unbalanced became easier prey for their associates. The huge tree trunk size feet of the dinosaurs and the velocity with which they charged, made it difficult for their opponents to strike any punitive blows or hinder their progress.

Intellect over stupidity especially in war, brought the Heavenly animals to eventually cut their opponents' forces in half, while suffering minimal injuries themselves. The importance of not exerting the extensive energy during the initial charge was an evasive tactic of the animals that helped them conserve energy for the lengthy battle. Despite their unusual tactics,

Heaven's animals fought with dignity and class, and they never succumbed to the thieving and conniving efforts of their opponents. The dynamic creatures provided by Lucifer proved to be a sterling challenge, although their non-cohesiveness became the reason for their demise.

The dinosaurs made a huge difference on the final battleground, as Hex eventually teamed up with its sibling, after the Saber Tooth Tigers adopted the technique of fighting with their backs against their peers. The dinosaurs combined to create the most electrifying team on the field, as Lucifer's creatures tried, to no avail, to eliminate either opponent's commanders. It wasn't long before the 'abstain from' message got through to the monstrosities from Hell, which found themselves being tarnished by the dinosaurs. The transitions through which the Devil's abominations went were astounding; as they began the altercation fully confident, before the savagery of war made them hesitant to attack. The animals from Heaven fought until their foes had all been extinguished, to which they celebrated by roaring and growling in expressions of their triumph.

The egotistical self-proclaimed ruler of the Earth motioned the troops at his disposal forward, as he remained stationary while they walked by him. The mixture of Dark Warriors and Demons were intent on protecting their king till death, as Lucifer refused to surrender until he had been completely defeated. Following the defeats of his generals across the Earth's continents, Lucifer refused to accept that his fighters were terribly outclassed. Satan had grown delusional with denial and was completely confident that he would prevail over the Angels and retain his command.

Those in attendance around Yahweh's Three Dimensional Screening were at the edge of their seats with anticipation, as the Angels' and Demons' Supreme Leaders clashed in the final war of Armageddon. Lucifer's most deadliest team of fighters, which also included the skilled members of his Honor Guards, proved inadequate to stopping the most dominating army in the Galaxy, as Michael and company swept through the Demon army like a bad flu.

It didn't take Lucifer very long to develop an agitated demeanor from watching his representatives, as the Angels made them appear lethargic with primitive fighting abilities. Watching the defensive assault launched by the Angels infuriated the Devil, who would never acknowledge the awesome display of physical dominance imposed by his former peers. The Angels, who saw their final fulfillment of a prediction encased in the historic scrolls of ancient past, fought with vigor and compassion to eliminate the forces before them; capturing and placing their leader in restraints.

After watching a third of his army getting eradicated, the infuriated Devil withdrew a whistle from a breast pocket and blew into it. The sound of the whistle remarkably controlled the Dark Warriors, who ceased advancing with Satan's Demon allegiance and returned to guard their king. The peculiar maneuver by the Devil's representatives caused the Angels to halt, and they protected themselves as a precautionary measure. Lucifer's representatives created a barrier in front of their king and stood their ground against the Angels, who were undeterred by their opponent's gestures. At the realization of the Demons' intentions, the Arch Angel Michael gave the order for the unit to disperse in order for them to bring an all point attack against their retreated opponents. Each Angel maintained their shield as their primary guard and thus scattered out and briskly walked towards the protective wall of the Devil.

The Ultimate Fighting Machines known as Heaven's Universal Army were magnificent individually against their opponents, as some wore their shields tied to their backs while others fought with their shields in hand. The Angels, who fought with their shields attached to their backs, had blades both hands, while those with their shields in hand fought with a singular spear. Despite their choice of weaponry, the Angels came at Lucifer's barricade like a bowling ball clearing away the pins at the end of a lane for a strike, with Dark Warriors and Demons getting stabbed and carved up like turkey. Lucifer, who nervously stood with his soldiers before him, could only see the rows of fighters ahead of him disappearing like erased sentences from a letter, as he watched his life of glory disseminate right before his eyes. Before long, the Angels had completely wiped away the millions of representatives that fought to defend Lucifer, which brought Earth's Demonic King to his knees with disappointment.

With Lucifer kneeling over in the snow on hands and knees, the Prince of Peace walked over to him and stood alongside him with his sword at hand, before using the blade to slap the throne from his head. "Bind him!" Michael commanded, as the triumphant Angels began shouting and celebrating.

Chapter 36

The Defender Angels travelled to every corner of the earth to recover alienated spirits that chose to disobey the Cycle of Life system. The Defenders went to foreign lands like Greenland, where they rounded up spirits like cattle and held them imprisoned until they passed judgment. Angels skewered the depths of the oceans and every crevice and corner known to men for disobedient spirits who aspired to cheat the Lord's judgment as they did the Cycle of Life. Spirits of all creed were captured by the Lord's Defenders, who implemented their martial law rules across the globe, against all intellectual life force.

Even though the powers attributed to God's Angels governed the spirits of humans, there were still those who daringly tested the bounty hunters, yet to no avail. With the wars predominantly erupting on the multi national continents such as Asia and Africa, one would believe that such continents would provide a host of sinful ghosts; but none so much as the tiny island of Jamaica. Even the Allah worshipping Muslims, who strap bombs to themselves, were less volatile than the Wicked Man Jamaicans. God's Defenders fought with the involuntary ghosts across the Island of Jamaica, to the point where the Angels had to bring in extra assistants to help subdue the hostile ghosts. Once it was reported that the spirits of those deceased had been captured, his Supreme Commander, who had secured the Devil and reclaimed the Earth, gave a briefing to Yahweh.

The citizens of Heaven celebrated the liberation of humans, after it was announced that the Universal Defenders had been victorious. With the grand celebrations transpiring across the planet, the Heavenly Creator and his Tribunal Members prepared to descend to the Earth to complete the final phase of the Earth's transformation. Yahweh, who hadn't visited the planet for centuries, (human time) waved both hands over the Earth, at which the ashes blanketing the sun dissipated and the widespread bad weather immediately ceased. The Planet Earth became as serene and quiet as a library, which offered the few thousands of survivors across the globe the opportunity to step out from the nightmare.

With his Tribunal Committee ready for the historical trip down to the reclaimed planet, Yahweh gathered with them in the centre of his Palace Hall floor, where he created an invisible bubble around them to transport them to the surface. Like the platoons of Angels before them, Yahweh ushered his entourage from the Planet Heaven down to the surface of the Earth, where they rejoined the Universal Army on the frozen terrain of Antarctica. The Members of Heaven's Holy Covenant received the welcome of kings, as the Angels gathered as if they were hosting an important function. The Lords of the Heavens were allowed to rest after their illustrious journey before attending to the matters for which they had travelled to the Earth.

The Arch Angel Michael sent the spy, Angel Tynias, to Lucifer's lair, to investigate the concerns his Father had concerning Lucifer's possible extended intentions. Tynias arrived at the Devil's abandoned lair, to find the place in shambles after Lucifer's messenger became destructive after his findings. After locating the deceased bodies inside Lucifer's palace, Tynias thought that all the human Devil worshipers had been slaughtered and thus continued his search for anything out of the ordinary. The Spy Angel, after checking several departments inside the humongous underground lair, found an area where several peculiar tunnels ran off in several directions. Curious to find out what lay at the end of such tunnels, Tynias followed one of them, which stretched for hundreds of miles inside the Earth's core. At the end of said tunnel the Spy Angel was surprised to find a cavern with a specially designed bomb, which had a remote control detonation device attached. Tynias' eyes widened with shock, realizing the Devil had planted a similar bomb in every one of the many tunnels he observed.

Above ground the Heavenly Father had began the Judgment Process, where Yahweh flew into the skies above and hovered amongst the clouds, before outstretching his hands and channeling his energy towards adjoining the many land surfaces across the globe. At the Creator's will, Europe, Africa and the Americas moved closer together and joined in areas, while Antarctica drew closer and connected with South America and Africa, as even the smaller islands of the Pacifics drew closer to their respective continents and attached. With the landmasses across the planet all connected for the first time in history, Yahweh descended to the ground where he went to speak with the self proclaimed King of the Earth.

"I have come to hear you admit your shame, before judgment is passed." Yahweh stated.

"My shame, my shame, I have never been ashamed for disobeying you Father! As I've mentioned, this is my kingdom and these are my slaves, and that will never change!" the well guarded Lucifer dictated.

"Have it your way, but you shall forever burn in the furnace of Hades!" Yahweh responded, before turning and walking away.

"I won't be the only one burning Father! I won't be the only one, Ha-ha-ha-ha-ha-ha-ha-ha!" Lucifer shouted with amusement.

The moment at which Lucifer instructed Doctor Flakiskor to destroy the Earth had arrived, as the Head of the Demons continued laughing in expectation of the globe exploding. Lucifer knew that reorganizing the planet was a process, and in order for the final judgment to occur certain events had to unfold; mainly the deaths of ever living creature on Earth. With the knowledge that such a catastrophic explosion would destroy the planet, there was no arguing the fact that Lucifer was on the verge of defeating his enemies.

Tynias realized he needed to locate the detonator holder. Hence the Spy Angel rushed back to the Devil's lair and went in search of the culprit. While the Spy Angel intensely searched, knowing that such an explosion would eliminate everything, the doctor had his assistant prepare two sedatives to relax them before setting off the detonator. Andrene, who had prepared many of the Doctor's bedtime tonics, prepared two cups of tea under the watchful eyes of Dr. Flakiskor, who was indeed ready to obey his master's bidding. The ex-airhostess pretended as if she would join the doctor in his consumption of the muscle relaxing fluids. Once the doctor turned his back and began walking to his studies, the short female used the stern brass teakettle and clobbered him behind the head. Doctor Flakiskor fell unconscious with the detonator in hand, which Andrene removed, in fear of any mishaps. The female picked up the detonator and went to exit the chamber, when she ran into the Spy Tynias.

The irregular laughter being expressed by Lucifer soon transformed to a chuckle at the realization that Yahweh was proceeding to the next phase of the Earth's judgment. Knowing that once all humans had been laid to rest his plans would become void, Lucifer attempted to stall the process by yelling profanity at the Creator and his Tribunal. Yahweh was intent on having no further dealings with the Devil, and he began concentrating before raising his hands from his hips and held them above his head, at which the oxygen supply on the ground level of the Earth climbed to ten thousand feet and remained there until the Lord lowered his hands. It became as if a vacuum sucked all the oxygen from the Earth and every living creature on the planet began dying from suffocation. Even the creatures of the sea began floating to the top of oceans and every body of water that housed them. After allowing enough time for everything to die, Yahweh then dropped his hands and the oxygen fell back to the Earth.

Humans have contended that God sees and observes everything at all times, but given the super computers or brains we're blessed with, the need for his constant observation was mitigated, as our brains record every bit of information experienced. Before we are sentenced to death or eternal life, the final phase of judgment came in the form of a brain scan, through which we divulged everything we've done and witnessed in our lives. The first to be scanned by the mind reading powers of Yahweh's Tribunal Members was King Lucifer, who revealed every detail about the different crisis he'd engineered since being created. Lucifer's Demons were scanned after their leader, which gave the Angels a detailed account of every facet of Lucifer's operation.

After scanning the Demons, the Heavenly Tribunal paused and went into deliberations, where they discussed their findings from the mutiny that occurred on home soil, prior to the Demons getting expelled from the realm of God. The Angles' findings were somewhat surprising, as Yahweh had always sought to know whether there were others who went unmentioned during the initial trial. After a short deliberation, the rulers and decision makers of Heaven emerged from their tent.

Yahweh appeared intensely focused as he walked out onto the snow and used his staff to mark a line, which measured approximately a quarter of a mile long. The instant the Creator began drawing the line in the snow, an eclipse began unfolding in space where the moon started blocking the sun, which was thoroughly completed by the end of Yahweh's line. The simple line resembled a deep crevice, which hurled far into the Earth's core, at which the fuming lava below became visible. The entire Earth had again fallen under darkness, where the multitudes of imprisoned spirits glowed under the shade of the moon. Yahweh again took to the skies, where he turned and faced the Planet Heaven and spoke a few words, at which a lightening bolt fired from the planet and struck directly into the crevice. The slight crack instantly expanded to a wide gorge, where the lava had been genetically enhanced into a foreign substance never before seen on Earth. The flames from the substance spouted into the air for hundreds of miles, at which Yahweh himself was forced to back away to a safer distance because of the scorching heat. While floating back towards camp, Yahweh used his left hand to create a wide road that led directly to the flames of Hades. At the same token, the Creator used his index finger on the opposite hand to compose a road opposite to the one that led to the furnace, which led to the promised land of Paradise on Earth.

I felt myself rise from the ground, as my eyes opened to the sight of my family and our adopted child floating in mid air. I looked down at the floor to the realization that my human body was stagnant, while my soul hovered about. "Oh shit we're dead!" I thought to myself, as I held tightly onto the hands of my wife, my son and the little girl, as an absorbing force began pulling us toward the south. Immediately after being drawn from the shack that housed us, it became evident that we weren't the only ones chosen for the trip, as there were a number of people floating in the same direction. After floating along for several minutes, a young woman and her teenage boyfriend came up to us and suggested they were the child's parents. There was no denying the little girl Taejah was conceived by both parents, who bore a striking resemblance to the child. Hence, we gave her to the youngsters and wished them all the best. The atmosphere was rejuvilant, as friends were reacquainting with friends, families with families, murderers apologizing to their victims, wrongdoers acknowledging their evil actions, even babies born deceased were reunited with their parents. There were several spirits that had to be escorted by Defenders, however, the tantrums came to a stop once that spirit came into contact with a grandparent, a parent, a friend or anyone who seriously inspired that spirit's life. It was amazing to watch suicide bombers apologize to their victims, police and soldiers begging forgiveness for harming the innocent, murderers of all kinds apologizing and being forgiven by their victims.

Sarah saw her mother and the rest of her siblings and dragged us towards them, as they marched along with a congregation of religious folks who were chanting gospel hymns. I was astonished to find the teller who I passed the robbery note to at the Toronto Dominion Bank amongst the congregation and I went over to her and apologized for scaring her during the ordeal. A former pastor, who sang proudly at the helm of the worshipers, with an elderly church member draped over his arm, led the congregation. While gliding back to Sarah and my son, my eyes gazed at one of the four females with whom I cheated. I surpressed a slight smile, as the thought of my infidelities caused my heart to skip a beat, knowing that I would not be accepted into God's arrangements.

I scooped up my son into my arms and held Sarah's hand tightly, seconds before someone kicked me in the butt. I didn't need a Genii to know who such a kidder was, as I simply shook my head while my kid brother Gilbert grabbed me around the neck.

"Rude Boy you don't hear your mother calling you all this time?" Gilbert questioned.

"Yow there is so many people around here screaming so many different names, that I make sure to hold on to one of the important parts of my family." I declared.

"See mama here, we just seen daddy and his other family over there somewhere." Gilbert reported, as he slithered away and traded places with our mother.

"You see how long I've been telling you boys to go to church, now look at this! Hello Sarah how you doing? Come here my grandson let grandma hold you." my mother implied.

"Hi mom." Sarah answered.

"Nice to see you too mom." I responded.

"Where is my baby Cassandra?" my mother asked.

"This thing caught her in Africa. She is the one I got my attention focused on finding right now." I responded.

With everyone travelling with companions, the opportunity to see people you haven't seen for a while presented itself often. Hence, it was fascinating to see people like my third grade teacher Miss Vicks, whom I had the greatest crush on. While I remembered my childhood fantasy, my wife interrupted me to point out Pastor Lester, who was walking hand in hand with his brother and the rest of his family. In another life I guess it might had been a thrill to see the Canadian Prime Minister and the United States President gliding along like commoners, but our predicament reminded us that we were indeed just commoners. While watching the United States President my daughter came into focus, right before she bumped into Julius who was on his way to reconcile with his parents.

Terry Duncan had found her parents and exhibited a huge smile while they hugged and floated along. The healthy glows from people who had suffered during their final moments before dying, was evident by Terry's mother and many others. While many spirits remained calm and behaved as if they had accepted their predicament, there were those who bawled as if they were too important to be judged.

Cassandra, who travelled with her friends, bid them adieu, as they separated and went in search of their own families. I fought with myself over admitting to certain infidelities, as I looked at the disgraced faces of people I had known to be vigilantes. With my daughter back into the flock, I felt it important that I reasoned with my family and advised them of my sinful ways, which would definitely hinder me from passing. I came forth and admitted to theft and other sinful acts that I have committed over the years, to which my family was disappointed to hear. Following my confessions, my family members simply drew closer and hugged tighter, as we drew closer to our destination.

The brain scan process was as easy as passing through a metal detector, where everyone's memories were recorded and processed, prior to being reprogrammed before sentenced. I had no idea how much time we had left before the judgment process, which was whispered to be our destination point by several spirits who claimed to be Jehovah's Witnesses. After hearing the predictions, I frightfully took my son into my arms and gave him my last will and testament.

"Listen Junior, whatever happens I want you to take care of your family. Help, love and support your mom and sister, I have nothing to give you to take with you but my heart felt love. If this is the paradise I've heard people speak about, then you won't ever have to worry about getting sick ever again. Cassandra honey, I love you and finish being that perfect young woman you have grown to be. I truly love you all!"

Once we arrived at our destination, the disorderly scatter of spirits began forming into organized lines, which brought the crowds to mingling spirits to silence. After every spirit born to the Planet Earth had been aligned, the Angels proceeded with their planned ceremony, which was highlighted by Lucifer's display to exhibit the cause of human's suffering. Despite our places in line, the advantage of being spirits allowed us the opportunity to witness the event as if we were front stage. With Lucifer and his Demons centre stage, the Supreme Commander presented himself and spoke to the myriads of spirits.

"My son the king." proudly acknowledged Michael's birth mother Mary.

"It is he; Our Lord Jesus Christ of Nazareth has returned!" whispered Michael's disciples and several ancient spirits, which existed during such times.

"I knew you would return and not forget me my Lord." humbly declared the thief who was strung up beside Jesus.

"The fulfillment of prophecies have brought us here; where your Heavenly Creator has returned to transform this planet into the Paradise it was intended. Sin was brought to these lands by these perpetrators of good, and as such they will be punished, as will anyone who have chosen to live by their examples. My Father had provided laws, through the great scrolls recorded by which you humans were to abide; and by these laws, you will be judged. To those promised the most marvelous of existence, your free passes will be acknowledged; but for those who fail the requirements necessary to enter the gates of Paradise; you shall burn forever with your master Lucifer in the flames of Hades!" Arch Angel Michael exclaimed, before a tentative pause at which he gazed across the faces of the myriads of spirits. "Your judgment starts now!"

Lucifer pretended to be a courageous soldier, as the turf beneath his feet and his Demons began moving them forward like a conveyer-belt. A number of his Demon colleagues began screaming from the pain, even before they tasted the flames to which they were bound. With absolutely no way to escape the judgment of the furnace, we all watched as Lucifer and his goons got thrust into the melting flames, under which they hollered from the excruciating pain. I couldn't help but to think to myself that for giants such as the Devil and his entourage to be screaming like attacked victims, the pain must be unbearable for a five feet ten inch human like me. With that thought in mind, the conveyer-belt began moving; a little too swiftly by my accord.

The cries of hearts being broken, was rampant throughout, as our lineup scurried along. Knowing I would be included amongst those designated to perish seemed surreal, like a convicted criminal on Death Row counting down his final minutes. I must have said the words, "I love you" nearly a million times to my family members, as I squeezed the hands of my wife and reminded my son of his obligations. The life force inside me felt just like a human's heart, due to the fact that it thumped and pounded like a nervous butt clinching defendant awaiting the verdict of their multiple count murder case. Then suddenly after one final "I love you", it was my time to be judged.

I was surprised to find a number of outspoken religious clergymen and their constituents on the wide path, which led to eternal destruction. The elderly woman, who was draped over her pastor's arm, was walking solo aside from her beloved preacher, who was also sentenced to pay for his sin in Hades. I was definitely not surprised to find extraordinary World Leaders on the road to Hades, considering the vast amounts of indiscretions prevalent to politicians. The vast amount of my personal family and friends had passed the BAR exam with me, which wasn't something I was at all pleased with, as I would have preferred to be the only one sentenced to death. I fought to get to the edge of the roadway, where Sarah had been hollering my name; to find a force field that encased us on our dreaded course to destruction.

There were massive screams from people who shouted every sort of sentiments, as they were tossed into the Furnace of Hades. Sarah kissed and hugged the children, as I watched with immense pride in knowing that my wife and children were eligible to enter Paradise here on Earth. Sarah told the children to look after themselves and never forget their parents, as she surprised me by leaping from her pad over to ours. I had not realized that those who chose to deny eternal life were free to transfer, which was not an option awarded those bound to Hades. With unconditional love in my arms, the flames of Hades consumed my wife and me, where our souls burnt until never.

The End

Objective

I was asked why I chose such a daring title and without any consideration said, "In respects to the Big Man." I was brought up going to Kingdom Hall with my grandparents, who were religious people that taught me the essentials of life, which are God, family, love, honesty and respect. As a teenager I broke away from my youthful teachings, as the reality and hardships to life began materializing themselves. I became a product of the system, but instead of being derailed I learnt to adapt and used my core principles to carve the future. Like every other child I've dreamt of the pinnacle to which I can reach, but never able to attain as an adult.

The objective of this novel is to bring God in the lives of many, who have forgotten the core principles of what makes us humans. Yes we are all imperfect, but that doesn't mean we are supposed to behave like cannibals. 'The Last Bible', which is how I've related to this novel, paints a graphic picture of the end of the world through the narrator's eyes and other events. 'The Big Man', or God as he is more popularly known, is my only inspiration for writing this novel, which I've dedicate to my family, friends and fallen soldiers.

Spirituality is the cornerstone of our beliefs, for a species that have no idea exactly from where we came. There will always be those eager to debate the truth, as will there always be Atheists, but regardless of the impurities of those with whom we pray, namely pastors, never abandon God. Mankind has done terrible things in the name of God, but that is because their God is Lucifer and not the true God Yahweh. Therefore, I say love and praise God unconditionally. JAH!!!

Special thanks to:

Derek Bateman
Sii Sam Ashoona